BOOKS BY BELVA PLAIN

BELVA PLAIN

LOOKING BACK

A DELL BOOK

A Dell Book
Published by
Dell Publishing
a division of
Random House, Inc.
1540 Broadway
New York, New York 10036

Cover illustration by Alan Ayers
Cover design by GTC Art and Design

For information, address Delacorte Press, New York, New York.

Dell® is a registered trademark of Random House, Inc., and the colophon is a trademark of Random House, Inc.

ISBN: 0-440-23577-4

Reprinted by arrangement with Delacorte Press

Printed in the United States of America

Published simultaneously in Canada

May 2002

10 9 8 7 6 5 4 3 2 1

OPM

LOOKING BACK

PROLOGUE

At a country inn on the coast of Maine, two men of a certain age, sitting on porch chairs some distance apart, watched the swollen, olive-green Atlantic crash on the rocks below. They were of a type that a careful observer would recognize by their old, well-cut woolen jackets, polished loafers, and reticence in the presence of strangers. They had not spoken at all.

Then one of them startled the silence. "Is this your first time here?"

"No. Every few years I come, whenever I feel the urge to see an ocean. Last time I went the other way, to the Pacific."

The waves crashed, the wind raced through the trees, and the silence returned. Then after a while, as if he were musing, the other man addressed the air.

"I read an interesting thing yesterday. Balzac is supposed to have said, 'Behind every great fortune there is a crime.' "

"Yes, that is rather interesting."

"I thought so. Apropos of it, I could tell you a story, if you care to hear one."

"By all means. Go ahead."

CHAPTER ONE

Books, purses, three empty bottles of Diet Coke, and the remains of a large pizza littered the card table that had been set up near the open window. Outdoors, green May was flourishing. Scented with lilac and wet grass, it was lively with walking traffic on the paths that crisscrossed the quadrangle from the Gothic library, to the glassy, modern science building, to the old red-brick museum, and beyond.

"Commencement. It's more like a conclusion, a funeral."

Startled, the two others turned toward Amanda. This doleful remark did not fit her. She was eager; her bright, blooming face in its frame of wavy, caramel-colored hair was always optimistic; she sparkled. Among these three young women, she was the one who would most attract attention.

True, there were some who would prefer the calm, classic elegance of Cecile. It was she who now said more cheerfully, "It's the beginning of something else, Amanda."

"For you, it is. You must be the only person in the graduating class who's getting married this summer."

"I know. Isn't it ridiculous? I feel like my own grand-mother. In her day, for Heaven's sake, you were expected to do just that. 'A ring by spring,' they used to say." Cecile's pink smile made fun of herself. "But we've waited four years for him to get through architecture in New York, and that's long enough. We haven't seen each other since February vacation, when I went east, and I can't wait." With a sigh of contentment, she added, "I'm sure if it weren't for all this, I would be terribly sad about leaving here."

"*Ave atque vale,*" Norma said.

Amanda asked, "What's that?"

" 'Hail and farewell.' It's Latin."

"Why on earth anybody should want to fill her head with that dead stuff, and spend the rest of her life teach-ing it to people who'll never use it except to teach it to more people who'll never use it, I don't know!"

"Surely not the rest of her life," Cecile protested.

"Why not? I happen to enjoy it," Norma said. "Any-way, I'm the family oddball. Always was."

Norma was plain, short of stature, and too broad of face. Yet, because that face with its keen roving eyes was so extraordinarily alert and intelligent, many a person, seeing her for the first time, had felt a kind of shock.

"You are not an oddball," Amanda said firmly.

"Oh, yes. Even my brother, who really loves me—

really, really does—even he says I am because I'd rather read than eat. Anyhow, enough of me. Have you decided, Amanda? Are you staying up here or going back south for good?"

"I don't know. I can't seem to make up my mind. One thing makes me mad, though. Nobody ever told me that a B.A. means almost nothing anymore, not my kind of a B.A., anyway. If I knew something *definite,* the way you know Latin, for instance, I could walk right into a teaching job, at least at a private school like yours where you don't absolutely have to have a degree in education. As it is, without graduate school, I don't see what there is for me." Amanda sighed. "So I might as well flip a coin. Spend the summer scorching here in the Missouri drought, or else cross the Mississippi and sweat in the soggy heat at home while I look for some kind of a job, though God knows what."

Cecile reminded her, "No matter what you decide, you'll have to come back up here for my wedding. You've got to be a bridesmaid. I'm paying the airfare and buying the dress, so no argument about it."

"Come stay for a couple of weeks with me," Norma urged. "I've a hunch that might help you solve your problem, if you know what I mean."

"No, I don't know what you mean." Amanda had a way of discarding at will, or else retaining, her native accent. Now, widening her eyes with puzzled innocence, she recrossed the Mississippi. "What d'y'all mean?"

Norma laughed. "You know perfectly well what. My brother Larry is more than a little bit crazy about you. He thinks you're absolutely beautiful."

"Well, so she is," Cecile said stoutly.

"Your brother Larry doesn't know a thing about me. I've been in your house only twice, for two weeks each time. What can you tell about a person in those few days?"

"You can tell plenty," Cecile declared, still stoutly. "Why, Peter and I both knew after the first three days, right here on this campus. Peter Mack, the senior, and Cecile Newman, the freshman! It was all unheard of, and still we both knew, no matter what anybody said."

Amanda studied her fingernails. Shell pink ovals with white tips in the French style, they were beautifully cared for by herself. She was thinking of Larry's latest letter that had come yesterday. By now, if she had saved all the letters, she would have more than a dozen of them, but she had not saved them. Thoughtful and quite correct, they were also far too frank and effusive. To be admired is one thing, but this was so sudden as to be absurd. And yet, here was Cecile with her tale of three days.

Obviously Amanda was thinking, Cecile saw, so she changed the subject. "Weren't we going to have some-body take our picture downstairs in front of the house before we leave?" she asked.

Norma said quickly, "Yes, but not today, and not a full-length picture. I need to press a long skirt first."

Automatically the two friends glanced at, and as quickly away from, Norma's legs. Shapeless and thick, the ankles measured the same as the knees. Held to-gether, they were almost as wide as somebody's small waist. These legs were the bane of Norma's existence, *bane* being *poison;* in a way, they had poisoned her life— or she had allowed them to do so.

In elementary school, the boys called me "piano

legs," until Larry, my brother, was old enough to beat them up for doing it.

"I have no time now, anyway," Amanda said. "Sundale's Coffee Shop awaits me," she mocked. "Will you be stopping at Sundale's later, either of you?"

"You're sure we don't bother you when one of us comes in?" Cecile asked gently.

"No, why should you? Come and admire me in my baby blue uniform."

"All right. If I can get through some more of this packing, I will. But just look."

The small space, cramped to start with, was jammed with possessions. Cecile's and Norma's rooms—or cubicles—were heaped with clothing and books, all seemingly flung at random on the beds. More books were stacked in boxes on the floor. Luggage waited to be filled; it was fine luggage, leather and tweed, Amanda saw, estimating its cost.

"Oh, well, I'll save some éclairs for you," she said. "If you don't come, I'll bring them back and put them in the refrigerator."

"Suddenly I feel so sorry for her," Cecile exclaimed when the door had closed. "She never seemed to be the kind of person you'd feel sorry for. In all the time we've known her, she never once complained about anything. Today is the first time."

"She's been wearing a mask all the time, haven't you realized that?"

"Do you think so? But she seems to get so much pleasure out of every little thing. It's almost contagious to be with her."

"No, no, no! What is a little thing to you is a big

thing to her. She must have been awfully deprived. I can't believe you haven't seen that in her."

"Probably," said Cecile with a small rueful smile, "I haven't because I've been too spoiled all my life."

"You're the least spoiled person, Cecile, given your circumstances. You're merely inexperienced."

"Well, I certainly know that it can't be exactly easy to be on a scholarship work-study program, but so many people do it, that it doesn't seem quite so—"

"She has more on her mind than that," Norma said, interrupting. "Things must be pretty bad at home, and being up here can only have made them seem worse. She's very torn between going back or getting away for good. I get hints of it when she's at my house, but only hints."

"Strange. So beautiful, and so smart. To look at her, you'd think she had everything."

When Sundale's closed at eleven o'clock, Amanda walked out into a clear, soft night. Most of the employees turned toward the avenue, there to catch the day's last bus for the long ride into the city; only one young woman, who lived in the town, took Amanda's direction toward the university. She was considerably younger than Amanda, only a senior in high school, yet in these fifteen-minute walks to the spot where their ways parted, they had developed a kind of intimacy. Perhaps it was the quiet neighborhood of sleeping houses and the solitary path on which their footsteps rang that had encouraged the intimacy.

"I see your friends didn't come tonight," said Terry.

"No. They're still packing up. Me, I can practically carry back all my stuff in my own two hands."

"You going to be sorry to leave?"

"In a way. In another way, I sometimes think I'm sorry I ever came."

"You aren't! Gee, if I could go there, I'd give anything, even though I'm glad I'm going to State U. It's half the price, maybe less. Gee, so much seems to depend on money, doesn't it?"

Under the sky's weak night light, Amanda glimpsed the girl's upturned face. Its innocence was not four years, but forty years younger than her own. And with a feeling almost maternal, she said gently, "You'll do all right, Terry."

The fact was that this girl very probably would. One Saturday afternoon, at Terry's urging, Amanda had gone over to visit her at home. The house was small and simple, but beautifully cared for by Terry's father, who was a carpenter, and by her mother, who worked in a pastry shop and kept the neat kitchen fragrant with good cooking. The little brother had been doing his homework at a table in the front room, while a fox terrier lay in his basket under the table. Leaving the house that day, Amanda had looked back. For a moment she had had a strange feeling, a pang of envy, as if a magic circle had been drawn around that house and all the people in it.

Terry was curious. "However did you get a scholarship? You must have been head of the class."

"Well, I was. I had A's all through, but all A's aren't equal to each other, you know. There wasn't much competition at home. Here, I got B-pluses, and believe me, I had to work hard to get them."

Terry, still curious, had another question. "How did you get to room with those two girls?"

"I was in three of Norma's classes. We got talking, and we liked each other. Then when Norma and Cecile got those rooms, they asked to have me assigned to the third bedroom."

"Who's the pretty one with the dark hair and the plaid pleated skirt? Sort of athletic looking and preppie?"

"That's Cecile. She is athletic. She plays lacrosse."

"What's the matter with the other one's legs?"

"It's something about her glands, Cecile told me. Pituitary, or thyroid, or something."

"With legs like those, you'd want to die, wouldn't you?"

"I don't know. I only know she's one of the nicest people I've ever met."

"Oh." There came a pause, and then another question. "Why did you say you're sorry you ever came here?"

"When I have the right answer to that, I'll tell you, Terry. Here's my street. Get home safely."

What indeed was the right answer? Two forces raged, one of them the longing for home, and the other a need to stay away from home and start another life. The conflict was sometimes almost physically exhausting, not the least so because of the effort to keep one's trouble to oneself. She had revealed too much today. It must not happen again.

All was dark and quiet except for a dim light in the hall when she went back to the dorm. Tiptoeing into the closet-size kitchen, she put the éclairs into the refrigerator, closing the door without a sound, so as not to disturb the sleepers. Sometimes when she caught herself tiptoeing, there came a sense of being, in a vague way, an intruder here, even though there was no sensible reason for feeling like that. Taken in one piece, this last year in these rooms had been wonderful. She would remember it as a collage of snow sliding on the windowpanes, of music on Norma's CD player, of food and drink, pretzels and chips, beer, and a crowding of feminine voices. It had been a curiously feminine time; Norma had no boyfriend; Cecile, wearing Peter's diamond on her left hand, most certainly wanted none; I, thought Amanda, had no time for boyfriends because when I wasn't studying to keep up, I was working every weekend and skipping half my vacations to earn something at Sundale's. No, you would never think that a year spent that way could still have been so wonderful. And that in spite of all, it could be so painful to leave it behind.

Restless now, not ready for sleep although it was midnight and she had been rushing around since five o'clock, Amanda went slowly through the nightly routine, repairing chipped polish on her nails, spreading lotion on her feet, and caring for her teeth, which were strong and even.

"You have a short upper lip," Norma, who noticed details, had remarked, "so your teeth show when you smile. You're lucky that they're so perfect."

Luck. Yes, she had had a good deal of it after all. She would never have been here if she hadn't come from Mill River and been a little bit—no, quite a good deal—different from the rest of her class. She was probably the only one in it who loved books so much. She was her family's *oddball*, as Norma was hers. And if the principal hadn't been an old-time college friend of some important people on the faculty here . . .

Yes, and besides all this, she had made these two friends, the first *real* ones she had ever had. In a way she felt closer to them than to her own sisters, although she hated to think so. But it was true, and it had nothing to do with any good things that Norma and Cecile had done for her.

Still, sometimes people think what they want to think. Isn't that so? Amanda asked herself. Perhaps if Cecile hadn't done so many warmhearted things, like giving me that sweater—

A little blue treasure, it lay in its original glossy box on top of her suitcase. It was a duplicate of one of Cecile's, which she had innocently admired. Desire for it must have been written on her face, for on her birthday, Cecile had produced that glossy box with a ribbon bow on it. The ribbon bow was still saved, tucked now under the sweater.

They were from another world, those two, Cecile and Norma, friends from their kindergarten year at some private country day school that, in the snapshots at least, was apparently surrounded by lawns. Some might wonder, judging by outward appearances, what Cecile might possess in common with Norma. But anyone who knew them both would understand. For in some ways, Norma was extraordinary. She had quite literally a photographic memory. You would have to see it to believe, Amanda thought now. She could scan a page in a textbook and then repeat the whole page. She played the piano very well, was witty, and could be amusing. Perhaps you might say that all these gifts were compensation for her miserable legs. Who knew?

But might it not be also, Amanda reflected, that Cecile

was attracted to Norma's way of life? Cecile always came
to town to visit when Amanda was there; living on a
farm fifteen miles out of town, she was probably glad to
leave it whenever she could. Norma lived on a fine suburban street in a marvelous house with a lovely garden in
the yard and a guest room with its own private bath.
There was even a woman, Elsa, who kept the house and
did the cooking. Amanda had loved it there. . . .

My brother's a little bit crazy about you.

He was nice enough, very calm and friendly. A large
man, seeming older than twenty-six, with hair already
thinning and a square face with brown eyes like Norma's.
Neither one of them had their father's cool, severe good
looks. His name was Lawrence. Lawrence Balsan.

Larry hated being a "junior." One night on the porch
he had confided in Amanda, and told her so. He would
gladly have used his middle name, Daniel, were it not
that his father liked the sound of Lawrence, Junior. That
seemed to be a foolish concession on Larry's part, unless
you reckoned the advantages of not angering a father
whose name was on signs scattered all over the county:
Balsan Real Estate.

The company had three offices. Larry ran two of
them. Five years ago he had been graduated summa cum
laude from this same university. Highest praise! Norma
was so proud of her brother that she might have been his
mother. Well, that was easy enough to explain: Their
mother had died, their father was remote, and the children had clung together.

Brushing until her scalp tingled, Amanda reflected.
People were so endlessly fascinating with their motives
and quirks. What was it about herself, for instance, that

had caused Larry Balsan to fall in love with her? Surely he must know dozens of pretty girls.

Yet surely, too, if she wanted, she could "catch" him. It was easy to tell when a man was teetering on the verge. But she really, really—as Norma would say—didn't want him. Those few embraces on the porch swing had been proof enough. She had felt nothing, and she wanted to feel everything.

At noon a few days later, Amanda stepped out of the bus into the pouring sunshine of central Mississippi. Along the length of Main Street, there were not more than a dozen parked cars and a not much greater number of people on the sidewalks. Four years ago she would most likely have recognized—or been recognized by—most of them, but long absences between brief vacations had rendered her almost a stranger. She walked on, not even glancing at the shops, for she knew by heart what was in each window and what had always been in them: the butcher's hams, the beauty parlor's array of toiletries, the grocery's canned goods stacked in pyramids, the shirts and jeans in Ben's Dry Goods—all unchanged. The town dozed. It was, in its torpor, extraordinarily ugly except perhaps for the sapphire sky above it. There was nothing here to give greeting or to please the eye. She had never noticed that before.

Her bulging suitcase, which needed new wheels that she hadn't had time to get, weighed her down on one side; she had to change hands after every few hundred steps. Over her arm dangled the lightweight carry-on that was Cecile's and Norma's going-away present. Striped in black and white, it was so pretty that her glance had kept returning to it all through this long day. In it were a book for the plane and the three bus changes that had brought her home; in it also was her diploma.

The family had no idea of what that piece of paper signified. They knew only that it was a proud thing to own, since most people they knew did not own one. And, trudging along through the heat that sweated her shirt onto her back, she felt how sad it was that they had not even been able to see the grandeur of the faculty procession, the tasseled caps, the gowns, and the insignia; nor had they heard the brasses ring out "Pomp and Circumstance," nor heard her name called as she stood to receive this proud piece of paper.

Too expensive. The plane fare was, and the hotel was, and the time off from the shirt factory where her sister Lorena and her father both worked was also too expensive. Yet, if Dad hadn't fallen and shattered his thighbone that week, he and Mom would have scraped together the bus fare and come.

In a spot of shade, she had to stop and sit down on a boulder to rest her trembling arms. Here were the familiar crossroads. The factory was on the other side of town, going back where she had just come from. The school was on the right, and home was two miles straight ahead. It seemed to her that everything looked gray. Apparently, it had not rained for a long time; the road, though tarred, was also gray. And the houses, so many of them in need of paint, as was her own, were also gray.

Mixed emotions were what she had. And she said it aloud: Mixed emotions. The here and the there. The here, where you could be yourself, not wondering what impression you were making.

"When you are beautiful," Norma had once confided in a wistful moment, "you don't have to wonder what people are thinking about you."

But Norma was quite, quite mistaken. There was much more to it than being beautiful. What impression, for instance, would Amanda make on her father's boss or on his son? A fleeting one. Two seconds' worth, she might be sure. To begin with, that assumed a meeting which, since such people generally lived far from the town in a house with a columned veranda, would never happen in the first place. They came from different worlds. You had to be realistic.

On the ground beside her feet were the suitcase and the carry-on. All at once, it occurred to her that the ground was dirty. And in fear that she might have damaged the carry-on, she picked it up to look. Thank goodness it wasn't soiled. In it was a collapsible umbrella that she had bought to protect it in case of a shower. The blue sweater was in it, too; this was for safety's sake, in case the suitcase should be lost. All her best possessions, the silver charm bracelet, the flowered summer bathrobe, and the soft, fur-lined gloves—no use for them here in this part of the country—were gifts from Norma and Cecile. Mostly, they were from Norma, who seemed to be so much better off than Cecile.

She stood up. There was only one more bend in the road, where, under the live oak, one of her sisters would be waiting for her. They would have consulted the bus schedule and timed the walk home, as the family always did whenever there was no car available to fetch anyone from town. There had never been enough cars for so large a family, with so many going to jobs in different directions. We're certainly not what you would call *poor*, Amanda reflected now, yet there had never been enough of anything.

There indeed and at last was Lorena with the large, cheerful smile on her still childish face. And with glad cries they rushed to meet.

Lorena's room contained a bed and a crib for the baby. They had had to bring in a cot for Amanda, since Tommy, now grown too old to share a room with another of the little girls, had had to move in with Hank and Bub. The house, especially since Lorena had come back with her three children, was bursting at the seams. There was no air in the room now, for it had begun to rain hard and the window was closed. Amanda had not had a bath this evening because Dad, her brothers, her youngest sister Baby, and Lorena's children had been using the bathroom until it was so late that she was too tired to take one.

It began to storm. A crash of thunder shook the house, and the baby awoke. In the dim light Amanda could see Lorena getting up to hold him. As he wailed, she crooned and rocked him. It had to be at least two o'clock by now, and Lorena got up every morning at half-past five to get breakfast ready before leaving for the shirt factory with Dad. It would have been impossibly harder for her if Mom had not been able to stay home and take care of the other children.

"You look different," Lorena had said immediately when they met.

"In what way?"

"I don't know. Just different since you were here at

Christmas. You always were different, Amanda, but now you're more so."

"Well, you look the same. Still pretty."

But it was not true. Lorena had puffs under her eyes and hollows in her cheeks; she was too thin; she had aged. Aged, at twenty-seven! A lump of pity stuck in Amanda's throat.

Of course, you didn't have to be like this simply because you lived in Mill River. You didn't need to marry a ne'er-do-well while both of you were in a state of ridiculous, thoughtless infatuation. You didn't need to have more children than you could afford, as Dad and Mom had done. It all depended upon how you, as a thinking person, made your choices.

Now, lying awake on the thin, lumpy mattress, Amanda's mind wandered back to the supper table where, a few hours ago, she had been enveloped by a loving welcome. Exactly as she had expected, they were taking it for granted that she had come home to stay with them.

"We need to get to know you again," Dad had complained. "You only came for a week last summer and went right away up there to that college."

The grievance was plain to hear. As gently as she could, Amanda had replied, "I needed to work, Dad. The job paid pretty well, with tips and a free dinner—I had to go back."

"With that diploma you've got, you could get a nice job here," Mom had said. Her forehead was marked with anxious wrinkles, and her voice was plaintive. She had made several trips to the stove, refilling their plates from the pot in hand, and with each time had repeated herself. "A nice job in an office at the high school. I'll bet you would get it if you asked, Amanda. I'll bet you would."

Then Dad: "Maybe even in the office at the plant. Hey, you and Lorena and me going off to work together, me and Lorena in our work duds and you trotting upstairs in your high heels with diamonds in your ears!" He chuckled. "How about that?"

"Yeah, but don't marry some bum and don't come back with no kids like Lorena's." Her youngest brother, Bub, had a way of shouting even when he was merely saying something like "Pass the butter." "Home is bustin' at the seams now."

Lorena, with the baby on her lap, leaned over to wipe brown gravy from Dottie's chin. Plainly, she was too tired to give Bub an answer.

Mom soothed, and worried. "Don't talk like that, Bub. Any girl of ours can bring her babies home anytime, if she ever needs to."

"Long as they're as pretty as these three," Dad said. "Look at them. Goin' to put them all in the movies, that's what. Then we'll all quit working."

"Us, too," Mom said. "You'll sing, Dad, and I'll dance."

That they could make jokes and be jolly here! Yet, here is where she had grown up and gotten used to it all, to the smell of fried grease and the littered, untidy kitchen. A person could very likely get used to all of it again, if she had to. And get used to the town, too, where nothing much ever happened, or ever would. Tomorrow would be like today, the day after would be the same, and the day after that . . . She had always been out of place here and was now still more out of place.

A desolate rain beat on the window. And Amanda, as the night wore on, had a strange sensation of being disconnected, of floating perhaps, with a fearful need to grasp something solid. It seemed to her at last that the only solid substance with which she had any contact was her friendship with Norma and Cecile. A family like Norma's especially—never mind her brother—would have a golden key that would open many doors.

Long before the dull, rainy dawn, Amanda had made her decision. Norma had invited her to spend a few weeks at her house before Cecile's wedding. So, then, she would stay home here until next Monday, would with some pangs of sharp regret kiss them all good-bye, and would leave for Michigan.

CHAPTER TWO

The porch swing creaked and jerked as it swung. Larry had an annoying habit of propelling it too high with his feet, and Amanda, sitting beside him, wished he would stop. After the third week here, these evenings were starting to produce a tension within her. There was a sense of expectancy in the atmosphere, as if everybody was waiting for something to happen, to be resolved. And everyone knew very well what it was.

"Tomorrow's the shortest night in the year," Norma remarked, making bright conversation. "It's after ten now, and it still doesn't seem completely dark, does it?"

Larry said, "I wish I could take the day off tomorrow and be outdoors, but there are two sales pending, and I can't let them slip. I should have been a schoolteacher like you. Then I'd have two months off in the summer. You knew darn well what you were doing, Norma."

He, too, was making conversation. But he had spoken with affection, and Norma laughed as though he had said something humorous. Then she stood, excusing herself, and covered a yawn.

"If you all don't mind, I think I'll go up to bed now."

"Leaving your guest?" The question was a reprimand, and it was the third time Larry's father had made it since Amanda had been here. She had counted the times. She had the impression that Lawrence Balsan was a perfectionist.

"I don't mind," Amanda said quickly. "I'm used to Norma. She was always the first one in the whole dorm to go to bed. And why not go, if she's sleepy?"

"Amanda knows me pretty well," Norma said brightly.

"Well, it's just not courteous," Mr. Balsan insisted, as if his daughter needed instruction.

"I can hardly keep my eyes open," Norma answered, ignoring the criticism as she opened the screen door. Amanda knew that she had gone upstairs to get out of the way. Larry had probably asked her to leave them alone. But the father was not about to get out of their way. He reveals himself, she thought, with those remarks about making sales to "the right sort of people" from "the right kind of background." That's why there have been all those questions—so polite, so casual—about my family and my home. God knows I understand him, and who better than I? Am I one to blame a person for wanting the good things? He's built his business from nothing, and he wants his son to marry up. It's as simple as that. The funny thing is, he knows I know it. I catch his glances.

A beam of light from indoors revealed Lawrence sitting upright in his chair, still wearing proper jacket and tie, although the night was warm. He had a sculptured face with no excess roundness of flesh to hide the bones, the very slightly aquiline nose, the resolute chin, or the curved structure surrounding the brilliant, youthful eyes. It was a haughty face. His employees were probably rather afraid of him.

An involuntary smile touched her mouth. She was thinking that this scene could come out of a nineteenth-century novel. Trollope or Dickens would reproduce it superbly with all its elements of potential tragedy and humor, of disappointment, ambition, and conflict hidden beneath the still summer night.

The sweetness of the night! Dark blue and shadowed under the trees, it was all white moonlight in the spaces between them. A bird, disturbed in its nest, gave a single, twittering cry. White iris gleamed along the path near the lantern.

"I've been thinking, Larry," said Lawrence, "we ought to take a small piece of that garden apartment. Naturally, they would like us to invest a serious amount, but I prefer to be cautious. It will probably do very well, yet there's risk of competition close by."

"From that vacant plot on the corner. Yes, I was thinking that it should be up for sale soon," Larry agreed. "I give it a year, maybe two, before they get moving on it."

Unlike his father's manner of speech, which was clipped short, Larry's was unhurried and calm. Up to this week, Amanda had not noticed it; nor had it occurred to her that the voice matched the man.

"Even our father knows that he's an asset to the firm," Norma had told her. "Everybody likes Larry so much."

Yes, everybody would. He had an easy manner that made you comfortable. Yet in his quiet way, he was firm. It surprised her that she had so suddenly come to take so much notice of his qualities.

As the swing moved, the creak that had annoyed her before began to lull instead. And that, too, was surprising. The minute his father should leave them alone, she knew that Larry would take her in his arms and kiss her. That action had become a pattern to which she made no objection. It was, after all, to be expected. He wanted her. Really, he was not about to hand her any golden key to open other doors. The only reason that they had never done anything more than a little kissing was the simple one that they were, after all, living in the family home. Larry was not the kind of man who would settle for the backseat of a car, for which, having had a few such experiences and having hated them, Amanda was thankful.

The two male voices, although so near, were yet so remote to her that she was barely aware of them; her mind had begun to fill with odd new thoughts. If he were to ask her straight out—and she had a feeling that it would happen soon, probably tonight—would it be at all sensible to turn him down? I could be fond of him in time, she thought. And thinking so, she began to feel shame at having, only in her mind and only very briefly, considered the possibility of using him as a stepping-stone toward someone better.

Fondness could easily turn into love, maybe a better

love than it would be if she were mad about him, infatuated, as he obviously was about her. People had always married for practical reasons, and their marriages turned out well, indeed often more successful than most. It had happened all through human history, and was still happening.

As the swing moved, it began to feel rather pleasant after all to have a man's shoulder pressing against her own. The shoulder pressed closer, as if he felt her willingness. His aftershave lotion smelt of pine or some aromatic shrub. Yes, she thought again, I could really be fond of him. Rosy scenes of herself becoming a good wife, while having the means for graduate study and learning to do something significant—the vision of such a life grew warm within her as she leaned more closely upon Larry's shoulder. Yes, I would be very good to him and for him, she thought again. I would never fool such a good man. He has all of Norma's trustfulness.

Curiously, the fact that his father disapproved of her only added to the excitement of this new vision, and to its challenge.

So much had changed, so rapidly, in these short weeks.

At last Lawrence said, "I'm going in. You need to get up early, Larry, and have your wits about you. Are you forgetting that those Fleming people are coming tomorrow morning? Nine sharp."

"I'm not forgetting, Dad."

When the screen door clicked shut, Larry smiled. "His bark is worse than his bite. Does he scare you?"

"Not at all."

"He has a big heart. You have to know him. He was father and mother to Norma and me after our mother died."

He stood up, and pulling her off the swing, took her in his arms. "Come here. Oh, Amanda, come here. I wish we could go someplace—you know, don't you? You know that I love you?"

They clung together. When she opened her eyes, she saw past his shoulder that there were thousands of stars in the sky. And she knew that she was being moved by the loveliness of the night, by the soft air and the rustle of wind through the trees. It was as if she were seeing herself, as if she had stepped outside herself, watching a woman emerge from a forest into the starlight.

"It is like a dream," she said.

"It isn't a dream. The first time I saw you, when you came here with my sister, I said to myself, 'I'd like to marry that girl.' And I haven't stopped thinking of you since that day. Norma knows. She told me how wonderful you are. She told me all about how hard you work, how smart you are. Not that I didn't see enough for myself— So . . . so, can you? Will you, Amanda?"

"You haven't known me more than six weeks altogether. Are you sure?"

"I couldn't be more sure if I'd known you since you were born."

When he drew away and grasped her hands, his plain face glowed. And she was touched by the joy that she saw there. The look that he gave her was so glad, and yet so wistful, that it filled her with tenderness, so that her eyes filled with tears.

After a while, long past midnight, Larry took charge

of practical matters. "We'll be married right after your friend Cecile's wedding. It wouldn't be right to steal their thunder. Maybe you won't believe this, and don't laugh, but in my daydreams this past month, I've been considering getting a house for us. There are four or five nice places for sale, a couple of colonials and a couple of ranches with everything on one floor, that you might like. Each one has a good yard, with old trees. I've noticed how you love trees."

A house right at the start? Marriage and a house, all at once?

"You look so happy," he said.

"I am happy."

And, as the unbelievable events of the last few hours became believable, as the shock of it ran like fire through her very bones, she really was happy.

They were whispering at the guest room door. "You don't know how much I want to go in there with you, Amanda."

"Not a good idea," she teased, glancing toward the father's door.

"Wait till we tell them in the morning." Larry was elated. "Norma won't be surprised, but my father will probably be stunned. Or maybe he won't be. He knows I have a way of making quick decisions."

"And standing by them?"

"And standing by them, Amanda darling."

Whatever his private thoughts might be, and Amanda had a good idea what they were, Lawrence Balsan said the proper things the next day. At least, in her presence, he did.

"Well, you've certainly picked a beautiful bride. As to

your wedding plans, this house and the yard are yours. Indoors or outdoors. You select."

Amanda had made clear to Larry that a wedding at her family's home was an impossibility, and he had obviously informed his father accordingly. As to her own people, Larry had a good conversation with each of them in turn, parents, sisters and brothers, cordially urging them to come for the wedding and stay here as long as they wished. Then, accepting with grace their explanation of why they could not come, he promised to keep in touch and to consider them all as his new family.

"Do you feel very sad that they won't be here?" he asked.

"Well, yes, but not as much as I would once have thought I'd be. After four years of college, you get used to being apart. In a way, I feel closer to Norma than to them. Yes, I've actually been closer to her, living there together."

Most generously Larry had offered to pay for her family's trip to Michigan, and also generously had accepted their reasons for not coming: the painful leg, and the time already lost away from the job. To these Amanda could have added: proper clothing and a certain shyness, for they had never been more than two hundred miles away from home.

It had not been necessary for her mother to explain this, so well did they communicate without words.

"Amanda, you know, you must know how happy we are for you. Later, as soon as you and Larry are settled in your own place—it will be more intimate, you understand. Oh, he sounded so nice on the telephone, I could feel that he'll be good to you."

*   *   *

For Larry, in the real estate business, the summer months were the busiest; on many an evening and many a Sunday also, he was out showing houses. Most of Amanda's time, then, was spent with Norma and her women friends at the town pool or the town tennis courts. These were lovely, leisurely days, the first leisurely stretch of time with no obligations that she had ever known.

Larry had given her his mother's engagement ring, a round diamond that called forth admiration, and undoubtedly some hidden envy, from Norma's group. Amanda had no idea of its value, since mere size could, as she had read, be deceptive. She had also read somewhere that round-cut stones have a special brilliance. At any rate, it was a great pleasure to stretch her hand out into the light so that the stone flashed sparks. Cecile's chip of a diamond had been too small to flash.

Cecile had been out of sight since Commencement Day. First there had been Peter's commencement in New York, then after that shopping for the wedding and for the apartment which they had taken close to his job, some twenty miles distant from the Newmans' house.

"We should go for a drive some afternoon," Norma said one day. "You haven't really seen anything of this city outside of the neighborhood, and you need to, now that you're going to live here. Maybe we'll go as far as Cecile's house, just to pass it, since she's not there now. Incidentally, I mailed her a clipping from the paper, the one Dad put in about you and Larry."

Amanda laughed. "I sent her one, too."

And she thought how odd it was that things like having one's name in the paper, just as Cecile had had hers, and wearing a ring on the left hand, just as Cecile did, made a person feel *equal*.

"We've grown," Norma told Amanda as they drove downtown one day. "Once we were a big town, one of the biggest in Michigan, but now we're a small city. Or maybe not so small. Here along the river is where we got started, with shipping. Mostly grain, later on tires, steel, cement—the works. Today, every big corporation west of the Mississippi has a finger in our pie. These past few years we've been getting the new technology. Look over there. Every few months another tower raises its head." Loving history, analysis, and explanations, Norma was a good teacher. "And naturally, people are spreading into the suburbs, farther and farther from the river, while this area that we're coming to is falling to pieces. Here's the old station. You can see how elegant it was, grand as the ancient Roman baths. One of these days, I guess, they'll be doing something with it, and with the switchyards, too. Twenty-seven acres of rusting rails and rotting sheds going to waste. The railroad is naturally holding out for the right price, the conservationists want it, and the whole thing's a mess, nothing's been done. It's all politics, anyway. Now here's Lane Avenue. Isn't it a disgrace for people to live in slums like these? Look at the school! Can you imagine spending all day in a dreary dump like that? The only cheerful-looking sights here are the prostitutes. Don't laugh. Look at these two. They may be prostitutes, but they are pretty, aren't they?"

"Who around here has money to pay them?" asked Amanda.

"Customers don't have to come from these streets.

They come from everywhere. Some of these buildings have rooms for rent, or even a whole flat to lease. A man can drive in from his country estate in half an hour. Very convenient."

"I'm certainly getting an education. I had no idea."

Norma laughed. She hadn't thought Amanda was that naive. "Country girl! Well, just don't ever accept any invitations to a party on Lane Avenue, will you?"

"Okay, I'll remember not to."

"Here we go, over the bridge to some fresh country air."

The landscape changed abruptly from concrete to grass. First the city fell behind, then there briefly appeared a few miles of suburban houses in their neat yards, and after that, as a curtain is lifted or a door is opened, came space. Wide, free, and blooming space.

Long driveways led toward great houses, glimpsed in their tall, protective groves. White fences enclosed a field where horses trotted around a training ring. Ducks floated on a pond. Brown-and-white cows grazed near their fine stone barn with a weather vane on its roof. A mild, softly gilded peace lay on the hills and the road that wound among them.

Amanda was unusually silent, and Norma began to wonder whether she might be bored by all this scenery, so she inquired, "Are you enjoying this trip or not? Tell me. We can go back if you want to."

"Oh, no! It's beautiful. It's a kind of paradise."

The moisture in Amanda's eyes moved Norma to cry out with all her heart, "I am so glad my brother found you!"

"I'm glad, too," Amanda said, smiling.

"You're so right for each other. You are lively, he's quiet; you are emotional, he's reserved. Opposites attract, and they should."

"Larry's not entirely reserved, I assure you."

"Well, I meant—oh, I might as well come out with all my thoughts while I'm at it. Larry's a strong man, but he's not using all his strength. This is hard for me to say, but truth is truth, Amanda. When a young man is in business with his father, it can get complicated. It's not that our father isn't a good one, and devoted to us, but—well, you've sat at the table with him often enough by now to have a pretty good idea of what I mean. He *rules*. That sums it up. He rules. It must have been hard on him when Mama died, leaving him with a twelve-year-old boy and an eight-year-old girl to rear. But he did his best, and we certainly didn't have any serious complaints to make. We had good care, and the house was peaceful. But it wasn't what you'd call a jolly or a *happy* house. So that's why I'm glad for Larry. Well, enough of that. Want to pass Cecile's place? It's only a few minutes away from here."

The long, low house lay gleaming in the sunlight. At the foot of the driveway, where the gates were flung back to their stone pillars, she stopped the car.

Amanda gave a low cry. "This? This is Cecile's house?"

"Yes. Pretty, isn't it?"

"I thought—she said she lived on a farm! I had no idea—this doesn't look like any farm I ever saw."

"Well, it is a sort of farm, what people call a 'gentleman's farm.' If you'd spent more time here I'd have taken you to see it before this. It's really lovely. They have animals and crops, and the house is what is supposedly farmhouse style."

"Can we go in, just for a peek?" Amanda was astonished and excited. "What do you think? Can we?"

It had not occurred to Norma that Amanda would be so totally astonished. But sometimes—rarely—you do get inside another person's head, and at this moment, only for a moment, Norma became Amanda in her blue Sundale uniform.

"We won't peek. We'll go right up and ring the bell. The Newmans knew me when I was five years old, and if they're not home, the maids still know me. Come on."

It was Cecile's mother, Harriet, who answered the door. As often before when she had not seen her for a long time, Norma was startled by her likeness to Cecile, having the same smooth, dark hair, the same figure, just slightly broader, and even, on this particular day, the same Scottish plaid kilt fastened by a large pin. No doubt Amanda, who noticed and remembered things like that, had also observed the kilt pin, nor would she have missed the welcome in Mrs. Newman's eyes. Even the house spoke welcome, with its comfortable chairs, its flowerpots, and its pair of barking retrievers.

"And this is Amanda," Norma said. "You had a quick glimpse of her on graduation day, and now she's here to stay."

"Amanda!" cried Mrs. Newman. "I knew all about you long before that quick glimpse; southern, very smart, very good-natured, and very pretty, Cecile told us. I'm so sorry she isn't here today. She's gone shopping in town."

"I thought you wouldn't mind if we dropped in," Norma said.

"Mind? Of course not. Wait till I get Amos. He's out in the garden, as usual. He should have been a gardener. Come this way. I'll show you where the wedding's going to be. Pray Heaven it won't rain that day. Oh, well, if it does, we'll all squeeze inside. How is everybody at home, Norma? Your father? Your brother?"

"Both well, thank you. Larry's doing especially well. He's going to be married this summer."

"Wonderful! I only met him once, but I remember that I liked him. He made an impression. Who's the bride?"

"Right here. Amanda."

"Really? That's so lovely, Amanda! You three room-mates staying nearby, like a family. I remember how all my best friends separated from one end of the country to the other. Yes, this will be lovely for all of you."

They had gone out through the wide central hall onto a terrace, from which a few steps descended to an expanse of greenery. Beyond these, in a rolling distance, rose a tier of low hills.

On the step, Amanda paused. "I've never seen hills," she said. "There are none where I grew up."

"Well, people think we're all flat corn and wheatfields in the Midwest, and mostly we are. That's why these hills are so precious. There's Amos in the rose garden. I see the top of his straw hat."

Amos Newman was so tall that the top of his hat could be seen above the brick enclosure. He had a long, lean head to match his height. When Norma and Cecile had been very small, he had used to let them ride, each in turn, on his shoulders. This memory returned whenever Norma saw him. Kindly memories, she thought now, as she announced Amanda's engagement to Larry, and went through the usual pleasantries. Kindly memories and kindly people, she thought, too; simple and unassuming in the midst of what almost everybody would describe as "splendor."

Amanda exclaimed over the roses. "Such marvelous colors! And the wedding will be right here?"

"No, no. This is much too small. It's my English garden, enclosed within four brick walls to keep the wind out. I built it for my special roses, and—look here—I've been experimenting with some fruit trees, espaliered, but I haven't been very successful with the fruit. I forgot this isn't France's or England's climate."

Amos's smile was rueful. Now, as long as he could be sure of a listener, he would get back to his roses. For a moment Norma waited, and sure enough, Amanda had at once perceived what Amos was waiting for.

"These are very unusual, Mr. Newman. I don't think I've ever seen them before."

"I'll bet you haven't. They're Near Eastern roses, called Phoenicia, accurately named. Very, very rare. I'm propagating more in my little hothouse. And these, come see, these are Autumn Damask. They bloom all summer until October. There are two rows of them in the main garden, right where they'll make an aisle for the wedding. You'd think somebody had planted them with that in mind, but I'll swear I didn't. Come, I'll show you."

"Amos," his wife protested, "not everybody in the world is a rose fancier."

"Oh, but I am," Amanda said quickly. "It's not that I know anything about them, I just simply love these colors. And the fragrance!"

"You need old roses for fragrance," Amos explained as the small procession left the walled garden. "These huge hybrid teas that look so gorgeous have hardly any."

Dutifully, the women followed him past perennial beds, box hedges, and althea bushes which, he pointed out, were members of the rose family, although one might not think so.

Amanda was following every word with deep interest, and Norma was amused, imagining how she would give the same attention to Larry's real estate ventures. Amanda knew how to please people.

When the garden tour was over, they were invited, almost commanded, to have tea on the terrace. Nothing had changed since Norma's childhood. In the field on the left, the Guernseys lay under the trees chewing their cuds. Next to the table, the dogs waited for a treat. A maid brought the silver teapot, the blue Wedgwood cups, and the big shell-shaped service plate bearing the cookies that were so familiar to Norma.

"Madeleines!" she exclaimed.

Amanda also exclaimed, "Then that's what they are! I always wondered when I read *Remembrance of Things Past*. So they're not cookies, but more like cakes."

Mrs. Newman was impressed. "You've read Proust?"

"Not all seven volumes, but I never mention that. It's nice to let people think you have read them all, though."

Amanda laughed at herself, wrinkling her little nose. She was charming.

The afternoon was drowsy. I could stretch out on the grass and watch the leaves quiver overhead, Norma thought. The conversation became only a soft murmur without meaning except for an occasional phrase.

"After the cow broke her leg, she had to be shot." This in a regretful tone from Amos.

"Peter has a starter job not far from here." This from Mrs. Newman. "I wouldn't be surprised if Cecile and he will be looking for a house before long and consulting Balsan Realty."

Now came the scrape of chairs as people stood up, and Norma became alert. Amanda was kissing Mrs. Newman and giving thanks for the lovely visit.

"This has been so beautiful. I'll never forget it."

"You won't have to think about either forgetting or remembering. You'll just naturally be coming here often as soon as Cecile is back."

"Let me take one more look!" Amanda cried in her silver voice.

At the edge of the terrace, she stood in her grace gazing out toward the violet hills.

"There's a beautiful girl," Amos whispered. "Your brother has good taste."

Isn't it a strange thing, thought Norma, that in all innocence a man can speak to me about another woman's beauty? Unthinking, he—and how many others besides him?—takes it for granted that I do not feel the contrast. I wonder whether Amanda can have any idea how lucky she is.

Back in the Balsans' guest bedroom, Amanda sat at the window with her chin in her hands, staring across the street at the house that Larry called a "sister house" to this one. They had been built before the First World War, and they were well constructed, he explained, made to last. That might be, but suddenly they looked ugly to her, square and boxy with bay windows bulging like frogs' eyes and a porch sticking out in front like a bullfrog's belly. Little kids were riding up and down the sidewalks on their toy tricycles, screaming at each other. Big boys ground by on skates with a noise that set your teeth on edge. The street was dreary and too crowded.

Her mood was depressed, or was it oppressed? How swiftly the spirit travels from one mood to the next! That house and those gardens this afternoon! And she had thought Cecile was the daughter of a farmer!

A "gentleman's farm," Norma said. "You might say it's a hobby. They're what you call 'old money,' not like us," she had explained with a smile. "Not like us. They're also the most generous people in the whole community, personally kind and helpful in every way. They're known for it."

I can imagine them, Amanda thought now, sitting there every afternoon, having their tea and cakes while they look out at the roses and the hills. On a cold or rainy day, then they will be indoors with a fire crackling under the mantel. Who would have thought that Cecile, with her simple ways, lived like that?

Everywhere I turned, it was so beautiful . . . the dogs running on the lawn . . . the monogrammed silver teapot . . . the cake plate, shaped like a shell . . . Cecile's mother, so calm and pleasant, pouring the tea. . . . *Mannerly,* it was all *mannerly.*

She was still at the window when somebody knocked on the door. A thought ran through her head as she went to open it: *At home, nobody knocks on a door.*

Norma was carrying a large, flat box. "Our dresses arrived! Just leave them in the box and peek under the tissue paper for now. Tomorrow we'll take them to the alteration people in case they should need anything. But look!"

Lustrous lemon-colored silk lay in long, flat folds. Cool and sleek to the touch, it soothed Amanda's fingertips.

She murmured, "We're to carry white rosebuds, I think?"

"Yes, won't it be lovely? This is my first time as a bridesmaid," Norma said.

"Mine, too."

"One of my cousins asked me once, but the dresses were practically miniskirts, and I couldn't see myself wearing one, so I declined. I'm sure she was relieved that I did."

"Long dresses always look better, anyway," Amanda said.

And feeling a sudden wave of pity for her friend, she put her arms around Norma, while for the second time that day, Norma cried out with a poignant gladness in her voice.

"Oh, I am so happy that my brother found you!"

CHAPTER THREE

Happy the bride the sun shines on, thought Norma. Usually at weddings, there is at least one person, often a nice old lady, who quotes the saying. And indeed today three people had already done so.

The sun, moving west, was behind them all, so that lightly, without glare, it touched the scene, the old yews that bordered the lawn, the ivy on the garden walls, the guests in the semicircle of chairs, and on every side, everywhere, the flowers. The breeze touched lightly, too, enough to freshen the air without ruffling Cecile's lace veil. In the stillness, the grave, poetic words of the ancient service rang like music.

Touched by fairy dust, thought Amanda in her enchantment, and in her hands the white rosebuds trembled.

Rapt, thought Norma, watching her. She is rapt. Why not? She thought for a word to describe this rite: The pinnacle? The peak? And all the awe and beauty was to culminate in the ultimate act of love, in the bed. No matter that for these two, Peter and Cecile, it would be far from the first time; this night would still be different, a culmination. In the eye of her mind, she saw them, stripped of their clothing and their solemnity.

Then almost immediately, as she stood there in the heart of the ceremony, she was ashamed of herself, and chided: Smile. All the ushers and bridesmaids are smiling. See how Amanda smiles?

Amanda was absorbing it all before in so few minutes it should pass away. Without fail, she must see and remember everything. How Cecile gleamed! Her dark eyes, her very white skin, her pearls—all were gleaming. Delicately shaped, in spite of lacrosse, she was perfection in a froth of organdy. She had class. That was the word: class. Perhaps it was her elegant repose? Or perhaps only the simple fact that she had grown up in a place like this one?

Peter was putting the ring on Cecile's finger, looking into her eyes as he spoke: "With this ring, I thee wed." He was an attractive man, with thick hair, a distinctive, mellow voice, and classic features, a male version of Cecile, strong yet sensitive. Quite sensitive, she decided. There was no mistaking his thoughtful eyes or his quietness. He was, after all, an architect, an artist. A man like him must be very, very interesting . . .

The mothers in the front row of chairs were wiping their eyes. Harriet Newman was really a handsome woman. All these people were dignified and handsome in their way. Everything was correct and orderly. At the proper instant, the musicians, hidden behind the shrubbery, broke into Mendelssohn's triumphant march, and everyone rose to let the wedding party pass down the flowery aisle. Yes, orderly and correct, orchestrated to perfection right down to the receiving line under the shade of the giant sycamores.

Cecile had turned pink with excitement. "Peter, Amanda, you two know each other well enough, goodness knows, but Larry, you'll get to know Peter better now—you've hardly met—"

"Twice," Peter said. "When Norma was visiting here one day, you gave me a lift. It was my senior year at college, and I was very impressed by you as a man of business, already out in the world."

Larry laughed. "I remember we were kidding about the girls, Norma, Cecile, and Amanda, even though I hadn't met Amanda yet. We named them the three musketeers, female style."

"Yes, and we're going to stay three musketeers now that I'm going to be here—"

Larry interrupted. "Say it. Now that you're going to be married."

"Isn't it marvelous," Cecile exclaimed, "the way everything's worked out? I haven't had a minute to congratulate you two properly."

"People are waiting," Peter reminded her.

"Yes, yes," Larry said at once, pulling Amanda by the hand. "Come on, honey. You can talk later."

"We three will meet once a month," Cecile called over her shoulder, "no matter what else we're doing. Business meeting once a month. Don't forget."

Walking away with Larry's hand holding and guiding her, Amanda was aware of a sudden, entirely new sensation: She belonged here. These were her kind of people. Warmth filled her chest. *She wasn't temporary, anymore. She had a place.*

"Nice, isn't it?" said Larry.

Nice? What a dull little word. It's thrilling, and I'm on cloud nine.

"The whole affair, so nice. You looked lovely standing up there, honey."

"You should have been looking at the bride, not at me," Amanda said gaily. It was a flirtatious, arch response, and she was aware of it. She didn't like to hear herself making it, yet she often made such responses when she talked to Larry, without knowing why.

"Cecile was lovely, but you were more so. Take my word," he said solemnly.

"You disappeared," Norma cried, rushing up to them. "I've been looking for you, Amanda. They want us right away for the photographs."

Now came another row to stand in, the ushers on Peter's side and the bridesmaids on Cecile's. While people watched, Amanda watched back. Groups were moving about on the grass, their voices blending in a sustained, high-octave murmur. If I close my eyes, she thought, it will sound like the ripple of moving water.

Far off on a side lawn stood an enormous green tent where they would have supper and dance. It would be buffet, family style, with no assigned tables, Larry had explained.

"You'll sit wherever you like, which is fine with me. The nice thing is, the Newmans like to keep things simple.

Homelike. Look, they've even let the dogs out." And as if in answer to Amanda's unspoken question, he went on, "I was at their dance here for Cecile's eighteenth birthday. The girls had to bring their own escorts, and Norma brought me."

Poor thing, she had had to bring her brother.

"She'll sit with us," Amanda said. Two positions had abruptly reversed themselves. Norma, who in a subtle way had been the dominant one, the authority in charge of Amanda, was now, also in a subtle way, to be her charge. When, inside the tent, the music began, it went straight to her head. She was stirred. Her heart began to race.

"Oh, how I love to dance," she cried.

"Do you? So do I. Hey, girl, put down your bouquet and let's go. Let's go!"

Larry had the same feel of the music's beat, the body's swing, and the foot's rap-tap on the floor.

"Hey, don't we go well together? Isn't this great, Amanda?"

He had a loud laugh, a boy's guffaw, an explosion of joy. He is a boy, she thought. An innocent boy in the powerful, tall body of a man.

"Isn't it great that they're bringing back the old dances? A man can hold a girl close again." He tightened his right arm around her waist. "Feels good, doesn't it?"

There was something about him, too, that touched her heart. He was sweet. A sweet man. And she smiled up at him, shaping her mouth as if about to kiss him.

"I love you, Amanda," he whispered.

The motion, the music, the man's arms—all were making her dizzy with the delicious, bubbling dizziness of the champagne she had drunk only one other time in her life. One time. When had it been? Yes, on Amanda's birthday in the dormitory room. Cecile had bought the bottle.

They went whirling now, whirling around the room. Some people were even noticing them. The guests at one table even applauded.

"Hey, look at those two fly!"

Yes, it was like flying, swooping through the air. Her skirt was billowing, and one of the musicians winked at her as they went past. She heard herself give a little whoop of delight.

"I love you, Amanda," Larry whispered again.

I'm happy, she thought. Of course I am. I have every reason to be so, so happy.

Norma had saved their seats. She had also taken their plates to the buffet table and filled them with the most delectable things there, including plenty of Larry's favorite lobster salad.

"As if she were my mother," Larry whispered aside to Amanda. "She's going to mother you, too. You'll see."

It did not disturb Norma in the least that she had overheard him. Their relationship was long-standing; although perhaps he had never thought to analyze it, she had. And it pleased her now to see that, as always, he was drawn at once into the play of talk that zigzagged around the table.

"You're Larry Balsan? Of course I know who you are. I'm Jason Bates, with Century Mortgages, hear your name ten times a week, for Pete's sake, glad to see you in person."

"And this is Amanda? I've already been hearing about you, Amanda."

"And this is your sister Norma. Glad to meet you."

No one had actually intended to exclude her from the buzz of conversation, Norma knew that. It was simply that they had not given her any thought. She was used to it. Unless the conversation was academic, or at least very serious, she was always left out. The other young women at the table, mostly older cousins of Cecile's, were either recently finished with graduate school, or else they were married. And they, naturally, would talk about weddings, furnishings and, possibly, babies. Their soprano voices, intermingled with their escorts' or husbands' bass ones, had been making a buzz in Norma's ears and now continued to do so.

"Did you know Peter before today? I've never met him before. They say he's darling, very bright. My husband met a man who was in his class in New York."

"Isn't this an absolutely unforgettable day? They're such a perfect pair."

"Peter? He's from some little town up north, practically in Canada."

"What about his family?"

"Nothing unusual. No money. He's had to work his way."

"They say it was like electricity, the first time they saw each other."

"Have you ever seen such flowers? Her father raises them, I hear."

"Not these. Orchids like these have to come from Hawaii."

Amanda was enjoying all this and holding her own.

You could tell by her body language that she wasn't missing a thing. Wherever it might be necessary to fit in, Amanda fit. Occasionally, she would glance at her ring finger, possibly to be sure the ring was still there, or possibly just to enjoy the ownership of it. Observing her, Norma was both amused and touched.

I suppose, if I were to make an effort and if I had to do it, she thought, I could make myself fit into all this. But where people all come in twos, as they do here right now, I can't.

She looked at her watch. It was later than she had thought, thank goodness, so it would probably soon be time to go home. She was thinking this when Cecile's father, accompanied by a second man, rose to make his rounds as a host. Amos was especially jovial today, possibly as the result of champagne, and the man who accompanied him was obviously even more so.

"No, no, sit down, all you people, please," he said as the young men rose to their feet. "You I know, Larry, but it's your sister Norma who should meet my friend Alfred Cole."

"Yes, yes, I want to meet Norma. They tell me she's going to teach Latin at Country Day, and my son Lester is going to be the assistant to the headmaster come September. Ah, Norma, Latin teachers didn't come so young and ravishingly beautiful when I was in school," he added, extending his hand to Amanda.

Larry said hastily, "This is Amanda, my fiancée. The pretty lady on my other side is my sister."

It seemed to Norma that everyone was flushing. She had an impression of red faces all around her, the reddest being that of Alfred Cole.

"Ah, well, please excuse me," he apologized, addressing nobody in particular. "So many pretty faces . . . It confuses a man. Anyway, I hope you and Lester will enjoy . . . I mean, I shall tell him to look for the lovely young Latin teacher . . . He's a very special young man, I guarantee. Excuse me for boasting, but he's my only son and he—"

"Come along, Alfred," said Mr. Newman, taking him firmly by the arm and leading him away.

Norma looked again at her watch. You could be embarrassed, sad, or angry. Angry at whom? The man hadn't meant to hurt her feelings, had he? Much ado about nothing, of course . . . to everyone except Norma. And she said quietly, "Cecile and Peter are leaving soon, flying to New York. And where to afterward is their secret. So it's almost over, and I don't need to see them off. I think I'll go home."

"Don't you want to see the rice or the confetti?" Amanda asked gently.

"Not really."

Larry urged, "Have one dance with me before you go."

"Thanks. But I'd really rather leave before the rush."

Laugh it off.

"Those damned legs of hers! I wish the doctors could do something about them and about her," Larry grumbled at the end of the day. "Those legs have changed her life. She tries. Does beautifully most of the time, but the bottom line is, they've changed her feelings about herself. So they've changed her life."

Amanda sighed. "That stupid man."

"He was a little woozy, that's all. It was just a dumb

mistake. Another woman wouldn't have cared that much. He's really a nice guy, Alfred Cole. A smart lawyer. Corporate work, with naturally some real estate thrown into a deal now and then. I guess he got invited because his wife was Mrs. Newman's best friend. Since she died, he told me, Mrs. Newman has sometimes included him in family events. Sort of an obligation, I suppose. Have you fastened your seat belt? I won't start the car until you do."

Larry was upset. Amanda had already learned that it was better to ask no questions until he had talked himself out. They had gone down the long drive and were on the road before he spoke again.

"You're so great with people, you've got such a great personality, honey. Maybe after you get set here and have a lot of friends, you'll be able to do something for Norma. I hate to think of her stuck in that school with a lot of middle-aged faculty grinds for the rest of her days."

"She'll make a good life for herself, Larry. She'll be fine. At college, everyone liked her. They respected her brains, and she's fun, good company."

"Who's 'everyone'? Only the women. She's told me. She wants a man. It's natural, isn't it?"

He's such a good person, Amanda thought. He's all heart. A man who worries about his sister this way will be good to his wife.

"I'll do what I can," she said, meaning it.

"I know you will. Move over, honey. Move closer." For a moment his big hand clamped down over hers. "God, you're lovely. What are you thinking?"

"Just that I feel good. It's been so marvelous today, and now I'm looking at all this wonderful scenery."

On either side the greenery overflowed; the trees were in full, heavy leaf, and the grass was thick and tender. Everything was prosperously cared for.

"Look at those horses, Amanda. Pretty sight, aren't they? This is real horse country. Want to take a ride or go home?" Without waiting for an answer, he made a quick turn. "Here, I'll show you something while we're out this far: Cagney Falls. Prettiest little town you'll ever see. You'd never believe it's only thirty miles from our house. Our temporary house, I mean. You and I need to do some talking soon about a place for ourselves. But not this minute."

They came abruptly into Cagney Falls. One minute they were passing gates and driveways like the New-mans', and in the next, after descending a hill by a road that became a street, they entered a genteel town square. Its sides were lined with shops whose window boxes and striped awnings made the whole resemble an elaborate toy, while in a corner of the far side stood a small white clapboard church straight out of a New England land-scape. In the center of all there was a flowery little park with a few benches under some old shade trees.

"This used to be a plain place, I remember. Hardware store, drugstore, feed store, dry goods, gas station—you name it. Know what I mean, Amanda?"

Indeed, she knew very well. "And now it's gentrified," she said.

"Come on, let's have a look. And take your time. Women always want to nose around the stores, don't they?"

There were people abroad, but nothing in the least

like a crowd, so it was pleasant to walk at leisure and stop to look into shop windows, to pass from ladies' sportswear to riding boots, children's hand-embroidered dresses, books, jewelry, antiques, chocolates, and finally, a quaint colonial bank with stockbrokers' offices upstairs.

"It sparkles like Christmas," Amanda said. "It seems as if you could buy anything you'd ever need right here."

Larry laughed. "All you'd need is the cash. Come on, I'll buy you some ice cream. There's a nice place around the corner."

"What? After all that food today? No thanks. Let's just walk once down that side again so I can get another look in some of the windows, and that'll be enough."

"Like it, do you?"

"It's charming. Quaint. I'd love to live here."

"You would, would you? Property around here is like gold, let me tell you. Like diamonds. Okay, we'll walk back once and call it a day."

The street was a little treasure trove: in one window, a pink cardigan; in another, a bracelet of gold daisies; in another, a handsome set of copper-bottomed kitchenware—

"We'll come back one night soon," Larry said. "There's a good restaurant up the road. Used to be a livery stable, and now it's chic. You need a reservation two weeks ahead, it's that chic. Lot of baloney, isn't it, in a way? But the food is good, I'll give them that. It's worth the drive.

"Speaking of drives," he said as they rode on, "we'll have to get you a car, Amanda. Can't live where we are without one. We've no such thing as a bus unless you want to hop the senior citizens' bus into town, and I doubt they'll let you on. What kind of car do you like?"

"Oh, I don't know. A small one. Maybe like that one ahead. Yes, something like that."

"Ho, ho. That's a BMW. You've got good taste, all right." He reached over and planted a kiss on top of her head. "But never mind. We'll find something you'll like."

The early exhilaration of the dance had left her, yet in its place there had returned the quiet feel of satisfaction and security that had been coming and going for the last week or more. Drowsiness began to overcome her, and she said so.

"I'm falling asleep."

"It's the sun. We're driving toward it. Put your head on my shoulder and relax."

Vaguely, she heard him humming to himself. It was a homelike sound, out of tune and contented. Vaguely, she roused when they rumbled over the bridge and entered the city.

"Can you believe, after where we've just been, that this is the same state? Even the same county? God, the mess! From the Lane Avenue slums to the terminal, it's all going to wrack and ruin. The problem, when you really come down to it, is the railroad yards over there. Twenty-seven acres of bare, unused land, loaded with junk and going to waste. Something's got to be done, and eventually it will be. I'd love to get my hands on it. But of course I'm talking through my hat. The railroad wants enough for it to pay off the national debt. Anyway, it's all politics, people knowing the right people. Hey, did I wake you? Were you still asleep?"

"Half and half." Amanda yawned. "Yes, Norma told me about the railroad yards, I remember."

In a part of town that was newer than where the Balsan house stood, the streets were laid out in a grid. Clean little houses were shaded by trees no more than fifteen or twenty years old. Pocket-size yards were half the size of the Balsans', and yet they contained probably every play apparatus that existed.

"If a house can look happy, I think these do," Larry said, stopping the car. "This one is trading up. Guy made quick money. They'll have to paint before we can show it, or I'd make an appointment to take you there tomorrow. I think you'd like this, Amanda," he said earnestly. "Have a look at the outside, anyway, while we're here."

She looked. Awfully cramped, she thought. Yet at least it was not a big old box like the Balsans' brown bulk. It was even rather cute when you thought about it. And you could always "trade up," as these people were doing.

Larry's arm went around her. And she saw in his anxious eyes that he was searching her expression; she saw how earnestly he wished to please her. And a flood of grateful warmth, like hot water on cold hands or hot tea on a shivering day, poured through her.

"What do you think? Do you like it?"

"Yes," she answered. "I like it very much. And I thank you for everything."

She was loved, really loved. She knew who she was. She knew where she was, and where she would be. Like the bride on this romantic day, she turned to him as if to give him her whole heart, and gave him her brilliant smile.

CHAPTER FOUR

Side by side on the float they lay, well anointed with sunblock, their faces covered by their straw hats and their toes pointed toward the sky. The float rocked to the rhythmical slap of the waves. Gulls called urgently. Cecile pushed the hat off to see what could be happening, but there was only a sailboat creeping along the line of the horizon. And in another moment, the raucous birds had slid away down the sky, leaving the blue air and the quiet as before.

Peter's hands lay still at his sides. The gold ring on the left one matched her own. How was it possible that such a small article, or that the few words spoken by an authorized person in the garden at home, or that the license signed in the town hall, could make such a difference? It was popular these days to insist that it made no difference at all; indeed, she herself had thought, whenever for a few days at a time they had gone away somewhere together, that they were already two people united. Yet now as she looked at the ring on his hand, then back at her own, she was filled with a kind of awe.

He stirred, stretched, and sat up. "Were you admiring my beauty while I slept?"

"I was thinking of how I love you. If you were to hurt your little finger, I believe mine would bleed, too. Do you understand?"

"Yes," he said gravely. "Yes. It is the same for me. Come, I'll race you back."

The tide was against them. But she was a strong swimmer, and the race would be an even one, as always, with Peter only one or two lengths ahead. It pleased her to be such a good match for him in everything they both did well: At tennis or on an uphill hike, or at a dance, they were in harmony.

Now, reaching the sheltered cove below the house, they sat together on the warm, sea-smelling beach grass, opened the picnic basket that they had left there, and talked. There was no end to the things they had to talk about. They were discovering a new world, filled with curiosities and wonders. And the golden day, like all their days, drifted.

Above them, the house stood in a circle of palms. Indoors, the rooms were cool, as the sea breeze swept through. Those that faced the water were aquamarine, furnished in haphazard charm with English antiques and Chinese rattan and, everywhere, with flowers.

"You know that famous Winslow Homer painting,

the lemon-colored house with the dazzling white roof? It could have been this house," Peter said. "He painted the house, or else your relatives copied his painting."

"Either one is possible. It's been in the family forever; I've forgotten how many generations. Dad's great-aunt is really generous with it. She goes somewhere else whenever there's a honeymoon or a convalescing relative who needs some rest in the Bermuda sun."

"You have such an interesting family. Some cousin of yours at the wedding was telling me about your mother's being on the governor's commission for slum clearance. Was that it? Or suburban sprawl? I wasn't really hearing things too clearly that day. I don't even know how I stood up at all. I was weak in the knees, and my head was in a fog. But tell me more about your mother."

"I don't know how to start. Well, maybe I'll just say that she gets things done. She doesn't only run fund-raising luncheons and have her name on letterheads, either, although she does do some of that, too, because it's part of the picture. She and Dad are real citizens. They've made a difference. For instance, the children's cancer department at the hospital is their doing. And there's the new park that they fought for against the syndicate that wanted to build an office park. Some park that would have been! I grew up hearing about all these things, and I'm sure they grew up the same way. My grandparents were givers, too."

"I had no idea there was that much wealth behind you. Where did it come from?"

Cecile shrugged. She had only a general idea that there were many sources and many legacies.

"Oil, and railroad stocks, a part of it. Also, one of my

great-grandfathers invented some machine that clamps metal parts together and—oh, I don't know how—but they use it all over the world in construction."

Peter smiled, and shaking his head as if to marvel, said, "People would never guess this stuff about you unless they happened to see where you live."

"We've been lucky," she said simply.

"Do you never feel uncomfortable with it?"

"No. Why should I?"

"Don't mind me. I'm only curious because I would."

"What, feel uncomfortable?"

"Yes. Of course I can't be sure. But I think I would."

"But you married me, and so now—"

"And so now it's still yours. It isn't mine."

"This is a silly conversation," she said, changing the subject. "I forgot to tell you that the maid gave me a message. One of Aunt Susan's friends wants to know whether we'd like to have dinner at their house one night."

"We only have four left."

"Okay, you've given the answer. I don't want to go, either. What do you want to do?"

"Tonight? Have an enormous dinner, as always. The woman who cooks here—what is her name again?"

"Sylvestrina. She likes to be called Sally, and I don't blame her."

"She's a fabulous cook. I told her so this morning."

"Well, that's fine so far. What about after dinner?"

"Sit in that wicker double chair and listen to music until the stars come out."

"Fine again. What music? There must be a thousand CDs in the cabinet. You choose."

"A pianist. The night's so still outside that an orchestra would tear it apart. Does that make any sense?"

"Perfect sense. And after the music?"

"Let's swim. Swim naked as fish."

"And after that?"

"Oh, I don't know," Peter said. "I do have a couple of possibilities in mind."

Although a month ago they would have sworn that they already knew everything there was to know about each other, their discoveries kept coming. They walked, they swam, they sailed, and always they talked. No subject was out of their range, from the number of children they might want, to their opinions about the political situation in China, and to their own tastes in food.

"I absolutely need something chocolate every day," Cecile told Peter.

"I can take it or leave it. What I really like is Indian rice and meat, spicy, with plenty of curry."

Each of them talked about work. Cecile had a special earnestness and pride. She was not, at least for the present, planning a "career" in the usual meaning of the word. Next month she was going to volunteer at the Children's Hospital, where she had worked for the last two summers. She had loved it there, and now they had filled her request for a five-day schedule, including time for some courses in social work.

"My sociology major helped me in my understanding of family problems. Sometimes I'm even surprised at myself, because the professional staff actually respects my work."

Then Peter talked about his plans. The new job was only temporary. As soon as he had gotten started, had made a bit of a name in his specialty, he wanted to be independent. Simply by hearing him talk about historic restoration, or by leafing through his photographs and books, Cecile herself had become interested. All of it meshed with history. The small brick inn from 1857 was supposed to have served a meal to the man who had shot Lincoln. True or untrue, the building was worth saving, as was the watchtower on the Atlantic coast where once great whalers had departed and arrived. She had even gone along with him last year on an expedition to a country railroad station; decked out in Victorian wooden lace and curlicues, it was being transformed into an inviting restaurant. Here, too, in Bermuda, he had been making quick sketches as they strolled.

Yes, the two of them, absorbed in their work and in love with each other, were going to be perfect together.

On their next-to-last day, wanting to waste not even one lovely hour, they rose very early. Peter had to check something on his sketch of the old Gothic church.

"You may wonder why I'm doing this," he said. "True, I may never actually need to know much about the construction of a Gothic church, but you never know. In that course I took last summer, we went to a fine nineteenth-century church that had been almost entirely wrecked by fire. There was a bitter struggle going on between those who wanted to restore it and those who wanted to destroy it and build a new church on the site."

"And what happened?"

"The usual thing. Last I heard they were still arguing about costs."

After their final leisurely breakfast on the terrace above the beach, they wandered slowly toward Hamilton. A cruise ship had docked, and the streets were bustling with shoppers. But the church, a good distance removed from the crowd, was blessedly quiet. They were, in fact, the only two people inside it, so that undisturbed by voices or footsteps other than their own, they wandered along the walls, reading national history and poignant personal histories on plaques and in memorials on stained glass.

Outdoors again, the yard, except for the chirp of sparrows, was just as still, and Cecile sat on the grass while Peter, for the second time, went about examining downspouts, looking for gargoyles, and studying the clerestory. She, in her own way as intent as he was, watched him. His tall figure crossed from sun into shadow when he moved around the building, and his face had a slight, intense frown when he braced his sketchbook against the wall. She was so proud of him! Why, that's what it was all about, this *union*, this oneness, as Norma would say, translating from the Latin in her usual funny way. One-ness. From now on they were *responsible* for each other, this Peter and this Cecile. There would be no severance, no "see you soon." Instead, they would rise from the same bed and eat breakfast together; in the evening they would eat their meal together again and return to the bed. After a while there would be children and serious things to talk about. There would also be the daily trivial things that must be seen to. Only a few days ago when going into Hamilton for lunch, had she not stopped him from wearing a brown sweater with navy blue slacks?

Now, reminding herself of her mother, Cecile had to laugh. Harriet Newman, for all her work in important public causes, was a thoroughly fastidious housewife. Yet why not? What's bad about having a tidy home, good meals, and clean clothes?

I never thought until now, Cecile thought, about how intimate this business of marriage would be, this being inside each other's heads, this taking care of each other for the rest of our lives.

"That's it," Peter said now, putting the sketchbook back in his pocket. "I'll probably never use it, but at least I have it. What's on the program now? Back to the house and the beach, I hope."

"Of course. But with one quick stop, really quick. We need a parting present for Sally, with thanks for all our marvelous meals."

"I have a nice big check for her."

"Yes, but a present, something in a box with ribbon on it, would be nice, too. They're known for sweaters here in Bermuda, really beautiful ones, something she would never buy for herself."

The crowds from the ship had thinned since early morning, most likely because it was now lunchtime. Holding Sally's gift in hand, Cecile kept slow pace with Peter, taking only quick glances at the shop windows as they walked past. Then suddenly, she stopped.

"Look, Peter. Those must be the most gorgeous girandoles I've ever seen. They don't usually come in such interesting colors."

Six porcelain arms, each holding a white taper,

extended from a graceful painted body with coral flowers and brown leaves.

"A perfect pair. So often on these old pieces there's something missing or chipped. They would be wonderful on the sideboard in a dining room, Peter."

"Must cost a fortune."

"No, I can read the sticker. Not bad at all. What about using my cousin Luke's wedding check?"

"Cele, you do what you want with the wedding checks. But where will you put these things? We have no sideboard and no dining room."

He was smiling as if in amusement at her "feminine" foibles. He looked the way her father looked whenever her mother bought something frivolous—which happened seldom enough—such as, once, a pair of pink velvet slippers with heels like steeples.

She smiled back. For two weeks now she had been keeping the most marvelous secret, waiting for the moment when he could behold the secret for himself. But suddenly her resolve broke into overwhelming excitement, and it burst right out of her mouth.

"Darling, we do have one! A house, with a dining room! I wasn't going to say a word until we got home. I wanted to surprise you, but I can't hold it in anymore. It's a house you will fall in love with. Wait till you see it."

"What are you talking about, Cecile?"

"There's a wonderful place in Cagney Falls. It's not in the town, but in the township, a lovely house with an acre and a half, maybe two. The people want to sell and my father knows them slightly—at least, well enough to have asked them to hold off until we get back to look at it. I've seen the outside, and it's just your taste, very simple, cut stone with white shutters and the traditional colonial doorway. You'd think it was built before the Revolution."

Peter said nothing, which seemed an odd reaction. He seemed to be staring over her shoulder into empty air.

"Well, what do you think?"

"Two acres? A miniature estate! I don't know what to think. I don't know what you can be thinking of, Cele."

"You're talking about the price? Nothing. It's a present, a wedding present to us."

"Oh, no, Cele. That's far too much. We've had enough presents already."

"But how silly! This is a lifelong gift, a home. Lots of people do that for their children if they're able to."

"Maybe they do, but I don't feel comfortable with the idea. We'll start out next month in the apartment we both liked and take life step by step."

"Peter, listen. As I told you, this is not an elaborate house. It's quite simple. Quite suitable for us. I promise."

"By your standards, perhaps. But I'm not a rich man, I'm never going to be one, and I don't want to live like one at somebody else's expense."

This decisive reaction was startling. It was puzzling, and it was hurtful.

"That sounds almost nasty, Peter," she said softly.

"I didn't mean it to be nasty at all. I'm being honest. These are my honest feelings."

"And what if"—she hesitated—"when my father's time comes, what will you do then?"

"Right now your father is still young, healthy, and able to work. I'm the same, except even younger than he, and I don't want to have him or anyone working to pay my bills for me."

Peter's mouth, set in a firm line, was unsuited to the rest of his face. She had never seen it like that before and was discomfited by the sight of it.

"Won't you at least look at it?" she asked.

"No. There's no purpose in seeing it when my mind's made up."

His voice had risen ever so slightly, with a tone that caused a passing couple to glance at him, and she knew that they looked out of place standing there in front of a window filled with porcelain and silver.

"Let's get away from here. I'm awfully disappointed, Peter. You don't know how disappointed I am. You really could go look at it. That's not much to ask, is it? You might change your mind if you were to see it."

"To begin with, Cele, you're not even being practical. You're not even thinking about the cost of maintenance. It's one thing to have a house given to you and another thing to maintain it."

"I would do all the gardening myself on weekends. Anybody can push a lawn mower."

"Now you're really talking nonsense. *You* going to mow the lawns! Of all the silly, childish—come on, let's go. This is our last afternoon on the beach, and we're using it up on a sidewalk."

Cecile was beginning to feel a rise of something close to anger. It was not only that she had fallen in love with the house, with the old trees and the rose garden, barely glimpsed from the roadway. But it was also the fact that her father's loving generosity was being so abruptly rejected. And she said so.

"Frankly, I think you are being very thoughtless. What am I to tell my father?"

"You won't have to tell him anything. I'll do it. I'll say that I deeply appreciate the offer, which I do, but I can't accept it."

"Don't you understand that he'll be terribly hurt?"

"I don't think he will be."

"How can you 'think'? You don't know him. I do."

"Then I'm sorry, Cele. I like your family very, very much, but I don't want to be one of their dependents. Keep your money to buy all the girandoles you may want. But it's my job to supply shelter for the family that we now are. My job, Cele."

The way he talked! He sounded like some Victorian husband, with that ring of authority. You're a hundred years behind the times, she wanted to say, but did not say it.

"Do you want to go back now and buy those things?" Peter asked. "It's only around the corner."

Now he was appeasing her, his childlike, delicate little wife.

"Since we'll have no place to put them, there's not much sense buying them, is there? So, no, I'm not going back," she added, with emphasis upon the "not."

"I only asked," he retorted, with equal emphasis upon the "only."

And there they were, still standing there staring at each other as if they were strangers who had been thrown together in some unusual circumstance and had no idea what to do about it.

"I don't understand you," Cecile said.

"Try."

"Why don't you try?"

"I already do understand you. You've seen something

that appeals to you, it's within your reach, and I'm being stubborn. I'm sorry to deny you, but—"

His slow, deliberate speech made her so impatient that she had to interrupt.

"But why? Why?"

"Pardon me," a woman said curtly in her attempt to get a better view of Cecile's girandoles.

"Let's go, Cecile. We're in everyone's way."

At the corner they waited for a taxi. Tourists whizzed by on motorbikes, many of them hooting, laughing, and obviously inexperienced. For no logical reason, their silliness depressed her, and she said coldly, "We haven't been on a motorbike once since we came here. I want to do it now."

"No motorbike. I've told you that before. I've never ridden one, and I'm not going to experiment with you riding behind me. We've already seen three bad accidents."

He was making sense. It was his scolding manner that infuriated her, that and the stern set of his lips. In silence she followed him into a taxi, and in silence they rode all the way back to Great-Aunt Susan's house.

For the sake of some abstract principle, he had upset her loving plans. In idle moments during these last weeks, her thoughts had been turning to that surprise, to the spacious rooms in that home: the bedroom they would have and the bed, no king-size in which two people lie apart, but rather an original double bed, in which they lie close; the bookshelves painted spring green, where they would combine their individual troves; the comfortable workroom, where Peter, undisturbed, would draw his plans. How could she ever have imagined that he would negate the whole thing? And adding insult to injury, now apparently *he* was upset with *her* because *she* dared to be upset. Now as he sat beside her in the taxi ostentatiously examining his sketchbook, he was apparently waiting for her to speak first. He was just going to wait.

They went into the house. Cecile, finding Sally in the kitchen, gave her the sweater and lingered purposely long to talk about Sally's children. If Peter was waiting for her to join him on the beach, let him wait.

Tonight was their last night, which was to have been a celebration for two. Instead there were guests, a younger-generation couple among Great-Aunt Susan's friends who had telephoned today to invite them to dinner. Adroitly, she had turned the invitation inside out by inviting them to dinner; in that case, Peter would have no choice but to participate as host. It would annoy him no end to spend this evening with these strangers. Let him be annoyed.

Late that evening she was reading in bed when he came into the room. With folded arms he stood looking down at her.

"You missed a perfect afternoon on the float," he said.

"I wasn't in the mood."

"You were cutting off your nose to spite your face."

"It happens that I was very content to sit alone on the beach with a great book."

"No, you weren't content, you were seething with

anger. Then you thought you'd get even with me by inviting those people. The funny thing is, I liked them and I had a nice time. You didn't think I would."

"I didn't think one way or the other."

"I went outside on the porch with Mark, and man to man I asked him a question, whether he and Rose ever had fights. I told him I was new at this business."

Was he actually twinkling at her?

"He looked at me as if he thought I was an idiot. 'Fifteen years married and you ask whether we ever have fights? Listen, young man, if anybody starts telling you he and his wife don't have fights, he's a sap or a damned liar, either one.' "

"On our honeymoon," she wailed. "A fight on our honeymoon, when we've never had one before."

"We never spent so much time in one place together before this, either, you know."

"You had such a furious face—"

"People don't make pretty faces when they're angry, Cele. Not that I was all that angry, really. It's you who were angry. I was just being very emphatic."

"We always agreed about everything. This is the first time—"

"Did you think we were going to go through life like a reflection of each other? I'm sorry if I was harsh today, and I'm sorry about the house. God knows, I want to give you whatever I can, Cele. But I just can't give that. It's a streak of independence, a need to prove myself. I don't know why, but it's the way I am, that's all. Please understand me."

Two large tears arose against her will and slid slowly down her cheeks.

"Ah, Cele, there's no reason to cry. Has this hurt you so much?"

Yes, it had hurt, yet not nearly enough to cause these tears. She wanted to tell him that all of a sudden a window had opened before her, that she was looking out upon the vast plain of life, seeing the long road on which two small human creatures would travel and, bound to each other as they were, would sometimes hurt each other and be sorry.

"Put the book down," he said, and with his fingers, wiped the two tears away.

Then she opened her arms.

CHAPTER FIVE

Lawrence Balsan, who liked to linger over a second cup of coffee at the table, was in an expansive mood this evening. "I think I've already mentioned that you're welcome to use the yard," he said. "It's certainly spacious enough for a small wedding. I must have had weddings in mind when I bought the double lot twenty-three years ago."

He was feeling expansive because Larry had closed a very profitable deal that afternoon. By now, Amanda was well on the way to an understanding of him, and indeed, of the family's dynamics.

"Of course, you will have to keep it small," he repeated. "Unfortunately"—this with a kind of good-humored mockery—"we can't have anything like that Newman wedding you went to. That must have been a spectacle. Who all was there? Anybody I know?"

"I saw at least a dozen people you know," Larry said. "Bates from Century Mortgage, Ralph Fried, the O'Connors, Alfred Cole, and—"

"In another words, everybody who is anybody. It must have cost plenty. Glad I didn't have to pay for it."

Yes, Lawrence, Amanda thought, I'm well aware how disappointed you are. A daughter-in-law like Cecile Newman is what you wanted. I know it, and what's more, you know that I know it.

His haughty, aquiline face had an ironic expression, as though he were trying to conceal some secret laughter. At the moment, he was judging her; his penetrating eyes seemed to be boring through her, or roving over her; he made her feel as if her face was smudged with the raspberry sauce that she had just finished, or as if her blouse had come unfastened.

"And you're sure you don't want to invite your people, your parents at least?" Lawrence asked, addressing Amanda. "We've plenty of room to accommodate them."

She would not expose her family to this man's keen scrutiny or his chilly courtesy. They would simply not fit, he with them or they with him and all his relatives. So she was about to say, for the third or fourth time, that they were unable to leave their work, when Larry answered for her.

"We're planning to visit them instead."

They had made no such plan at all. It was he who had suggested it. But even though he was surely no judge nor snob, how could she let him see the derelict, rusting car in back of the barn, or Lorena's latest baby crawling about in his unchanged diaper, or the greasy pot of stew in the center of the supper table?

"Whatever your plans are," Lawrence said as he rose from his own mahogany table and left the room, "I should think you both had better start making them."

"You don't have to have a wedding here," Larry said when they were alone. "I know you don't want to."

"That's true, I don't."

Either you did the thing the right way, which meant family, music, flowers, and friends, or you didn't do it at all. There was no beauty in a meager compromise.

"You know, Amanda, I've been thinking that a quiet elopement to some country town, with a justice of the peace, is really much more personal. It's more romantic, when you come down to it, than all this public fuss. Of course, women do like satin sleeves and lace veils, I know that," Larry said with a tolerant smile.

The smile was also a little worried. He understood her.

From her days and nights at Sundale's, she had saved a few hundred dollars. Since it was already August, whatever remained of summer clothes was on sale in the shops, thus allowing her money to stretch.

"Take swim stuff," Larry said. "This place is right on the lake. I was there once, and I know you'll love it." So, well equipped with her own clothes for every day, new dresses for dinner, two negligees, and a blue linen suit in which to be married, Amanda was ready before a week had passed.

Actually, Larry had asked her where she wanted to go on their honeymoon, and she, having never been anywhere, had replied with a question: "Bermuda?" But he had explained that Bermuda might better wait for a time when they could stay away longer, so she had left the choice entirely to him.

The night before they left, he smuggled their suitcases into the car, and after putting a note on the breakfast table, they crept out of the house without making a sound, at dawn.

"They won't mind," Larry said. "They'll probably be relieved by our little trick. My father's overwhelmed with work this month, and Norma isn't crazy about weddings, anyway."

In a portable refrigerator he had put an old-fashioned bouquet in paper lace and two bottles of champagne. "The bouquet is for now. The champagne is for later, when we get where we're going."

Larry was right, Amanda thought. There really is a kind of clandestine excitement, a Romeo and Juliet effect, in running away together like this. They were heading north. After a drive of four hours, they arrived at the town where, by Larry's prior arrangement, a justice of the peace and two witnesses were prepared for them.

They climbed a few steps at a small, drab building, probably, Amanda supposed, a town hall. Her impression was vague, for all of a sudden the delightful excitement had left her completely, and a flooding of fear took its place: No matter how easy it is to get a divorce, this is still so *final*. Divorce was certainly not part of her life's pattern. Her parents were celebrating their twenty-ninth year together—if you could call it celebrating. Well, maybe you could. Probably you could. And Lorena was waiting to take her worthless man back.

What am I doing with these thoughts at a moment like this?

No doubt it was the dreadful thought that caused her to stumble and drop the bouquet.

"Take it easy, honey," Larry said in his kind voice as he put the flowers back in her hands. *He is the soul of kindness.* Amanda held up her head and walked with him to where an old man stood waiting behind a table. There was a young man in the room too, probably one of the witnesses, and she saw in his eyes that she was beautiful. . . . When she placed her hand on Larry's arm, his mother's diamond flashed rainbow colors. The ring said: Permanence. It said: Goodness. Honesty. Truth.

It was strange to compare the few quick words of this ceremony with the solemn, long injunctions of a clergyman. Still, the result was the same. Two rings were exchanged, a kiss was exchanged, and they left the commonplace little room just as married as if they were marching away to the tune of the Mendelssohn wedding march.

"Are you feeling any different?" asked Larry after the first few minutes of dumbstruck silence as they drove away.

"I don't know. I'm probably numb," she said, which was true.

"Read the license to me."

"Funny. It looks so—so official, like the income tax: *Amanda Louise* and *Lawrence Daniel.*"

"I always wanted to be called Daniel. Dan. Doesn't it sound better? Don't I even look like a Dan? Larry's a name for a kid on the soccer team in junior high. It's a name for a junior. But my dad likes having a junior, and it's not worth a squabble and hard feelings to change it."

He was sensitive. You wouldn't think so to look at him. You wouldn't think he would care that much about a thing like a name. Now, when you looked at a man like Peter, for instance, you could easily imagine that he might care. Funny.

"You're going to see some mountains, honey. This inn's practically on the Canadian border. You didn't forget a swimsuit, did you? The lake's a little gem. The whole area's filled with lakes, from Canada right down to our own Great Lakes." Nervously, he prattled. "The food's wonderful at the inn. Some nights they have a campfire. And there's trout, fresh from the brook. Do you like fish? There's so much I still don't know about you."

Of course he was thinking about the night that was only a few more hours away. Of course he could hardly wait. It was almost unheard of today that people's first time in bed together and their first night married were one and the same. And it wouldn't be the case here either, she thought, if Lawrence's bedroom didn't happen to be just down the hall.

Larry was humming. "Remember that song? The melody keeps running around in my head, but I'm darned if I can think of the words."

A feeling of tenderness toward him rose in her chest and trembled there. It seemed as if every kind of emotion had been churning inside her, on and off, all during this day. No doubt, though, that was entirely natural. After all, it was the most important day in her life. It was the most important day in anybody's life, Amanda felt.

"Darn it, I can't think of the words," Larry said again. "I know it's an oldie."

"It's a very, very oldie, from the 1930's, I think. I heard it on cable. 'Always and always, I'll keep on adoring'—something like that."

"Right! 'The glory and wonder of you.' That's it."

Amanda had always been an early riser, from childhood through the university years during which she had had to prepare her work in the mornings because the evenings were spent at Sundale's. So it was not long after dawn on the first morning of her married life when she stood at the porch rail and looked out over the scene.

Log cabins like this one were scattered, comfortably apart, all along the lakefront. A little distance above them, on a low rise at the end of the dirt road on which Larry's car had bounced through the darkness last night, stood the hotel center, a large structure, also built of logs, with a surrounding lawn and a flag, now whipping in the breeze. The lake shimmered and the air was bright as crystal. As far as Amanda's eyes could see, in every direction, the earth was covered with pine trees.

"Mostly spruce," Larry had explained, "but if you walk far enough, you'll see plenty of hemlocks and junipers, too. They have guided hikes here, of three or four miles or even longer, if you want. One time I took a ten-miler. Sounds like too much, but actually it isn't. I felt great afterward."

A flock of Canada geese came honking overhead, disturbing the peace, as if on a city street a hundred automobiles had sounded their horns at once. She watched them race toward the south, leaving behind the silence that they had ruptured. Minutes after they were beyond sight, she was still looking up at the distant sky that had enveloped them, down at the motionless disk of the gray-blue lake, and then at her familiar hands with their two unfamiliar rings, these hands that seemed to belong to somebody else.

It had all been so different from what she had expected. . . . The adoration, murmured words, and passionate endearments, the clasping, the enfolding—it was being seized, possessed and swallowed, eaten alive. . . . None of her past experiences had prepared her for this fever of emotion; surely none of those few quick encounters in an automobile or on the rough grass in a back pasture could have prepared her.

"Good morning, honey. Taking in the view? Gorgeous, isn't it?"

He had had a shower and stood now dripping in the doorway. She looked at him with curiosity. He was well built, with sturdy shoulders, narrow hips, and no flab. Still, she had no desire to embrace him.

"I don't see anybody down below. It's probably too early for breakfast. How about going back to bed for a while first?"

There was no possible way she could refuse, or even show reluctance. When, in the bed, he whispered, "I love you so," she said the same to him. How could you not return such a fervent declaration? Lying there with his arms around her, she was tense and confused: It was dishonest to pretend what she did not feel, yet in a strange way it would be cruel not to pretend. He believed in her love. He trusted. And yet in another strange way, she really did feel some love for him.

Afterward they got dressed and went up to breakfast. The rustic room was charming, with tablecloths of blue gingham and an earthenware jug of early asters on every table.

"You're delightful when you smile," Larry said.

She must remember to smile often. . . . It was not hard to do so that day. They swam, went out in a canoe, and ate an enormous lunch. Larry was sociable. The other guests, all older than they, were retired couples and couples with children, which disappointed Amanda a little, for she had hoped for people their own age. Still, these were all very pleasant folk, warmly welcoming and interested in the honeymooners. And Larry, in his usual fashion, made friends with them all, helping a ten-year-old boy with his crawl stroke and spending half an hour with an elderly gentleman discussing real estate.

"Tonight we'll dress up and drink the champagne," Larry said. "This is our wedding dinner."

Sometimes, when Amanda saw herself in a mirror, she was disappointed: Her hair was in need of a trim, or else the shoes were wrong with the dress, or her face was pale and tired. On this night, though, there was no fault to find. The sun had flushed her face with health, her hair was at its best form, and the simple white silk dress, flounced at the neck and hem with touches of pink, was lovely. So, in the perfect mood for celebration, she linked her arm through Larry's, and they entered the dining room together.

In the doorway she stopped and cried out, "I don't believe it!"

Everyone had stood up and clapped. On their own table, where at breakfast time the jug of asters had stood, there was now a spread of traditional white flowers, gardenias and freesia wreathed with smilax. In one swift glance, she saw that champagne was in the ice bucket next to the table, and in the next glance, she saw that every other table had its own ice bucket, too. Flustered and smiling, she turned to Larry, exclaiming, "It's you! You arranged all this."

Red with pleasure and a little bit of embarrassment, he admitted it. "I won't say I didn't."

"You ordered champagne for all these tables, too?"

"I won't say I didn't." And when in her surprise she had no comment about that, he said, "This is a once-in-a-lifetime night, Amanda. It's your time to shine. You're the bride."

He is remembering Cecile's wedding, she thought. He wants to make it up to me. And curiously ashamed, she kissed his cheek.

The management had considerately moved their table into a corner that was almost private, so after a few smiles and waves in their direction, they were left to themselves. Only when an enormous cake was trundled in on a cart did they become the center of attention again. Toasts were given for them, glasses lifted, and a whole roomful of strangers suddenly was transformed into family and friends, warm with goodwill. Everybody received a slice of the cake. The tiny bridal couple on its top was lifted out of the white icing, wrapped, and presented to Amanda just as the nightly dance band was arriving in the adjoining room.

Then she danced, and Larry with her, whirling and flying as they had whirled and flown at that other wedding. Her heart soared. Through the open door she could see the white flowers still on the table. How sweet of Larry to think of that! How sweet all these people were! *Sweet. Sweet* . . . The champagne has gone to my head.

Men asked whether Larry would mind their having a dance with the bride. He wouldn't mind. *He* was *sweet.* After a while, though, he made her sit down and ordered black coffee for them both. He was laughing.

"What a night! Let's take a slow walk up the hill. The cool air will do us good."

Back in their room, he watched Amanda undress, and she saw in his eyes what was to come. When his arms went around her, she was aware of some comfortable contact with a warm body, but she felt nothing more than that simple contact, and the need to sleep. Then she slept.

Never without consulting Amanda first, Larry made plans. One day they would picnic on that speck of an island near the opposite shore. The next day they would sign up for a five-mile hike. Would she like to have a trail ride? It didn't matter that she had never been on a horse; it was easy to sit on a western saddle, and besides, on these narrow trails, with so many overhanging branches in the woods, you only walked the horse. So the days were lovely, vigorous and bright.

Still, August was on the wane and here in the north one day, there came a hint of chill in the air.

Late on the next night it began to rain and was still raining when day broke. The temperature made a sudden drop, so that the rain felt like ice on the skin. In the dining room the talk was of the weather.

"It's nothing new to us up here. You folks'll need to buy some raingear if you haven't brought any. This'll probably keep up all week."

They drove to the town for some raincoats. When they returned at noon, the cold rain was still falling; it dimmed the view of the lake and darkened their room. All night and the following morning the rain beat on the windows.

"Nothing much to do today," Larry said. "One thing that they should have and don't have is a television in the rooms. Guess I'll go up to the front desk and get some magazines. Want anything special?"

"No, thanks. I have some books here."

He peered over her shoulder. "*Shirley,* by Charlotte Brontë. What's that about?"

"Well, it's an old story, more than a hundred years old, about an English girl who goes to Belgium and falls in love with a teacher who's married. Of course, there's a lot more to it than that—"

"Gotcha. Got the idea. I don't go for that stuff, but I see you do, bringing three books, enough for six months' reading at my speed. Don't know how you do it."

His admiring tone was annoying. It was as if he were talking to a child who has just learned to read *Peter Rabbit* all by herself.

"Fact is, I don't read much, ever. Being in the business school, I never really had to, except business, naturally."

He stood there, still with that benevolent admiration in his smile. "Norma and you, with your books. Except that she's even worse than you. Latin! At least you're reading English."

For three days the rain continued, softly and steadily. On the fourth day, after having dwindled during the night, it began to swell again into a tangible form; like a sail, it billowed in the wind; like a wayward curtain, it slapped the windowpanes; and like an overflowing stream, it splashed out of the downspouts. Cold seeped indoors through the walls. It was so dark that by noon they were reading by electric light.

Amanda had finished *Shirley* and begun *Bleak House*. Larry had read through all the magazines on the rack in the main building.

He turned from the window where, for the last quarter of an hour, he had been looking out while jingling coins in his pocket. By now she had learned that this was another of his irritating habits, along with loud out-of-tune humming while he shaved.

"*Bleak House,*" he read over her shoulder.

Reading over her shoulder was another irritating habit.

"Yes, 'bleak.' A good word for the last few days."

"I know, I know. But nobody can help the weather."

"The natives say it's nothing unusual for this time of year."

"Well, maybe. But we're snug here. The food couldn't be better, and I still think it's a great place for a honeymoon. I picked it," he went on somewhat anxiously, "because I didn't think a fancy, dress-up place would be as much fun. I still think this place and our little wedding beat the Newman affair all hollow."

"Their wedding was perfect. It was in beautiful taste," Amanda said, raising her eyes from the book.

Why she should be defending Cecile, who needed no defense, she had no idea.

"Oh, there's no question about their taste," Larry amended. "They're what you call 'understated,' don't you think so? I always say that they're remarkable for being so plain in their ways, that family. So simple, with all their money."

What was so wonderful about being "simple"? He and Norma, both of them, always raving about how plain the Newmans were! As if it were such a great virtue! She was tired of hearing it because, anyway, it wasn't true.

In one of Cecile's pictures, Peter and she were standing on a terrace. Behind the balustrade were palm trees and the ocean. On the side you could see what was probably a wing of the house, lemon yellow, with a bright, white roof. Bermuda must be heavenly.

Then a wave of shame brought heat into her cheeks. It was beautiful here, too! Those mornings, standing on the porch in the stillness with all that fresh pine scent in the air! And Larry is so kind, so good, the salt of the earth, as Norma says in her old-fashioned way. He is just purely good.

"Hey, honey, how about going for some tea and cake?" he asked now. "It's something to do."

They had been having enormous meals these last few days, and cake was the last thing she needed, but she rose at once, put on the new slicker, put her arm through his, and went up the hill in the rain.

There they found a tea and cake display in an almost empty room. Half the guests had already left the inn, while the rest, having heard the prediction about the thermometer's drop into the fifties by morning, were in their rooms packing.

"We should have known better," one man remarked in passing Larry and Amanda. "Nobody with any sense comes this late in August."

"I suppose we should leave, too," Larry said, looking as forlorn as a little boy who's been scolded. "Do you want to go, honey? Or do you want to wait and see?"

"Whatever you decide." She spoke with cheer. "We've had a great time here in spite of the rain, haven't we?"

Late in the afternoon they rumbled across the bridge, past the deserted railroad terminal, across Lane Avenue, and headed uptown.

As once before, Larry remarked, "It's a disgrace to the state. All this land going to waste, and the station itself, one of the grandest buildings of the nineteenth century. And Lane Avenue is—is a cesspool. That's all it is."

Amanda gave a mental shrug. Every time she had crossed the bridge, either he or Norma had made the same comments. It was boring.

"Guess where we're going," Larry said brightly.

"Home, of course." There was a little shudder in her chest as she said "home." It was almost hard to believe how once she had seen that ugly brown box as a *pleasance*. The word, unused for a century or more, popped into her head out of *Bleak House*—no, more likely from some book older even than that, out of the eighteenth century. *Pleasance*. A park, a garden, a place where you had pleasure.

There had been little pleasure in that house this past

summer. Every time she looked up from her dinner plate, she seemed to meet Lawrence Balsan's eyes. They confounded her with their alternating expressions of indifference and mild interest. Always she turned away as did he, and always unwilling, she met the eyes again.

Now that she had his son's wedding ring on her finger, he should at least pretend some warmth! But the sooner they could leave that house, the better. The atmosphere there was too heavy.

As if he had been reading her mind, Larry said, "We need to get into our own place as soon as possible. If you're up to it now, we can even look at that house I once showed you. The people have moved out, and I have the key in my pocket. Do you want to, or are you too tired after riding all day?"

Was he going to be this way all the time? So carefully considerate? Most men were not.

"Let's do it now," she said.

The little houses stood row on row. One had blue-green shutters, another had a red door; some had picket fences, and most had a jungle gym. Many had "For Sale" signs on the lawn, while others had "Sold" signs, and almost all these signs said "Balsan Real Estate."

"Buying and selling," Larry said. "That's where the money is. Still, someday I'd like to build something really spectacular. I'd like to make a name for myself."

When the car stopped before a house that sparkled white in the sun, he explained that he had had the outside freshly painted, but had left the interior to be done to her taste.

"In case you decide on the house. I think—I hope—you will, because it's a real buy. These owners made a lot of improvements. The kitchen is brand-new, and they built a flagstone terrace in back with nice shrubbery, so it's more private."

The kitchen was indeed new; it was sunny, and the appliances were complete, even including an indoor grill. As she followed Larry through the house, she had to admit that it was spotless; even the unmarked wallpaper needed no replacement.

"Nice thing is," Larry said, "I didn't tell you, but the school's only five blocks away."

Amanda laughed. "School! What are you thinking of? I'm just out of college. I'm twenty-two, and you talk about schools."

"Well, in time, I meant."

"In plenty of time. I first have to find some kind of job, and soon, before I go crazy inside four walls."

Perhaps she had spoken too sharply, because he gave her a quick, puzzled look, and she corrected herself, saying more gently, "People start families much later these days."

"A lot do, but a lot don't. Guys I knew in school, guys twenty-seven like me, already have a kid. But that's neither here nor there this minute. What about the house?"

Amanda looked out of the window. A lovely maple stood in the backyard, more than half grown and in full leaf. Sunlight sprinkled the grass.

"We can move in right away. I can set the closing for next week, even."

Under the maple, in a birdbath that had been left behind when the owners moved, a pair of mourning doves were splashing.

"We can move that quickly?"

"Why not? All I have to do is write the check."

My house. It's nothing fabulous, but it's nice, and I can make it look nicer. And it's mine. My mother would be thunderstruck. I'll take lots of pictures and send them home with the one of me in my white dress, with Larry.

"I just don't know what to say, Larry."

He twinkled at her. "Say you'll be glad to get away from my house. From my father."

"I would never say that."

"Okay. Say you love me."

"That I do, Larry."

"Well, show it then."

She put her arms around him and kissed him. For a long time he held her there, holding the kiss. When he let go, it was to take a pad and pen from his pocket. For a minute or two he made notes while she watched him. When he looked up at her, his mild brown eyes had narrowed in concentration.

"I have it all figured out. What's left of my available cash will be just enough to furnish here. We'll need a living room set complete, so we can start having friends in. You'll need to get acquainted fast. Then a dining room set, ditto. Eight regular chairs will fit. We can always add folding chairs if we ever do anything on a bigger scale. The second bedroom upstairs can be a den with room for a TV and a computer and a couple of recliners for solid comfort. Then our room—and no twin beds." *If only he would stop twinkling . . .* "So it's a deal, right honey? Hey, it's almost time to eat, and they'll be waiting for us. Let's go."

*　*　*

Amanda liked the way Larry took charge. Her father, the only other man with whom she had lived, had depended entirely upon her mother.

"He brings his wages home," Mom always said, "but as far as he's concerned, and as long as it didn't wreck his chair and the TV, the roof could cave in."

Now Larry was giving a brisk report to the family. "It's a good buy, Dad. The guy made some quick money, he was in a hurry to move into his new mansion, and he didn't want to take time dickering. As for the furniture, I'm going to see my friend Tom Rich. Remember Tom? He's got that furniture place out on the pike. He'll be glad to give me a break. Matter of fact, Amanda, you and I'll go see him tomorrow and see what he has on the floor. If he hasn't got what we want, he can get quick delivery."

"I'm so glad for you both," Norma said. "And you both look so happy! It's wonderful." Her warm smile spread across her round cheeks. "Remember, I take responsibility for it. You'd better give me credit, you two."

Amanda nodded. "We do, we do. But enough about us. Let's talk about you."

"What's there to say? School starts the week after next. I take a second-year Latin class, Caesar's Gallic Wars. And some French classes. And something that's called 'Music Appreciation.' "

"That's some schedule," Larry said heartily. "Very challenging, I should think."

But Norma would rather have a husband and be furnishing a house, Amanda thought. Not that every woman these days wanted that anymore, but a whole lot of them, whether they admitted it or not, still did, and Norma was one of them.

"And what are you planning, Amanda?" asked Lawrence.

Although he had kissed her and wished her joy when she had arrived half an hour ago, this was the first personal remark or question he had directly addressed to her. As a matter of fact, she reflected scornfully, once he had determined that she was not part of the city's elite, or of any elite, he had scarcely ever addressed her at all.

It was Larry who took his question. "Amanda plans to fix up our house first."

"But after that? Amanda is not the sort of woman who can lock herself up at home, away from the world. Amanda wants to *live*." And saying so, Lawrence turned for a bare moment to rest his brilliant, youthful eyes upon her.

Although she was both astonished, and for no plausible reason uncomfortable, she found a quick answer.

"I had been thinking I might learn to be a paralegal. I love words, and besides, it wouldn't take too long to get through the course. It's not like working toward a graduate degree. It's not as expensive, either."

Larry exclaimed, "You never told me!"

"I wasn't sure."

"Well, you can't do it this minute. The house comes first, and that will surely take a couple of months."

"Larry is right," Lawrence said. "Take your time, Amanda. These are precious days. Don't rush them."

Such thoughtful advice was the last thing she would have expected from Lawrence Balsan. Well, you never knew about people, did you?

When Larry took their suitcases upstairs, he set them down in the guest room where, only a short few weeks before, he would have been an intruder.

"Every night, whenever I passed this closed door, I used to go half crazy with wanting to get in. Weren't you lonesome in this bed by yourself?"

"Of course I was, but we couldn't help it, could we?"

"Just looking at your happy face would make anybody feel good."

And now again came the confusion, the vague fear that she was acting a part. But then she protested: But I do love him, don't I? Are there not more ways than one to love?

She began to undress while he watched her, smiling, and she smiled back.

CHAPTER SIX

Miss Elizabeth Jenkins was retiring. Norma, going through the hall after her last class on Friday, was suddenly reminded of this when she passed the third-grade room and saw Elizabeth packing a cardboard box.

"Oh," cried Norma, "I feel so guilty! I had planned to do something special on your final day, but the time ran away from me, and I didn't look at the calendar. Will you forgive me?"

Tired eyes, too old for the owner's age, looked up at Norma. "I'm glad that you've come at all," Miss Jenkins said simply. "It's nice to say good-bye to somebody on your last day."

Apparently nobody else had come into this room to mark the day. They were just too busy to take the time, or they had forgotten. It was shocking. It was a silent tragedy. Norma hardly knew what else to say except to offer some help, to speak superfluous, dull words.

"Are you packing these books on the desk? Do you need another box?"

"No, thanks. The books belong to the school. I've only packed the contents of my desk."

There she stood, a thin little woman with gray-brown hair and a perky, small face. A sparrow.

"How long has it been?" asked Norma, needing to say something. "How many years?"

"Thirty-five. It hardly seems possible, does it?" Miss Jenkins had a habit of asking rhetorical questions. "Sometimes it seems like a long time, and other times it seems like yesterday. But people always say that, don't they?"

"You'll be missed," Norma said. "To tell you the truth, I usually don't enjoy this new lower-school language program all that much, but I have enjoyed teaching French to your class. Your children seem so interested, so bright. Just—different from most."

"Oh, do you really think so? I'm so glad to hear that. I've always wanted to bring out the best in them, to make them listen and look about them at everything, at people, birds—"

Norma followed the gesture to where along one wall hung a row of nicely framed bird prints, each with its proper title.

"Oh, those are lovely. I'll help you take them down."

"No, I'm leaving them here. They liven the room for the children. They're better off here than they would be at home."

Elizabeth Jenkins, seeing a broken piece of chalk on

the floor beneath the blackboard, stooped to pick it up and dropped it into the wastebasket. In thirty-five years, Norma thought, she must have picked up thousands of broken pieces of chalk.

"I must say something about you, Norma. I've seen many language teachers before you, and from that first day last September when you came into my classroom, I knew you were going to be special. So young and inexperienced you were, yet you already had that special touch."

"Thank you, Elizabeth. Thank you."

In the year since Norma had come back here as a teacher rather than as a schoolgirl, her contacts had chiefly been among young faculty members; she would have been embarrassed to approach on an equal basis anyone who had once been her teacher. But since Elizabeth Jenkins had never been her teacher, it was easier.

"What are you going to do with all the wonderful new time you'll have?" she asked.

"Oh, I'll be busy enough. Mother and I have been living in a nice apartment, but it's on the second floor of a house, up a steep flight of stairs. So we'll have to move. Last month she fell on those stairs, going up, thank goodness, but she cracked a bone in her ankle nevertheless. Our lease runs out next Tuesday, so that's why I'm leaving here a week early, because we have to move." And Elizabeth Jenkins smiled, although there was no evident reason for a smile.

She smiles out of habit, Norma thought. It is a way of ingratiating oneself. An old woman, going home to an old mother! No companion, no husband, no child! A silent tragedy, yes. And there are millions of other personal tragedies all around us, although because they are so private, we do not see them.

"Well, Norma, I guess I'd better go. It's been nice knowing you. Keep up your good work."

Together they carried the box to the car and parted.

"I'll be calling the office with my new address, Norma, so people can keep in touch with me."

Not many people will. Right now I think I will, but most likely after two or three attempts, I won't. For in all this year we haven't spoken as much as we have just now.

Norma stood watching the car back out, start away, and stop.

"Norma, I forgot. Do you mind running back to check the window? I'm afraid I may have left the casement open, and if it should rain, it will stain the floor. They've just been polished."

"Right away. Don't worry."

She cares, she really cares about the floor. . . . Back in the classroom, Norma stood at the window, feeling the three o'clock silence of the deserted school. Thirty-five years, she repeated. Classes come and go, new faces appear and fade, the oak leaves fall, the pink azaleas bud and bloom. Thirty-five years, and then home to Mother.

"Is that you, Norma?"

Turning, she saw Mr. Cole. Occasionally, at a faculty tea with no students to hear, he was Lester. Otherwise, he was Mr. Cole, and she was Ms. Balsan. Two or three of the women old enough to retire were still, out of habit, called "Miss."

"Yes, I came in to see Miss Jenkins off."

If he could address her as Norma, then she should be

allowed to voice her feelings. "There was no one else here. It was sad."

"You're right. We all get so busy that we don't have time to consider what's important. . . . I don't know. But I did have a talk with her yesterday in my office to show appreciation. Recognition. It's hard. What thanks can there be for so much devotion? All those years?"

Lester looked troubled, as if he really cared. He does care, Norma thought. She had heard of so many incidents involving both students and teachers, to know that he did. He was a quiet man, often dressed in brown tweeds; you saw brown eyes and hair, all of him brown, with the warmth of bronze and russet. He looked like a teacher, too, which is an absurd thing to say because what does a teacher look like, for Heaven's sake? Still, she thought, if you were to stand him next to my brother, you would easily see that Larry is not the teacher.

Melanie Fisher had a crush on Lester. She had never revealed it to anyone, yet it, too, was easy to see. Everyone knew that he had taken her out once or twice and then not again. People had also seen him in restaurants, once with a "stunning" young woman who had red hair and a foreign accent; another person had seen him with a young girl who could have been a model.

"She forgot her bird prints," Lester said.

"No, she left them on purpose for the children."

"They're very good ones, you know. This parrot's extinct. Not that I know so much, but I am a birder, and I happen to have read about this particular parrot. Well, I'm calling it a day. You, too?"

"I don't know. Maybe I'll stay awhile to use the piano

in the music room. It's better than the one we have at home. If you don't mind."

"Mind? Help yourself. Just watch when the janitor leaves so you won't be locked in overnight."

This was not Norma's usual Friday mood. As with most people, Friday meant welcome rest and pleasure. She laid her pencil down on the pile of Latin finals that were to be graded. Ordinarily, she really liked these tasks; Latin was, for her, the same tool or toy that mathematics might be for somebody else. But today she had carried home a load of self-pity and dread.

Was she, in the end, to become another Elizabeth Jenkins? She was seeing her life escaping from her control. Once she had watched a beach ball, a light, careless thing, round and bright, caught in a receding surf, carried far out, tossed back into the shallows, then carried back again, each time a little farther out, until finally it was gone from sight and would never return. It had occurred to her then that, like the ball, a life could simply flow away.

It was absurd—she knew it was—that a person only twenty-three years old could feel that way. Nevertheless, right now, she did feel that way.

From across the street there came the mingled ring and screech of soprano laughter. Two girls no more than sixteen or seventeen years old lived in that house; they were already luring boys in droves, and had been luring them since they were in grade school. What was it? Why them? And why Amanda or Cecile? Or why Elizabeth Jenkins? Or herself?

On the back of the closet door, there was a full-length

mirror. With a sudden wrench, she got out of the chair to stand before it and examine herself, bit by bit. The hair was good enough, especially after the expensive cut that Amanda had coaxed her into having. Her skin was unblemished. Her eyes were nothing unusual, just nice, average brown eyes like Larry's. Her cheekbones were too broad, also like Larry's. The nose was a bit broad, too, but certainly it was no monstrous affliction such as you sometimes see. The mouth was just a mouth. Sound white teeth, brighter than many people had, were pretty when she smiled. Her figure was slender, not alluringly curved, but average, as good as most young women's and better than many.

But now the legs. Dear God, how can You have made such legs? Columns, they are, without any shape, the ankles thick as the knees, crammed into the shoes so that the flesh bulges over them. Do You know how it feels at a school dance to see a boy approach with invitation written on his face, then to watch when his eyes go downward to my legs, as he changes his mind and walks away? *Wallflower:* a grandmother's or perhaps a great-grandmother's term that describes the one who sits there smiling, who hopes, and who is never asked to dance. *Unless her brother asks her?*

It's all very well, this talk about how unjust it is for women to be judged by their beauty or their lack of it. Tell that to the girl at the dance, or to the woman at the dance of life. Of course it's unjust! But that's the way it is, no matter how many articles are written about why it shouldn't be that way. Yet, it's really quite a simple matter: Everyone loves beauty, and not only in a woman, but in a man, or a landscape—or in a dog.

Angrily, she tore off her skirt and pulled a pair of trousers from a hanger. If it weren't for that stodgy head at school, she thought, that so-distinguished scholar Dr. Griffin, she could wear these every day. But as long as he remained in charge, he would have his way. Perhaps if someone were to speak to Lester Cole? No, no. A young assistant, himself new in the job, shouldn't be asked to challenge his boss. Not fair.

Lester would listen, though. You could tell that he was kind and open-minded. He had felt for Elizabeth Jenkins . . .

I wonder whether he's in love with anybody? I imagine he would be very tender. Heaven knows what makes me think so, I who's never had any experience. What can I know?

And she sat there gazing out onto the street. The soft spring air blew between the curtains, and the light began to change as afternoon moved toward evening. Big boys, the grind of whose noisy skates had once disturbed Amanda when she had occupied the guest room, were scattering. The little hopscotch players were being called in to supper. The old man who apparently spent the whole day working at his perennial border was putting down his tools.

How long she had sat there, Norma did not know, until a gong was struck in the hall downstairs. It was the dinner gong, which her father had installed because people in great houses always had a dinner gong.

As she rose to answer it, she had the feeling that, gradually, her mood was changing. Was it a kind of reassurance that had come from watching the healthy, common life on the street? Perhaps. And perhaps it was also the working of her own inner toughness, which had reawakened of its own accord. *Seize the day.* She always did seize it, didn't she, every morning? *Head over heart.* She was used to doing that, too.

CHAPTER SEVEN

Amanda heard Norma lightly tapping the horn outside. She took a last approving look around her home. Finally, finally, it was finished! The "set"—long curved sofa and matching easy chairs, all wine-colored with the shades on the twin tables made to harmonize—filled one wall. On the opposite wall stood a huge, impressive piece of furniture of some pale, highly polished wood, the newest thing on the market, as the salesman had assured them. In addition to space for books and curios, it even had a wine closet with room for every kind of bottled drink that anyone might desire, along with a mirrored bar. Beyond the open door of this room stood the dining room set: table, chairs, china cupboard, and sideboard, all glossy and all matching.

Mine, she thought with satisfied approval. Owning

good things like these made you feel warm within. All else was secondary.

As she rode away in Norma's car, she could not help turning her head for another glimpse of the little white house that was her own.

"I'm glad Cecile thought of these monthly luncheons," Norma said. "They seem to prolong the college years. Keeping us under the same security blanket, I suppose." She laughed. "But people do drift apart if they go too long without seeing each other."

"I can't imagine that could happen to us three."

"I hope not. Wait till you see Cecile's apartment. What paint and new wallpaper can do! You'll hardly recognize it. Their first anniversary's next month, and they've just now got the place in shape, can you believe it?" And again Norma laughed fondly.

"I can believe it. It's taken us fairly long, too," Amanda said, feeling complacent.

Some half an hour later, as they stopped before a hollow square of garden apartments, she felt complacent again. "I would hate to be cooped up here in a little apartment," she said.

"When you see what they've done with that little apartment, you may change your mind. I know I'd love it, and someday, sooner rather than later, I intend to have one. I want a place of my own."

Cecile and Peter had made an indoor garden of their three rooms. Vines on a silvery background climbed the spring green walls and tipped over into a border on the ceiling. A scattering of blossoms that might have fallen from the vines lay on an earth brown rug. In a corner next to a table piled with books was a scarlet wing chair; on its other side an enormous, living fern grew out of a scarlet Oriental pot.

Amanda stood and gaped. "Whatever have you done?"

"This is all just odds and ends that my grandmother left, along with paint and wallpaper. Come have lunch," Cecile said.

The table was set in a green-and-white nook, where more plants stood on the windowsill. On the floor, in a hooded wicker basket, lay a white Persian cat.

Cecile introduced her. "That's Mary Jane. Isn't she gorgeous? Look at her blue eyes. Peter saw her in a pet shop window, and he couldn't resist her."

It had been a long time now since Amanda had felt this awkward. The last time had probably been on her first visit to the Balsan house. She had not even felt awkward on her first visit to the Newmans' country house. But she was feeling that way now.

If there could be such a thing as perfection, it was here, even to the cat. The monogrammed white linen place mats had crocheted edges. The silver was polished, the salad was crisp, and the rolls were warm. Cecile's pink cotton dress was untrimmed, and her only jewelry was a wide gold bracelet. Even in college, she had looked different from other people, and this past year had made her more so. The fact was simply that Cecile had class, and most people didn't. That was it: a thing indefinable, and yet a thing that you recognized when you saw it. Maybe everybody doesn't recognize it, thought Amanda, but I do.

Her eyes went wandering. On a shelf within view stood the wedding photograph of Peter and Cecile. There they were, caught for all time, in front of the rose hedge. Autumn Damask, they were, she remembered, as she remembered everything about that day. Wouldn't it be wonderful to have something like that to remember?

"It's a good thing Peter didn't go into that firm in town. This way, he has only shared space and a shared secretary with another man, so he's free to take courses toward the advanced degree."

"What in?" asked Norma. "Historic preservation?"

"What else? He loves it. We'll be in Washington this summer, and of course that's a treat, with the Virginia countryside, Fredericksburg, the plantations, and all those lovely houses to browse in. But believe it or not, I'm going to miss my work, too. My God, the things I learn can tear your heart! There's the most darling little girl who has lung cancer; they've operated, and maybe she'll be all right, but her mother's a prostitute. They live down on Lane Avenue, and what care is she going to have when she goes home? It makes you sick."

There was sober silence until Cecile broke it. "Looking at those books on the floor, Amanda? We're running out of space. Someday we'll have to have a room, a large one, with shelves floor to ceiling and wall to wall, for Peter's books."

"I can sympathize. I'm always buying books, paperbacks because hardcovers are too expensive, but paperbacks are better than nothing."

I never get around to reading much, Larry says. When I get home, I like to relax in front of the TV.

Amanda wondered about Peter. What was he like, really like? What did they talk about when they were together in the evening?

"Is anything happening with you yet on the job front, Amanda?" Cecile asked. "Any decision?"

"I've looked into paralegal work, but I haven't decided on it."

Norma nodded. "I didn't think you were ever really enthusiastic about it."

"Then Larry said they might be opening another branch office out in Derry, and I've been thinking maybe I could work on their computers, keep records for them or something."

Norma objected. "It's a bad idea for a wife to work next to her husband all day. What does Larry think?"

"I haven't even mentioned it to him."

Now Cecile asked, "What do you really want to do?"

"Go on to graduate school for a degree, probably in English literature. That's what I'd really want if I could. But it has too many problems. I don't see myself as a teacher, so the only other job would be in publishing. And practically all of the publishing companies are in New York. Anyway, there's no university here, and if there were, it would cost too much."

Amanda heard her own voice dying away. Did everybody's moods fluctuate as hers did? Only a few hours ago, she had felt closer to contentment than she had ever felt in her entire life.

"I have an idea for you." Cecile spoke decidedly. "I had planned to keep it till after lunch, but now you can hear it along with dessert. It's this: My mother has a friend, Mrs. Lyons, who owns a beautiful shop in Cagney Falls, right on the square. It's a fashion boutique, mostly European imports, expensive stuff. It's been a hobby of hers for years, buying things and getting ideas in Europe every year. Now she's getting older and doing much less. But even though she certainly doesn't need the money, she wants to keep the shop going. She needs somebody young and energetic to take charge. So here's where I thought you might come in."

"Who, me? You've got to be joking. What on earth do I know about running a shop?"

"No, listen to me. I've already told her about you, naturally without mentioning your name, and she's interested. You don't have to be trained to do this, Amanda. All you need is to be a responsible person. There's a seamstress for alterations who's been there from the beginning; there's a saleswoman, Dolly, who is great with the customers, lots of friendly personality; and there's a bookkeeper who comes in regularly to keep the books straight. All you need to do is to see that everybody works smoothly with everybody else."

"Who's been doing it up till now?"

"A young woman who's leaving, moving away. She can show you everything before she goes."

Here I've just said my idea is an advanced degree in English literature, Amanda was thinking, and this is what she recommends. She ought to know better.

"It pays very well," Cecile continued. "I was surprised. And you said you're in a hurry to earn some money."

Had she really said she was "in a hurry"? She must have. It must have slipped out somehow. But it was true. She was in a hurry. Still, a dress shop?

Cecile was urging, "This won't last forever, in case that's what you're thinking. And you can still take night courses while you're working, you know. After a while, you'll have a baby and you'll quit."

Amanda was still searching for a valid objection. "The only work experience I've had is at Sundale's, waiting tables. I'm too young to have had much experience."

"You're not too young. The woman who's leaving is twenty-eight, and you're nearly twenty-three, which isn't much different. And you're a whole lot smarter than she. I know because I've met her."

A dress shop, she thought again. It may pay very well, but it's not what I wanted. Still, it's probably not nice of me to refuse without taking a look at it.

"All right, I'll go see it," she said. "Tell me when."

"How about now? It's a lovely afternoon to go prowling around Cagney Falls, anyway."

"Just looking today, Dolly," Cecile said. "I'm not buying a thing. I only wanted to show the shop to my friends."

Dolly was the kind of woman who, while still in her thirties, behaved like a chatterbox teenager. During the ten or more minutes they had been in the shop, she had not stopped following them.

If I were to work here, Amanda decided, we would be friends. You can see that Dolly is a very nice person. She bubbles. Customers must like her.

"Beautiful stuff," Norma murmured, "and beautiful prices."

"True," Dolly said, having overheard, "but you don't find things like this on every street corner." She held out a white cashmere cardigan embellished with flowers. "Look here. Hand embroidered. No, you'll never see yourself coming and going when you wear this."

Not at these prices, thought Amanda, echoing Norma. Every nook, shelf, and corner held a treasure: a paisley handbag with a tortoiseshell handle, a suit of rough, peach-colored wool, silk dresses pleated from neck to hem, a plain black evening gown with a cascade of marvelous white lace. Amanda was fascinated.

Perhaps, after all, it might be fun for a little while, at least . . .

Outside again, they began to walk back to the car.

"It was an eye-opener," Amanda said. "This whole town is an eye-opener."

"Well, what do you think about it?" Cecile asked.

"I surprised myself, and I suppose I'll surprise you. Yes, I'll try it if Mrs. Lyons likes me. I really would like to try it, for a while, anyway."

"Good. She'll like you. I'll phone her the minute I get home so that you can meet. Now, shall we start back?"

"Can we just walk around for a few minutes? I was here one day with Larry, but everything was closed, and besides, he hurried me, the way men do. This is a place where you need to take your time and feast your eyes."

Cecile agreed. "It's a beautiful little town. I wouldn't mind living in this area, not right in the town, but near it."

Norma pointed out a clock in a window. "It looks like brass, doesn't it? But it's not. It's lacquered wood. I saw one when I had dinner at the home of one of my students. Pretty, isn't it?"

"Look at those silver frogs! And the music box!" Amanda cried. "All these beautiful, beautiful things that people make with their hands! Let's go in for just a minute."

A spacious interior was crammed with chests, pictures, chairs, clocks, objects of porcelain and of silver, all of them in orderly display. Amanda was dazzled.

To the dapper, dignified gentleman who approached them, Norma said, "We're just browsing, if you don't mind."

"Please do, and if there's anything you want to know, just ask me."

"Oh, look at this bureau!" exclaimed Amanda. "Isn't it pretty? Our bedroom set has two bureaus, but one's much too small. There's an empty space on one wall, and this one is really lovely. Look how delicately it's painted."

The gentleman, who had been hovering nearby, corrected her. "Oh, dear, no. Not paint. That is inlay, called marqueterie, the most painstaking woodwork, all satinwood." Murmuring, with his eyes upon Amanda, he seemed to be exceedingly amused.

"All you need is money," remarked Norma, nudging Amanda to the other side of the room, where Cecile, who had not heard the little encounter, was examining another chest of drawers.

The gentleman, following, now approached Cecile, who had a question. "This block-front chest. I have one very like it. Is it about 1770, would you say? That's my guess, at least."

"You're close. This is dated 1781, made in Rhode Island, like most of them."

"I thought so. It's typical, isn't it? I'm curious. What are you asking for it?"

"We're asking seven. It's in excellent condition, as you can see. This is the original hardware."

"Seven hundred dollars for *that!*" cried Amanda with intent to thrust her scorn into the man's smug face. "For one piece of furniture, four drawers on four feet, simply because it's old and bears the term 'antique'? That's ridiculous."

"Well, it may seem so to you." The gentleman was now unmistakably on the verge of laughter. "But there are those who would think it a find at the price, which is, as it happens, seven *thousand,* and even though it's not part of a *set.*"

"Come on," said Norma. "It's already half past three, and we all have to get home. We've no time to waste in this place, anyhow."

On the sidewalk again, Amanda spoke out of her raging sense of humiliation. "He positively smirked! Did you see his face? Trying to make a fool of me. Who does he think he is?"

"He's an insignificant snob, that's who he is," Norma said roughly. "Forget him." And no doubt seeing the tears starting in Amanda's eyes, she said more gently, "One has to expect every now and then to meet a person who's completely insensitive. Get used to it."

Ah, yes! Her legs. She still hasn't gotten used to insensitive people, though.

With her usual calm candor, Cecile gave advice. "Of course, he was horrible. Why should everyone be informed about expensive antiques? Most people couldn't care less. And anyway, all there is to know about them, all the basic information you need if you should ever care to learn, can be found in a handful of books. It's no big deal."

Norma was in a hurry. "Let's put a move on. You haven't forgotten that you and Larry are eating with us tonight, have you? And that my father is one man who can't stand it when people come late?"

* * *

Larry had looked reproachful when Amanda and Norma arrived barely two minutes ahead of the dinner hour. Now he was listening with severe disapproval to an account of the day's achievement.

"What is this all of a sudden? You've been wanting to be a paralegal. What is this?"

"I guess I didn't want it enough."

"What? Amanda, if you told me once, you told me a hundred times that it's what you want."

They were sitting side by side, so that when she turned to him, their faces were only inches apart. It was incredible that she had never before observed his eyes so clearly: They were not really brown, as she had assumed, but a queer yellow kind of brown.

"Taking a long drive every day to stand on your feet in a shop and sell clothes—it makes no sense."

Norma came to her assistance. "It's not a long drive, Larry. Only three quarters of an hour from your house, that's all."

"No matter. It's stupid. Why did you say you wanted to be a paralegal if you didn't want to?"

"It popped into my head. You wanted an answer, and I said the first thing I could think of."

Lawrence Balsan was listening. He actually looks as if he's enjoying this, Amanda thought. His expression was ironic, as it often was. His son, on the other hand, had a baffled expression.

"I can't understand the whole thing," Larry muttered.

"I suggest that you stop trying," Lawrence said abruptly. "This argument has been going on for twenty minutes by my watch." Drawing back his sleeve to reveal the heavy gold watch, he continued, "Amanda wants it, and there's no harm in it. Take the job, Amanda, if you can get it. You won't be married to it. You can quit whenever you want and go do something else. So let's not have any more wrangling."

It was astonishing that this man, of all people, should come to her rescue, and that he should flash in her direction the brilliant look that so rarely illuminated his rather austere face.

It was less astonishing that Larry should accept this dictum at once. The surprise would have come if he had dared to disagree with his father.

So it was settled. Yet now that it was, Amanda was not so sure that she wanted it. Is it possible, she asked herself, that I only wanted it the more because Larry opposed it? For it had been such a strange day, beginning with lunch at Cecile's apartment, then the delightful shop, and then that horrible man with his antiques. Her very spine still felt his sting.

At home, preparing for bed, Larry asked for the third or fourth time, "So you had a good day? Pretty out there, isn't it?"

"It's beautiful. Cecile wants to move there eventually."

He shrugged, as if to acknowledge the obvious. "Why not? With the Newmans' money behind them? They'll probably spend two years in the apartment and then move. I'm surprised they didn't get a house right away. Gee whiz, we did."

We're not talking about the same kind of house, she thought, or the same kind of anything. And as she sat down to remove her shoes, she looked around the room at the "colonial" matching set—the bed, the night tables, and the bureau with the wedding snapshot of herself and Larry standing among the tables at the inn. None of all this had come cheaply, either, but it was so drab, without imagination or charm; it was tasteless and banal, like every other house on this street that she had seen. It was commercial factory stuff turned out by the millions for people who didn't know any better. And she had been one of them. . . . She saw again the cascade of green vines on the ceiling at Cecile's apartment, and the silver-framed wedding portrait near the eighteenth-century chest. She saw the treasure-filled shop, and felt again the sting of that man's insolent smile.

And without meaning to burst out, she cried, "You should see Cecile's apartment!"

"Nice, is it? Well, it can't be much nicer than this. God knows, we paid enough for all our stuff. But it's worth it. Good furniture lasts a lifetime and more." Unbuttoning his shirt, Larry stretched and yawned. "The only thing we might have to do is add more to what we've got if we should ever get a bigger place."

"A bigger place? You know, with your real estate connections, it might not be so hard to find a house near Cagney Falls. You can't be sure."

"Honey, I can be sure. That stuff is just about doubling up while you look at it. No, if we ever do move, and I don't say we will, we'll probably take my father's house. You know, Norma's been saying she wants a place of her own, a nice convenient apartment near Country Day. Then maybe my father won't want to rattle around by himself in the house. Gee, I wish Norma could find some nice guy like Peter, for instance. Somebody to take her out to dinner, for God's sake. She's too young to live the way she does. It must be hard on her to see her friends, Cecile and you, being so happy, on top of the world. All she does is go to the movies with a couple of women, or sit home by herself to read or play the piano. Even my father goes out more."

That was interesting. "He does? With women?"

"Sure. What do you think? It's a question you don't ask your father, but after all, he's still a young man, fifty-two last birthday. Good-looking, too, don't you think?"

Balsan—in her mind she thought of him so—was nothing if not distinctive. It had been quite a startle this evening to see his haughty face, with its high-ridged aristocrat's nose and his cool gaze, light up like a candle.

"Yes, in a way," she said.

"Not like me. He's even got better hair than I have. His isn't receding, and mine is." Larry grinned, as though it were all a big joke.

For a moment, the grin touched Amanda's heart. It was pathetic, although why it should be she did not know, for if Larry exuded anything, it was confidence in himself.

Lying in bed while he took his shower, she wondered about her own self. The older I get, the less I know, people said, and it seemed to be true. Surely she *wanted* to be happy with this man! I want, she thought, I want, as everyone does, to be happy. But I want beauty, too. I want to hear beautiful music, to read, to learn, to see the world, to feel a passionate love. And most of all, admit it, I want beautiful things around me. I never knew before I left home to come here that there were so many beautiful things.

*   *   *

Late in the fall, Amanda's mother came to visit. "Dad couldn't come," she explained, "because some big company's bought the factory and he's afraid of losing his job. Lost so much time on account of his leg, of course. They might want to let him go."

A light snow was falling as they left the airport. In her thin coat Mom shivered.

"I'll buy you a warm coat," Amanda said. "We'll do it first thing tomorrow."

"I don't need one. Thanks, but save your money, dear."

"I guess I can give my mother a present, can't I?" She was making her voice sound jolly. Mom looked so tired. . . . "I'm so glad you're here, Mom. And Larry will be, too. You're going to like each other right away."

"Oh, I like him already. I feel as if I know him, talking on the phone every week the way we do. My, I can't believe I'm as far away as Michigan, visiting my daughter in her own house. It looks beautiful in the picture you sent. Is it far?"

"Not very. Sit back and let me point out the sights."

Mom was more excited about this trip than were Mrs. Lyons's customers about a cruise to the Orient. She was overwhelmed by the house, the yard, and the two new cars in the garage. When Larry hugged her, she looked as if she was about to cry.

He wanted to take her out to dinner, to the movies and on drives through the countryside, but all she wanted was to stay in "this wonderful house" with them, playing checkers and watching movies from the video store. One day she made a pecan pie, because Larry had never eaten that authentic southern pie.

"She reminds me of my mother," he told Amanda.

His expression was tender and again she was affected by it; behind his extroverted personality she seemed to be seeing another personality, one vulnerable and frail.

On her last day Mom baked two more pies for the freezer. This freezer, the electric wall oven, and the whole machinery of the kitchen were rubies and emeralds, in her eyes.

"Even your floor is beautiful," she said.

Amanda looked down at the smooth marble tile. As if he had read the meaning of her glance, Larry reached into his pocket, fetched an envelope, and handed it to her when they were alone.

"Give this to Mom at the airport when she leaves. It's for a rubber-tiled floor," he said, still with that tender expression on his face.

When they went upstairs for the night, Amanda received some unexpected counsel from Mom.

"Treasure what you have. I wish my other girls had men like yours. The goodness shines out of him."

Yes, she knew that, and knew very well too what she ought to be feeling. So later when he lay down on the bed beside her, she understood at once what he wanted. He had his own little way of beckoning her to himself. Never in any mood to respond, she was even less so now. But since her willing response was expected, she gave it now.

CHAPTER EIGHT

Welcome clouds were moving across the sun's orange glare, and a small, moist breeze, also welcome, began to drift in from the Mississippi. But it had been, nevertheless, a wonderful summer day of exploration in New Orleans. In the restaurant's shady garden, Peter was being anxious and proprietary.

"We're taking a taxi back to the hotel, Cele, and no argument about it. You've done too much walking today and it's my fault, I shouldn't have let you do it."

"For goodness' sake, don't you know that pregnant women are supposed to have exercise? I feel absolutely marvelous! I'm floating on air."

Indeed, she was. Now, in the third year of their marriage, a baby was on the way, and Peter, having earned his graduate degree with distinction, was also on his way.

Just this week his work was about to lead to bayou country and an unusual eighteenth-century house. She was so happy for him! So proud of him!

"I'm still amazed that anybody tracked me down here in New Orleans," he said, "amazed and excited, too. I didn't know that they knew I was here."

"You're making a name for yourself! You love the work, and it shows. All those marvelous old houses, all the history, the romance in it—"

"Of course. But preservation isn't all romance and George-Washington's-mother-lived-here history, fascinating as that is. It's also how ordinary people lived; it's connected to town planning and how a building is connected to the environment, to the climate and family life. It's a hundred things besides brick and mortar and accepted styles. Not long ago, people turned up their noses at the Victorian; it was dowdy, fussy and illogical. Now you suddenly see developers copying Victorian front porches; they're neighborly, they're sociable—" Peter smiled at himself. "Heck, I'm giving a lecture. You should stop me when I do. I'm no professor."

"One day you may be, if you want to."

"We'll see. We'll see. Now taste this gumbo, will you? Best food in the fifty states."

In a dove gray twilight, they walked back toward the hotel. "We'll compromise," Cecile said. "Right after the bookstore, we'll get a taxi. I saw a lovely book of New Orleans photographs for Amanda."

"All right, but that's all. I want you to get to bed early."

In a way it bothered her to be ordered about as if she

were a child or an infirm old lady, yet in another way she, an independent woman, was enjoying this temporary babyhood.

"All right, boss," she said.

"I wish you were going with me tomorrow, but I'll probably be there for a week, and you need to go home and keep your appointment with the doctor."

"And should I go look at that house again?"

The subject of a move had been analyzed and discussed to the limit. Their two-year lease on the apartment was almost up; if they were to renew it, the landlord was now asking for three years; in three years, the baby would be an active child with no room of its own. Their apartment had simply not been designed for children. Clearly Peter understood that a move was necessary. Yet, she knew he was feeling anxiety.

"It's a quaint little house," he said. "Yes, I guess I can handle the mortgage. In fact, I know I can."

Quaint it was and little it was, too. Back in the 1890's, it had been the gatehouse on an estate that had not long ago been turned into an upscale development. The builders had retained the gatehouse, perhaps because it was picturesque; built of the same stone and in the same style as the original mansion, it was surrounded by a tiny, bare yard, which meant almost no upkeep.

Back in the hotel, Peter reflected. "We'd have to fix up the kitchen, that's about all. Yes, it's a good start, a first house, a nice living-dining room and two bedrooms, just what we need. Yes, go ahead."

"I do plan to use some of my own money for decorations, painting and paper, you know that?"

"Hey, I don't want to be fanatic about never using

some of your money, Cele, but be careful. Keep it modest. I'm having a good start, thank God. Only don't count all my chickens before they're hatched. Here, let me help you pack. This darned book weighs a ton. I can pack it with my stuff."

"No, I'll manage. It's for Amanda's birthday. She's learned so much about art and decoration lately, and she'll love it." Cecile paused to stare at Peter. "Why the sour face all of a sudden?"

"Well, maybe I'm just not that fond of Amanda."

"Oh, that's mean! And it's not at all like you. You always like people."

"True, but I can't like everybody."

"But why Amanda? She's one of my closest friends."

Peter, folding ties to pack, seemed to be considering the question. Then, with a slight frown, he replied.

"Maybe it's because I feel sorry for Larry."

"Sorry for Larry?"

"Yes. I think she belittles him."

"Really? I don't know what you mean. They always seem so compatible, so comfortable."

Peter shook his head. "It's very subtle. Her conversation, whenever we've been together, seems to consist of other people's vacations, jewelry, clothes, and houses. Stuff she picks up in that place where she works, I suppose."

"She never had anything, Peter. I don't mean that she was like you, needing to be very careful about money. I mean she never had *anything*."

"Then she ought to be more careful of what she has now." He spoke shortly. "She ought to appreciate Larry."

Those were troubling words. And as Cecile absorbed them, certain incidents, which obviously must have made enough impression on her to be recalled now, came to mind. There was the flowered silk dress that Amanda wore when they all went out to dinner a month or two ago: nine hundred dollars, it had cost. Cecile had seen it in the shop and had not bought it because it was overpriced. There was a bracelet Amanda had worn; quite innocently she, Cecile, had mentioned it with admiration while talking once to Norma. And Norma had changed the subject too abruptly. Had she, Cecile now wondered, taken my comment to mean disapproval? Or to be, worse yet, a piece of disloyal gossip? I meant neither, she thought uncomfortably.

"You're sorry for Larry, and I'm sorry for Amanda," she said, "or I will be if things are not good between the two of them."

"Well, you can be sure Amanda will take care of herself, no matter what. With that body and that face, she'll be fine."

"How can you say that?"

"I've watched her among people. She's a magnet. You mean you haven't noticed?"

"I never pay that much attention, I guess."

"Don't sound so wistful."

"I'm not wistful at all. I'm only thinking about what you've been saying," said Cecile. And then added wistfully, "It must be nice to be a magnet."

Peter laughed. "Oh, not like that, my lovely darling. Definitely not like that."

*   *   *

"Are you sitting down?" asked Cecile. "I have a tremendous surprise for you. I wanted to keep it until you got home next week, so I could see your face, but I find I can't wait. We're having twins!"

"What? You're joking!"

"Why on earth would I joke? It's definite."

"Can the doctor be sure?"

"Of course he can. Twins. Can you believe it?"

"Twins. Can you see us pushing a double baby carriage, strangers coming up and smiling at them?" Peter was chuckling. "You know what? I like the idea! I do! You're sure the doctor is sure?"

Cecile laughed. "You big idiot! Of course he's sure. Oh, Peter, I'm thinking of two little boys who look like you."

"No, a boy and a girl, and they should look like you. Especially the girl should. I wish I was there with you right now. If I could rush things here, I'd get the next plane, but I need a few more days with builders."

"Take your time. I'll keep the champagne chilled. And Peter, we can't buy the gatehouse. It only has two bedrooms."

"Can't two cribs fit in one room?"

"Of course they can. But babies do grow out of their cribs. They'll need space to play in. And if one's a girl and the other's a boy, they'll eventually need two separate bedrooms."

"What do people do who can't afford separate rooms?"

They weren't going to have a repeat of the street-corner argument they'd had that time in Bermuda, were they? Was she imagining a strain of stubbornness in his tone?

She replied calmly, "People like that have to make do. They put up a bed in the living room, which isn't the worst thing in the world, but it certainly isn't the most comfortable arrangement, either, and if you don't absolutely have to do it, why should you?"

"Well, yes, I guess you're right."

"Actually, we could take the gatehouse for now. It's charming, and we could stay for a year, maybe two, but then we'd have to move again, which doesn't make any sense to me."

"Yes, yes, you're right.

"Oh, I'm happy, Cele, a little dazed, but happy." The familiar laugh rang over the wires. "So you'll have to go out looking right away. Just—oh, you must be tired of hearing this—but keep it modest. Don't forget, I'm only getting started."

"I won't forget."

More than once, her father had praised Peter's independence. "Many a man in his position would be only too glad to relax and enjoy his wife's good fortune. I admire Peter. I liked him the first time I laid eyes on him. You know that."

So, carrying faithfully in her mind Peter's desire to pay his own way, Cecile set out on the search. Her first thought had been to call on Larry. But then two other thoughts occurred to her: One of them was that the Balsan company was not active on this side of the city, and the other was about Amanda's vague discontent with her own house, her ambition being to live in the very area where Cecile was about to go searching.

It was surprising to see how many houses were unsuitable. Some were too small, others too large. Some were too formal in style, others too gaudy; several had beautiful, large yards that were too expensive to maintain, and a few were simply too expensive altogether. Not until the fifth day, after having seen some thirty-odd houses, did she come upon the one that was just right. The tired broker, who had probably given up hope of ever satisfying this client, simply stared at Cecile when, after a ten-minute inspection, she announced, "We'll take it."

"But you've hardly had a chance to think. And your husband hasn't seen it. Are you sure?"

"I'm positive. I love it, and he's going to love it."

Surely, Peter would. An architect had duplicated for his own use a house in Williamsburg. It was simple, authentic, and the next best thing to an original. She had during her tour brought to life in her mind all the plans that had long been dormant there. Here were the children's rooms, with gingham curtains at the windows; there the piano, now in storage, would stand in the left-hand corner; down the rear hall, where Peter might study and draw in quiet, was his wonderful room, where northern light filtered through windows that opened onto the porch.

Seeing this enthusiasm, the broker rose to meet it. "As you see, the house is vacant and you can have early possession, which is quite unusually good luck."

It wasn't that unusual, but it was luck. And with a lovely, peaceful sense of completion, Cecile wrote out a check that would hold the house until Peter's return.

Here was their lifetime home. Children would grow

up in it; grandchildren would come to visit; holiday dinners, P.T.A. teas and civic community meetings, political events—all these would fill the rooms. Oh, she was letting sentiment run away with her, but why not? This was a tremendous event in anybody's life.

Still, after a while, a faint shadow began to creep over her sun. Careful as she had been about price, she had nevertheless overstepped Peter's limit. She had not forgotten the lesson learned in Bermuda: Here was no two-acre miniature "estate" this time; her father was not making any gift this time; the extra funds were to come from her own fund bequeathed by her grandmother. It had never been a large amount, and she had already dug into it; now with this purchase, it would be completely used up. They would then have to live very, very carefully on Peter's earnings.

But she was no spendthrift, and they would manage.

"I can't believe it," Peter said. "I thought we had this out over two years ago in Bermuda, and now you've done it again."

They had just come back from viewing the house. His suitcases, still unpacked, lay on the floor beside the basket from which Mary Jane, the placid cat, now looked up as if puzzled at the unfamiliar voices of anger.

"I have not done it again! My father has nothing to do with this." Cecile was furious. "How many times do I have to tell you that I'm using my—"

"Don't tell me again about your grandmother's legacy. It should be put aside for these twins we're having instead of being squandered on a fancy house."

"It is not a fancy house! You were just there and you

fell in love with it until I gave you the details about the price. You fell in love with it."

"All right, I did. People fall in love with a lot of things they can't afford. That's half the trouble with most people, and I won't be one of them."

"Now you listen to me. It's my turn. I'm trying to tell you, but you don't seem to understand, so I'm going to get pencil and paper and write everything out in dollars and cents, and you'll see that with economy, because I won't spend a penny on myself— We can wait to furnish. You've been doing very well and you're always pessimistic; you never thought you would start out so well. I wish you wouldn't be like that. Give me your pen—no, I can't find one—take it out of your pocket and give it to me, and I'll show you how we can manage—"

"Yes, from hand to mouth. Beautiful. Wonderful, living from hand to mouth in a house filled with empty rooms. Wonderful."

The doorbell rang. "Oh, for Pete's sake, who's that? Go answer it, Cele. I don't want to see anybody. I've been traveling all day from one airport to the next and I want to unpack this stuff."

"It's my parents. They've hardly seen you since you got your degree last May, and they wanted to welcome you."

Amos and Harriet Newman were embarrassed. In these apartments with their flimsy Sheetrock walls, one heard everything, and Cecile, when she admitted them, knew at once that they had overheard the argument.

Peter knew it too, for after giving his greeting, he at once apologized. "I'm sorry you happened in on a bit of trouble, but thank you anyway for the welcome home."

As Cecile could have predicted, her father came right

to the point. "I'm guessing that it's about the house. If it is, do you want to talk about it or not? It isn't Harriet's business or mine, so be frank."

Peter sighed. "I can put it into a few words: Cele has found a wonderful house, but it's more than I can afford. It's that simple."

"You don't want her to use her own money."

"No, sir, I don't. It's that simple," Peter repeated.

Amos nodded. "I thought so. You're determined to get on without any help, and I've admired that. I've told you so more than once. But may I be equally frank?"

The two men were still standing in the center of the room. They were a pair of strong men, one very young and the other still remarkably young. Each was a man who was fundamentally gentle, yet could also display on occasion a good deal of righteous anger. And Cecile, through the fog of her own anger, was tense with expectation.

"May I be equally frank?" Amos questioned again.

"I wish you would be."

"All right, then. Like any other good thing, like vitamins, exercise, and even charity, independence can be taken too far. When they're taken too far, they lose their value. They become false."

For a few moments, Peter seemed to be considering Amos's words. "False pride, you're saying."

"Yes, it can be."

"It's very hard for me to be a taker." The murmur was barely audible.

"Whatever made you that way, whether something in your genes or something in your past," Amos was saying, "I surely can't know and maybe you can't, either. In any case, it doesn't matter. The fact is I didn't come here only to welcome you back, but also with an idea." He smiled. "Cecile, may we use the dining table? And your mother could use a cup of coffee and a piece of cake, if you have any. I rushed her out before she had a dessert, and you know her sweet tooth."

Out of his pocket Amos withdrew and unfolded a sheet of paper almost as large as the table and began to explain it.

"Here you see a very rough sketch of the enormous, unused railroad yard, twenty-seven acres stretching from the old deserted terminal to the river. There it lies, pristine land piled with rusty cars and junk, as far as Lane Avenue, which is also a stretch of junk, although people live there. It's a disgrace to the city and to the state, and has been one for too long."

Cecile, having provided coffee and cake for Harriet, stood beside Amos to observe. She was still too sore and hot to stand on Peter's side of the table.

"This wound has been bleeding for so long that most people in the city have gotten used to it. The ones who aren't used to it are divided—but you must have read about all this. Every now and then some editorial writer brings up the subject from his point of view: Either we keep the marshland for migrating birds, create a park, build some decent, affordable housing on the Lane Avenue end, make a low-rise, small-town commercial area near the bridge for convenience shopping—in other words, construct a community—or else we turn the whole thing to high-rise, high-technology office space and big profits."

"Yes, sixty stories tall," Peter said with some scorn.

"Glass boxes stood on end. Don't they know that those things are already outmoded? Cold in the winter and blazing hot in the summer, unless you're prepared to waste money and electric power on heating and air-conditioning."

"Plenty of people are quite prepared. You know that."

"Who's going to win the battle?"

"It depends pretty much on the elections. A governor, if he has the legislature with him, can almost wave a magic wand. It's all a tangle. Banks, environmentalists, zoning fights—a tangle. But eventually something will be done." Amos paused. "You haven't asked me why I'm telling you all this. Aren't you wondering?"

"Well, yes, I guess I am. This is all way out of my line."

"There's one thing that isn't, Peter. Whichever way it goes, my way with the bird sanctuary and the rest, or the other way with the glass boxes, there will be the terminal to consider. These grand old terminals all over the country are being restored to use, aren't they? And isn't restoration right up your alley?"

From across the table, Cecile was able to see the light in Peter's eyes. Apparently overwhelmed, he almost stammered.

"You mean that—I'm only a beginner—wouldn't people want one of the big names, those big firms?"

"They all got started somewhere. And if you can come up with a good design, why not you? You're trained, you're talented, and a job like this would give you national recognition." And before Peter could reply, Amos continued, waving the pencil in his enthusiasm.

"The terminal would probably be a museum, wouldn't it? We lack a good one in this city." The pencil made a flourish in the air. "The possibilities are tremendous, and no matter what else is done, the terminal will be the hub." He paused again, scanning Peter's face. "So, what do you think?"

Peter blinked. "I guess I'm stunned. I'm honored by your confidence, and I thank you. Yes, I'm stunned."

"I have to repeat that this isn't going to happen tomorrow. It will certainly take a couple of years. But it will happen. It's bound to. I have plenty of contacts who keep their ears to the ground. When it does happen, it'll be the biggest thing to hit this city in the last half century. But that's all right. You'll have plenty of time that you can squeeze out of your present commitments to think about how you would do it. Go down there and walk around. Make some sketches for yourself." Carefully, Amos folded the paper back and put it into his pocket. "But I have to caution you. What I've said here must not leave this room, not ever."

"Of course not," Peter said.

"This room," repeated Amos. "I'm glad you heard it, too, Cecile. Not a word, ever. One idle, thoughtless word, totally innocent, can start a train of thought in the mind of a hearer who might also be totally innocent; the train speeds away and ends in a wreck. Remember that. So, Peter! It appeals to you, does it? I thought you'd like the idea."

"It appeals to me very much. How can I thank you?"

"You're asking me how, and I'll tell you how. Let your wife have the house. She wants it. She loves it."

"He loves it, too," cried Cecile.

Peter looked down at the floor, raised his eyes to meet hers, and murmured as he had before, "I want to give it to you, Cele. I want to give you everything, but I'm not able to."

When I went home after my first visit to your family, it seemed to me that I was on my way to making a terrible mistake. I am out of my league, I thought. The paintings, the sheer size of the place—this girl was not for me. I had heard people say that the Newmans were "simple" people, without any airs, and that was true, but "simplicity" depends on the point of view. I thought and I argued with myself for days, but always I came back to the beginning: We are so right for each other.

She seemed to be hearing his voice. And they stood there with eyes connecting.

Then Amos, obviously moved, spoke again with deliberate heartiness.

"Consider accepting Cecile's money as a loan, Peter. Whenever you can, replace her grandmother's legacy, if it'll make you feel better."

"As if I would accept it," Cecile cried. "I don't earn anything. But he works and buys my food! Am I supposed to pay him back for it?"

Amos and Harriet were both laughing. "Go kiss and make up. Don't be silly, either of you," said Harriet. "Go take care of your twins."

CHAPTER NINE

Now and then, on her way to work in Cagney Falls, Amanda would make a five-minute detour onto a winding rural road past Cecile's house. Even on a raw, bare winter morning, the sight of it, square and sturdy as though it had stood for two centuries, was oddly pleasing to her. It was also, and she well under stood why, more than a little disturbing.

The house had an elegant simplicity. The window panes, six on top and nine below, the dark green doorway with its harvest wreath of autumn leaves and sheaved grain, the shallow, semicircular steps below it, all were exactly right. Amanda had been sufficiently exposed to what she thought of as "class" to recognize it. Everything that Cecile and Peter owned, or said, or did, was exactly right. They had even known enough to choose each other. . . .

Somewhat subdued, she would continue on her way. Not until she had entered the town square and parked the car, a really smart little car that looked like an import but was not one, did her spirits return to their natural high.

This job was, after all, the best thing that could have happened to her. Who could have guessed that working in a boutique would be so satisfying to a woman who had once thought about a graduate degree in English literature? She had certainly never given herself any credit for having a "head for business," but apparently she possessed one, because Mrs. Lyons was leaving more and more responsibility to her. Mrs. Lyons, who in manner, speech, and style could have doubled for Cecile's mother, was shrewd besides. She wanted to keep Amanda because, with her in charge, she was free to travel and stay away for weeks; then, too, Amanda attracted customers, especially men shopping for gifts. On her part, Amanda wanted to be kept, and Mrs. Lyons knew that, too. She also knew that Amanda coveted fine clothes, so if a little discount, or more than a little one, could make the girl happy, it was worth the cost. In this way, a wordless contract between the two women was cheerfully struck.

The entire atmosphere in the shop was cheerful. Even the seamstress hummed while she worked. Dolly was still noisy and, in Amanda's opinion, not too bright, but very likable all the same, and for some reason a bit in awe of Amanda, too. In the mornings before the doors were opened, when the three had coffee and doughnuts together in the back room, the little shop almost felt like home.

It was such a pretty place in which to spend one's days! In winter, especially, it was snug; outside on the square, the rain or snow might be turning the scene to a dim gray, yet indoors, on the table where small objects were displayed, there was always a brilliant bouquet ordered weekly by request of Mrs. Lyons. The clothes themselves were brilliant. Mrs. Lyons had a taste for rare shadings and striking combinations. The clothes, in fact, were irresistible. It was astonishing that, despite their shocking prices, very few people came inside without buying something, even if it was only a scarf.

As it happened, Amanda's very first purchase was a white silk scarf sprinkled with poppies and cornflowers.

"Wear it with a white suit," advised Mrs. Lyons, who had just brought back from France a small selection of treasures.

When Amanda replied that she did not own a white suit, Mrs. Lyons advised her further. "You ought to own one. Take one of ours. You may have it for twenty-five percent off."

So easily did it begin. So easily did it become a habit. When you had the right clothes, you felt like a different person. They made up for, or almost made up for, whatever else might be lacking in your life.

It was already dark at five o'clock when, one day in early December, Amanda locked the shop's door and walked toward the parking lot. On the square a few lights still gleamed; in the porcelain shop on the corner they gleamed invitation, where a lovely green bowl lay in the front window. For several weeks past it had been attracting Amanda's attention. Since it had not been sold, she reasoned, it must be outrageously expensive, yet this evening she stopped again to look at it.

From somewhere, probably from the music store across the street, now came the sound of some familiar, ancient Christmas music. Otherwise, the square was quite deserted. A few walkers on her side of it had halted in the evening darkness, apparently to catch the pure, exalted melody. Then a couple, holding hands, smiled at her as they passed, as if they, too, were feeling the beauty of the moment, that sudden keen thrust in the breast.

Ah, you only live once! Take all the beauty that you can, while you can! And she went inside to buy the lovely green bowl.

"It's an unusual piece," the young salesman assured her. "Turn of the century, I should think, maybe 1910, but no later. Expensive, and worth it."

He had a sensitive face, with calm, harmonious features, reminding her of Peter Mack. His hand, with a wedding ring on it, was resting on the counter beside the bowl. His cuff was worn. When he looked up toward Amanda, their eyes met for an unmistakable instant, and quickly disconnected. She knew what he was thinking, but he could not know what she was thinking, or feeling, about him: that he was only a salesman here, marketing objects that he would never afford; that he had a wife and probably some children at home. Poverty row, she thought, and felt pity.

Something needed to be said while he wrapped the bowl, and so she remarked that she loved porcelains, yet knew nothing about them.

"There's a lot to learn," he answered. "Porcelains date back to the Greeks and earlier—no, to Egypt before that. Maybe you want to buy a book about it? They're on the shelves over there."

So she bought a book, a heavy volume filled with illustrations, and feeling quite powerfully lavish, took that with her, too.

It was such a pleasure to arrive at home bearing something new to be carefully unwrapped, and then, after equally careful deliberation, placed in the spot that was proper for it. The splendid, glossy book, too tall for any shelf, belonged naturally on the coffee table. Between it and the graceful potted plant, the table seemed not quite so ugly. With the bowl, she had to experiment: the sideboard in the dining room, or the stand between two windows?

When she removed the sticker on the bottom, the price leaped up at her, bringing a chill of unease. It was not that Larry had any right to object; if she wanted to spend her next two weeks' salary—no, more than that— on this bowl, it was her own affair, wasn't it? Still, it would be more sensible not to tell him.

She was still admiring her two fine little additions to the commonplace room when he came home. First he kissed her cheek, and then made his usual quick, prideful glance around at that room.

"Hey, when'd you get that?"

"Today. Like it?"

"I dunno. What's it for?"

"What's a bowl for? Whatever you want to put in it. I'm going to put flowers in it."

"Expensive?"

"Not very. Not at all."

"That's good. You ought to be putting away a nice

little nest egg with that nice raise she gave you." At the mustard-colored bar, he poured a drink. "Want to keep it a secret, hey? Well, that's okay. I don't mind. But you could look at everything I'm saving. It's all in the left-hand desk drawer upstairs." He sat down on the club chair, stretching his legs out onto the ottoman. "I was thinking on the drive home just now, the thought just came to me, what you said about Mrs. Lyons wanting to retire soon, maybe you'd like to buy the business, you like it so much. I could raise some cash with no trouble, and with a little help from you, we could swing it without my touching any real capital. You'd like that, wouldn't you?"

Real capital. She wondered how much there was. Very much, she thought. The business was old and solid. All the Balsans were personally frugal, prudent, and shrewd. She had listened at many a dinner table to the father and son discussing deals, conservative stocks and no-risk bonds. Yes, it would be a great thing to have them start her in a little business of her own.

"I would love it," she said.

"Imagine you going to Europe on a buying trip some-day! I might even take time off to go with you. But that's putting the cart before the horse. First we should have a couple of kids."

"We will. There's no rush."

"Hey, what's that on the coffee table? D'you buy an-other book? Hand it over."

"You won't be interested. It's a history of porcelains."

He laughed. He had no intellectual curiosity.

"Porcelains? What the heck, let me look."

When she put the book on his lap, he turned a few pages and then, while starting to hand it back, cried out with some indignation, "Sixty-five dollars! You paid sixty-five dollars for this garbage?"

She answered quietly, "It isn't garbage. You know better than that. It's art. It's history."

"All right, so it's history, it's art. But sixty-five dollars is too much to pay for a book, Amanda." He was indignant. "It's wasteful. You're—we're—not in that class. There's a very good library not ten minutes' ride from this house."

"I use the library. But I don't understand how you can say that buying a book now and then is wasteful. Books are an investment." Needing to defend herself, she spoke with heat. "They feed the mind. Is that a waste?"

"I'd like to know how much this one is going to feed your mind. You'll take a look now and then when it needs dusting. And the house is already full of books that you buy but don't read."

It was rare for Larry to be so exercised about anything, and whenever he was, he was quickly over it. So her best response was silence. She was at a window pulling the shades down for the night when he spoke again.

"I haven't wanted to mention it, Amanda, because I'm a peaceful guy, but I had a look at your closet as I walked by it yesterday, and it looks like a dress shop. You must be Mrs. Lyons's best customer."

"That's ridiculous! I need clothes. I have to look decent there, don't I? Besides, I should think you'd want me to look nice for my own sake, and for your sake, too."

"Sure I do. But there are only seven days in a week. How much do you need? And at the prices you've been telling me about?"

"I get them at cost. They cost me practically nothing. You know that perfectly well. Why shouldn't I take advantage of it?"

As her voice rose, his softened. His pique was a balloon, deflating.

"Okay, it that's true, okay. You did tell me. I guess I forgot. I still think the book is silly, though."

"I'll take it back if it will make you happy," she said, softly now.

"Oh, forget it. Listen. My father wants to celebrate Norma's birthday tomorrow night. It'll be kind of a double celebration. I pulled off a great deal today, and he's proud of me, really tickled. It's a farm way out where the highway is going to be extended. Probably will be another five years till they get around to it, but in the meantime, I've got a tenant. Rich guy who wants to raise buffalo."

Really tickled. L.B.—in her private thoughts, Amanda had named him so—had of late been visibly mellowing. He seemed to be seeking their company, buying tickets with them to sports events, inviting them to family gatherings with cousins, who varied from young and lively to old and dull, or taking them to expensive restaurants.

"Dress up, Amanda," he would say, "and show off."

She remembered his first cool inspection of her four years ago. She could never have imagined then that such words would come from L.B.

"We're going to dine Français out past Cagney Falls. Costs an arm and a leg, as I've told you fifty times, but it's worth it, and anyway, the old man likes being a sport."

This description was totally inaccurate. L.B. was no old man; you would never believe he was old enough to be the father of this particular son or that particular daughter, both of whom appeared to be older than they really were. L.B. was also not a "sport"; regardless of the mellowing, he was still too remote and he still had too much hauteur to be one.

"I wish Norma had a guy to invite," Larry complained as always. "Isn't there somebody at that school for her to like, for Pete's sake?"

Someone for her to like? Very likely there was more than one. There was, for instance, Lester Cole, assistant to the headmaster. In one way or another, Norma seemed to drop his name whenever she talked about events at the school.

"I think there is someone she likes."

"So?"

"It's a two-way street, isn't it?"

Larry sighed. "She's such a good gal. It's a pity."

Yes, it is. Somehow, being a "good gal" is never quite good enough.

Cecile looked about and was satisfied. A medley of poinsettias, the familiar red interspersed with her favorite pale green, framed the fireplace in the dining room. On the table at Norma's place was a birthday gift for her, crystal bookends, a copy of Lincoln in the Memorial. It was said that he had been homely, but that was not true; his gentle, grave face was singularly beautiful in Cecile's eyes, and surely, too, Norma would see it that way.

It was a lovely winter day, one of those when the air is cold but without wind, so that every twig is drawn against a scrim of sky as pens draw lines of ink on paper. From any window in the house you could look out upon this scene. Through every window there came light; there was never a dark room in the whole house. And walking through it now, she felt satisfied with everything.

They had made great headway in these three months. Two of the four bedrooms were complete. The nursery furniture had come just yesterday as the last wallpaper, scenes from Winnie-the-Pooh, had been hung. The shelves were filled with stuffed animals and books, for these days people knew that it is important to read to infants. As soon as Norma and Amanda arrived for lunch, she would rush them upstairs to look at everything.

It was too bad, though, that she wasn't feeling quite right. In fact, for the last few days she had been slightly feverish. There were colds going around in the neighborhood, as they always seemed to do when holidays were approaching. And her back had really been aching; you might say from time to time it was more a pain than an ache. The weight in her enormous belly had begun to hurt, too. At times it almost seemed as if she were about to burst apart.

Downstairs again, passing the hall mirror, she turned her profile to it. She looked like an elephant! Peter had fun with her, gauging her growth almost day by day. He liked to feel the twins turn and jump. For the last few days, though, they had been very quiet. Probably eating, he said. Greedy already. They'll eat us out of house and home.

Oh, it was going to be such a happy home. It was that already, for Peter was so glad they had done this, almost more glad about it after his deep doubts than she was. His room, the workroom that she had wanted for him, looked out upon what would be a garden. No doubt her father would help them with that. Roses would be perfect against the fence; there would be plenty of sun for them there. Peter's desk was at the window on the shady side; there he would be able to draw away from the direct glare. And for evenings when he wanted to work, she had found a perfect double student lamp.

For a minute she stood there with these pleasing thoughts in her head. He was doing really well, restoring an old wooden church and turning a hosiery mill into condominiums. And he was also giving serious thought to Amos's proposal.

She sat down suddenly. Here again was the pain in her back, the one that had been so sharp during these last few days. But now it was something else! It was an attack. And she cried out, clutching the arms of the chair. After a minute or two, it subsided. After another minute or two, it went away. And then, still trembling from the shock of it, she stood up.

Comes with the package, she thought. For Heaven's sake, this wasn't the first muscular pain she had ever felt! In any kind of athletics, and she had done practically every kind, you were bound to bear some pretty bad, needle-sharp pains.

It was almost twelve-thirty, and the two musketeers were always prompt. Still, there was time to take the harvest wreath from the front door and put on the Christmas wreath. She was hanging it up when her neighbor Judy Miller drove past and lowered the window of her car to call out.

"How are you? Any more aches or pains?"

"Oh, not many, though I had a pretty bad one just now."

"You really should see your doctor, Cele. At least call up and ask some questions."

"He's away this week, and I've never even met the man who's covering for him. I'll wait till he gets back. Anyway, it's nothing."

"You don't know that."

"I hate being a hypochondriac, one of those pregnant women who make their husbands get up in the middle of the night to fetch strawberries or ice cream or something."

"That's utterly stupid. Have you told Peter?"

"No. Why bother him with a few pains? Look at me, I'm big as an elephant. It isn't surprising, is it?"

"I don't know. I'm not a doctor, and neither are you. If you don't tell Peter, I will."

"All right, all right. You probably make sense. I'll tell him this afternoon. He may be home early."

"I wouldn't wait. Don't be foolish, I tell you."

"All right. I will. I will."

For a few moments Cecile stood watching the car drive away out of sight. Maybe Judy was right. But still, you can't expect to go for nine months without some aches and pains. On the other hand, maybe the doctor would know whether or not she ought—oh, God! Here it was again.

It tore at her back. No, not her back, but the huge

mound where the babies lay. It tore, it wrenched. It was inhuman; she heard herself scream; the screams bounced back and echoed.

And leaving the front door wide open, pressing that huge mound between her two hands, racing up the stairs, weeping and pleading as she ran, frantic and terrified, crashing into the bathroom, crashing her head against the basin, with everything gone black and dark, Cecile fell.

Norma, waiting in her car not far from Amanda's shop, was wondering why she sometimes felt vaguely sorry for Amanda. The reason was truly unfathomable. You had only to think about Amanda's first arrival at the Balsan house, carrying her old suitcase, and then to think of her now, married with a house of her own, a man who was insanely in love with her, and a job that she enjoyed. So why feel sorry?

Possessing a defect that she considered almost a disability, Norma had become extraordinarily aware of nuances that many other people would not notice. Standing in front of a classroom, even while concentrating on Latin grammar, there was a fragment of her mind that could detect hidden laughter or possible signs of trouble. For a long time, for instance, she had been puzzled by the unkempt appearance of a lonely girl named Jessie, who could certainly afford to look kempt. Then one day when the mother came to school looking like a fashion model, it all came clear; she understood that Jessie was a pathetic, unloved daughter.

Well, what troubles could Amanda have? Here she came with a smile and wave, with an independent stride and beautiful, thick curls grazing a cashmere collar.

"I'm starved for something sweet," she announced in her lively way. "Cecile will be sure to have a marvelous cake for your birthday. I've been thinking about it all morning. Did you really like my present?"

"I told you I did. I'm wearing it." And Norma unbuttoned her jacket to show a fine embroidered blouse.

"I told Cecile to put one away to wear after the babies come, but—can you believe it?—she said it was too expensive."

"Well, maybe it is for her right now."

"You've got to be kidding. As if there's anything that could ever be too expensive for her. The Newmans must have millions locked away. I don't mean that I envy them—"

But of course she did, and had done from the moment she had seen their rural mansion. How far we have come from the innocent days in the dormitory, from the laundry scattered on the bathroom floor and the pizza crumbs on the table!

"She's living within Peter's means. I think she deserves credit."

"Well, I think it's nonsense. They can be a little tight, the two of them. Haven't you noticed?"

Without responding, Norma concentrated on the road. They had never used to talk about each other, even in a harmless way. But lately she had noticed these prickly little innuendoes, far more of them on Amanda's side than on Cecile's, or perhaps never on Cecile's. Anyway, it was a bad precedent. Real friends didn't gossip about each other.

Her silence might have spoken for her because Amanda said quickly, "Of course, it's none of my business and you know how I adore Cecile. I only meant, she's so considerate of people's feelings—she shouldn't deprive herself of a single thing."

"I'm sure she doesn't."

They rode on quietly, which was unusual for them. On either side lay pleasant houses with cars in the driveways; there came a skating rink with children in bright woolen hats; here came a young couple walking a pair of golden retrievers. And suddenly a window seemed to open in Norma's mind.

It is the green monster, of course, as simple as that. Now that Amanda has more than she ever had before, she wants more. Poor Amanda! Well, poor me, too. Do I really like visiting Cecile's house where in every room there is something, whether it is Peter's picture or the new baby furniture, to make me think of what I have not got? We are all, in our different ways, hungry. Maybe Peter and Cecile are not because life goes so smoothly for them, but most of us are.

"She's been waiting for us," Amanda said as the car slowed. "Look, she's left the front door open."

"In this weather?"

They went inside, shut the door, and called, "We're here. Only five minutes late, too."

There was no answer.

"Are you in the kitchen?"

They walked through the first floor, calling without answer, and stopped at the foot of the stairs.

"Cecile? Cele? Where are you?" There was no answer, and they stood there looking at each other.

"Robbers?" Norma whispered.

"They wouldn't leave the front door open."

Norma's heart raced. Questions hung in the air.

"Shall we call somebody? Neighbors or police?"

"She might be taking a nap. I'll go look."

"This is too queer. Don't go up, Amanda."

But Amanda was bold, and Norma had to follow her. At the top of the stairs, the first thing they saw was the open door to the bathroom. The next was Cecile on the floor, unconscious, in a puddle of blood.

It was the worst week. It was a singular stretch of time that Norma would recall and relive perhaps for always, with every detail of faces and voices, even of weather, sharply defined against a blur of fear. It was like the week in which her mother had died, or the week when the family down the street had lost their son in a plane crash over the Atlantic and the whole street had mourned with them.

If school had not been closed for vacation, she would have made any excuse to stay away. Nothing else mattered, not on this continent or anywhere on the globe, except that Cecile should live. Had she really ever been ignorant enough to think that Peter and Cecile had been touched with some golden charm to leave them forever unscathed?

She lay on one of those high, white hospital beds that for some reason always reminded Norma of a stone catafalque on which slept a long-dead queen whose young face asked for pity. Next to her sat Peter, himself almost as frozen as a figure carved in stone. His hand lay on Cecile's, and his eyes rarely left her.

"I don't know when he goes home," a nurse replied to Norma's question. "When I go off my shift at night, he's still here, and when the next shift comes on in the morning, he's already here."

Once, on her daily visit, he spoke to Norma. "Her blood pressure soars and sinks. Now today I learn that there's an infection. What is the cause? Talk and talk. It all comes down in the end to some 'internal malfunction' that I don't understand. All I know is terror . . . Excuse me, I'm not thinking very clearly." His voice was unnatural, and on his face there was an unnatural alternation of pallor and flush. "What shall I do if she—"

This suffering was perhaps even greater than whatever Cecile was undergoing, for she was mercifully able to sleep, and unaware of Peter's terror, spoke only of her lost babies.

"She doesn't seem to realize that she can have more children," he said. "There's the difference between us. I don't care. No, I don't. I only care about her . . . my world . . . from the first day."

To lose yourself in another human being, thought Norma, to be so united with another, is to open your heart to grief like this; why then do we long for it? And still, if I could once feel it, how willingly I would take the risk! And on tiptoe, she left the room.

In the end, thanks to the miracle of antibiotics, Peter took Cecile home. It was a foggy, wet morning, quite still except for the occasional, dismal call of a crow. Upstairs, while waiting for their car, Norma had tidied things, taken the toys from the nursery shelves and closed the door so that Cecile would not have to see the sad room. What else would musketeers do, she was thinking, but stand by to help when help was needed?

Downstairs, Amanda was preparing a light lunch. "Funny," she said when Norma came in, "my sister's having another one that she can't afford and didn't want. Doesn't make much sense, does it?"

"I wonder whether Cecile will ever have another."

"That's one more question without an answer. Oh, the car's turned into the driveway. Here they are."

Leaning on Peter, Cecile came slowly up the shallow steps at the front door.

"Both here!" she cried. "Oh, how good of you!"

"Didn't you know we would be? We're the three musketeers."

CHAPTER TEN

S ome days, everything goes wrong. The alarm clock
fails and you oversleep. Then the weather, which as
Christmas nears ought to be cold and bright, is
damp and dark instead, while sleet turns the roadway
into a dangerous, greasy slide.

So did Amanda complain to herself as she neared the
shop. No doubt it would be crowded with last-minute
shoppers, chiefly men who needed a gift in a hurry and
had no idea what they wanted. Naturally, you needed
customers, but sometimes they could be a nuisance.

Even when people were as pleasant as can be, their
inane chatter could be annoying. There was, for instance,
name-dropping: *Oh, she doesn't look like any of her
mother's family, they're all much taller and thinner*—
implying an intimate relationship with some prominent family. Or implying the personal possession of old

wealth: *They made everything they own in the last stock market boom, you know.* And then there was the traveler's one-upmanship: *Fiji is delightful, yet you can't compare it with Bora-Bora.*

And the things these women bought, disposed of, and in no time replaced! Another world, that's what it was. Another world.

How nice it would be to get away for a little while, to go *someplace,* almost anywhere, over the holiday. Peter had taken Cecile to a Caribbean island for a few weeks. True, Cecile had been very ill and deserved a tranquil rest. Amanda was certainly not comparing herself with Cecile. But Larry was almost always too busy to go anywhere; even the neighborhood movie house was sometimes too far for him. Stick-in-the-mud, he was.

So Christmas would be the same as last year. The Balsan house, according to tradition, would be filled with cousins; Larry's father would present the usual gift certificates to the local department store; admittedly the food, roast beef and turkey, would be delicious and the house most beautifully adorned with holly and mistletoe, according to tradition. All was *tradition* in that house, even to the red dress that Norma, on the occasion of Amanda's first Christmas with the family, had advised her to wear.

Now quite suddenly, and in spite of herself, Amanda had to laugh. The weather and the extra work, along with a vague, nameless boredom, were weighing upon her and put her in a cranky humor. But that was really inexcusable. Why, she had only to think about poor Norma! Another year had gone by, and it had been the same for her as the last one, or the one before that. And a shudder moved Amanda.

Once in the shop, and after all this vexation, she was cheered by the bustle. An extra hand had been hired to wrap gifts in holiday red and gilt. There were cookies and eggnog ready for the customers. There were also, in the back room, some new deliveries.

"Believe it or not," Dolly said, "some spring stuff is already coming in. This arrived yesterday just five minutes after you left. I started unpacking a few pieces."

"What's there?"

"The usual stuff. You know Mrs. Lyons's taste."

Amanda knew indeed. And feeling like Ali Baba in a dazzle of riches, she peered and lifted each treasure as carefully as if it were a work of art. And suddenly, she gave a cry. "Dolly, come look at this jacket, will you? What would you call this color? Apricot? Peach? No, neither one exactly, but isn't it gorgeous? We should put one out in front right now. I give it five minutes before it walks out the door."

"I don't know about that. Have you seen the price?"

Amanda looked and sighed. "Oh, my."

A young woman, one of the steady customers who could well afford anything, was the first to see it, and remarking that it "looked good enough to eat," tried it on, admired it, hesitated, and said that she would really have to think it over and would let them know.

When in the late afternoon the last customer had left, the jacket still hung there. Now Dolly put it on and stood before the mirror.

"It's to die for, isn't it? There's no place like Paris, is there?"

Amanda corrected her. "This happens to come from Milan."

"Well, anyway. It's to die for. Cashmere. Feel how soft. Now you try it on."

She wanted to, and also did not want to. The luscious color, the curve of the lapels, the jaunty swing of the back! It was such a pretty thing, and conflict stirred within her, as if her mind were directing her to run, and at the same time, to sit down.

"Oh, just put it on."

If she were to try it on, she would not want to give it up. If she were to buy it, guilt would plague her. If she were not to take it, she would regret it.

"You want it. I see it in your eyes."

"People want lots of things they can't afford."

"You can afford it. You're always buying stuff. So treat yourself to one more thing. Make it a Christmas present to yourself. Here, now button it. Or leave it open. Either way. Look at yourself. It was made for you, Amanda."

Yes, it really had been. The shoulders, the swing of the back that she had remarked, the rare color against her pale hair, all were perfect. And she stood quite still before the mirror.

Dolly was urging again, without any trace of envy, and as if in awe, as if acknowledging that such luxury was fitting, not to herself, but to Amanda.

"Yes, the price is crazy," Amanda said, thinking at the same time that the jacket was really practical: You could dress it up or down; it was a classic that would never go out of style; you could wear it with so many colors, and she ticked them off on her fingers: gray, brown, navy, tan, white, black—

"I'll leave a note to Mrs. Lyons for when she gets

back," she said, not giving herself any time to change her mind. "It'll be deducted from my money every week, as we always do it."

"It's stopped raining, but bring the car up to the door, anyway, Amanda. I'll run out with the jacket."

Dolly doesn't crave, Amanda thought as she went to the parking lot. It must make her life less complicated, working here and not wanting things. From now on I'll have to call a halt myself. I suppose I sound like an alcoholic, having just one more drink, only one more, before I quit.

In the trunk there was another box, the result of last week's visit back at the porcelain place. Whenever people came to dinner, their table was a picture, she reflected, admitting frankly that, by observing Cecile, she had learned how to do it. Most of their guests very likely took no notice of the fine linens or the Royal Doulton. And Larry definitely did not. But that was unimportant; these were her treasures, and they gladdened her. So, in a far better mood than the one that had been hers that morning, she drove home.

Norma was sitting in her car in front of the house. She had forgotten that Norma was coming to supper, as she did sometimes when her father was not going to be home. You couldn't blame her for not wanting to sit all by herself in that big barn of a dining room.

"You've been shopping today?"

The intonation was unclear. It might have been a statement or a question. Either one might have been casual—or not quite so casual; on several occasions recently Amanda had detected, or thought she had detected, a puzzling, critical expression on Norma's face.

She answered lightly, "Yes, I picked up a few things," adding when Norma offered to help, "Be careful, don't drop the box. There are dishes in it."

She had just hung the jacket in her closet when she heard Larry's voice. It was his way to give loud greetings. Often they rang so loud that she wanted to put her fingers in her ears. Often they were simply hearty, especially so when greeting Norma. Remembering her own family as well as other families she had known, Amanda was continually being surprised by this pair of siblings.

"I'm home, honey. Home and starved." The voice came roaring up the stairs, while the feet came pounding with it.

"I'm coming right down. We eat in half an hour." It pleased her to feel efficient, with meals always on time, and excellent meals, too, in a house so well ordered.

She was in the kitchen when she heard another roar from above. "Amanda! Come up here!"

He was standing at the top of the stairs holding the new jacket on a hanger. "What in blazes is this?"

From head to foot, Amanda quivered. She saw that he was enraged, and this was so unlike him that she had no idea what to expect.

"I asked you: What the hell is this?"

"A jacket. For my sister Lorena. You know I send gifts home."

"Not like this. You don't buy presents at this price to send down to anybody living in the kind of one-horse town that you've described."

"It was on sale, nowhere near that price. Nowhere near, Larry."

"You should have remembered to take the ticket off if

you hoped to get away with your tall tale. I wasn't born yesterday. Listen to me: You're a compulsive shopper, no better than a compulsive drinker, or gambler, or anything else. Yes, I see you clearly. I haven't wanted to say this, or even to think it, but I see that there's no limit to your wants, and today, right now, I've reached *my* limit. You treat money like water, although people should be more careful with water, too."

They had moved toward the bedroom; her eyes now moved to the bed, on which her quilt, sparkled with leaves and buds, concealed the ugly varnished headboard. Never once in all those hundreds of nights had she experienced a moment of pleasure on that bed, except in sleep. He saw her clearly, did he? He saw nothing. He didn't begin to know her.

The sight of that bed, and of him absurdly standing there with the jacket dangling from his hand, was turning her tremor into defiance.

In some way, though, he was also pitiable, too old for a man barely thirty; he had gained weight, and in not too many years he would be bald. This outburst of temper did not become him. Yet it was strange that she could feel such a growth of power over him, while at the same time, feel sorry for him.

She spoke quietly. "Even if I am a spender, Larry, there's no reason to get so excited about it. It's my money I'm spending."

"No, it's a matter of principle. A person who works eight hours a day should be saving something, or else she might as well work for nothing. Otherwise there is something sinfully stupid about the whole business."

"I do save. And I send things to my family."

"I'm not talking about that. You certainly should do that. I'm talking about—but we went through this once before. I didn't believe you then, and I don't now. If it's true, show me."

"I don't have to."

"You agreed that we should both put money away to buy the shop for you. You said you wanted it. So why won't you show me what you have? I'm willing to show you again. I have nothing to hide."

From a box at the back of his closet, he drew a folder and, laying it on the bed, flipped through some pages.

"Here, on the bottom line. Read. Here's my net worth as of last June thirtieth."

Amanda, reading, was surprised. The amount was pitiable. She had expected a great deal more, and she said so.

"Considering the hours you keep and the deals you make for the firm, you're not being paid enough. Your father should do better for you."

Deeply offended, Larry snapped his retort. "That's his business and mine."

"Well, then, my business is mine, too."

"It is and it isn't. If you want to work, it's your right to do so. But if out of all your earnings you're not saving anything for our mutual benefit, then I have a right to ask you to stay home and start a family. Give me a child, a couple of children. I'll be glad to support them and you. I'll take good care of you."

"There's something burning on the stove," Norma called from downstairs. "I've turned it off, but the pot's ruined, I think."

They both ran down to the smoky kitchen and the scorched pot.

"The beef stew!" Amanda lamented. "I was heating it."

"Give me some hamburgers for the grill." Larry, still angry, took command. "I'll have to do them outside. Where are my gloves? It's freezing. Hey, what's in this box?"

"Leave it alone, will you? Here, take your gloves."

"I want to know what's in this box."

"It's not important. I'm busy, and I'm not about to open it now."

Norma, standing in the corner near the door, looked anxious.

"In case you're wondering what's going on," Larry told her, "I'm upset about the way my wife spends money. She's got enough clothes to open a shop here in this house."

Here was a nice little morsel for Cecile and Norma to chew on! Not that Cecile would relish it, Amanda thought. But Norma might well do so. There couldn't be very much to talk about in her uneventful life. And out of her own mouth, words shot like bullets.

"You think I have too many clothes? You don't know what you're talking about. You should see what some other women buy. You should see what I see every day."

"You're talking about three generations of wealth in that neighborhood. Quit the job if you can't accept the fact that we're not in that class. If you can't stand the heat, get out of the kitchen."

"Speaking of kitchens, look around you. We need a

new floor. Have a look. And while you're at it, have another look at the dish closets, and the new blinds, and the breakfast room set. The best things in this house were bought by me."

"Did I ask for them? It's you, not I, who wants every gadget that's advertised. Not that I wouldn't be willing to buy them if I thought we could sensibly afford them, but we can't. So get that through your head."

"We could afford them if your father paid you what you're worth."

"What the hell are you talking about? He pays me very well."

"No, he doesn't. Not fairly. Did you get any reward after those last two big deals you made? No. You should talk to him about it."

"You keep out of this, Amanda."

"If you aren't brave enough to talk to him, maybe I should."

"And maybe you're losing your mind. Keep out of this, I said."

When Larry banged the door and went into the yard, a cool silence followed, until Amanda broke it.

"Don't get the idea that this sort of thing is natural for us, Norma. It isn't. He's been awfully tense lately," she said, although he hadn't been.

"Oh, who knows Larry better than I do? He's lovable, but stubborn. Once he's made up his mind about something, nothing will change it."

Amanda smiled to herself. Larry was as malleable as putty; if you just used a little patience, he would always come round to your way. Of course, that was true to some extent of most men, was it not?

"From childhood on he's had to adapt, you know. And I have too, except that a boy's situation is psychologically different from a girl's. Our father, as you have seen, was not always the easiest person to live with. He's made a remarkable change lately. He used to be very critical when we were children, very determined to have everything done the right way. So now Larry is probably doing the same with you."

More amateur psychologizing, Amanda thought. Everybody's an expert these days. You read an article in a magazine, and right away you're an analyst.

Back and forth, following her as she set the table, went Norma in earnest talk.

"He's always been, in spite of what I've said, a very caring father. A man as young as he was when Mother died usually remarries, but he never did. He worried, I'm sure, that a stepmother would want children of her own, and then Larry and I might be neglected. He never raised his voice to us, either. Never. He was always kind, just cool and quiet—oh goodness, I needn't tell you any more, need I?"

Indeed she need not.

Still Norma was not quite finished. "I've told you all this because of what I had said earlier about how a father can influence a son, making him an opposite, or else a copy of himself. This last year, though, it looks as if the father is copying the son a bit, doesn't it? Those dinners and shows he takes us to are something so new—" She broke off, and with anxiety in her voice, asked whether Amanda had really meant all that about Larry's pay. "He wouldn't want to hurt Dad or make him angry, either, you understand."

"Of course I understand," Amanda retorted, concealing impatience. Norma meant well, but she could talk your head off telling you what you already knew.

The cold air must have cleared Larry's head because he seemed a bit mollified when he came back inside bearing a platter of hamburgers.

"French fries? Better than any perfume you can buy," he cried, sniffing the air. "Well, I was starved, so I've already sampled a burger, and I feel more normal."

"The way to a man's heart," Amanda said to herself, quoting her mother.

Tipping the bottle to pour ketchup on his potatoes, suddenly Larry looked like nothing more than a hungry boy. When he caught her eye, he gave her a faint, embarrassed smile.

"You haven't told me," he said, "what's in the box."

"Porcelain. I'm returning it."

"What kind of porcelain?"

"A pair of plates."

They had a raised pattern made in the eighteenth century for a British aristocrat who had been blind. She had read about them and had recognized them at first sight.

"You like them? You really wanted them?"

"I did like them, but I don't really want them that much anymore." And that was the truth.

He nodded. "And the orange jacket?"

"It isn't orange, and I don't want it." But that was not the truth.

He said quietly, "Keep it. You must have wanted it very badly to pay that much for it."

Half an hour ago they had each been boiling with

anger. Anger is simple, she thought now; it's strong, and it fills you. But when it leaves, all sorts of confusing things rush in to take its place: shame and guilt, regrets and longings, pity, and yes—yes too, a kind of love.

For some reason, the Christmas dinner, offered as always in the time-honored way, was subtly different this year. Amanda looked around her and enumerated the ways.

The room was entirely lighted by candles. There must have been two dozen or more of them, giving a flickering bloom to the unusually luxuriant roses on the center of the table, and to the faces around it. The champagne this time was one of the most costly imported brands; she was amused to think that only a few years ago she would not have recognized the name. It was astonishing how, working daily where she did, she picked up so many scraps of information.

This year, the seating was changed, too; always the places on either side of the host had been given to a pair of respected elderly cousins, but tonight it was Norma and Amanda, with Larry on her other side, who were seated there.

"Well," said L.B., "what do you all think of the dessert?"

Set before him on a silver platter lay a long *bûche de Noël*, richly, smoothly chocolate, in a frame of holly. This, too, she recognized, having seen it once before when L.B. had taken them to the city's best French restaurant.

"It's my favorite," she told him.

"I thought so. Yours and Norma's favorite."

"This is a feast, a banquet tonight," Larry murmured into her ear, as if he too had sensed something different in the atmosphere.

L.B. was more talkative than usual, holding everyone's attention. He was, actually, vivacious; his aquiline, shapely face, relaxed now with smiles, was younger than ever; he could have been Larry's older brother. It was as if, so thought Amanda, he had suddenly decided to be the center instead of the keen and probably critical spectator. There came to her then a totally groundless suspicion, which she immediately dismissed, that he might be having a love affair. More likely it was only the champagne.

After dinner, there were as always the presents, given out in the living room. The cousins received suitable mementos: books, ties and sundries, or more practically, the department store certificates, chosen as always by Norma. Tonight though, at the end of the list, came total surprise, as L.B. presented to Norma, Larry, and Amanda three little velvet boxes.

Startled, the three looked toward each other while L.B. waited, pleased and expectant as adults are on a child's birthday.

"What are you waiting for?" he demanded. He was enjoying himself. "Open them!"

Larry, finding a pair of gold cuff links in his box, remarked with thanks that now he would have to wear French cuffs.

"I'll have to buy new shirts," he said in mock complaint.

Norma took from the little box a fine gold chain with a pendant in the shape of a pavé diamond heart, and Amanda received the same. Then, with all the elderly cousins watching and smiling, L.B. fastened the chain around Norma's neck, where it disappeared under her red turtleneck collar.

"It doesn't show," he said, kissing her cheek. "You'll have to wear it with a different kind of dress."

Amanda's red velvet dress was cut so that the pendant lay and sparkled exactly where her discreet cleavage began. In the tall, old-fashioned mirror that hung between the windows, she had a glimpse of herself and of L.B. leaning close to her neck as he fastened the chain. A preposterous thought flashed through her head: *I've never felt his touch*. And she hoped that he would not kiss her cheek. Ashamed of herself for having such queer thoughts, she was relieved when he did not.

It had begun to snow by the time everyone left the house. The first hesitating flakes swirled ahead of the headlights, and houses along the route disgorged people who, like themselves, had been celebrating. Amanda was feeling a pleasant excitement that she had not expected to feel.

"You did pretty well for yourself," Larry said when they were in their bedroom. "That's a nice piece of jewelry."

He laughed, poking his cold finger into her cleavage. He had sometimes the most annoying ways. "I'm freezing. Let's get into bed fast. Okay, honey?"

"I'll need to make some hot tea and take an aspirin, Larry. Suddenly I'm not feeling right."

"Maybe you ate too much, or drank too much champagne. I know I did."

"No, more likely it's a virus. Aspirin and sleep are what I need."

She simply did not want what he wanted tonight. Tomorrow she would be good, though, and make it up to him.

I really don't know myself. Most of the time I think I do. I know I want too much, and I think I understand why, but maybe I really don't understand. For instance, I would have expected that the diamond pendant would make me enormously happy; diamonds were far out of my reach, yet when I look at it, I feel flat. Yes, that's the word: flat. Do I feel that I don't deserve it? Yet that makes no sense because no one ever really *deserves* luxury.

Such were Amanda's thoughts on the Sunday after Christmas. Larry had taken a client to see a property, and Norma had invited her to go ice skating, but these other thoughts filled her too full to accept. So she had gone for a drive.

Whatever had induced L.B. to do it? He could possibly have been feeling a trifle sorry for Norma. Larry was always talking about his anxiety over her. At any rate, he could obviously afford what he had done. Otherwise he never would have spent that much.

Next, her thoughts returned to the nasty quarrel of the other night. She dreaded quarrels. There had been too many of them while she was growing up at home, none serious enough to cause any rupture, just anxious squabbles, caused by overcrowding and job worries, squabbles quickly made up—and yet remembered. (Was that why she, once away from home at college, had been known for having such a happy disposition?) The fight with Larry, though, must not happen again. He was right when he attacked her for having saved almost nothing out of her salary, and she was right in her complaint that he worked too long and hard for too little.

He feared his father, and feared to admit it. Oh, yes, both of them, Norma and he, were quick enough to assert that L.B. had always been very good to them; what then was it that they feared? Nothing more than a lofty manner, a certain hauteur, like that of the father, the head-of-the-house father in a century gone by. They were too sensitive, both of them; although on the surface Larry did not appear to be so, she had lived with him long enough to know that he was so. Their mother must have been a timid soul, and they must be like her. They looked like her; in all the photographs of her you saw Norma and Larry.

I really believe I could talk to L.B., she thought as her car rounded the corner, and she saw the brown bulk of the Balsan house at the top of the street. Yes, I will talk to him, she declared as she neared it. An earner now, able if necessary to take care of herself, she was no longer the first-time visitor carrying that unforgettable shabby old suitcase. And strikingly aware of the difference between then and now, she mounted the front steps.

The housekeeper, Elsa, opening the door, appeared to be surprised at this disturbance on the part of Amanda.

"Why, yes, Mr. Balsan is at home. You know he reads the newspaper early every Sunday morning," she admonished.

"I won't keep him long."

"Well, he's in the sun parlor."

He presented a picture, the kind of subject that Wyeth might have painted: a man in a high-backed chair that hid all except the top of his head and his long legs, sitting with his two dogs in front of a window where bouquets of snow were clustered on the hemlocks beyond it. When he heard her and stood up, he presented a look of alarm.

She said quickly, "There's nothing wrong. I only wanted to see you for a couple of minutes."

"Then sit down. I have to go out at ten o'clock," he added, indicating the clock on the wall.

Now that she was really here, her confidence ebbed. In profile his face really did look forbidding, like those haughty faces on ancient coins. She ought to have rehearsed her approach to the subject before making this impetuous attempt. And abruptly, with a small shock, it occurred to her that this was the very first time she had ever been alone with L.B.

"Well, Amanda?"

Some instinct told her to sit tall, be straightforward, and get it over with. The worst thing that could happen would be a negative, sharp response. Or his disapproval might make future contacts somewhat uncomfortable, but nothing more.

"I think Larry should get better pay. He has complete responsibility for the new branch office, and he's never been given a raise."

"Discontented, is he?" The bright eyes widened with the question. "So he sends you to me? Instead of talking up for himself?"

"Oh, no. Don't blame him. He doesn't know a thing about this. And he isn't discontented, he loves his work. Right now, on Sunday morning, he's out with a customer."

"So it's you who's dissatisfied?"

"Not for myself."

There was a long pause. Blankly, she was aware of silent scrutiny.

"I don't believe you. It is for yourself. You have expensive tastes. I have eyes. I can see."

She had a queer feeling that he was not angry, but rather that he was secretly laughing at her.

"It's not for me. I'm telling the truth," she insisted.

"Oh, you have your nerve, Amanda. You never in your life had it so good, and yet you want more."

These were stinging words. The snow bouquets, now glittering as the sun circled past the hemlocks, were giving her a headache. What exactly was it that had brought her here to plead for Larry? His meager savings and her extravagant orange jacket, which wasn't orange at all, were somehow joined in opposition to each other; yet they were a part of whatever had brought her to this place.

"You have your nerve," he repeated. "I don't know how many women would go to the husband's boss and complain about his wages."

"But you're his father. It's not quite the same."

"You feel that intimate, do you?"

His lips had twitched with something that might be the start of a smile, or of laughter, but if it was either one, it was caustic, bringing an instant's hot rush of blood to her swimming head.

"Respectfully intimate," she said, pleased to have come up so quickly with an apt and cutting reply. "I was just trying for fairness."

Again there came that quirk of the lips. Was it revealing sarcastic amusement, or only amusement without the sarcasm?

L.B. stood, and Amanda followed, so that they confronted each other. Obviously she was awaiting an answer, so he gave it.

"Let's say you made a good try."

"That's it?"

"That's it."

He had made a fool of her. Now all she wanted was to get out of his presence. And with no intention of saying good-bye, she turned to walk toward the door. Then, remembering something, she stopped.

"Please don't let Larry know I was here. At least, promise me that."

"You have my word."

In the front hall, there was another mirror. Apparently Larry's mother had liked to decorate the house with them. In the instant it took for L.B. to unlock the door, the mirror reflected his alert, patrician face just above hers, which was still flushed beneath a diadem of windblown hair.

"Be careful. The steps are slippery," he warned.

She did not answer, and the door made a sharp click behind her. The interview had been short, but it would take a long time, she told herself, if ever, to forget the indignity.

Late on Monday afternoon, Larry arrived home with news. He was scarcely through the door, when he shouted it.

"Honey! You won't believe it, but I got a raise. Ten grand a year. Out of the blue! Just like that. Dad even said he should have thought of it sooner. Can you believe it?"

There he stood, grinning in his excitement. He looked like nothing but a great, big, good-natured kid, and she was happy for him.

But what on earth had moved L.B.? People, people! You never knew what was going on inside them. For that matter, you often did not really know what was going on inside yourself.

CHAPTER ELEVEN

Where are you?" asked Cecile.

"At school, at lunchtime, using my cell phone. I couldn't wait to talk to you. How are you? How's everything?"

"I'm fine. Everything's fine. We didn't get back till after midnight yesterday, but it was wonderful. It did us both so much good, being away in the sun. Peter was the one who needed it more than I did, really. Do you know, he lost eight pounds while I was sick? And he surely is one person who doesn't need to lose weight."

Awful visions of Cecile on the bloody floor, and of Peter at the hospital bowed over her white face, flashed before Norma. "I'm glad," she said. "You both needed it."

Even the dearest friend, she thought, especially one

who has seemed to be blessedly invulnerable, becomes even dearer after having suffered a misfortune.

"I swam, snorkeled, and danced. About the only thing I haven't done is tennis, and I'll be going back to it soon."

"I'm glad," repeated Norma.

"After we'd had enough of the island, we took a detour on the way home and spent a few days not far from New Orleans, where Peter has rehabilitated that row of Victorian houses. You remember, we showed you some photos of it? Well, you wouldn't recognize it. By now every house has a garden patch between the front door and the sidewalk, so that the whole street is blooming with everything from hollyhocks to pansies. Peter took a ton of pictures to show some people who are trying to restore more old neighborhoods."

"Maybe he'll tackle Lane Avenue someday. It needs it." Norma laughed. "I'm remembering how he worried about being able to afford your house."

"Well, we still have to be very careful, Norma. I told him that maybe we should sell it now." Cecile's sigh was audible. "It's a big house for us two to rattle around in. But he won't hear of it. He's sure we'll have better luck next time. He won't have the babies' room disturbed. 'Keep the door closed so it won't be a daily reminder,' he says, 'until we need to use everything again.' Peter's an optimist at heart in spite of his caution."

"He's right."

"I know. Whenever I work at the hospital and see what I see, how people strive and how brave so many of them are, I marvel. Next Monday I'll be back. I miss it.

But enough of me. How's Amanda? I must call her tonight. Did you have Christmas together as usual?"

"Yes, as usual. It was lovely at Dad's house." Then something compelled her to go further. "As to Amanda, she really is changing. We've both mentioned her extravagance. But lately, it's grown to be disgusting. She had a terrible fight with Larry just before Christmas."

Why did she have this compulsion to talk about Amanda? Ordinarily, she disdained the common gossip that is called "girl talk," even among a group of schoolteachers in their sixties. Nevertheless, she continued.

"I happened to be at their house, and I'm sorry I was there because it was really, really hideous. Would you believe that she hasn't saved a cent out of her salary? She'd been buying everything at that shop, and you know what their prices are. She buys enough to fill any other woman's clothes closet three times over."

"Try to understand it. She never had anything."

"You always say that. Neither did most people ever have anything—at least the things she wants. Who does she think she is, some ancient potentate's bejeweled mistress at the bazaar?"

"Come on. You're taking it far too seriously, Norma. You always do."

I may take things too seriously, thought Norma, but Cecile oversimplifies. She always did.

"Actually, Norma, the truth is that you're worried about your brother. You're worried that she's not making him happy. How did the quarrel end?"

"Well, I must admit that it seems to be all right now. She hasn't been buying much since the big blowup."

"How do you know?"

"She told me. I guess she was sorry that it happened in front of me."

"No doubt. Listen. People have squabbles and forget all about them in no time. You certainly know that Peter and I had plenty of them about buying a house, and yet now I can barely recall how they started or exactly what we said."

"This is different. I feel it in my bones whenever we're together. And that isn't all that often anymore. She used to love having dinner when Dad invites us all to a good French restaurant, but the last few times she's had an excuse—a previous date with friends or a cold coming on. She just doesn't want to be with us."

"Well, whatever it is, there's nothing you can do about it. You analyze too much, Norma. You probe too deeply. Take care of your own life."

"Oh, I'm taking care of it, all right. I've started a Latin text for beginners, something entirely different from what we're using now—oops, there goes the bell. Call me over the weekend if you have time."

For a few minutes after the call was disconnected, Norma sat with the phone in her hand. Perhaps she really did analyze things too deeply. As far as these recent events were concerned, she had admittedly done a good deal of analyzing. A certain event at the Christmas dinner had rankled, and she had allowed it to go on doing so.

The way Amanda had looked with the diamond pendant, the red velvet dress, and the fire in her eyes! After dinner, in the living room, everybody, the old and the young alike, had been staring with open wonder at the picture she made, smiling while Dad fastened the clasp at the back of her neck.

It had rankled, and Norma, recalling how much it had done so, was bewildered at how it could have done so. Perhaps, she thought, it was because when a person is down-and-out as Amanda had been when they were at school, it is easier not to be envious of her beauty. But now she is no longer down-and-out . . . And I should be ashamed of myself. . . .

Late in the afternoon, she was still correcting a pile of tests when Lester Cole passed through the corridor. Seeing her at her desk, he came in.

"You must love Country Day," he said, "to stay this late."

This was not the first time he had made a similar remark. It occurred to Norma that he might be curious about the reason she often stayed so late. She could hardly tell him that the classroom, even now on a dark, bleak day in February, was more cheerful than the house at home; vacant all day except for Elsa down below out of sight in the kitchen, it was so still that the occasional crack of settling wood was a shock. Here people walked and talked in the hallways, as teachers held conferences with parents and students stayed late to work on the school paper.

"I do love Country Day," she answered simply. "It's been home since I was in kindergarten here."

To her surprise, he drew up a chair and sat down. "I've been hearing some interesting things about you," he said cordially, "that you're writing a Latin text. I'm impressed."

She felt herself flushing. "It's quite elementary. I'm no great classicist."

"You mustn't belittle yourself," he said in gentle reproof.

"I'm not. I'm only seeing myself clearly. When you go to ancient Greece or Rome and you see—"

He interrupted. "You've been there?"

"Yes, and to Sicily, to Agrigentum the summer before junior year. It made me wish I'd studied Greek. Maybe someday I will, but not now."

She was wondering why he was sitting there, relaxed as if he were going to stay for a while. Had she perhaps committed some offense? Had a parent complained about her? Something must have brought him here for a serious talk.

"Another interesting thing I've heard about you is that you have a photographic memory. Is that true?"

Still puzzled, she replied, "Yes, I do seem to remember things very easily. I don't take any credit for it, though. It's no different from being born with the ability to run fast."

Lester smiled. "Slightly different, I should say. I've always been fascinated with memory, the way, for instance, an actor can repeat hundreds of lines. I can't imagine how it's possible, when for the tenth time in a month I have mislaid my car keys. So I'd like to know how you do it—although that's foolish of me, because you can't possibly say *how* you do it. But would you mind demonstrating for me?"

"I wouldn't mind at all." Naturally flattered, she was also a trifle—but only a trifle—amused.

Cole went to a bookshelf and withdrew at random a copy of the Constitution.

"How about this? Okay?"

"Anything will do. What page?"

"Any. All right, this. How long do you need?"

"Let's say, two minutes."

Aware that he was watching her, she had a sudden thought about her hair, which she had not combed since lunchtime. Well, it was too late now. And turning to the page, she began to concentrate.

Facing the opposite wall, she closed her eyes, letting the vivid image of the page stand unhindered and alone.

"Time's up," said Lester, seizing the book. He, too, looked amused.

"Here goes. It starts in the middle of a sentence: '. . . nobody who holds office should accept a gift from any king or foreign state without the consent of Congress. No state can make treaties, coin money, or grant titles of nobility. No state without consent of Congress can charge import duties. No state may make a compact with another state or engage in war, keep troops or warships in time of peace.' Then in the middle of the page, it says Article Two, Two, in Roman numerals, I mean. Then it tells how the President is elected—this is no good. We both know this, anyway."

"I certainly didn't know everything on the first half of the page. But I'll get another book. Here's a Hemingway story. Try this."

Again she read until "Time's up." Then she spoke.

"Somebody sees an old man sitting. He asks him what kind of animals they were. The answer is three, two goats, a cat, and four pairs of pigeons. Then he tells that he has to leave them. There's a war on. He says the cat will be all right. Cats take care of themselves. He's worried about the others. In answer to a question, he says he isn't a political person. He's tired and sits down. He asks where the trucks are going. The answer is to Barcelona. Then he says again that the cat will be all right, but he is worried about the others, and he asks the narrator what he thinks. The narrator says he thinks all the animals will be all right. The last sentence at the bottom of the page is the old man asking what they will do under the artillery, since he was told to leave because of the artillery."

"Great!" exclaimed Lester. "Ninety-nine percent accurate. Well, maybe I'd give you a ninety-five. You omitted the old man's age."

Norma frowned and thought for a second or two. "Seventy-six?" she queried.

"Seventy-six is correct."

When he had taken the book and replaced it on the shelf, he said to Norma, "I am in awe of you. You have a marvelous little machine inside your head."

That may be, but why must she also be so awkward? So awkward that she was unable to accept a compliment with grace, and then go ahead with some entertaining subject? She had no social graces. The very presence of this pleasant man was inhibiting. And she sat there looking at her hands, splayed out upon the pile of papers. They were nicely manicured, thanks to Amanda's well-meant nagging.

"Don't be embarrassed," Lester said, chiding her.

"I'm not." She had to defend herself. "I'm not," she repeated.

"All right, you're not."

She wondered what he could really be thinking of her and was wishing that he would disappear, when he asked whether she was hungry.

"I forgot my watch," she said irrelevantly.

He pointed to the big clock above the blackboard. "What has time got to do with it? Can't you be hungry whenever you're hungry without looking at the time?"

"I guess I am, a little."

"Well, I had no lunch, and I definitely am. Would you like to go with me down to Stuffy's for a hamburger? Nothing fancy, just the usual hamburger."

This was so strange! What could he want with her?

"Yes," she said.

"Put the tests away. You can finish them tomorrow."

In Stuffy's entryway there was a mirror where, in a passing glance, she was able to see that her hair was smooth and becomingly curved along the line of her cheek. Around her neck was a handsome black-and-white scarf, a present from Amanda, who had shown her how to tie it.

"Frenchwomen can do wonders, just with a little thing like a scarf," Amanda had said.

This brief glimpse of herself was encouraging. A good many of the younger faculty would be astonished to see her here with Lester Cole. Yes, astonished and disgruntled, too.

"*I am in awe of you,*" he had said.

Lester was one man who fitted the definition of an intellectual. Perhaps he was interested in having conversation with her because, on account of the Latin textbook, he—quite mistakenly—thought that she was one, too. He was probably in a mood for good conversation tonight, that was all.

For Heaven's sake, it was infuriating that she had absolutely no idea how to begin! Could she start talking about the headline in today's newspaper? Or maybe about the Second Punic War? Simply because he was male, not female, her mind went dead.

Then suddenly, anger entered her embarrassment. It came with one of those clear glimpses of herself that ought to come more often. Why, it was absurd that she should be so humbled by this man's mild attention! Absurd. And yet she waited passively for him to speak.

"It's plain that you love to teach," he began. "Unfortunately, some people do it because it's a respected profession with long vacations."

Norma felt her eyebrows rising at this rather unusual remark from the assistant headmaster. "Do you really mean that?"

"Well, not most people, but many. For people who don't like to compete, it's easier. It's not like, for instance, being in a first-class law firm striving to become a partner." Lester smiled, and his eyes had a reminiscent look. "My father always accused me of wanting what he called 'the easier way.' He's a lawyer, naturally."

"Well, I certainly wouldn't call teaching the easier way," Norma protested.

"No, but it's not clashing wits against wits. You're not fighting all day. You're helping people. Teaching is really compassionate. It's humane."

Now this topic was alive! It brought to mind a chronic problem that Norma had encountered again this very morning.

"But when you try to help and find yourself talking to deaf ears, what can you do? Just sit by and watch a human being going to ruin? A fifteen-year-old girl staring out of the window with tears in her eyes?"

"Her name doesn't happen to be Jessie, does it?"

Norma was astonished. "Why, yes. How did you know?"

"I've had a few sessions with her mother." Lester's tone was grim. "She's quite a character, isn't she? Poor child."

"I've talked to her many times, and to the mother, too. Jessie knows she needs counseling, but her mother thinks it isn't necessary. She thinks Jessie should simply 'pull herself together.' "

"Just pull yourself together." Lester sighed. "Simple, isn't it? So, what do you think we can do for Jessie? Anything?"

Another part of Norma's mind was running parallel to the conversation. He's really nice. I do believe, behind the authority that he shows in school, he's fundamentally shy. He must have ten different suits, all shades of brown, from tan to mahogany. It's funny how different he seems here, putting sour cream on his baked potato and spilling a drop of coffee on his tie, from the way he looks behind the podium at a school assembly, so dignified, even a bit austere . . . Yes, he's really nice, and not hard to talk to, not at all.

The crowd in Stuffy's place had peaked and was now emptying out, while at the booth where Norma was barely aware of passing time, the conversation had traveled away from school to a concert, to an old movie, and to a camping trip in Alaska.

The waiter was hovering near their table, which caused Lester to look at his watch and apologize.

"I've kept you over two hours, Norma. We're the last ones here. They're ready to close the doors."

Inevitably, she had to precede him on the way out. From the rear, her legs must look horrendous. But why only from the rear? And was it conceivable, anyway, that in over three years' time he had not noticed them before this? But perhaps he had never noticed her enough even to become aware of them. If so, there would be no next time. And thanking Lester with a mind both pleased and perturbed, Norma went home.

"You missed dinner," her father said. "I was worried that something had happened."

"I'm sorry, Dad. I should have telephoned, but we got talking and time flew by."

"Who's 'we'?"

When she told him, he nodded his approval. There was a little twinkle in his eyes. "Do you know who he is? He's Alfred Cole's son. Cole, Armistead. One of the half-dozen most prominent law firms in the state. We have dealings with them all the time, on real estate matters, of course. There's talk that he always wanted his son to grow up and join the firm, you know."

Cole, the man at Cecile's wedding who had made that horrible gaffe. "He told me."

"Well, as long as he's happy where he is at the school. Do you like him?"

"Yes, but—" As her father's expression spoke of too much eagerness, she quenched it with her next words. "Please don't get any ideas, Dad. Please don't. We had a hamburger together and talked school, that's all."

"Fine, fine. Live one day at a time, as I always say. And I never get 'ideas,' as you call them."

But he did "get ideas." He had most surely had them for Larry! It had taken a long while before he had learned to accept and finally to welcome Amanda.

Come to think of it, Norma thought for the second time that day, since Christmas Larry and Amanda have hardly been in this house. But then, they have their own lives and their own reasons, as they should have. How little we all know about each other! We present the surface, and often a good deal more than that, but the engine, the hot, vibrating power that moves us, remains unseen.

CHAPTER TWELVE

April was chilly. The sky, like a soggy gray blanket, hung low above the earth, and the wet trees dripped. Then a steady drizzle began, so that Amanda pulled the hood over her head. Not having expected such weather, she had gone jogging too far from home and, suddenly tired now, stopped to rest by leaning against somebody's high stone wall.

The scene was really, in its way, quite lovely. To begin with, it was silent. There never was much traffic on the winding roads of this exurbia; at midday in the middle of the week, and in such weather, there was hardly any. Daffodils that had been naturalized on the sloping lawn across the road were beginning to bloom. A small family of robins was seeking worms on that same wet lawn. Two boys on bicycles went by, whistling; when they had passed, the quiet surged back. A great artist could paint this silence, Amanda thought. That was a queer concept, painting silence! But she knew what she meant.

Waiting for the rain to stop, her mind drifted idly from one thing to another, from the shop and dear, silly Dolly's troubles with her current boyfriend, to the place that she still thought of as home. How far away and long ago it seemed! Her mind leaped to the package that she was going to take to the post office this afternoon before it should close at four o'clock. Then she thought about the three musketeers; come to think of it, they had lately not been calling one another by that name. Indeed, they had not had their monthly lunch for several months. Cecile's babies would have been almost six weeks old by now, if things had gone right. Norma had been seeing Lester Cole quite often, or so Larry had reported. Why does she not confide in me? Amanda wondered. I'm glad for her, anyway. She's a kind soul, like Larry. He wants to start a family. I don't want to. My best times are my days at work. Even right now on my day off, I would just as soon be working.

A car drove by, slowed, backed up, and stopped.

"Amanda! That is you, isn't it? What are you doing here?" called L.B.

She wished he had not seen her, but it was necessary to approach the car and to reply.

"Waiting for the drizzle to stop," she said.

"What a day to go jogging! Get in before you're soaked through."

On the car radio a Mozart piano concerto was playing. It surprised her that L.B. should be listening to the classical station and that he was sensitive enough to wait until the piece was finished before he turned it off.

When it ended, there followed a minute or two during which neither of them spoke. The front seat was a tight enclosure, both their tall bodies confined in a too-small space, or so it felt to her. For no reason at all, she remembered that this was only the second time since her marriage when she had been alone with L.B., the other being that morning in his house when she had gone to ask about a raise for Larry. Uncomfortable with herself, she seemed to be wriggling inside her clothes.

"Going home, I assume?" asked L.B.

"Yes, but the rain's almost over with, so if you'll let me out on the avenue, I'd like to jog the rest of the way."

"That's foolish. I pass your house on the way to the office, anyway. But first I have to make one quick stop, ten minutes at the most."

It was hard to disagree with L.B. Well she knew.

"It's a Victorian house on a triple-size lot. They've had it in the family for four generations, but the present owners have moved east and it's up for sale. They're conservationists and also sentimental, very interesting people; they don't want to sell to just anybody who will divide the land. Of course, that's the obvious practical thing to do these days. So my job is to find someone who'll want to live in this relic and keep it as it is. I might as well find a needle in a haystack. Still, you never know."

On a wide street where new houses had been fitted in among the grand old mansions, L.B. stopped in front of one of the grandest, a gloomy pile of dark brick, complete with porte cochere and a pair of iron deer on the front lawn.

"Come," he said, inviting Amanda, "you can give me

your opinion. My only thought is that young people with a lot of money, a lot of children, and a lot of energy to spend on fixing it up might take it. Maybe."

They entered a wide, high space, dim and cold as the inside of an empty barn. But unlike the simple, pungent scent of hay, this scent was mingled: clean dust, faint cooking spices, wafts of powder and perfume—or so she imagined—were the remnants and reminders of the lives that had once been lived here.

Standing at the center of the huge parlor, turning her head toward the huge, vacant spaces on either side of it and up the broad staircase that must lead to further huge spaces above, she felt suddenly a vague, romantic melancholy. It was as if from somewhere in the deserted house, she was hearing voices and strains of music.

L.B. was looking at her with curiosity. "What are you thinking of?" he asked.

Feeling too self-conscious to tell the truth, she gave a prosaic answer. "Of the construction. They don't build like this anymore."

"How true! Look at the doors, solid chestnut. Come into the dining room. Look at the wainscoting, the workmanship." L.B. spoke enthusiastically. "And the fireplace marble. I imagine that this brown-and-white coloration must be fairly rare. At least, I never see it, and I see a good number of pre–World War One houses. Take notice of the fireplaces. There's one in every room, even in the kitchen opposite the coal stove. Come see."

The stove was a great big crouching bear, Amanda thought, letting imagination run away with her.

"They kept it, too, out of sentiment, I suppose. Great-grandmother must have cooked on it." L.B. shivered. "It must have been cold here in the winter, and probably it still is, even with natural gas. Everything's too big, windows and ceilings too high. Do you want to see the upstairs?"

She had no particular interest in seeing it. Nevertheless, she followed him up the steep staircase, down a long hall, all through the big, high-ceilinged bedrooms and the big, antiquated bathrooms, while he pointed out every feature of style and construction as if he were trying to sell the house to her. This friendly change from his former distant attitude, let alone his former stinging rebuff on that Sunday morning, puzzled Amanda—not that it mattered.

Did it matter? Well, yes, it did. When a person's behavior toward you is inconsistent and causes you to feel puzzled, you want to find the explanation.

"Be careful," he said, preceding her down the stairs.

His back and shoulders in the well-tailored dark blue suit were impressive. And if that was an absurd reflection, it was no more so than the commonly used one about uniforms being aphrodisiac.

When he stopped at the bottom of the stairs and turned to her, she was still a step above him, so that their heads were level with each other. A steely light from the window fell on his face, and amazingly, for the first time, she saw that he had a cleft chin. It was almost a dimple, a strange, soft feature to see on that commanding face, and strange to discover it only now after so long.

"Well, will you buy it?" he asked with a touch of laughter in his tone.

"A few million dollars for a makeover," she responded, giving back the laughter, "could turn it into something delightful. The first thing it needs are yards and yards of brilliant colors to get rid of the gloom. Then rugs and silver and many paintings on these long walls. The Hudson River School, big ones, each to cover half a wall, would help."

"Yes, a good deal, it would. You've learned a lot for a country girl since you came to live here. You talk like an interior decorator."

"Yes, I was a country girl," she acknowledged. "But in the shop, the boutique, among those women, I've seen how the other half of one percent lives."

"And you learned from books. Norma tells me your house is filling up with books."

He was still blocking her way so that she was unable to descend the last two steps. His direct, bold gaze, so typical of him, was a sharp reminder of that humiliating Sunday; yet something else, perhaps the sight of the just-discovered dimple, provoked her into a boldness of her own, and she said directly, "You could come and see our house for yourself. Why have you been staying away from us?"

"I could ask you the same question." And when she failed to answer, he answered for her. "Because you—you, not Larry—did not want to see me, either."

"Why should I want to see you? You were nasty to me when I came pleading for Larry. And then you gave him what I asked for, anyway. You gave more than I had ever dreamed of asking."

He did not reply directly, but said instead, "I wasn't angry at you. I was angry at myself."

"For not having thought of giving Larry a raise?"

"That—and other things." He moved away, allowing

her to pass. "You haven't seen everything," he said abruptly. "There's a big back porch with a nice view over some gardens. They've been neglected, but can easily be restored."

On the porch roof the rain no longer drizzled, but drummed, and the east was visibly darkening as clouds raced overhead.

"Looks like a storm, Amanda. Good thing I came along, or you'd still be jogging through it two miles from home. Come, I'll show you the library. It's got shelves from floor to ceiling. You'll need to stock up on books if you buy this place."

She was not feeling right. These odd, occasional spurts of laughter, along with that remark a few minutes ago, *I was angry at myself*, were baffling. They were not what they pretended to be.

"As far as I'm concerned, this is the best room in the house. I wouldn't mind having one like it. Have you ever seen windows like these?"

No, she had not. At right angles, touching each other, a pair of windows filled a corner, bringing indoors the western sky, still lurid in the face of the dark advancing storm. The sky, the tossed trees, and the gloomy house all heightened her mood; this was a fearsome setting out of a Grimm's fairy tale.

"I wish the storm would come and get itself over with," she said.

"It doesn't look that way."

Just as he spoke, there came a crash of thunder; it was as if a hundred brutal, giant fists had clobbered the roof. Lightning tore across the sky as if it were aiming toward these very windows.

"Away from the windows, Amanda! You know better than that, country girl. Come over here."

She had not noticed that he was sitting on the sofa, nor even observed that there was a sofa against the opposite wall.

"Only piece of furniture in the place. It must have been built in the house. The way the doors and corners are placed, they couldn't possibly have gotten it into the room or out of it, either. It's fifteen feet long if it's an inch. A crazy thing."

"Yes, crazy."

"But comfortable, and still clean. The people moved out only last week."

Obviously, when there was a place to sit, it made no sense to stand at the window watching the storm. And still she hesitated.

He spoke again. "You've changed your hairdo."

"I've let it grow. It's not as curly now."

"Either way, it becomes you."

"Thank you," she said formally.

"So straight hair is 'in' again? Am I right?"

He was twinkling, teasing, and in a nice way, making fun of what he would probably call "feminine foibles." Understanding that, she replied in kind.

"Of course. Height of fashion. That's me. The best part of my life is spent in a fashion shop."

"The best part? Really?"

"Yes. Yes, really."

"I find that sad, Amanda," he said, seriously this time.

"Why so?"

"Because it means you aren't happy with the rest of your life."

What could she tell him? That her life at home was dull and drab? That there was so little purpose or meaning in it? Yes, Larry was a good man, the kindest and best, but his touch, which had never lured her, was now a nuisance; no, it was more than that, because she dreaded it and did everything to avoid it. And Larry was too obtuse to realize what was going on. And he was too decent for her to tell him the truth, letting come what may. So here she stood confronted with a question that could not be answered, a situation which, out of pride or compassion or a combination of them, could not be discussed with anyone, least of all with this man.

But it was her own fault, having let slip that careless remark about "the best part of her life." Some silly slip of the tongue about fashion had led into this.

"What is it, Amanda? What's your trouble?"

Tears rush uncontrollably into eyes, and her eyes were suddenly filled with them.

"Nothing," she said, shaking her head. "It's nothing."

"It has to be something. Why won't you tell me?"

"Why should I tell you anything after the way you acted toward me?"

"I'm not treating you badly now, am I?"

"What difference does that make? You were mean, you were nasty to me, and for no reason."

"I know I was, and I apologize, Amanda. But I should tell you why I was really angry at myself, and so . . . Why are you staring at me?"

"Well, you're the only person in the room," she said.

"And if there were others, you mean, you wouldn't be looking at me."

"I didn't say that," she retorted.

They were sparring and fencing. They were standing on the edge of someplace—where? They were playing some game—what?

"You have your nerve," he said with the familiar twist of amusement on his lips. "But I like it. Even when you came that morning, I liked your nerve."

Another savage crash of thunder shook the house. Lightning flared at the windows and he cried out, "Never stand near a window when there is lightning! I told you!"

"I know. I know. I grew up in the country, remember?"

Wind and rain rattled the glass. You could imagine that a storm like this one was directed at yourself, that its lashing wind was intended to whip you and its lightning to burn and blind you. Subdued by the storm, side by side they sat, not speaking.

Then suddenly, regardless of his warning to Amanda, L.B. got up and stood at the window. For a long time, he stayed with his hands in his pockets. From where she sat on the sofa, she had an angled view of his face. It is a face on an ancient coin, she thought as she had thought so often in the past. It is proud, and changeable, and passionate, too. Never before had she allowed herself to use the word *passionate* in connection with L.B. Was it the storm here in this queer, vacant house that was bringing to light, and to her bewilderment, these wild, prohibited thoughts?

She did not want such random flashes like those she had from time to time experienced when in the presence of Peter Mack, or even with the neighbor out mowing his lawn in back of the brick bungalow next door! She wanted to wipe such things away, wipe them out, for they were useless; no good would come from any of them, and certainly not when these thoughts were about L.B. or his thick black hair, his tall narrow back, or his touch.

And yet right this minute she was wondering what it would be like to have his arms around her, and wondering with whom he lay down, for surely he must . . .

"The worst of it is over," he said suddenly. "It's only rain now, heavy rain."

"Can we start back?" she asked.

"It's still coming down too fast for the windshield wipers. Wait a little." He sat again. "Maybe I should explain what I meant by being angry at myself that day. Do you want to know why I was?"

His face, although the ridiculous sofa was long enough to seat eight or nine people, was only a foot or two distant from hers. Now looking into his steady gaze, she knew the answer. When she did not give it, he gave it.

"I was angry at myself because of my thoughts about you."

They stared at each other. His eyes, fixed upon hers, were dark and vivid. Wanting to look away, she was held fast.

"I didn't want to see you. I've been fighting this for a year at least. After that Christmas—you were so beautiful—I knew I mustn't see you. And it was the same for you, Amanda. Don't deny it, because I know better."

Her heart was quivering so that she was sure its beat

must be visible through her thin shirt. And those reluctant tears that had been lying between her eyelids now flooded and rolled down her cheeks.

"Ah, don't," he whispered, pulling her to himself. "Lovely, so lovely, Amanda."

Easily, willingly, she moved within his arms. Enclosed in warmth, his mouth pressed upon hers. Vaguely she was aware of his fingers opening the buttons and fastenings on her clothes; she heard his murmuring voice. Vaguely she was aware of her own deep sigh, of her own surging heartbeat and the rush of her blood.

When she opened her eyes, she found him looking at her from a height. He was fully dressed, and she was covered with his raincoat.

In a panic she cried out, "How long have I been asleep?"

"Maybe ten minutes. I don't know. Oh, Amanda, what can I say? It happened—"

In a wave of terror, she was drowning. "Oh, my God," she whispered.

L.B. collapsed with his head in his hands. Then he clapped a hand to his forehead, and his body rocked.

"My fault. All my fault," he repeated.

In spite of the terror, she was able to refute him. "No, it was mine, too. I wanted—" She stopped.

Yes, she had wanted, and now she knew. This was what she had imagined, had gone without, and if it were up to Larry, would never have known.

And yet she was drowning, struggling under the waves, and filled with terror. And she sat there, staring at L.B.

After a while he roused and spoke. "This was crazy. We must think of it this way: It was simply something that happened. Things happen. And then," he said steadily, "they don't happen again."

"I know."

Water was gushing and gurgling through the downspouts. In contrast to the sound, the stillness of the house was eerie. Through the long windows came the specific light of late afternoon, the lateness adding to Amanda's sense of doom.

"I have to go home," she said. "I have to go right now."

When she stood to fasten her clothes, he tried to help her, but she moved away from him. And he, understanding at once, dropped his hands. When they walked to the car, she looked uneasily up and down the street. And he, understanding that, too, assured her that no one had any cause to be suspicious.

"I am simply the owners' agent, the sole person outside of themselves who has the key. So don't be afraid, Amanda. Only you and I know what happened, and nobody else will ever know."

She was still shaking when they were in the car. My God! His father! Had it happened with anyone else, one would condemn it for being dishonest and unfaithful, but this—*this!* Oh, any other man, just not *his father!*

They drove in silence, L.B.'s profile sternly fixed upon the road. Cars passed, an SUV filled with little boys, the mail truck, and a delivery wagon bearing in red letters the words "Queen's Market."

People were out on the sidewalks now that the storm was over. Everything was normal. And everything outside had been normal, too, on the day they found Cecile inside, lying on the floor in a puddle of blood.

"I'm going to drive you as far as your corner," L.B. said, "and you will walk to your door. If anyone asks where you've been, since it's rather late, say that you were jogging, say anything else you can think of, but tell the truth about my driving you home. I passed you on the street a few minutes ago and naturally offered you a lift."

Her heart began to go wild again. "What about the time in between? What was I doing during the storm?"

"You were at the library. You took refuge there when the lightning came." He looked at her. "Are you all right?" And when she nodded, "You're sure you're all right?"

"I have to be," she said, straightening her slumped shoulders.

"That's it. Remember what I said. Things happen. Life doesn't always turn out the way you plan. Things happen. But you get back on track."

"Do I look all right? Can you tell that I've cried?"

"No. Act as if you're exhausted. You've had a long walk, caught in the storm—well, you know what to say."

When the car stopped, he laid his hand upon hers. "I think the world of you, Amanda, and I'm terribly sorry if I've harmed you and if I've given you something to worry about." His voice, although it concealed a slight tremor, was still deep and strong. "All I can say is, don't worry. Please don't. Forget it. It didn't happen. Can you do that? Okay?"

"Okay."

She got out of the car and watched until it had disappeared down the avenue. Then she rounded the corner, walked down her street, and had not taken more than a few steps before she met with another shock. The enormous old sycamore in front of her house had crashed diagonally across the lawn, with its top branches only a few inches from her dining room windows. A small gathering of people stood surveying the wreck.

Then Larry, catching sight of her, called out and ran toward her. "Where in blazes have you been? Somebody phoned me at the office to tell me about the tree, but she wasn't clear, and I didn't know whether it had destroyed the house with you in it—" He gasped. "I just got here, half out of my mind, haven't been inside yet, where've you been?" And he grabbed her, kissing both cheeks.

"Jogging, until the storm struck. Then I took shelter in the library. Then walking home I met up with your father passing on Hampton Avenue. He gave me a lift the rest of the way."

"Ah, good. Thank goodness."

So the lie had been spoken, and been easily received. She said calmly, "My, what luck. Saved by inches. I'm going to miss the old sycamore. It was lovely."

The neighbors were marveling and clucking. "Tsk, tsk. Tore up your lawn pretty well, didn't it?"

"You'll have to reseed, but it'll come back in no time."

"Going to cost a few dollars to get that thing sawed up and carted away."

"Look how the lightning stripped the trunk, an even cut right down the middle. Anybody inside the house would have had the fright of his life. Good thing you weren't home, Amanda."

No. How much better it would be if she had stayed home all day. . . .

"All's well that ends well," Larry said.

She had been waiting for him to say it, in fact she would have taken a bet that he would say it. No matter how slight the misfortune, he always did.

Supper was over, the evening news had come and gone; the usual suitable comment on the news had been spoken by Larry and heard by Amanda; both back and front doors had been locked and checked, so now nothing remained to end another day but bed.

"How about a bowl of ice cream for a change before we go up?" he suggested.

She wanted to tell him that he was getting too fat, but he resented being told it, and anyway, she was in no state of mind to argue. Besides, to be fair, he was really not getting all that fat; it was just that he had a pudgy build, heavy bones that made him look too broad. Suddenly she recalled that once she had thought, or talked herself into thinking, that this was "manly." Oh, but how her taste had changed! And regarding him now, she felt sorry, sorry for him and—sorry about everything.

"How about it, honey? Strawberry, chocolate, or what?"

"You choose."

"Strawberry. I'll get it."

"No, you sit there." She gave him a benign smile. "You worked all day."

"Right! I did. And you had the whole day off. Enjoyed yourself, I hope?"

Already past the kitchen door, she pretended she had

not heard. The panic was coming back, and it was a terrible, terrible thing. What if she were, in some passing situation, to lose control? What if she were to get sick and become delirious, or else perhaps need an operation sometime. They said people talk under anesthesia. Or was that not true?

"What's wrong with the ice cream?" Larry asked.

She had not been aware that the spoon was still lying untouched on her dish. "Wrong? No, nothing. I'm just not hungry. My stomach—I stopped at Stuffy's for a hot dog. It must have upset me."

Larry frowned. "How often do I have to tell you to see a doctor and stop neglecting yourself? You have too many stomachaches and headaches for someone your age. You're always telling me you need tea and aspirin or something before we go to bed. You're sick too often. What's wrong with you?"

This time he was really impatient. And seeing him so, she knew she must placate him.

"I'm sure it's nothing much," she said cheerfully. "You do exaggerate so, Larry. But I'll do something about it, only because I want you to be satisfied."

Thus mollified, he went to bed without making any demands on her, for which she was thankful. She could not have borne it tonight.

My God! His father!

If I could only tell somebody, she thought, lying awake. And she wondered whether L.B. was also lying awake in the same panic, with the same need to tell somebody. But most probably he was not. L.B. was strong.

The room was white with moonlight; unkind to

Larry, it exposed his thinning hair and his open mouth, from which there came a rhythmical, gentle snore.

My God! His father!

The face, the eyes, the mouth, the arms, the miracle! What had he meant by the words "get back on track"? To forget and not ever to have it again? Of course that is what he meant. What else could he have meant?

Tomorrow Larry would remind her of their weekly phone call to her family. How was she to pull herself together and talk naturally about natural things, about Mom's recent visit or her younger sister Doreen's pregnancy?

How was she, indeed, going to look her mother in the face again?

The clock downstairs struck twelve distinct notes, and still Amanda lay awake. Yet she must finally have fallen asleep because, as she would later remember with horror, she opened her eyes to the sight of a terrifying, enormous, green-white moon poised on the windowsill. It blocked out the night; it had collided with the earth! It was about to absorb and destroy the planet!

She screamed, and screamed again, awakening Larry, who shook her gently.

"Wake up. You're having a nightmare. Something must have frightened you today, most likely the fall of the sycamore. Close your eyes, and you'll go back to sleep."

CHAPTER THIRTEEN

The bus jerked, stopped, crawled, and rumbled through the city for what seemed like many miles. It had indeed covered a long distance as it zig-zagged from the suburbs' edge through neighborhoods that Amanda, in spite of having lived near the city for going on four years, had never seen before. Most of these neighborhoods were dispiriting in their mustard-colored monotony; once off the main prosperous avenues, the streets were a repetition of shabby, cramped dwellings, little stores, garages and filling stations, restaurants, and dark brick schools.

Occasionally she closed her eyes. Occasionally when the bus stopped, she half rose in her seat as if prepared to get off, and then sat down again. Her hands were tightly clasped on her handbag, revealing the tension of her body, revealing it so distinctly that after a while she became aware that people were observing her.

A group of four girls seated two by two across the aisle were in fact staring. She had attracted enough attention for them to whisper together. One gave a raucous bellow of laughter that caused an elderly gentleman to turn around and look at them. They're laughing at me, she thought indignantly, they in their shorts and outrageous miniskirts high to the crotch, with their heavy thighs exposed, their hairy calves and their not-quite-clean toes exposed, too, between the strips of their gold leather sandals. Tough. Tough and rude, they were, and she sat up straighter, her hands still clasped on her patent leather bag, her feet in their matching patent leather pumps resting properly on the floor.

They were still whispering and laughing. "Stuck up," they're thinking, because I don't look like them.

Then she saw that one of them was showing the others a magazine. Was it possible that they had been looking and laughing not at her, but at something in the magazine? And if they had for whatever reason been judging her, had she not been judging them? And what did she know of them except that they were not well groomed and had no proper manners? What did they know of her except that her clothes were fashionable and expensive?

They don't know what I'm doing, she thought. They might be shocked if they knew, or perhaps only titillated, not shocked at all. Nobody really knows very much about anybody else. We are only strangers sitting temporarily in a bus, coming from different places and going to different places.

Her lips moved: *Forward or back?* One foot tries to step forward, while the other tries to step back. But that way, you can only stand still. Decide. Decide now. I am a hungry woman who wants to break the window and steal the bread. I am a thirsty one who has had no water and is weak with thirst. I am a needy woman who has only to reach out her hand and seize what she needs. Does it matter that I have no right to do it, even if no one will know and no one will be hurt if I do?

And if that is so, it doesn't matter all that much, does it? Why then should she keep trying to resist? Anyway, it is beginning to appear that she really does not have the power to resist. Every day and half the night for weeks on end she has had but one thought, suspended between a strange sadness and a great joy.

Her heart began to race and her head to whirl, as the bus slowed to turn the corner at the bridge and enter Lane Avenue. The last time she had seen it was on the way back from her honeymoon. The first time was when Norma had made one of her little jokes: *Don't ever accept an invitation to a party on Lane Avenue.*

And suddenly, she was terrified: What if he wasn't there? Would there be another bus back? She ought to have come in her car. No, he had said; if something were to go wrong with the car, a flat tire or a slight fender bender, you would have to explain what you were doing on Lane Avenue. Nobody you know ever comes here. That's why it's a safe place for us.

He thought of everything, and she was safe with him. Of course he would be here, right on the corner. She stood up and was waiting to step off the bus the minute it stopped.

"You're late. I was worried," he said. "I thought maybe you had changed your mind. I've thought of nothing else since that day. It's seemed more like a year than a month."

His eyes beseeched her; there was a deep tenderness in them. Even so, he could not help but be in command; as she looked up into his face, he was, as he always was, regal. She gave him a small, shy smile, and holding hands they walked away down the street.

"Your smile, Amanda, lights up the sky."

One day in early fall, Cecile telephoned Norma with an invitation to go to the airport. Their mutual friend Liz, on her way to Europe, was to be there for two hours between connecting flights. Cecile, with all her wonderful qualities, could still be annoying sometimes. No doubt Liz had done some urging; Cecile was always obliging; and she, Norma, was not much better at saying "no." Hence had come the long ride to the airport, an admittedly pleasant coffee hour with Liz, whom neither of them had seen since Commencement Day, and now the long ride back to school where she had, for convenience's sake, left her car.

"The traffic here, getting off the bridge, is getting worse every day," Cecile complained as the car crept around the corner.

Norma yawned. "It's a good thing you're driving. I can hardly keep my eyes open."

"Too bad Amanda couldn't come. This was supposed to be her off Saturday, but they're too busy, she said. She really does work hard."

The car, idling behind a truck that was being un-loaded, was almost at the turn to Lane Avenue.

"Look down there," Cecile resumed. "Those places can't have had a coat of paint in a hundred years. It's awful. Just look."

Norma was looking. When her sleepy eyes came awake, her heart made a terrifying leap. Surely that is Amanda over there, and my father with her? Walking arm in arm . . . The jacket, the famous coral, orange, or whatever you call it. No, that's crazy. It isn't possible. They're half a block away. I'm not seeing straight.

Out of the corner of her eye, she watched Cecile. Were they both seeing the same thing? But no, if Cecile had recognized Amanda, she would have exclaimed. Or maybe she would not have done so? The concept was so absurd that no one would want to believe it, and so would not want to make a foolish mistake.

At any rate, the truck moved ahead and they were able to move around the corner. Cecile turned on the radio.

"Let's have some music," she said.

Norma's heart was thudding, steadily thudding; her whole body was shocked. Could there be any doubt in her mind about what she knew she had seen? But perhaps she was only imagining she had seen it. The eyes and the mind play tricks.

Her nerves were throbbing along with the music. That long, vivid hair and the coral jacket were not seen everywhere. And her father! Was it likely that a person would not recognize her own father, even from half a block away?

So she wrestled, her will not to believe in dire conflict with the growing certainty of fact. Sweating, she wiped her hands with a handkerchief. Impatient with the slow progress of the car, she could have jumped out of it, to run, to do something. But to do what? When she *knew,* she already *knew,* what she had seen.

What were they doing there, when Amanda was supposed to be at work? What would they be doing in that neighborhood, or doing together anywhere? It made no sense. There was never any love lost between them.

Cecile observed, "You're very restless, aren't you?"

"I am? I didn't realize it."

"You're uncomfortable. It's been a tedious drive. I'll drop you off at school in five minutes so you can pick up your car and go home. It's been a nice day though, hasn't it?"

At this minute the word "home" was distressing. Her father might come back there before she would have had time to collect her thoughts. She needed time. She was afraid of herself, afraid that some queer phenomenon might be taking place in her mind, that she might have had a hallucination, such as people have when they see water on a desert.

As soon as Cecile was out of sight, she drove to the theater building at the far end of the campus. The door was open. Next to it was the headmaster's house, where some sort of meeting must be taking place because there were a dozen cars on his driveway. Feeling safe because of their presence and yet at the same time needing to be let alone, she went into the music room and sat down to think.

The thought came to her that she was being unduly

suspicious. Facts were what was needed. Taking her cell phone from her handbag, she telephoned the shop in Cagney Falls and asked to speak to Amanda.

"Amanda's not here today," came the bubbling voice of Dolly.

"She's not? This is Norma. You remember me, Dolly? I thought she was there."

"She was supposed to be, but she's at home. Called in with an awful cold, bronchitis or something. Could hardly talk. I just phoned to see how she is, but there's no answer."

"Thank you, Dolly."

Cold fear came now with the sweat. This isn't possible, she murmured to herself. After a minute or two of utter bewilderment, she called Amanda at home and got no answer. Then she took up the telephone again and called the main Balsan office.

"Mrs. Flanagan? This is Norma. Is my father there? I have a message to give him."

"Dear no, didn't he tell you? He took the afternoon off to drive out to Creston. There's some property he needed to look at."

"Thank you, Mrs. Flanagan."

Her voice was natural and calm, which was a miracle. Creston was at least fifty miles away, far enough to account for an afternoon's absence. So could she still tell herself that she had not seen what she saw? She was in the kind of shock that happens when one has been a witness to some disaster. And laying her head on the back of the chair, she sat staring up at the ceiling.

"I saw your car," said Lester Cole, "and wondered what you were doing alone here. Are you all right?"

She sat up. "Yes, yes. Just tired all of a sudden."

"Excuse me, but I don't believe you."

"I'm sorry if you don't," she said almost angrily. She must look a fright here, hot and flushed, with her hair all this way and that. It wasn't tactful, it wasn't decent for him to barge in like this. He ought to know better.

"What are you doing here all alone?"

Now came his stern look, the one that befitted the assistant to the headmaster. Maybe there was some rule about entering the building without having a legitimate reason? She didn't know.

"I wanted to play the piano, to practice," she lied. "You remember, I explained to you several times that the pianos at school are so much better than the one we have at home? You said you didn't mind."

"And I don't mind. Why not play something for me now? Play what you were playing before."

Either she had to read and memorize for him, or she had to provide him with musical entertainment! She wanted to scream at him: Let me alone! Can't you see that I'm suffering? I don't know whether I'm coming or going.

But obediently she went to the piano and began to play from memory the Mozart Serenade in D. The notes went briskly, brightly rippling toward the doorway and the sun; then, as abruptly, they ceased. For, suddenly overwhelmed, she had to stop.

"I'm ashamed that you should see me like this. It's not *me*," she stammered.

"Surely I know that by now. I won't question, I won't probe, but I'm not going to leave you until you feel better."

What was ever going to make her feel better? Unless perhaps proof of some sort were to turn facts inside out? Meanwhile this man, this nice, well-meaning man, was just sitting there while she, too, was just sitting there staring at the piano keys.

"I've been meaning to tell you," he began, meaning obviously to break the silence, "how much we appreciate the way you stepped in and took over the A.P. French class when Mme. Perrault got sick. The way those kids swirled right through the finals and did so wonderfully well! You deserve an award."

"It was nothing."

"Far from that. It was a crucial time, and you had four Latin classes along with it, not to mention third-grade French. You're a born teacher, Norma, and a born linguist, too. Why don't you take up Urdu or Bulgarian in your spare time?"

This little attempt at a joke falling flat, Lester bent forward to see her more clearly. Three parallel lines marked his troubled forehead.

"Sorry," he said. "That wasn't funny."

Then silence came back. If he would simply *go,* she wanted to cry! Let me sit here till the cars have all left and I can run out to mine without having everyone see my red nose and eyes.

"Have I ever mentioned to you that I've often stopped in the corridor over in the Hale Building to hear you play? Have I?"

"No."

"You're a gifted woman, Norma, in many ways."

This time, too, she wanted to say something and did not: If it's even true, what good is it doing me right now?

"Thank you," she said, "although I don't agree."

"Tell me, apropos of that, what's happening with Jessie?"

Poor lost, lonesome Jessie! She at least was worth talking about. "I think she's doing better. She's happier."

"I got that feeling when I saw her on the Great Lawn the other day. She had on one of those silly shirts that girls are all wearing this year, she was walking with one of the boys, and she looked almost pretty. What have you done to her? I have a hunch you got her father involved."

"How did you guess?"

"I didn't guess. Given the hopeless mother she has, it would be the logical thing to do."

"Well, I told her to speak to him about having some money to choose and buy her own clothes, so she can dress like everybody else. That mother's a self-centered fool with, in my opinion at least, a large problem. Maybe she wants to keep Jessie an ugly duckling so that she can preen her own swan feathers. That can happen."

How long would he insist on staying? He's being the good Samaritan, she thought, diverting me with talk about Jessie, and he will stay until he has found out what's wrong with me. But never, never even under torture, will I reveal this.

Suddenly there were voices outside, and the sound of engines starting up. A couple of passersby looked in at the pair who were sitting there together in the deserted theater building.

"We should go someplace else," said Lester.

Understanding that it did not look exactly suitable for them to be there as they were, Norma got up at once, went toward her car, and was stopped by Lester's tone of command.

"We'll walk down to the playing field. They're having softball practice, and we can watch."

She understood that, too. It was natural for faculty people on one of these golden afternoons to come over to the school and relax at the playing field. She understood also that in his position he could make a reasonable request of her and expect to be heeded.

When they were seated on a shaded bench, he returned to the subject. "I thought we were friends, or I wanted to think so. But to be frank with you, Norma, I sometimes have a feeling that you really don't want to be."

She was astonished. "What do I do that gives you such an idea?"

"You really don't do anything. It's just that you have a distant manner."

Still astonished, she cried, "I have? I never mean to be 'distant.' I'm a quiet person, and always have been. You misunderstand me."

"If I do, I'm sorry. But sometimes in school as we pass each other, I know you pretend you don't see me. And I'm looking straight at you."

She always thought he was looking at her legs . . . She could think of nothing to say. Everything was going wrong today. Everything.

"I'm not myself right now," she blurted. "I had a bad experience, and I'm terribly confused."

"A bad experience here in school?" he asked with immediate concern.

"No, it had nothing to do with school."

If it were possible to reveal the truth to anybody, it might well be to this kind, intelligent man. With great tact, as her voice broke, he looked away from her toward the field where girls in yellow uniforms were running on the grass.

"What would you do," she cried, "if you caught people you loved and trusted, people close to you, doing something terribly wrong? Let's say you saw your—" she fumbled for words "—your grandmother stealing something in a store. Of course it wasn't that. It was something just as wild, something very, very ugly. What would you think?"

"Why, I would think that your poor old grandma was ill and needed help."

Norma shook her head. "No, no. I gave you a poor example. These people are not ill. I trusted them. It's unbelievable. I could scarcely believe my eyes."

"There's a difference between suspecting and knowing. Maybe you really shouldn't believe your eyes."

"What do you mean? I know what I saw."

"Do you know how many witnesses in criminal cases, honest people who were sure they knew what they saw, have been proven wrong?"

"Yes, but I really, really do know what I saw."

"Those people thought so, too—under oath, moreover."

"No, no, Lester." And yet only three days ago she had seen Larry and Amanda together, quite unchanged. Would they have been so if—if the other were true?

Yes, maybe.

Lester persisted. "So let us say that you actually did

see something so shocking. Let's say that your grandmother, having lost her mind, had become a shoplifter. You would still have to go on living your own life, wouldn't you? I should hope you would."

She did not answer. He was reasoning with her as a good teacher reasons with a child in distress. Perhaps he was right. It could have been an illusion, there on the corner of Lane Avenue.

"You would still have to go on with your own life," Lester insisted.

Norma smiled weakly. That, at least, was true. There was nothing else you could do. She could hardly confront them: *Was it you I saw on Lane Avenue near the bridge? And if so, what were you doing there together?*

"Don't jump at conclusions. That's my advice, Norma. Things unfold, for better or worse, but inevitably they do. Take my word for it. One day you will find out whether you were hallucinating or whether you saw what you think you saw. In the meanwhile, how about dinner tomorrow?"

Cecile was in a hurry. The excursion to the airport had taken longer than she had expected, and there were some preparations yet to be made for the evening's meeting at home. Her father was to bring some investment bankers to meet Peter for a discussion about the railroad land. A subject that had long lain more or less dormant was now awakening; recently there had been a noteworthy editorial in the morning paper protesting the long delay in making some good use of the "valuable acres."

Driving homeward, her mind was on the simple refreshments she had prepared for the meeting. Her father, ever a canny judge of human nature, had wanted the introduction to be an informal one at Peter's own home.

"I want him to be the memorable centerpiece of the discussion in his own environment," Amos had declared, "because he is the centerpiece. There are any number of syndicates that can slap up a mighty profitable heap of what Peter calls 'glass boxes,' but we want a work of art here. Not that works of art aren't profitable. They can be even more so in the long run than are the merely mundane. We need to create something here that will bring people from all over to have a look, and maybe to emulate it. We want something to be proud of."

Thinking about all this and feeling quite exhilarated herself as she entered her driveway, Cecile was at the same time vaguely troubled by something else, a sight that seemed to persist in her mind's eye just as a midge bite continues to itch long after the midge has flown out of sight. What had she really seen that afternoon? It was the oddest thing to have seen—or to have thought to see—Mr. Balsan and Amanda walking with linked arms on Lane Avenue. It was in fact so very odd that she could only think she had imagined it. Yet there was that jacket, that beautiful, distinctive color; there was Mr. Balsan, so unusually tall; there was also Norma, who had annoyed her by squirming in her seat and who had been so unnaturally silent. All these things, of course, were conjectural. Not admissible, or not really so, in a courtroom. Quite probably she had not seen them at all.

At any rate, right now she was too busy to think anymore about it. At home Peter, already there ahead of her and very excited, had spread his papers on the library table, arranged the chairs, and checked the portable bar.

"Amos said Mr. Baker likes a bourbon and soda. Roland drinks Perrier."

"May I listen in when the meeting starts, or is it strictly private?" Cecile inquired.

"It's strictly private, as private as any conference or get-together of the CIA. But you're thoroughly trusted, darling Cele, and you're welcome. In fact, I'll enjoy showing off before you."

By eight o'clock the four men were gathered around the table. Peter, by request, was holding court, explaining, answering questions, and illustrating with eloquent gesture, while Cecile, in the leather wing chair against the wall, comprised the sole audience.

"The museum, according to my plan, must be the pivot, the center, as the terminal was in its heyday. The restored terminal becomes a museum, a cultural center for the city, just as the original terminal, surrounded by hotels, offices, and great stores, was the center of the city's business. I don't know how long it is since any one of you has explored the old pile, but I've spent a total of, well, I guess, three months' worth of scattered days, and let me tell you, it is full of treasures. The ceiling—does any one of you remember it? Lord, they knew how to spend money back then before World War One. The murals alone are magnificent. Each section is a depiction of some American natural wonder, from Niagara Falls to the Sangre de Cristo Mountains—you name it. All they need is some cleaning and the right lighting, which they've never had. Now, the great thing is that these murals do not cover the entire ceiling but are concentrated in the shape of a fairly large, but not too large, cap around the center of the dome."

Peter gave a bright, almost boyish smile. He was enjoying himself. This was the first time Cecile had heard or seen him in action; his fluency and his elegance as he stood there gave her a warm thrill. Sometimes she wondered whether it made sense to believe you could really know another human being, but whether it made any sense or not, she was often certain that she did know him through and through.

Immensely proud, he insisted on his independence; had not experience taught her that almost from their very first day? But there was no arrogance in his pride; far from measuring himself against other people, he measured himself only against an ideal in his head. Once he had told her that every human being, when he opened his eyes in the morning, should be able to look at something beautiful, if it was merely a row of spreading trees on a narrow street. That, then, was his aim, to preserve and create some kind of beauty where none had been.

"I see in that old terminal," he was saying now, "a science hall, a museum, a community theater, and more. I would add wings for lecture halls, or anything else that comes to mind. Here," he continued, indicating the sketch, "this is the hub of the wheel. From it, these roads connect with downtown and with the wetlands on the river. Along them I would have housing in every price range, nothing higher than three stories, small hotels to accommodate the people who will come to the great museum or to hike through the wetlands, or both."

When he paused and narrowed his eyes for an instant, he seemed to be seeing, far in the distance, the finished project, the magnificent hub, the tree-lined roads, and the circumference of the great circle, all the way to the river.

And of course, Cecile knew, he is seeing himself as the acclaimed creator. But why not? A composer must see in his mind's eye the crowd applauding in the concert hall. The painter sees the quiet crowd lined up at the gallery doors.

"This will be a marvel for the city," said Mr. Roland. "If we don't do anything more than clean up the Lane Avenue area, we'll deserve a medal."

Everyone laughed. Amos had an I-told-you so expression as he turned to the other two men.

"When, quite a while ago, my father-in-law first talked to me about this project," Peter said, "one of the first things I thought of was that sick Lane Avenue area. It needs medicine, and plenty of it. Nobody should have to live like that."

All nodded in agreement, and Mr. Baker reminded them that the next thing was to get the financing. "But I'm confident that, with a striking plan like this in hand, we'll have no trouble."

"If we can get one of the important chains to put up a hotel between the museum and the river, we'll have it made," said Amos.

"The hotel must be in keeping with the rest of the plan, though," Peter warned.

Amos teased him. "No seventy-story glass boxes stood on end?"

"And no casinos, either," Peter answered, laughing. "No imitation rajah palaces."

"So," said Roland as the meeting adjourned, "it's settled and we all agree. We're on our way. But not a word, not a breath, outside of this house. I can't emphasize that enough. I really can't."

"We all know it," said Amos. "Don't worry."

Once the other men had left, he was jubilant. "You've made amazing progress," he told Peter, "and I'm proud of you, especially when I think of all the other work you have to do, and what you have been through this past winter," he added soberly.

That last was quite true. Regardless of the vacation under the palm trees and regardless of all their determined efforts, these last months had been far from joyful for Peter and Cecile. The vacant room upstairs was a daily and nightly reminder of loss. Almost, as they passed in the hall, it seemed to be asking a question: Will you ever be able to fill this room with life? One good thing about this grand project, Cecile liked to think, was that it kept Peter's mind busy as he worked at his desk almost every evening. As for herself, she had the blessing of work all day. But the evenings, at least until Peter left the desk, were very, very quiet. . . .

Amos clapped Peter on the back. "You'll be one of the most prominent architects in the U.S.A. if you can accomplish this. And with that thought, I'm going home. Good night."

"You didn't dream," Cecile asked later, "when Dad first talked about this, that you were going to care so much about it, did you?"

"No, I didn't. To tell you the truth, I started to work on it because I felt an obligation. I didn't feel that it was my kind of thing. But now I see that it is very much my kind of thing. I feel challenged, Cele, and I enjoy the feel."

"I know. You looked so happy tonight. You deserve to feel happy."

"We both do, Cele. And we will be. We'll be ourselves again."

Much later while in bed, she remembered the thing that had bothered her earlier in the day. And touching him on the shoulder before he should fall asleep, she told him about it.

"Such an odd thing happened. At least I thought it was. When you all mentioned Lane Avenue, it came back to me. I'm almost sure I saw Amanda and Mr. Balsan walking there arm in arm."

"On Lane Avenue? You're sure?"

"Well, I think I am. It was the coral-colored jacket that caught my eye. The scenery was otherwise so drab that it stood out like a bright speck in a mass of brown mud. And I thought I recognized Mr. Balsan, too. Such a very tall man in a dark business suit would be conspicuous on Lane Avenue, wouldn't he?"

"He certainly would."

"So what would they be doing there? And being there together? Doesn't make any sense, does it? The more I think about it, I'm sure I couldn't have seen what I thought I saw. It's impossible. And yet—"

"No, Cele, when you're dealing with human affairs, almost anything you can think of is possible. But I very definitely wouldn't mention it to a soul. Just forget about it."

"Of course," said Cecile.

CHAPTER FOURTEEN

On Lane Avenue on the other side of a dirty windowpane, an ancient oak, which a farmer might have planted before the Civil War when the avenue was a dirt road, flared red in the October sun. Indoors the room had had some rudimentary sanitizing by a hand-held vacuum cleaner, but otherwise it remained a slum, its sallow green paint peeling and stained, its scuffed baseboards and broken light fixtures serving as reminders of the numerous families who had been tenants here.

None of all this, not even the broken light fixtures, distressed Amanda. To begin with, they never occupied the flat at night. It was strictly an afternoon meeting place, and only for two, or at most three, afternoons in a month. But it was secret, it was safe, and one could import one's own comforts.

These at present took the form of a cheap couch wide enough for two, a pair of equally cheap soft armchairs, and between them, a low, collapsible table on which lay a handsome wicker picnic basket fitted out with cutlery, fine china, and proper glassware fit for any drink from water to Château Lafite-Rothschild, if such were to be on the menu.

Today's menu, provided by L.B., consisted of grapes, imported cheese, French bread, and a wine that, if not exactly Château Lafite, was not too many notches below it. L.B. knew how to celebrate.

"An anniversary," he said, "or half an anniversary. Six months to the day since that April storm, Amanda. Could you have dreamed then that it would ever come to this?"

Wrapped in a plaid robe, he lay on the sofa, while she, at the table, ate grapes. When she looked over at him, his eyes were fastened upon her with a look of profound tenderness.

"No, never."

How could she possibly have dreamed of this betrayal, this crime? It was a crime before God, nothing less, and she was aware of it every day. Yet life had never been as full and gratifying as it was now.

She had never known what it was to love. Longing for it, trying to imagine it, she had even begun sometimes to think that romantic love was nothing more than a trick of the arts, invented and vividly sustained by gifted dramatists and musicians inspired by the troubadours of long ago. But this cynicism came to her only when she was in a mood of profound discouragement; in most of her moods, knowing better, she had merely longed and hoped. Then suddenly, the miracle had happened.

Her memory reeled backward to that night of horror when the moon had stood on the windowsill, to the astounding event in the vacant house, and then—yes, then, before that, to her own growing physical awareness of the man whom she had once feared and disliked. Who was to explain the how or why of all this?

There were a hundred ways, large and small, in which this man and this woman, during the long summer, had met and merged. At very first there had been her own faint hope and fear that he would summon her to him. He, too, had fought between hope and fear that he would summon her, and that she would accept him. Like her, he had fought with himself and lost, and been radiantly glad of it ever since.

"I knew you wanted me," he had told her, "as much as I wanted you. Both of us knew how right we were for each other."

How different he was from the Lawrence Balsan who sat at the head of the table in his gloomy dining room! And she glanced now at today's small gift, a book of American poetry with a rosebud wrapped in wet foil alongside it.

"Take the rose home," he said, having followed her glance. "You can say you found it on somebody's fence, the last of the season. Maybe it will keep until we meet here again. And there are some poems of Edwin Arlington Robinson's in the anthology. You might like them. They're unusual."

She smiled, and he caught that, too; his dark, vigilant eyes saw everything.

"You're smiling?"

"Yes, because I'm not altogether used to it yet, your being so different from what I thought I knew."

"I've been bottled up, I guess. Who knows why? I'm no psychologist. And it isn't important. What's past is past." He paused. "And who knows anyway what is cause and what effect? All I can tell you is I married too young, we were too different, then she died, and I tried to do the best I could for the children. I haven't known love since I was in my twenties, and even then it was nothing like this, Amanda."

Again L.B. paused, while between Amanda and him the name *Larry* wrote itself in tall letters. "I knew it was wrong, and I fought it. One time, the first time, last Christmas, I gave in. That dinner, that sudden whim, was arranged for you. Did you know that? I wanted to put things off, but I wasn't able to anymore. I wanted to see you glow, not that you needed an occasion or a setting, because you glow right here in this hovel. And after that when you came that Sunday morning, I didn't want to be alone with you, and I was nasty."

"Yes, you were. Haughty and cold. But that's what I had always thought about you from the first time I saw you."

"Here's what I thought the first time. I saw a fire that wouldn't be hard to set ablaze. And it made me very uncomfortable—in the circumstances."

"However would you know anything like that about me? I was a proper young lady that day. I even held a pair of gloves in my hand. I wasn't wearing them, but I had them."

"I can't explain. I seem to sense things, that's all—for

instance, the second time. On that afternoon last April in the storm when we walked into the old vacant house, I felt what was going to happen. I myself had no intention of making it happen, that I swear. But all the same, I felt it."

They had had this dialogue more than once before. It was as if, still stunned by events, they had a need to go over and over them. Were they repeating themselves merely to marvel, or was it to exonerate themselves—if that were possible? Amanda wondered.

Other people, many people in these days, revealed their transgressions on radio and television in talk shows. Unashamed, unafraid to speak in public, they told of affairs such as one young man's with his mother-in-law. A newspaper reported a woman's affair with her husband's father; when it became known, she committed suicide. And Amanda shuddered.

Huddled there in her silk robe, she had a too-familiar sensation of sinking in her chest. It was sad that a woman could be so deeply, blessedly in love and yet in the midst of it, have all these sudden poignant moments of sadness. How would she bear it if everything should come to an end? This man, this love, had become the very core of her life.

"What are you thinking about, my Amanda?"

"That you and I are an unfolding story. We're not writing or reading it, we're living it, and I am praying, desperately praying, that it will have a happy ending."

"It will have. I know this is wrong. It's like any adultery, only more so. But listen to me and remember that nobody is being hurt and nobody will be. As long as no one is harmed, any sin is forgivable. If that were not so, half the world would be damned and doomed. Oh, come here, darling. Take off that robe and come here."

"I don't want to leave here," she whispered.

"Even a place like this?"

"Even a place like this."

Somewhere, not far away, a wood fire burned, sending its tart fragrance through the open window. Sunlight, sifted through moving leaves on the ancient oak tree, speckled the ceiling. In perfect peace and satisfaction, Amanda thought, a woman rests beside her lover, but an ignorant young girl assumes that this is the way it always is. And the swift, unpleasant contrast to that honeymoon, a hundred years ago, darkened her memory.

L.B.'s voice dispelled the darkness. "You deserve a better place. This room is dead, and you are life, Amanda."

"Yes, with you, I am."

Whatever zest she had once possessed—and she knew she had possessed that quality in an extra-generous amount, knew it not only because other people had told her so, but because she herself had felt it—during these last years she had felt it slipping away. So gradually had this slippage occurred that she had not actually realized the total loss of it until L.B. had so splendidly revived it.

There was no end to her yearning. She carried it, and it carried her in its own rhythm, just as a tide declines and swells again.

"It's time," he said. "We have to go."

"Ah, no! A whole week. It's like a year."

"I worry," he said thoughtfully. "You meet so many people. Yes, I'm jealous. A woman like you, all radiant, your eyes, your hair—what man wouldn't be jealous?"

"Don't say that. You have no reason to be, and you never will have," she answered, giving him a long, steady look.

"I believe you. Darling, it's time to go. We can't take any chances. Hurry."

When instantly she stood and reached for her clothes, he caught her hand and kissed it. And when he raised his face, she saw a film of tears in his eyes.

"That's a beautiful jacket, that coral," he said as they were leaving, "but don't you need another one, too, a new one?"

"No. It's my good-luck jacket, and I love it. And somehow I don't have that mad love of clothes anymore. I have another love. Larry has even noticed that I'm not extravagant now. I hardly ever bring anything home anymore."

L.B. winced. "Please never mention Larry. Please."

"I'm sorry. It was unthinking."

She must be more careful, must remember—and of course she did remember—that his relationship to Larry was immensely different from hers.

The car was rolling away down Lane Avenue before L.B. spoke again. "Don't I know on every one of our wonderful days, as well as in all the time between, how wrong this is? With all my soul, I know it. But tell me, are we to stop?"

"We've been over this often enough," she cried in distress.

"Yes, and we know we're not able to stop it. Neither you nor I. Not able," he repeated. "Oh, I feel so helpless sometimes. I would like to stand free and open before all the world with you. I would like to do the things a man

does. I would like to bring you a gift other than an innocuous book—"

She interrupted. "I love books."

"Or meet you and make love to you without having
to hide in a hole down here where no one can possibly
find us."

"But that's why it feels so good, don't you see? It feels
safe, and permanent. That's what people—I speak for
women—want when they are in love. They want permanence."

"Many men do, too. At least this man does."

Driving with one hand on the steering wheel and the
other hand clasped over Amanda's, L.B. took them
slowly by unfrequented routes toward home. As always,
he let her out five or six streets distant from her house
and quickly drove away.

"When?" he asked as they approached the parting.

"Not this Saturday. It's my time to work. Call me on
my car phone around Thursday or Friday. Then I'll know
about the next Saturday."

There was no need to be more specific, it being understood that if Larry were to have his tennis game, she
could say she was going to the gym.

"If I could only take you home with me," he began,
and stopped.

She knew what he would have said: We'll take a walk
before it gets dark, we'll go out to dinner, or take our
plates into the sunroom at home, we could—but it would
have been no use, and besides, they had gone as far in the
car as they dared. So she stepped out quickly, he drove as
quickly away, and Amanda walked rapidly back to arrive
before Larry could.

*   *   *

"Another book?" Larry, stretched on the sofa after supper, yawned and reached for the remote control. "Nothing decent on tonight. Let's see the book."

"It's poetry," she said, handing it to him. "American poets. I bought it secondhand, but it looks new."

After riffling the pages, he handed it back. "Nice. You get a lot of pleasure out of this stuff, don't you? I always think poetry is a very feminine pleasure."

"That's odd, considering that most of the world's major poets since long before Shakespeare have been men."

She had not intended to speak sharply, but too often when he made a statement that she found irritating, words like these came out of her mouth. So now she made amends with a friendly question and a smile.

"How was your game today?"

"Okay. Phil and I make a great team, so it was good except for interruptions. I feel like a doctor, being tracked down even at the tennis court. The lawyer for the buyer wanted to ask about the closing. Couldn't wait till Monday to ask."

He yawned again. He never covered his mouth, so that the whole wet, pink interior, almost as far back as the tonsils, was exposed. Norma would never do that. How different these siblings were, she a walking encyclopedia, and he what he was! L.B. would never do it, either. How was it possible that father and son were so utterly different? Of course it was possible. Larry had had a mother, too, hadn't he? *I married too young,* L.B. said. They might have been fairly miserable together. They must have been.

"Lord, I'm tired," Larry groaned.

Only a short while ago, it seemed, he had been a sturdy man, filled with energy. Vigor and cheerful good humor had been his attractions. Something had happened to him; sprawled here like this, he seemed to have turned into somebody vulnerable, a child or a very old man, arousing pity.

True, she thought, he works very hard. People say that he brings in more than half the business. He's smart, they say, innovative, with a head for business.

"Sometimes," he said, breaking into her thoughts, "I feel that you really don't love me."

There was a sickening flutter in her stomach. The room shrank close, entrapping her. Yet she managed to reply.

"That's ridiculous. What on earth do I do to make you think that?"

"I can't say exactly. It's more what you don't do, I guess."

"I've never been a touchy-feely person, you know that. I can't help it. But I show my feelings in many other ways, don't I?"

"Yes, you're very good to me, very kind. It's just—oh well, drop it. Forget I said it. I guess I'm tired tonight, not making sense . . . You're looking especially beautiful right now, Amanda. Flushed, as if you'd been out in the fresh air all day."

"I took a long walk."

"Good. By the way, I was thinking, we never see Dad anymore, except when I see him at the office, I mean. And not often, even then. He keeps me way out in the branches practically all the time now, not that I mind. But wouldn't it be nice to get up a dinner with him again? And with Norma and her date? It's getting to look a little bit serious between her and that fellow Lester, I think. What do you think?"

"About Lester? She hasn't said anything definite, yet I do get a feeling when she mentions him."

"Great! She deserves a good man, a life. So what about the dinner?"

It would be unbearable, impossible! L.B. had exclaimed when Amanda had once before transmitted this message from Larry.

"Well, sometime soon," she said now, "but not just yet. I don't think Norma and Lester are quite there yet." Her stomach still fluttered, and she stood up.

"You never sit still. Where are you going now?"

"Outside. I forgot to fill the birdfeeders."

"Well, do it, and then come upstairs. I feel like going to bed early tonight."

In the little yards and houses all along the street, lights were going out, but the sky above glittered. She stood and gazed. "Universe" was a misnomer: There wasn't *one;* there were many. There were unknown numbers, for with each telescope more powerful than the previous one, still another universe was revealed. Beyond, she thought, always beyond. We know nothing. We do not even begin to know ourselves, let alone the galaxies. We do not understand why we do the things we do.

Surely some other woman would have been much better for poor Larry. Yet he wanted me. Surely he's forlorn now and depressed, very probably through my fault. I understand what he wants, yet his touch is almost more than I can bear. But leave him, he who has always been

so good to me? Impossible. Unless, unless L.B. and I—
but L.B. never would. He's Larry's father.

Lacking a handkerchief, she wiped a few tears on a
fallen maple leaf and went indoors. On the kitchen
counter lay the rose. Still damp, it was barely starting to
wilt. So she put it into a bud vase with cold water, carried
it upstairs, and stood it on the table beside the bed. When
she opened her eyes in the morning, it would be there,
and with joy—oh, with what joy!—she would remember
who had given it.

CHAPTER FIFTEEN

Norma, too, was marking a date. It was just half a year ago that, stricken by what she had seen or thought she had seen on Lane Avenue, she had taken shelter in the vacant theater building at school and been discovered there by Lester Cole.

"You broke the ice that day," she said to him now.

He had indeed. Their dinner on the following evening had begun a train of events and marked a colorful new era in her life. Many candlelit dinners, concerts, and lectures had come after it, enriching their friendship. Both of them were introverted and reserved people, which probably made them very comfortable with each other. They looked at life in the same way.

Sometimes she asked herself whether she was in love with him, and found herself unable to answer her own question. She did not even know how it would feel to be "in love." Too many of her acquaintances were in and out of intense relationships all the time; angry and brokenhearted when one ended, it never seemed to take very long for them to be equally "in love" with someone else. So what could you make of that kind of thing? Of course, there was always the case of Peter and Cecile to prove the exception.

For the present, she was enjoying herself. On this particular evening, the famous country restaurant near Cagney Falls, a favorite of theirs, was particularly enjoyable. Under the stone mantel a fire burned, not for warmth on this mild spring night, but strictly for rural atmosphere. Miniature hothouse roses were a pleasing change from the usual daffodils or tulips.

"Broke the ice, did I?" Lester asked.

"Yes, I had a very bad problem that day, as you know. I don't think there is anyone else to whom I could have admitted that I even had one."

"You haven't yet told me what it was."

It was a cloud, one of those that hover in the bright sky and threaten the day's events; then when the events are about to be canceled, the cloud disappears beyond the horizon and the sun returns.

An impression is not enough, Lester had told her on that awful afternoon. Every day people swear to the truth of what they have seen and are proven wrong. She remembered that. He made sense. He always did. There was a firm, quiet wisdom in Lester. You would never go wrong by listening to him. So she must cleanse her mind once and for all of that lingering cloud, that taint.

"I can't talk about it," she said, shaking her head.

"Okay, I won't ask you to. But as to breaking the ice,

I hope you won't mind too much if I break a little more of it."

"I won't mind. Go ahead."

"This ice may be a bit thin, so I'm going to order a re-fill of my coffee cup to fortify me."

"Oh, for goodness' sake, what's it about?"

"About your legs," Lester said flatly.

She could not have described her reactions. She felt that her eyebrows had risen, that her forehead was wrin-kled, that her cheeks were hotly flushed, and that brutal embarrassment was draining through her. She had been caught naked on the street. She wanted to get up, run and hide from his eyes; she was furious. And she could think of nothing to say.

"I don't mean to hurt you, but it's time that some-thing be said," he went on. "Do you suppose that in all these months I haven't noticed how you try to pull your skirt down to hide them? Or that you surreptitiously keep glancing at them?"

Still she was unable to speak. No one had ever talked about her legs—no one except Amanda and Cecile in the intimacy of that flat on the campus—since early adoles-cence, when she had been taken to doctors, none of whom had been able to do anything for her.

"Why are you cringing?" he asked. It was almost as if he were angry. "So you have bad legs! Look at yourself, at your fine, sensitive face and your beautiful eyes. What if you had Pinocchio's nose? Or my ears?"

Involuntarily, she glanced at Lester's ears as he con-tinued.

"For a while at school, I was called 'Taxi.' Somebody

started it by saying that I looked like a taxicab going down the street with the doors open."

It was true when you looked carefully. His ears grew out of his head at an angle and were too large, anyway, for the size of his head.

"What? You never noticed them before?"

Well, yes, and then again, no. He was an otherwise attractive man, so probably one didn't notice his ears so much.

"Well, yes, and then again, no," she said.

"These ears haven't stopped me from forging ahead in the world, nor have your legs stopped you."

Little did he know about the ordeal of school and college dances. Even now on occasions when she had to sit on a podium, or worse yet, pose for a group photograph there, it was an ordeal.

He spoke indignantly. "Okay, I'll amend that. Women do suffer more over things like this. Yes, they do, and they shouldn't have to. They feel inferior when they have something wrong that makeup can't hide. It's unfair, but that's the way it is." Shaking an admonitory finger at Norma, he continued his lecture. "Don't be like Elizabeth Jenkins! Remember her, going home to Mama every day after school? She was a prisoner of her mother, and you have been a prisoner of your legs. I've been waiting for months to tell you, but I haven't had the nerve until now. You're not too angry at me, Norma?" he asked wistfully.

She was, and yet, should she be? He had been blunt and he had been clumsy, but she saw in his eyes that he had meant the best for her and would never willingly hurt her.

"You're a lovely woman. You're a remarkable woman, Norma."

Wiping her eyes, she sniffed. "It's only that life would be so much easier at school if Dr. Griffin would let us wear trousers."

"Listen, he's a marvelous person, although in some ways he's from the year one. But the hell with hiding under trousers, Norma. Wear your skirts freely. Wear a miniskirt! People be damned. Let them look. Do you know what? Ninety-nine people out of a hundred care too much about their own affairs to care about your legs. Come on, let's get out of here. Let's go home now that we've cleared the air. We can sit on your porch and watch the moon come up. That is, if you're not too angry at me."

"I'm not," she said softly, and took out her compact to powder her red nose.

He had indeed shocked her, but he had done it with honest emotion, and as the minutes passed, her own honest shock receded. Along with it any self-conscious discomfort that she had ever felt while in his company was suddenly gone. Her legs, at least as far as Lester was concerned, would no longer be a problem.

She had never, she reflected as they sat on the old swing, heard him speak on any subject with such vehemence. Even when at a faculty meeting he expressed himself, as he often did, with unmistakable firmness, the effect had not been like this.

"A comfortable old house," he said as the swing creaked. "How long have you lived here?"

"I was born here. But I'm making plans to leave it fairly soon." She did not know why she was saying this, yet she went on, "I've been feeling that it's time to be on my own. It's true that my father will be alone here when I leave, but I can't help that. There are some really nice new apartments not too far from the school, so that's what I'm considering. It's been in my mind for quite a while, and now it's time for some action."

He made no comment, which did seem odd, so she continued to cover the pause. "I still won't be too far from Dad. I don't want to desert him. But I'm earning more than enough to take care of myself, and I've suddenly been seeing myself as a spoiled teenager living here on his bounty."

"You're hardly spoiled, Norma, but easily able to pass as a teenager. You probably haven't changed a bit since you graduated from college."

There now came another pause during which he made a sound like a forced cough and said, "It's a good enough idea, yet I wouldn't be hasty if I were you. I wouldn't sign anything until I was sure. What I mean is, that's a big change, and you should be absolutely certain before you make it."

Puzzled, she waited while, after coughing again, he proceeded to talk about himself.

"Yes, you should always be absolutely, one-hundred-percent sure. Now confidentially, I must tell you that Dr. Griffin is going to retire at the end of the school year. In May, that is," he explained as if she did not know. "And he tells me that I'm almost certain—in fact he used the word unqualified—'you're certain,' he said, 'to take my place.'"

"Why, that's wonderful!" Norma cried. "Really wonderful, Lester."

"And so I thought that perhaps you and I, I thought that maybe you would, that we could talk about—"

"About giving me a promotion?" she said eagerly.

"I don't know whether you'd call it a promotion. Actually, it wouldn't, in certain circumstances, be suitable for you to remain on the faculty at all. It could lead to complications: I to be the headmaster of the school, while—should you accept me, and I hope to high Heaven you will—my wife works there, too."

In the summer, the Balsan yard underwent a transformation. An enormous air-conditioned tent striped green and white, a dance floor and first-rate orchestra, tables clothed in pink and garlanded with dark red roses—all these evidences of gaiety and celebration were the products, not of the bride's brain, but of her father's. Everything inside and outside of the tent, from the newly planted floral border leading to the latticework gazebo where the marriage ceremony was to take place, was in the best taste; nothing was overdone; it was perfectly splendid, and yet it had an elegant simplicity.

If that isn't a contradiction, thought Norma as from an upstairs window she observed the preparations.

She, if given the choice, would certainly have preferred a small family gathering, a fine dinner for the same few, and maybe, in some bow to the tradition that both her father and her brother seemed to want for her, a scattering of rice as the bride and groom departed for the airport and their flight to Greece.

Lester had urged her to go along with all the plans. "They're happy. Aren't you glad they are? Your father's a self-made man, and this is an opportunity to show what he's able to do for his daughter," he said, showing his usual discerning wisdom. "And the same goes for my father."

He took Norma's hand and held it to the light, in which the five-carat emerald-cut diamond on her finger flashed its magnificence.

They both laughed, for they were thinking of the same thing: her astonishment and his almost sheepish explanation on the day he had given it to her.

"For Heaven's sake," she had exclaimed, "you can't afford this on your salary!"

"Not on my salary, but on a lifetime of savings. Birthday and graduation presents, and a small inheritance from my grandparents that I have never touched, not a penny of it. And now it all sparkles on your finger."

Norma had really been shocked. And for some reason, she had thought of Amanda, whose ring was half the size of this one and who would have appreciated the glory of this one far more than she did.

"I hope," she said, "you don't mean to say you've spent it all."

"Indeed I have. I hadn't intended to, but my father shamed me into doing it." He gave her an amused, mock rueful smile. " 'Live while you can,' he told me. 'You and Norma will enjoy seeing this every day. You've got a good job and you won't be in need of the cash, so why let it molder in a bank where you can't look at it?' I'm a very prudent man and my father is, too, but this time, he was right."

Having said all that, Lester had given her a memorable kiss.

Once we got started, she thought now, everything has come in a rush. After four years of covertly observing each other, then one year of what one might now call "feeling out" the situation, after the usual quiet dinner, with no prior hint at all, had come the proposal given to her as though it were simply a matter of fact which they should both have known all along.

Wasn't it odd that Alfred Cole, the man who had made that hideous mistake five years ago at Cecile's wedding, should now turn out to be her husband's father? Norma really liked the man, too, not only because he liked her, but also because he was so obviously proud of his son. Good reason enough!

So here now was the ring and there in the closet hung the wedding dress, white taffeta studded at random with rosettes of ribbon. In this case it was Cecile and Amanda who had done the choosing. She herself would have worn a white day dress, a short one now that she had at last triumphed over what Lester frankly termed her "neurosis," and certainly no veil.

What really was all this about? Two people liked each other's company so much that it seemed very sensible for them to continue the relationship. And pledging to do so, they announced it to the world. That was the sum total of it. Religion for most people was an essential element, although for many these days it was not; they simply moved in together. No, that would not be Norma's way. But all this expensive, elaborate folderol? Photographs, announcements, gifts, and bridesmaids—whom she refused to have—what had all these to do with the essence of it?

Lester and Norma, however, were in the midst of it all, and oddly enough, it was he who made no objections, when so often it was the man who made them, or would have liked to make them.

But he had only to think about putting on a suit and making sure not to forget the travel tickets, while she was now waiting for the hairdresser, and for the florist to deliver the bouquet on time while hoping that, tent or not, it would not rain.

It was eleven-fifteen by the bedside clock. There were five hours and fifteen minutes to wait before "half after four." Why didn't the invitations read *four-thirty*, which is the way people talk? Why? Well, because it just isn't done, that's why.

And why am I smiling to myself? Because I am just so happy, that's why, just so happy.

"How pretty Norma has turned out to be," remarked Cecile's mother to Cecile. "You have to admit," and Harriet Newman lowered her voice, "that she never was a pretty child. It's as if she's been transformed."

The ceremony, complete to the final notes of the Mendelssohn wedding march, was over, and the crowd, a very large one, was moving about the yard with drinks and hors d'oeuvres in hand. Receiving kisses and congratulations were Norma and Lester, a couple so well matched that one could almost swear that these among all people would endure together.

An acquaintance had already remarked to Cecile that "they must be having great sex to have made Norma look so much softer. It does make a change in a woman, especially in one who always looked so deprived, if you know what I mean." That surely was a thing Harriet Newman would never say!

"It was darling of her to invite your father and me, we thought."

"Oh, she really wanted you. You're old friends. She remembers so many things about you, how good you were after her mother died and how you took her shopping for her junior-high graduation dress. She hasn't forgotten a thing."

"Well, she's married into a fine family, I must say. Alfred Cole has an outstanding reputation."

Cecile was amused. She must have heard that at least six times today.

"We're going inside now. I've already peeked in—they've got long tables, twelve people at each, I think, the same as we had, or maybe more."

"It seems like yesterday," said Harriet, "and then again it seems like a hundred years, although it was only five years last month."

When she sighed, Cecile understood it was because she was thinking again about the great blot on the history of those years, about the dozens of names that had been talked over and the double carriage that still stood in the basement covered with plastic wrap.

This was not the time for such talk, if ever there was a right time for useless mourning. "Come on," she said, "they're already at the table."

At the head, side by side, sturdy and steady as any old couple, sat bride and groom, these two who had become a couple only half an hour ago. Now Peter and I, thought Cecile, were no doubt the most flustered couple in history. I was in a fog, while Peter's face was so hot that he might have just returned from a ten-mile hike.

There was, naturally, a sameness about these wedding parties, especially at this kind of table where you were bound to find yourself making conversation with total strangers so that they would not feel excluded by the others who knew one another. The strangers here at Cecile's end were people from Country Day: new faculty members, very young, along with the recently retired Dr. Griffin, very old. Luckily, their conversations were all interesting.

But then, and also luckily for her, Cecile found most people's conversations, indeed their very lives, most interesting. If she had had the necessary talent, she often reflected, she would have attempted to write a novel. For in her daily experience, from the poor and sick at the hospital's social service department to the suburban ladies who were her chief contacts around and in Cagney Falls, there was a rich variety of human character, enough for an endless series of novels.

She was also a good listener, full of curiosity and quite content in certain moods to sit and contemplate the scene. The action here this afternoon was lively. People interrupted their eating and drinking to get up and dance. They visited other tables to give a greeting and were visited in turn. Above all, they talked. Occasionally she recognized Peter's voice in the midst of the crisscross chatter at the other end of the table. Lester and he were being very earnest about something; they were evidently agreeing with each other, which was nice to know because so often among couples a pair of good friends would find that their husbands did not like each other. Peter and Larry, for example, were less compatible than she would have liked; it was not that there was any disapproval between them, but merely that they were too different from each other.

Cecile's glance moved across the table to where Larry and Amanda were seated next to Alfred Cole. Larry was intently listening to Alfred and to Amos, across from him, who were discussing their experiences in World War II. Amanda was especially quiet. But all she ever had to do was to sit still and wait for everyone's eyes to turn to her, for eventually everyone's did; even those of the old retired headmaster were drawn to that pale crown of hair and that piquant face.

"True," Alfred was saying, "nobody who wasn't there can ever understand. I was in a tank in the first wave on D-Day, and no matter how excellent the movie or the book may be, it can't begin to approach the reality."

"You were down there in the muck and blood," Amos said, "and I was a couple of thousand feet up, but we had blood up there, too. On my eleventh mission over Germany—God, I'll never forget that mission—I was standing next to the flight engineer, nice young guy from Pawtucket, Rhode Island—flak took his head off. I got some scratches, a few still bother me, but I still sometimes dream about that death."

Alfred nodded. "I know. On the fourth day in Normandy, we'd already reached a couple of miles inland. There was a village, deserted except for some dogs and cats, where we stopped in an empty barn. Somebody said, 'There ought to be some food around here, maybe in that shop down the street, some eggs or cheese or something.' So I said I'd go see, and I went, and I was coming back with a bag of stuff, ripe peaches were in it I remember, and when I saw the barn, I saw it had taken a hit. It was gone, and all the guys with it."

"We were lucky ones," Amos said. "We went through it, got home, and kept on being lucky. We've had a good life, you and I, sitting here in good health with all this happiness around us."

Now he is going to get emotional, Cecile thought with affection, as he always does when the war is the subject. And sure enough, Amos was reaching across the table to shake Alfred's hand.

"We ought to see more of each other, Alfred. I know we say that every time we meet, but somehow time passes, we're both busy, and we don't do it. Do you still play tennis?"

"Not as often as I'd like to, or as I should."

"Then come on out to us and play. I keep the court in shape, and it's a pity it's so little used. We're only half an hour's drive past the bridge at Lane Avenue."

Rarely, almost never, did Cecile hear any mention of Lane Avenue and the bridge, so it brought now a nasty little shock such as she always felt whenever the car passed there on the way to her old home. It was exasperating that nature should play such tricks, retaining in your memory against your will some ugly, senseless thing that you wanted to forget.

Larry, who had been paying close attention to the two men, now remarked that Alfred Cole was the lawyer you wanted whenever you had a real problem.

"I heard that from everybody when I started to work, especially from my father. He's a great admirer of yours, Mr. Cole."

"Hey, Larry, now that your sister's married to my son, you certainly don't have to 'Mister' me anymore, do you?"

Larry replied gallantly, "Okay, Alfred, it will be my pleasure."

"By the way, where is your father? Why isn't he sitting with the bride and groom?"

"He's over there, with some relatives."

At two tables' distance sat Lawrence Balsan, presiding over an array of gray and bald heads.

"Six of those folks came from Vancouver," Larry explained. "They're my mother's Canadian cousins, and we haven't seen them in years. But they decided to come for Ella—that was our mother's name—for Ella's daughter's wedding."

Turning to illustrate, he caught his father's eye. When they waved to each other, Lawrence stood up at once and came over to Norma. At that moment the orchestra, which had been silent for a while, began again to play, and he seized the bride by the shoulders, kissed her, and whirled her away.

"I'm taking your wife, Lester," he said. "Go get yourself another girl to dance with."

And so the dancing began. It would last awhile, as it always did, to provide a welcome gap between the main course and the cutting of the wedding cake. On the day they had all shopped for her dress, Norma had mentioned to Amanda and Cecile that there would be real music and romantic dancing, with "no tom-tom beat or jigging around by yourself." Cecile was just telling this to Peter as Amanda passed, dancing with Mr. Balsan. What a striking couple! she thought.

"You shouldn't have asked me," Amanda wailed. "What are you thinking of?"

"For God's sake, people can hear you."

"I wasn't loud. I only cried under my breath. Do let me go. I want to sit down."

"What, sit there alone at the table? Or better yet, should you and I sit there together? What are *you* thinking of? Now smile, will you? We're having a jolly conversation, we're dancing, having a good time. Smile!"

"All right. I'm sorry. I'll be okay. But it hurts so much."

"Yes. Try to think of something else."

"I'm not able to."

But she was. And every single thing that she did think of only increased the palpitation of her heart, the lump in her throat, and the sting of all the tears suppressed in back of her lids. There was the remembrance of Cecile's wedding and the sight of her right now, dancing with Peter. Most probably they, too, were talking about it; she had tilted her face up toward his, and he was kissing her neck. Five years ago, it was, and he still did that, and she still wanted him to.

"Think about Norma, your best friend, and how wonderful this is."

Yes, it is wonderful, because a blind man would know that she has gotten the man who is exactly right for her, the kind of man she needed.

"She's got a man to suit your specifications, L.B. She's married up, to the son of one of the most prominent real estate lawyers in the city."

"Don't be bitter, Amanda. And do keep smiling. People notice things."

"How can I help being bitter? I'm in your arms, where I want to be and have no right to be."

Tonight Norma would be with Lester in a wide bed at a hotel. Tomorrow they would be in Greece, in sunshine together, climbing a hill or lying on the sand, talking about the future, perhaps about that house they've been considering. For her, Amanda, there had been only that mockery of a honeymoon, that total disappointment, and now an empty, drab unknown.

"Is this music ever going to end? I need to sit down, L.B. You shouldn't have asked—"

"I asked you because Larry told me to. He thought it looked strange that I had danced with every woman at your table except you."

There was no answer to that.

"I wish we could go someplace together and stay forever," he murmured. "I wish I could have a clear conscience."

"Don't, L.B. I'll cry, I tell you, I can't help it."

"Don't cling. You're too close to me. And smile, I tell you again, we're at a wedding."

"As if I don't know where we are."

When she raised her face to show him her proper, dutiful smile, she saw behind his equally proper expression a tender concern.

"How do you feel about us?" he asked. "That we ought to stop?"

"That we ought to stop? Of course."

"But can we do it? Can you?"

Sorrowing, Amanda shook her head.

"It's wrong, it's wicked, but it's the way it is. I keep reminding myself that no one is being hurt, and you must do the same. We love each other and we can't help it."

CHAPTER SIXTEEN

S hortly before noon, Cecile came home. When she reached the door of Peter's workroom, he looked up from the table.

"Nothing," she said.

"What did the doctor say?"

"Nothing. What can he say? Oh, yes— to be patient."

It had been almost three years since the miscarriage. She stood there, all her muscles gone loose as if it were too much trouble to raise a leg and take a step, even too much trouble to move her lips and talk.

"Well, that's true," Peter said. "Being patient may be just the thing to bring it about, so I've very often heard. Or we could give up and adopt."

"I want our own, Peter," she said brusquely.

He looked down and drew a line on the drafting board.

"Peter?"

"Yes, dear?"

"Are you as terribly upset about this as I am?"

He sighed. "Not being a woman, I suppose my feelings may be different from yours. Yes, I'm disappointed, but I'm not going to devote the rest of our lives to the disappointment. We have each other. And if you ever finally decide you want to adopt—and you may want to— we'll do it."

The gentle tone of his voice and the pity in his eyes distressed her. What was she doing to him, spreading the pall of her sadness over them both?

"Every time I'm like this, I'm sorry," she said, making a quick apology. "I hope I don't do it too often. Do I? It's really only when I go to the doctor and come away empty."

"You've no need to explain yourself. No, you're never a complainer, and I understand."

"Thank you," she said. Planting a kiss somewhere between his cheek and his ear, she leaned over his shoulder. "I swear I think you've come to love this project, and I'm sure you only took it originally to please my father."

"Well, there was more to it than that. But during these last few months I have to admit this work has actually filled my mind, here and at the office. I turned down two jobs this month so I could spend more time on this."

"I woke up after eleven last night when I missed you in bed. Then I looked down the stairs and saw the light still on in this room, so I didn't disturb you."

"Genius at work, hey? Funny, I'm no landscape architect and I haven't the least idea what one will do here, but still I have my own mental vision of trees on the inner side of the pedestrian paths, shading the walkers without affecting the drivers' vision on the roads."

"I don't think I've ever seen anything like this design anywhere, the spokes of the wheel going out to the rim, to the river, the houses on Lane Avenue, and way out to the bird sanctuary. And you've got the circles inside the terminal building, those beautiful round murals over the doorways—no, I could swear that this whole work stands by itself. When do you think you'll be finished?"

"About a year, or a year and a half. The business end, the syndicate, won't be ready much before then anyway, Amos says. Hey, aren't your three musketeers coming to lunch today?"

"Not until one o'clock. Amanda works half a day."

"Well, I'll be leaving soon after I put all this stuff away. I'm meeting some people who want to remodel an 1890's barn out in Jefferson. I'll be back about five, I guess, time to take my girl out to dinner. Hey, give me a kiss, not on the ear this time."

Amanda took her coat off in the vestibule. "These miserable fall rains," she said. "Aren't you lucky to have a place for wet coats? In my house you step right into the living room with your wet coats and boots."

"Don't complain," Norma said. "Your house is half again as big as our bungalow."

"But you wanted a bungalow," Amanda retorted.

"Come in. Lunch is waiting, a hot one to make up for the weather."

Cecile soothed. It seemed to her that there was always

a vague animosity between these two, a carping tendency to snap at innocent remarks. She wondered whether it harked back to that old business of Amanda's extravagance and Norma's protectiveness toward her brother.

"I always say this place should be photographed for a decorator's magazine," Amanda remarked.

In a way, the remark was discomfiting to Cecile; it almost sounded as if she, Cecile, was in the habit of making a special display of her possessions.

"Through no effort of mine," she said, which was of course not quite true. Everything in the dining room, except for the asters in the centerpiece, was inherited; everyone knew that the way you combine things is what matters. The handsome chairs, which had been covered in a fusty brocade, were now covered in a soft green bird print, and the matching brocade draperies had been replaced by white curtains with tiebacks of the bird print. "Everything here is ancient," she repeated, "from some dead relative's house."

"No one-upmanship from you, Cele," said Norma. "I, too, have been offered my choice of anything I want at home. Any old treasure that I want, because my father wants to move to someplace smaller now that I'm gone."

At the thought of the dark, elephantine bulk of the Balsan furnishings, she laughed, and the others could not help but laugh with her. Norma was cultivating a humorous streak that no one had known she possessed.

"I love your new place," Cecile said then. "You might not expect me to like your modern furniture because I'm not a fan of the modern, but the truth is that I like yours very much. Even though it's not for Peter and me, it's right for Lester and you and I admire it, especially with all your wonderful books and prints to warm it up. It looks as if you've lived there for years."

"I'm surprised you bought a house with only two bedrooms," said Amanda. "What will you do when you have a family?"

Norma answered promptly, "We're not going to have a family."

Cecile was astonished. "What do you mean?"

"What I said. We don't want any children. We don't believe people should have them unless they really, really want them. We don't. And if you don't want any, it's wrong to bring them into the world." An odd, unpleasant thought, an old thought, ran through her head: *Especially if you have a girl with legs like mine.* "At Country Day we're surrounded by children, or at least Lester is now, and he loves it. They're family enough. And in between working on my book and my translations, I tutor, as you know."

"Still, it's hard for me to understand," Cecile said wistfully.

"Not for me," Amanda asserted. "I'd just as soon not have any. I like my work, like being out in the world every day. Believe me, I can see and hear remarkable things every day instead of being shut up in a house."

Norma said sharply, "That may be for you, but I hardly think Larry sees it that way."

Amanda shrugged, and there was an abrupt though subtle change of atmosphere at the table. It seemed that what was all right for Norma was not all right for Amanda.

We never used to have this swiping, thought Cecile for the second time that day.

"Shall I heat some more rolls?" she asked.

Amanda said quickly, "I hope you're having a bit of encouragement, Cele."

That was one thing about Amanda; she was sensitive to other people's feelings; it was as if she had seen inside Cecile's head. And Cecile told her so.

"You do understand. Without having my wants, you feel them. No, there's no change. There are all kinds of things, pills and whatnot. You know. You read the papers."

"Be careful what you do, and don't have sextuplets," Amanda teased.

"Believe it or not, I wouldn't mind."

The sorry little remark seemed to echo in the room. And Cecile, aware of it, said brightly, "I see you have a sale sign in your shop window, Amanda."

"It's nothing. It's silly. We've only a few summer pieces left over—after all, this is fall, and winter things are coming in. Mrs. Lyons wanted the sign and she's the boss until she retires. Then we'll see . . . Oh, let me tell you something really wild. The things I hear—or rather that Dolly hears. People seem to confide the craziest things in her, not me! You want to hear the latest? It's about this woman—she lives in Cagney Falls, so I won't spread her name—but she has had five husbands, and the last one, you won't believe—"

Amanda related the absurd story until they were all choking with laughter.

Like magic, the atmosphere changes when she's in a room, thought Cecile, and was sorry when, soon after lunch, Amanda left, pleading a doctor's appointment.

"It's only for my annual checkup, but I forgot all about the lunch when I made it, and it's too late to change it. So thanks, Cele dear, and kiss Peter for me. See you soon."

"I felt for a while recently," Cecile remarked when Amanda had left, "that she was a trifle melancholy. But today she seemed to be her own lively self again."

"Yes, I have seen some changes back and forth."

"I see one in you, too, if you don't mind my saying so."

"What do you see?"

"Oh, nothing fundamental. You're still a walking encyclopedia, but—well, but you never talk about your legs anymore. Is that Lester's work, by any chance?"

"Smart girl. Yes, it's all his work, that and more."

"I'm so happy for you, Norma. For you, and for Amanda, too. Everything has turned out so well for you both. When we were in those rooms above the quadrangle, could we ever have imagined being where we all are today?"

Across the street from the post office was a pocket park with benches set among evergreens. The rain had stopped, but the benches were still damp; nevertheless, Amanda, drawing her raincoat tight around herself, sat down.

Alongside the post office was a short row of stores, a stationery, a pharmacy, a convenience store, and a filling station. For a while she sat and watched the activity, although there was not much. Cars entered the filling station, were serviced, and departed. A woman took her small, hairy dog, wearing a pink leash and collar, into the stationery store. Three small boys came out of the convenience store, each one holding a double-dip ice-cream cone. And all of these received Amanda's undivided attention, as though she were about to write about them or to paint them.

Eventually, she would have to get up and leave, or somebody would assume that there was something wrong and that she needed help. It happened that she did need it. If she could have called or run to her mother, she would have done so. Young soldiers, fighting men and brave, when they are wounded or terrified, are often known to cry out for their mothers: *Mother, Mother, help me.*

So she sat, afraid to move and not quite sure anyway where to go. The doctor's friendly, fatherly chuckle was still sounding in her ears. Imagine that! He had chuckled! Halfway through a sentence, he had actually chuckled.

"You'll have something nice to tell your husband this evening, Mrs. Balsan. By next April, there'll be three of you. An April Fools' baby. Not as good as a New Year's baby because they get their names in the paper. But good all the same."

He had probably thought he was being humorous. Obviously he hadn't been noticing or understanding what was happening to her.

"I thought," she had said, "that those tests people do at home aren't always accurate. That's why I came to you."

"Well, relax. There's no doubt about it. You're well into the second month." Suddenly he was in a hurry, there being at least six women with enormous bellies in the waiting room. "Outside at the desk they'll give you a list of instructions and an appointment for next month. Congratulations, Mrs. Balsan."

In her handbag there was a small notebook with an attached pen. She took it out, held the pen poised and struggled with words. So much depended, as it often does, on the words one uses, whether they are heavy and ominous, striking fear into the listener, or whether they are spoken by a person who renounces doom, sees the glass half full, and is in charge of a situation. But how in the name of Heaven could anyone call this glass half full, when it was empty?

Also in the handbag there was a cell phone. With a shaking hand, she pressed L.B.'s number, praying to reach him in his car. There was no answer.

Half an hour, she thought. I'll try him again in half an hour. In the meantime I must stabilize myself, watch the life in the little street, speculate about the passersby, and keep my sanity. Remember the people whom Cecile describes, how dreadful are their troubles and how brave they often are. Take that old woman going into the dry cleaner's; all crippled with osteoporosis, she must look at herself in the mirror and wonder how she had ever come to deserve this. Or take that battered car driving out of the gas station. You'd be afraid to take it on the highway for fear it might break down. You had to be in desperate straits to risk your life in a wreck like that.

Again she tried L.B.'s number, and reaching him this time, heard her voice crack. Make it short, then.

"I need to see you today. Can you get there by four?"

"Today? It's impossible. I'm up to my ears. No, I can't."

"You have to," she said.

"What? Talk louder, I can hardly hear you."

"I said, 'You have to.' It's very important, very serious."

"Amanda, I can't. It's only three days till Saturday—"

"Oh, please. Oh, please." With that she began to cry, and hung up.

He was there ahead of her. When he helped remove her raincoat, he felt her trembling and was angry.

"What is it? Talk. Anyone sick? Have you been in an accident? What is it? What's the mystery? Hanging up like that, crying. You frightened the life out of me! What was I to think?"

She sank into a chair, holding her head in her hands. "Don't be angry at me, L.B."

"I'm not, really, I'm just reacting to my terror. Your tears—what's wrong?"

"I'm pregnant," she said softly.

"You are? Oh, for God's sake." He sighed. "Oh, for God's sake. But don't cry like that," he whispered, stroking her bent head. "Ah, don't, don't. Ah, poor sweet Amanda! It's not the absolutely worst thing in the world. I know you don't want it, but really it's not the worst thing."

Large tears broke loose and rolled down her cheeks. "You don't understand," she wept. "It's yours." She raised her head and looked into his eyes.

He stared at her. "How the hell can you be sure of that?" he demanded, he who almost never swore.

"Don't you think I know how to count?"

L.B. was too stunned to reply. He simply stood in front of her and waited, still staring.

"He's had the flu off and on, and anyway, I try to avoid"—she sobbed, wiped her eyes on her sleeve, and gulped out the rest—"to avoid—it makes him angry, but anyway, we go for weeks with no—so I know it isn't possible," she finished.

"Does anyone—I mean, will anyone else know that?"

"You mean, will he know? The answer is absolutely not. But I know. God help me, I do. There's no doubt."

"Are you sure?"

"Yes. No chance I'm wrong."

"I'm trying to think—what happened? How? We did everything right—"

"Nothing's a hundred percent sure, you know that."

L.B. groaned. Now it was he who sat holding his head in his hands. The silence was smothering. She had a sudden vision of being in a tunnel sealed at the ends with no way out.

The alarm clock rattled and struck the hour. Thirty minutes had already passed when she raised her pleading eyes to L.B. "I don't know what I'm going to do. What am I—what are we—going to do?"

More minutes passed before there was any answer. At last L.B. got up and knelt at her feet.

"Listen to me," he said, almost whispering. "It's a damned ugly thing, but it's not the worst thing. I thought when I heard you crying over the telephone—I don't know what I thought. I don't know what I'd do if anything happened to you. Forgive me for being impatient when you came in. I'm sorry. I apologize. Please understand and forgive me."

"But what are we going to do?" she insisted.

"We'll do nothing. Remember the case that was in the

papers a while ago? You were the one who told me about it, that they had been in love for fifteen years."

"She didn't get pregnant, L.B. What am I going to do?" she repeated, imploring him.

"Nothing. You'll get through this in the usual way, and nobody will ever know. That's all we can do."

Although he spoke calmly and logically, she was not fooled. When he rose from his knees, he went to the window and, in his usual contemplative pose, stood there with his hands in his pockets. He had not given way to any emotion, no recriminations, no lamentations; all were held back in control. "Head over heart," as Norma so often liked to say. Yes, he would use his head now because he was strong and able to, but she knew that his heart was stricken. She knew that he was seeing his son's face before him, and that he despised himself.

Rising, she touched his shoulders and murmured, "I'm sick, too."

He touched her cheeks. "You're all red from crying. I'll get some cold water."

Tenderly, he pressed a cold cloth to her eyes and, as tenderly, spoke. "We'll manage, Amanda. Don't I always say to you that as long as nobody knows, nobody will be hurt? That's the important thing. Only keep remembering that. Now we need to drive home."

"I'm not sure I can do it. I'm still shaking. Do you realize what I'll have to do when I get there? How am I going to get the words out and pretend to be happy?"

"Give yourself a rest and wait till tomorrow. Now you're going to follow me. I'll drive very slowly and watch you in the rearview mirror. You'll do all right, darling. You will. We'll both do all right because we have to. Just keep remembering that. We have to."

The night passed. Amanda slept, probably, she thought, because of exhaustion; she had been beaten down. The day at work passed until about three o'clock in the afternoon, when suddenly the cheerful voice, the upbeat manner, and the fortitude collapsed.

Dolly noticed it. "You look sick," she said. "You've got no color in your face. I hope you're not coming down with something."

"I don't know. I feel as if I might be."

A totally bizarre thought came when she looked at Dolly. What if she were suddenly to blurt out, "Dolly, help me," and then tell the whole story? Dolly would stand there with her eyes popped open and her mouth dropped open. Dolly, who made no secret of what so many people, although not all, would call her "raggedy" life—roaming from one man to the next—yes, even good-natured, easy-living Dolly would be shocked.

So she went home, although not to bed but to the kitchen, where in a frenzy of nerves she kept herself busy preparing a dinner fit for a holiday celebration. If she were not doing that she would need to keep running around the block, she thought. She thought too that perhaps, if she were to postpone telling Larry for a few more days, she might be better pulled together. Then she corrected herself: Postponement was nothing but cowardice.

"What's the reason for the feast?" Larry inquired, wrinkling his nose at the scents of gravy in the roasting pan and pie in the oven.

"There was nothing much doing in the shop, so I left early, and when I walked into the kitchen, I suddenly became inspired."

"Well, it's a good thing you're not inspired like this every day, or I'd soon be a tub. But right now I'm not going to think about that. I'm going to eat."

He enjoyed his food. If things were different, if she were different, if those *ifs* were not what they were, it would have been a pleasure to see his enjoyment. Between mouthfuls he talked, complimenting the biscuits and describing an encounter with an eccentric customer.

Part of Amanda listened to him and made appropriate responses. Part of her relived yesterday's luncheon meeting of the three musketeers. How far they had come from the days of their innocence, when they had felt themselves already so old and wise! Now Cecile longed for a child that perhaps she was not destined to have; Norma had made a flat decision never to have one, while she, Amanda, had lived recklessly . . .

From where she sat, it was possible to glimpse in the living room a small, round table cluttered with photographs of those who were part of her years: the family on the front porch at home, herself as a child, Larry as a Little Leaguer, the three musketeers in cap and gown, and herself in the long white dress, standing with Larry next to their wedding cake in that frostbitten honeymoon lodge.

And she cried out inwardly, Ah, Amanda, act your age! *Face the music,* they say. *Be a man,* they say. In your case, *Be a woman.* Go ahead.

She interrupted him. "Larry, I have some news. I'm pregnant."

"You're what?"

He jumped up. His fork clattered on the plate. His chair overturned and clattered.

"You're sure? When did you find out? Why didn't you tell me right away?" He raced around the table to hug and kiss her, cheeks, lips, neck, and hands, in a frenzy of excitement.

"You sure? When did you find out?" he repeated.

"Today. I saw the doctor and came right home," she lied, and lied again. "I made a special dinner to celebrate."

"Oh, my lord!" he cried. "I've just won the ten-million-dollar lottery. I've been elected president. I'm on a rocket trip to Mars. When is it going to be?"

"April."

"My lord!" he repeated. "And we weren't even trying! I've had the flu one week off and one week on practically all the darn winter, and you've been working hard, not feeling tiptop—it goes to show you, doesn't it? But you're feeling all right? Everything's fine?"

"Everything's fine." She smiled. Was it not a miracle that she was able to? Some good fairy must be propping her up.

"Are you sure you're feeling all right? You're so quiet."

"I guess I'm just stunned," she answered, still smiling.

Larry glanced at his watch. "Hey, I've got to call Dad and Norma."

"Let your father enjoy his evening in peace. You can tell him at work tomorrow."

"You think it'll disturb his peace to hear that he's going to be a grandfather for the first time? He'll burst his buttons, he'll be so proud!" Larry moved to the telephone and stopped. "But what am I thinking of? You should have the first turn. Call your folks. Then I'll go."

"Thanks, but I'll call my mother tomorrow when everyone's left for work and we can have a long talk. We do it a lot anyway, as you can see from the telephone bills."

"You're sure?"

"Sure. You make your calls while I clean up."

"No, no. You did all the cooking and I'll do the cleaning up. You just sit down and rest."

There was no use arguing with him, because she would not win. Obviously, he was going to treat her like an invalid or a princess for the rest of her term. So without further speech, she would simply do what she wanted, and what she wanted now was not to overhear his telephone call. Alone in the kitchen, she closed the door.

A few minutes later he opened it and called in. "My father was stunned. I could tell because he barely said a word."

"He didn't say anything?"

"Oh, surprise and congratulations, of course. You know how he is. He never says very much, but I could tell he was happy. Really, really happy. And Norma was thrilled. She's so different. Now let me scrub that roasting pan. It takes elbow grease. You can put the dishes in the dishwasher if you insist on doing something."

"Larry, you're being quite silly. Very dear, but silly. I'm not sick, and I'm not a queen."

"You're my queen. And in there," he said, patting her stomach, "is the heir to the kingdom."

Ah, Larry, poor Larry! She wanted to weep for him, and could not.

"I get a kick out of seeing you so happy about the news," Lester said, as he came back for the second time into the room where Norma was working on the next edition of her Latin reader. "I never saw you rejoice over anything the way you're doing now."

He was also, Norma saw, somewhat puzzled. His expression seemed to be asking in a nice way what all the fuss was about. Most people who wanted children did, after all, have them without much trouble. So it really wasn't such a remarkable happening, was it?

No, it wasn't. But in her particular circumstances, which she would have liked to describe to him and never would, this was an exquisite relief. A baby anticipated with such joy as Larry was so clearly feeling is the best possible evidence that the couple is a solid unit. So she reasoned.

"I can't wait to see Larry's face," she said. "He's been wanting this for so long. Not that he ever said so directly, but I could tell from hints and by the way he behaved with little children."

The cloud that had been hovering above her since that memorable afternoon in the school's theater building was now dispelled for good. True, through a combination of her own reasoning powers and Lester's excellent advice about the tricks one's eyes can play, the cloud had faded to a shred. Yet, she had to admit that at rare moments when the wind shifted, it had reappeared in a clear sky and lurked there, a small, dark menace on the horizon.

All that remained to trouble her now was a quiver of

shame as she recalled her own suspicions, so nasty, dirty, and obscene. Well, at least nobody else knew about them, and now she simply would toss them into a refuse heap where they belonged.

Outside on Lane Avenue trucks ground by. Heat smelling of gasoline poured through the open window. Completely dressed, without desire or energy of any kind, Amanda and L.B. lay on the dusty couch. For many minutes past they had not spoken.

After a while L.B. asked, or said, for it was impossible to tell whether he was making a statement or asking a question, "So he is happy."

"Very."

"Yes, he's been going around the office these last few days talking about it. I go to the other office. I stay away as much as I can. I can't look at him."

"*You* can't? What about me? I have to do a lot more than look, you know."

"I do know. Does he never question your dates? You said you so rarely—"

"No, never. Why would he not trust me? Anyway, it's the woman who keeps count of herself."

She gazed about the room, the safe haven for which the world outside and time itself, every hour apart from here, had existed only as a framework. All golden it had been, beautiful and beloved as a summer afternoon in the country. Would it, could it ever be restored?

This guilt that she bore around her neck, this albatross, was hooked and fastened so tightly that it would never be removed. It was going to be with her for the next seven months, and after that, for the rest of her life.

In one way she wished the seven months would pass quickly, while in another, she wanted them not to come to an end. The physical presence of a child—of this child, poor innocent being—was going to be a daily, an hourly reminder that it had arrived unwanted by its mother.

How was she to love it, or even look at it, without feeling that way? How was she to care for it without ever letting it sense that there was something unnatural in its mother's way of caring? For no matter how intense the effort she might make, surely she would never be like other mothers, who hug and kiss and laugh and who have earnest discussions about which parent's mouth and eyes the baby has inherited.

Yesterday there had come a fancy card, signed by all her family at home including Lorena's vagabond, now-and-then husband, congratulating them on the news. Last week her mother, over the telephone, had half sadly and half humorously remarked on the difference between her two sons-in-law: The one kept producing babies without wanting them, and the other, wanting them, had taken years to get one.

After hanging up, Amanda had sat down and given way to more miserable reflections about families and complications. L.B. would naturally be given a name such as "Grandpa," "Grand-daddy," or "Gramp." How would they two, sitting in the same room, even be able to look at each other?

"Are you going to keep your job, or what?" he asked now.

"I'm going to work right up till the end, and as soon as I can, start again after it's over. I'd go crazy otherwise. As it is," she said bitterly, "I may go crazy anyway."

He pressed her hand. "You won't. You're too strong." And then, as if in pain, he cried out, "I'm so sorry. You can't know how sorry I am. What have I done to you?"

"Given me the best years of my life, L.B."

"I don't mean that. I mean this business."

"How can this be your fault? Darling, there's never a one-hundred-percent guarantee."

"The last thing I'd ever do is cause you any pain. Or cause Larry any, either."

In two years they had used his name no more than a dozen times. Always they had circled about to avoid it, finding another way to say whatever had to be said.

In myriad small ways, everything had changed and would continue to do so. The contacts that they two had avoided had already begun: Nothing would do, Norma had insisted, but that L.B. take his two offspring and their respective spouses to a gala dinner in celebration of the new event. Once there they had not dared to meet each other's eyes. Amanda had spent the time talking earnestly to Lester, and L.B. had managed to concentrate on Norma. After the child arrived, there would be more of these forced meetings; was Larry's father not to play his expected loving part in the life of the child?

And this room, this safe haven, what of it? Were they to play their parts at a two-year-old's birthday party on Tuesday and then meet here on Wednesday?

As if there were someone who might overhear, L.B. whispered. "I see your tears. Listen, it's all too sudden and too soon for any clear thinking. We simply have to remember what we've been saying all along, that no one will be hurt, and we will manage."

"Hold me. Comfort me," she whispered back.

"Always. I'll always comfort you. I love you so, Amanda."

In spite of the heat and in spite of the noise from the street, she closed her eyes, wanting and needing to float away in a familiar peace. Quietly, they lay, with their hands clasped.

Quite suddenly then, a terrible foreboding disturbed Amanda's peace: *You are going to be punished* . . . But because she loved him, she did not tell him.

CHAPTER SEVENTEEN

Amanda watched snowflakes drift past the hospital window. It was the beginning of spring, and the belated snow was a strange way to welcome Stevie Balsan into the world. It seemed as if even before this morning, when for the first time a doctor had addressed her cheerily as "Mother," she had been living in a sort of waking dream.

Pretty soon her mother would come on one of her cheerful visits. You would think she'd be blasé about grandbabies by now, having had so many of them. But no, she declared, each one is different from the rest, born of different parents, in differing circumstances.

Differing circumstances.

Now there would be an excuse not to pay the visit to Mississippi that Dad had been asking for—with a new job and a raise he had been able to straighten out the house a bit. But even so, they would not expect people to travel with a new baby.

Her hand went to her stomach, as if the hand were trying to test whether it was really flat again. It was, or nearly so. The former occupant of the space was in the nursery down the hall, calmly asleep. She had awakened early with a start and plunged at once into a frightening conflict of emotions, chief of which was a frank dread when she realized that they would shortly be bringing him to her.

What kind of a monster was she? She had no feeling for the child! What did that mean? Everything was remote; the snow, the voices in the corridor, the white bed, and the baby—*her* baby—wrapped in a blue blanket. Stevie. The name was Larry's choice. Wasn't there some funny expression: Even Steven? Her head was behaving strangely.

"Let me feel," he had said one evening a few months ago. It was he who had first observed what is called "life," the child's first thrusting of little arms and legs within the mother. Yes, it was the miracle that everyone said it was. Yet to Amanda it was something else, too: fear. What kind of a monster was she?

She thought now of all those weeks during which Larry had been kindness itself and full of cheer. "Most women feel sick in the morning at the beginning. It must be miserable, but at least you know it's part of the game."

He was a mine of information, some of it accurate, and much of it not. Most women did not go through as many months of nausea as she had endured. But then most women did not have a body as heavy with fear as was hers.

"I've heard that something sweet, some jam on toast before you get out of bed, will help."

That piece of advice at least did help. And so early every morning for many, many mornings, she had lain flat until Larry should appear with the plate of toast and jam. It would have been so much easier if he had been mean to her.

The most unexpected people, especially as the winter progressed, had shown their friendly interest in this birth. It had been astonishing and unsettling to see so much of it. A neighbor had knitted a carriage cover. People gave advice about buying the right high chair and crib, or going to the right pediatrician. Cecile, who had received enough gifts for three pairs of twins, had already parted with luxuries: a satin quilt, a CD player for the nursery, and a silver mug. Norma had bought a collection of books, children's classics, to be read to him, and a size-two snowsuit on which his name was being embroidered. With affectionate laughter, she had reported that "Dad is giving money, a big, fat check, too. He said he had no idea what to buy for babies, and I believe him."

Oh, he knew very well what to buy for anybody on any occasion, only not for this particular baby, born as it was, born like every human being, helpless and without fault! What were they to tell him? The question was absurd because the answer was plain: nothing. As long as you or he may live, he must know nothing.

To look at his little face, which had not the slightest imperfection, was like looking at a wound. One is filled with pity over a wound, while at the same time one is filled with horror that any human being could have inflicted it upon another. And one looks away.

Once she had told L.B. that she wished they could confess to someone, and he had understood. He always did understand.

When now the telephone rang beside the bed, she felt it was he. It had been ringing all morning, but she had not yet heard from him.

"Are you alone?" he asked cautiously.

With equal caution, she replied, "Yes, I can talk. How are you?"

"I've been somewhat better since I got the news that you're all right. Before that I was an interested spectator who didn't dare show too much interest. Was it awful, darling?"

"Not bad at all. Nothing unusual, they tell me."

"Nothing unusual," L.B. said bitterly.

There was a silence, as if the telephone had gone dead. Then she said, "I can't bear to look at him."

"I don't want to do it, either."

"But you'll have to."

"I know that, too."

"I'm not thinking about us. I'm thinking about him. What kind of a life will he have?"

"A very good one. The best life, at least, that the best of care can give him. The rest only depends on luck, doesn't it? Isn't that true of all of us?"

This resolute optimism was meant to help her, she knew, and so she replied in kind. "I'll think of that next time they bring him to me."

"Think, too, that I am with you. I am with you all the time, every day, all day."

"I already do that."

All she could see from where she sat in the bed was

the blank sky and the unseasonable snow. A sudden loneliness overcame her in spite of her resolve, so that she
could not help but cry it out. "The loneliness is the hard-
est thing. It has been so long for us, L.B."

"You'll be all right. You're very strong, Amanda. I'm
a fairly good judge of people, and I know that you can
weather anything. Let's just take one day at a time. Today you're going to have visitors, Norma told me. She's
coming, and Cecile will come, too, since she works right
downstairs at the hospital. So put on your best smile for
them."

"Why do they have to come? For goodness' sake, I'm
going home tomorrow. I don't want them. I'm not in the
mood."

"Darling, it's not hard to understand why, but you
have to be in the mood, don't you? From now on, both
of us will always have to be."

He was right. It was already noon, and rousing all her
energy, she got up, washed, put on a pink robe, and
forced herself to walk around the room. At the window
she stood to watch the snow. In a book L.B. had given
her, there was a poem with lovely words about "silent
snow, secret snow"; she tried to remember the rest of it,
but was not able to, nor to remember the name of the
poet. Her mind was not functioning clearly. And yet, she
could precisely recall the book's green jacket and the
long-stemmed rose that lay on the table beside it. He had
lain on the couch watching her open the book. Always
her memories returned to him. And she stood there resting her arms on the high sill while the snow fell past. She
was still standing there when the bright sounds of joyous

greetings came from the doorway. Cecile and Norma had arrived together.

"We met by accident in the elevator. Shouldn't you be resting?"

"No, I should be on my feet."

"Your husband," Norma said, "is the limit. He came to our door practically at the crack of dawn with a turkey sandwich for your lunch. He made it himself the way you like it, with whole wheat bread. I was to take it to you today because you will have been up half the night, and you'll be hungry before he gets here later."

"He was up half the night here himself," Amanda said.

"He looked it, all worn out. The funny thing is, you did all the work and you don't look it, does she, Cele?"

"She looks beautiful, the way she always does. We cheated on you. We stopped first at the nursery to get a peek before seeing you. He's adorable."

Put on your best smile, L.B. said.

Amanda smiled. "Oh, they all look alike, round and red like apples."

"No, if you saw as many as I do," Cecile objected, "you'd know that's not true. This baby has a beautiful head, and his nose isn't pug, it's—don't laugh—it's going to be aristocratic."

Norma did laugh. "Aristocratic! That's a good one. But you're right. You really can see that it's chiseled, like his grandfather's. Oh, won't Dad be pleased to hear that!"

"Lucky boy," Cecile said. "God bless him with all these people to love him, a grandfather and all the rest of you. I just left a family downstairs, a broken family. The father left home last week with another woman, and this morning the mother's going home with their third baby."

"Poor little thing," Norma said. "But what's new? It's all luck for every one of us. Yes, lucky Stevie, God bless him as you just said."

Can I blame them? Amanda asked herself. What they're saying is perfectly normal. It's the kind of thing people always say when a child is born.

The sandwich, made with Larry's habitual generosity, was enormous, and an almost untouched pitcher of orange juice remained from breakfast, so she had enough excuse not to talk. It would have taken too great an effort to pick her cautious way through conversation. Slowly she ate and drank, keeping an unfocused gaze upon the snow as it drifted and fell sadly, without purpose, onto the earth.

Now and then, in answer to some question or remark that took no effort to acknowledge, she turned toward the others. In her strange state of mind, and she was aware how strange it was, she seemed to be seeing them in broken segments, as in one of those modernist paintings where features have been deliberately misplaced, or exaggerated, or left out. Norma was a small-shouldered body with huge, anxious eyes and a mass of bulging legs; Cecile was elongated with huge, perfect teeth in a head too small for them . . .

She blinked, grasped the chair's arms, and sat up straighter.

"Are you okay?" asked Norma.

"A little woozy, maybe. I think, maybe."

"You'd better get back into bed. Or at least lie on it," Cecile said quickly. "Here, let me help you."

It was better there with the pillows behind her. Things came back into shape. Norma's eyes were her own. Cecile was wearing her warm Irish tweed overcoat, four seasons old, but still rich looking. Waste not, want not.

"We're going to the nurses' station and ask somebody to take a look at you," Norma said. "Maybe you need something."

"Norma, you worry too much," Amanda protested.

"No, she's right," Cecile said. "This is only your first day, after all."

It had been very good of her to come and see the baby; it must have hurt her terribly, although she would never show it, or maybe not even admit it to herself. She was like a calm ocean with only a few ripples in it now and then. Storms did not brew in Cecile. She would never be where I am now, Amanda thought. Nor would Norma, either, she added as their voices faded away down the hall.

Reality struck Amanda as she stepped through the front door. It was as if a trickster had suddenly jumped out of the hall closet and said, "Boo!"

So here you are, said Reality, with proud husband at your side and new baby sleeping in your arms. Here you are with diapers, bottles, formula, and the rest of the paraphernalia. Here comes your good neighbor Joan with a hot dinner, and your good friend Cecile has left another hot dinner. Your good sister-in-law has stocked your freezer so that you will not have to market or cook for two weeks. There is a pile of unopened baby gifts on the floor. There is a bouquet of white tulips and white narcissi in the living room. This welcome, given what is in your heart, is enough to break your heart.

Joan, who has three children and is expecting another, has advice. "They send you home too early these days, Amanda. You really should go right upstairs and get a long night's sleep in your own bed. You'll probably think that's pampering yourself, active as you are. But it isn't. Take my word for it. You'll be needing all the energy you've got. That seven-and-a-half-pound person you're carrying has as much energy as you have, maybe more. You'll see."

"I'm taking the whole week off," Larry said. "She's going to rest. After that, she'll be on her own. Hey, you haven't had a good look. Pull the blanket back, honey, and show him off."

"Look at his hair!" cried Joan. "I think it's going to be fair like yours, Amanda."

She only wanted to be free of them all, free of their friendliness and their talk. Lightly and cheerfully, she replied, "Hair? It's merely fuzz."

"No, I think he'll be blond. But you know what, Larry? He looks a lot like your father."

"Do you think so? Here, honey, I'll take him up and lay him in the bassinet. Go on upstairs with Norma. Norma, make her lie down. Have you called Dad? Did he know what time we'd be home?"

"He said he'd try to come over this evening."

"Try! What does that mean? He hasn't seen Stevie yet."

"Calm down, Larry. He'll be here."

"You'd think," Norma said as she went upstairs with Amanda, "that Larry had just given birth, wouldn't you? Men really are funny."

Now that Norma's married, Amanda thought, she knows all about men, doesn't she? She thinks she does, poor soul.

Alone again, she lay back on the pillows, staring at the ceiling. Larry had left the newspaper on the night table. Norma had brought a small plate of fruit. Cecile had gone home, and the house was still except for the murmur of voices across the hall where Norma and Larry were tending to the baby. It was he who had listened to all the instructions that the nurses at the hospital had given. And a good thing, too, because they had simply passed through her head and been at once forgotten. There was no space in her head for anything but fear.

After a while when she thought she heard the doorbell, the fear seized her by the throat. She knew who it was before Larry came into the bedroom.

"I just wanted to see whether you were awake, honey. It's Dad. He's coming up to see Stevie, and he'll want to stop in and say hello."

"No, no!" she cried. "I'm only half awake, I'm not dressed—"

"For Pete's sake, you're under the blanket, and it's only family, anyway."

"Larry, I said no. I don't care who it is. Close my door. I just got home, and I want some privacy."

"Okay, okay. It's ridiculous, but I'll tell him another time. He'll understand."

Listen to me, he told me. Take one day at a time.

* * *

Is it possible that she didn't want the child, that it was an accident? Norma wondered on the way home. Her face looked like stone when she walked in. And not to see Dad when he came was really inexcusable, really rude, and one thing I've always said about her is that her manners are perfection. Yes, I wonder.

And later Cecile, at home, was thinking about the lovely baby. Perhaps if I had some marvelous talent, if I could create, as Peter does with his whole mind and heart devoted to the Grand Project—he thinks of it in capital letters—I might not have such painful longings for a baby. To have one of your own is to create the most marvelous— Her thought broke off. I am so envious of Amanda.

Larry was disgruntled. "If I were a healthy woman like you, I would want to breast-feed the baby. Look at Joan next door. She's nursed all three. It's nature's way."

"Joan's a lovely person, but I'm not Joan," Amanda said. "What I want is to go back to work. I'm hardly the only woman who wants to these days."

"I don't know how you can bear to leave him. I can't wait to get home to him every night. He smiled at me when I changed him just now."

Let him think so if it makes him happy. At one month, babies don't smile. Soon, though, he will smile, and I'll want to look away. For why should he smile, my little boy? A sword hangs over his head. I am the one who hung it there. Larry can't bear to leave him, and I can't bear to be with him because he breaks my heart. So dear and innocent! What have I done to him?

Larry complained, "Sometimes I can't make any sense

out of what you do. I told you my father was going to stop in yesterday afternoon. He's so darn busy, I had to lasso him. And when he gets here, he finds the sitter, the kid from down the block, instead of you."

"I'm sorry, but I explained to you that my tooth bothered me and that was the only time the dentist could see me."

"I don't know what Dad thought."

"He didn't think anything. You're super sensitive, Larry."

"It seems to me that you are. You've got the world in a jug. Nice house, loving husband, baby boy, and you act as if you're in a fog. I don't understand it."

"I told you I want to go back to work."

"Well, who says you can't eventually? But right now, you belong here. It costs a fortune, anyway, to get first-class care at home. That's if you can even find somebody."

I have to get out of here, she thought. I can't be cooped up here all day with my guilt. I can't.

"So it's not unusual," the doctor concluded. "You're undergoing a slight postpartum depression. I'll give you a mild prescription, and I'll recommend again that you not stay isolated in the house all day. Get together for walks or a little tea party in the yard with other mothers. Your neighborhood must be loaded with them."

"But will you please tell my husband that I want to go to work? Not a year from now, but now? Please. I need to."

The doctor looked at her. "Is there something else you want to tell me?" he asked gently.

"Thank you, no. Only that I need to go to work."

"I'll tell him," he said, still gently.

He knows there is something really wrong with me, Amanda thought as she left. After a while, unless—unless what?—everybody will know it.

Larry had predicted that it would not be easy to make arrangements, but he had been mistaken. A pleasant young woman, Elfrieda Webb, had been found to take care of Stevie while Amanda was at work, and Mrs. Lyons was happy to have her back.

Now that she was out in the car, it was possible to reach L.B. by telephone. Without having any contact with him, she had been feeling as if she were floating alone on a life raft in mid-ocean. All this she explained to him as, for the first time in months, they met in the familiar room two flights above Lane Avenue. They were sitting side by side in the pair of chairs. She had thought that perhaps, after so long, they would—but no, it was impossible, anyway, so soon after giving birth. So having said all that she could think of to say, she fell silent, and since L.B. was also silent, they simply sat there staring at each other.

Amanda spoke first. "Don't mourn. Now it's my turn to remind you that we love each other and we are not hurting anyone. I feel a little better already, just being in this place with you."

"I hate this place, Amanda, you know I do."

"There isn't any better one for us, is there?"

"That's why I hate it, and hate myself," he said vehemently.

"Yes, I know. Don't you think it's the same for me?

How do you think I feel when I hold that baby? I can't even look at him sometimes. I think—I think, if he ever has to suffer because of what I did—and then I run to pick him up and hold him and cry."

L.B. put his hands over his face. "Oh, my God, my God," he groaned.

She got down on her knees and cradled his head. "Don't, don't," she whispered. "You're the one who told me that we'd get through it."

"That was before I saw him, and Larry holding him with that look on his face. Such joy and pride—oh, my God!"

That simile about the raft on the ocean had meant nothing other than that she depended upon him to guide it. He had always been the stronger of the two. Now he was clinging to her, literally clinging, and she was suddenly very afraid. There was no one; her family, her mother who was so gentle and loving, were out of the question as confidantes or guides. And now L.B., the rock, was giving way.

"I wish you hadn't told me," he murmured.

"Told you what?"

"If I thought he was Larry's, don't you see, we could go on."

"And now we can't go on? Is that really what you're saying?"

"How can we?" he repeated.

She jumped up. "You're saying that it's over, that you and I will forget it all as if it had never been?"

"What do you want me to say? Whatever can we do?"

"We can go on somehow. Haven't you always told me that as long as nobody is hurt, we'll be all right? We can

see each other once a month, or every second month, I
don't care. There's always the telephone in between
times. As long as I know you are there, and that you are
thinking of me."

"I am always thinking of you. But there are always
the others, especially my son."

"Now you think of him? Now? Why not before we—
we became what we are to each other?" She paused for
breath. "Oh, you shouldn't have done this to me, L.B."

"I didn't have to coax you, did I? Be realistic. It happened. It was something both of us wanted."

Her eyes went to the couch on which they had so often
lain together. "What can we do?" she asked, very low.

"The best thing that could happen is for me to go
away."

"And leave me with Larry, when you know what that
means for me?"

"Maybe if I were gone, then you and he—"

"You know very well that can't be! You who know
me, my heart and my soul, as nobody else ever has
known me, how can you even say such a thing?"

"Do you think I want to say it? Look at me. But if
there is no other way, then I have to say it, don't I?"

"If you are serious about this, then I might as well
give up."

"I have to be serious, Amanda. Oh, please."

"I can't believe what I'm hearing, and hearing from
you." In terror and anger, she lost control. And snatching
her handbag, she went to the door. "I'm going. My life is
in shreds. I'm losing my mind. I'm getting in my car and
driving home. With any luck, a truck will hit me and
smash it."

"Where are you going? Sit down. You can't go out this way." L.B. caught her arm, but she wrenched it free. "You drove here in your car? You know you can't do that. If you should be seen—"

"Is that all you care about?" she called back when she was halfway down the stairs. "I was so eager to see you, I hadn't the patience to ride in the bus. I was so eager—"

"Stop!" he cried as they clattered downstairs.

He beat on the car door, but it was already locked, and in a blur of tears she drove away, leaving him almost in tears on the curb.

No doubt each of them knew even then that this was no final break. It lasted, in fact, only until the next morning, when the phone rang in Amanda's car on her way to Cagney Falls.

He had not meant what he said. He had been at a low point, fearful, desperate, and overloaded with guilt. He had clutched at the thought of moving away. And it had been cowardly, he admitted. More than that, it had been impossible, because he loved her. He loved her too much to do it. And therefore it was impossible. Surely she knew that.

And so they would go on as they had been doing, seeing each other whenever they could, no matter how seldom. The simple knowledge that they were still *together*, would that not be enough to sustain them?

When she entered the shop a few minutes after the call, there had been such a change in her that Dolly remarked it.

"Now Amanda looks like herself again," she said, and the seamstress observed that motherhood must be agreeing with her.

* * *

How well motherhood agreed with Amanda was ar-
guable. Surely the little boy had not lived for nine
months within her and left her with no awareness of that
blood-and-bone connection. Yet when she gazed at him
asleep in the crib with his fists curled and his eyelashes
resting on his cheeks, or when she met his curious
scrutiny as she changed his diaper, or when at six months
he sat up and reached for the rattle that was held out to
him, she had an awful feeling that he was a stranger. She
was seeing him through the eyes of pity and horror, as
one would see a lost child abandoned on a public street.

And as if there were some devil at work in the background, Larry kept asking her and everyone who knew
L.B. whether Stevie did not look "exactly like my dad."

"I don't know," she replied one day. "He looks like
himself. He's a beautiful child."

"You always say 'the child,' as if you were talking
about John Doe's baby in the next block. His name is
Steven. Stevie," Larry said crossly.

His moods, since Stevie's birth, had changed. Indeed,
he had rarely had any "moods." Had not his placid, dull
good humor been an irritant to her? But lately, so it
seemed to Amanda, he was given to these small, cranky
reprimands, or else on the other hand, to bursts of eu-
phoria when he walked around the house humming to
himself, or more often, to Stevie, whom he liked to carry
around like a trophy.

He was the father of a son; now he could proudly
measure himself alongside any other man on the street:
prosperous householder and father of a handsome boy.

He wanted to assert himself. It still angered him that Amanda had had her way about working in the shop. Old-fashioned as he might be, he still believed that there was something unnatural about a woman who, without any real need, could choose to leave her baby with somebody else all day.

How could he know that the shop was her savior? It kept her mind busy. It kept her away from Stevie. Nobody could know that the long, long walks she took, pushing the stroller on weekend afternoons when sometimes Larry was not home, had their reasons: One was to quiet her nerves, and the other to avoid having to play with Stevie at home. This way the stroller was in front of her, and she did not see his wisps of new hair, unmistakably curly like her own, or his face, already so like L.B.'s.

How she could have rejoiced in this baby if things had been different! There was such a struggle within her not to love him too much, because—well, because who knew what lay ahead? What punishment waited? She wondered about L.B.'s confidence. Was he really feeling it or was he, for her sake and for Stevie's, only pretending?

Nothing, nothing must ever happen to hurt this little boy of hers, he with his fat little legs, his fat little fingers clasped around his bottle, and his big, serious eyes! Often she imagined that those pretty eyes were asking her a question: *Who am I?* And once, without meaning to, she had given a cry, weeping into her hands while he in his innocence stared at her.

I am walking a tightrope. I am standing on the edge of a cliff where a gale wind may blow me over.

Yet, she thought, to the stranger's gaze we probably

make a fine picture. And apparently they did, because one day when Larry was photographing them on the lawn, an old man out for a walk paused to watch.

"Too beautiful to resist. Frame it," he told Larry. "You're a lucky man."

One framed copy was now in the living room, and the other on Larry's desk at Balsan Real Estate. He had offered another to his father, but L.B. had graciously refused it because, he said, he did not display family pictures in the office. Larry thought that rather odd, especially so for a grandfather who had been so generous with a bank account in Stevie's name, yet almost never came to see him. Didn't Amanda agree?

Well, she thought it was understandable. After all, he was a busy man, and he did have his own life, too.

Like her, L.B. had a hidden life. There was far less pure joy in their relationship than before the baby's birth, and yet it was a deeper relationship; there was less of the body and more of the spirit in it. They comforted each other. These days the room on Lane Avenue was bare, without flowers or gifts or festive picnic basket. Often they lay without speaking until it was time to leave, then embraced and parted. Weeks often passed before they met again.

Months did pass. And before long Stevie Balsan was one year old. On Lane Avenue Amanda was obliged to issue an invitation to the party.

"Larry's going to tell you about it, so I'm warning you in advance. He's invited the cousins, the ones who always come to your Christmas dinners. And of course the next-door neighbors will be there. There's no way you can avoid it."

L.B. groaned. "I can't look at the child. I want to dig a hole in the ground and crawl in."

"You can't avoid it," she repeated. "If only we could go away somewhere!"

" 'If' is a great big word."

"Need it be? Couldn't we? Stevie doesn't need me. He'd be better off without me. I try, oh, God knows, I try. But I'm not going to improve as time goes on and he grows older. I'm going to get worse, and he will feel something without knowing what he's feeling or why. Yes, my poor little boy, he will be happier without me. What am I going to do?" When no answer came, she wrung her hands. "Yes, he would be better off not knowing me. Larry adores him. And Norma does, too. She even likes to baby-sit some evenings. I've told you, she and Lester come over, bring their books and watch Stevie. Oh," she cried, "how can I talk like this? He's my own baby and I love him so. What am I saying? And yet—"

L.B. spoke gently. "You're talking nonsense, darling, and you know it. Don't you know you are?"

"I suppose I do." When she sighed, a gray sadness filled the room. "But enough for today. You have to come to the party. There's no possible excuse that would make any sense."

Larry had arranged it all; the long tables, the rented chairs, and the balloons had been his work that week while Amanda was in the shop at Cagney Falls. Although the day was warm and blue, her mind was a year behind the date, remembering the snow and the sadness in it.

Just yesterday, Stevie had begun to walk. Dressed in a yellow linen suit hand-embroidered with ducks and roosters that Cecile had brought, he trotted bravely across the lawn between the hands of Larry and Amanda. Then, smeared with icing and in the best of humor, he allowed himself to be passed from the lap of one elderly cousin to another.

"Adorable!" they crowed in their delight. "What a beautiful disposition! Is he always like this?"

It was Norma who answered. "Yes, isn't he blessed to be so good-natured? And aren't we blessed to have him? But, Stevie, you haven't given your Grandpa a turn! Here, take him, Dad."

Amanda grew very busy picking up paper napkins and discarded paper cups.

"Oh, leave the stuff. We can clean up later," Larry protested. "Where's the camera? Have you got it, Amanda? We need a picture of Stevie with Dad."

One of the cousins made a suggestion. "Let me take a family picture. Grandpa will hold Stevie with Dad and Mom standing on either side of Grandpa. Let me do it. Everybody says I have a hand with photography. Over here, so you don't face the glare. That's it."

How, thought Amanda, are we going to get through this day? And she glanced at her watch. It was still only two o'clock, and they would all probably stay until four. Larry would encourage them all to stay. Plainly, most of the neighbors had come because of him. He was always the friendly one, while she was Larry Balsan's wife. She felt weak. Voices crisscrossed the lawn, sounding faint and far away.

"Come, Stevie, let's play ball." That was Norma's voice. She had spent the morning showing Stevie how she rolled the ball, which fascinated him.

Bent over the table, Amanda fought the weakness. Busy cleaning up, she did not turn her head.

"You play so well with him, Norma," said one of the cousins, adding with more innocence than tact, "Don't you want one of your own?"

Unfazed, Norma replied, "No. But I could take Stevie," she teased, and everybody laughed.

"Come, see the pretty ball."

A cheap thing, made of felt, striped red, white and blue, it was her family's birthday present. She had a vision of her mother and the *other* grandfather wrapping the package and taking it to the post office, three doors down from the intersection of Church and Main. It was so long since she had seen them, any of them except Mom. Regret surged like a lump into her throat, and she wiped her eyes with the back of her hand.

She had to talk to L.B.! As soon as everyone had departed, she got into her car on the pretext of returning some books to the library. L.B. had not yet gotten home, and she was able to reach him on the car phone.

"Hell, wasn't it?" he said. "Sheer hell."

"Poor Stevie. And poor us for doing this to him."

"I've told you before that Stevie will be all right. Who's going to question his paternity? You're not going to abandon him, and neither is Larry, and what Stevie will never know, what nobody will ever know, won't worry him."

Only once before had L.B. spoken at all brusquely to her. And understanding that this day had been a torture for him, she told him so.

At once he apologized. "Yes, I'll admit it was a torture, and for you, too. Listen, Amanda, dearest girl, I keep telling you that we will weather this. I keep telling you that we must. Don't you hear me? I'll be waiting for you Saturday after next. Can you do it?"

"I don't know what might be going on that day, but it doesn't matter. Nothing, and I mean nothing at all, will ever keep me away."

His confidence was like water to someone who has gone two days without a drink. But she needed to be alone for a while to savor that good drink, so instead of going right home, she drove to the library, there to select a few books at random, and provide an explanation for the extra half hour's absence. Then she drove home.

Stevie, tired out from the day's excitement, was in his crib.

"I put him in early," Larry said. "He was starting to get cranky, and that's rare for him. What a doll he is!"

"He has your disposition," Amanda said, meaning it.

There sat Larry, comfortable at the kitchen table in his sweaty shirt, stained with the mashed carrots that Stevie had had for supper. With a soup spoon, he was eating from a carton of ice cream.

"Left out on the picnic table in the sun," he explained. "Almost the whole quart, too. Very wasteful, so rather than throw it out, I'm eating it. Tastes better when it's soft, though." And he grinned his familiar, childish grin.

It did not fit his other persona, the one in the business suit who put through all those smart deals. Still, she thought, who of us hasn't got several sides? And as expected, she sat down at the table, prepared to keep him company.

She felt compelled to look at him. For the last two

years, she had been warning him that he was putting on too much weight. There was an unmistakable bulge of belly over his belt, and under his chin, a roll of soft flesh. Above his pudgy cheeks his eyes looked small. She had never noticed them until this minute. Definitely, his eyes had grown smaller. A feeling of revulsion caused her to shrink within herself.

"Ahhhh, chocolate chip," he said, smacking his lips.

Such mouth noises were always disgusting. He was clean, very clean, and yet he had such disgusting habits, like sitting on the bed while cutting his toenails and letting the pieces fall onto the rug. It was strange how you could feel kindly toward another human being, and at the same time dread the touch of his body.

"Hot for April," he said. "Remember how it snowed a year ago today?"

Yes, she remembered.

"If we had a swimming pool, I'd go in now, April or not. Skinny-dipping, that's what I'd do. Sound good to you?"

"Oh, yes," she said dutifully.

He stood up, shoving the chair against the table so sharply that everything clattered and tumbled. Then he yawned.

"Since we can't go skinny-dipping, how about a skinny shower together? I'm right in the mood. How about you?"

"Another time," she said. "It's been such a long day."

The yawn, the grin, and the eyes' laughter were instantly wiped away. A hard stare took their place.

"You never want anything I want!" he cried.

"That's not true, Larry. I—"

" 'Not true, Larry!' " he mocked. "How often have I heard that for one reason or another? What is it? You never want *me!* I'm always the one who makes the first move, and then you'll go along unless you can wangle some excuse as you're doing right now. You think I don't see? Look at my eyes. Am I blind?"

She looked. The small eyes were wide now, and glaring with anger. This was an attack, and she had had no time to prepare any defense, so she was able only to respond weakly, "No, no, Larry. No, no."

"Yes, yes! What is it? Am I filthy or diseased or something?"

"No, Larry, listen, you're wrong, I—"

"Have you got another man? Yes, that's it. You've got somebody out there in Cagney Falls. Yes, that's it."

Hold on, hold on, she was saying to herself. *There's the baby. Angry voices in the house can damage even one that young.*

"You're wrong," she said. "There's nothing out in Cagney Falls except a shop and the women who shop in it."

"Can't you see how I feel?" he cried out again. "You're so cool. You're like an ice cube. How can I melt you?"

"I don't mean to be cool, Larry. I never want to hurt your feelings. If I do, I'm sorry. It's only my way, the way I'm made, just as you are the way you're made." And seeing that his brief, hot flame was already starting to die, she continued, "You always tell me how kind I am, and how good to you. Isn't that true? Don't you always say so?"

"I guess so," he muttered.

"Of course it is. And here we are in a fuss about taking a shower," she said with a small, reproving smile such as one gives to a darling child who has somehow misbehaved.

He muttered again, "Well, I guess you're right."

It was so easy to manipulate him that it was pitiable. And with this thought, true tears of pity began to gather and glisten in her eyes.

Seeing them, he was all contrition. Naturally, he misunderstood them as having been caused by his anger.

"Ah, don't cry, Amanda. I said a stupid thing. A man in Cagney Falls—forget I said it. I'm too sleepy for a shower right now, anyway. Shouldn't have eaten all that ice cream. I'm stuffed."

So fast had that explosive anger evaporated. It was like the thread of pure smoke that is left after an explosion; it rises, floats, and disappears into the sky. Grumbling good-naturedly, Larry went up to bed.

"She was positively rude again," Norma said on the way home. "Do you mean you didn't notice it, Lester?"

"I wasn't paying much attention. I was sitting in the shade, talking to Peter. He's a very interesting guy, an artist, entirely out of my line. I know almost nothing about architecture."

"That family shot with Dad holding Stevie," she persisted. "You must have seen her face."

"Her face is a work of art, too," Lester said, laughing. "You can't deny that."

"I'm not trying to deny anything. She has a new expression. It's stony, it's frozen. I wonder what's wrong. Something is. I've sensed some kind of rebellion ever since Stevie was born. I still think she never wanted a baby."

"Let's not get caught up in pop psychology." Lester knew how to chide with good humor. "If what you say about her expression is true, it was probably a sick stomach, or she's coming down with a cold."

"No. Something is wrong. I'm not fooled, Lester."

In another car traveling in the opposite direction, Cecile remarked that she distinctly felt some enmity between Amanda and Mr. Balsan. "I wonder what it could be."

"It doesn't have to 'be' anything. Sometimes people just don't like each other, especially when they're in-laws."

"They're both such fine people."

" 'Fine'? That doesn't mean anything. Fine people tear each other apart every day, especially in families. Usually it's about money."

"You know, now and then I recall that day—how long ago now?—when I was sure I saw them both on that horrible street, Lane Avenue, near the bridge. I wonder why I still think of it."

"Who knows? But it's funny that you should mention Lane Avenue: Just today, I finished my final plan for it. You won't recognize the grand, curved boulevard I've made out of that street."

CHAPTER EIGHTEEN

Give me time," said L.B. "This is like unraveling a knot, or finding the exit out of a maze."

"Well, can you unravel the knot? And is there any exit from this maze? Are we perhaps trapped in it?"

"No, but I need to think. Just give me time."

May passed, and June arrived with birdsong and early roses. Lavish with breezes and greenery, with fragrance and butterflies, the earth outdid itself this summer. Larry walked around the yard singing: "Oh, what a beautiful morning, Oh, what a beautiful day." The maple planted last year had grown half a foot. Stevie said "Mama," after which Larry was ready to enroll him at Harvard.

It was all unbearable. Amanda was floundering. Her nerves wore thin. She cried at a television movie about a starving, mistreated dog. She cried one day when Stevie, when she gave him a cookie, put his arms around her neck.

What was to become of them all?

The bus lurched. It gave off fumes that made her almost as sick as she had been on those nauseated mornings during her pregnancy. She put a sugary mint into her mouth as Larry had recommended then, and closed her eyes. Ahead of her a pair of middle-aged ladies, no doubt on the way to the midtown department stores, were having a discreet conversation. Their voices were well modulated, and their accents pure. Very likely they were teachers; they looked like the guests that Norma and Lester invited to their little dinners. And she wondered what they would say if they knew that she, as quietly dressed as they in a dark cotton suit, as well mannered and well educated as they, was on her way to a room to which she possessed a key, there to meet and probably make love to her husband's father.

Once past the central avenues where the bus lost most of its passengers, it struggled through the narrow streets that by now were so familiar to Amanda that she could have described each structure in detail, and rumbled around the corner of Lane Avenue, where she left it.

At the entrance of the building that now seemed more like home than the place that was officially her home, she was greeted by some teenagers who lived in the flat across the hall. They did not exactly smirk at her, but an unmistakable glint in the eye and a half smile on the mouth showed clearly that she was not fooling them; they knew why she was there. This small incident so dismayed her that she ran stumbling up the stairs and pounded on the door.

L.B. took her into his arms, where she clung and buried her face in his shoulder.

"What is it? What happened?"

"It got to be too much for me today. I don't know why. It's one of those days."

"Yes, yes," he murmured, holding her tightly.

"It's very hard to live two lives, L.B."

They stood together feeling their unity breast to breast, while she wept softly.

"Go on, darling, cry. Don't hold it in. Crying will help you."

A siren startled them. "Noon," he said. "We've never been here this early in the day, so I brought lunch—chicken sandwiches, salad, Georgia peaches, and a nice wine—to celebrate."

He was beseeching her. He wanted to lift her out of her mood, but the mood lay too heavily upon her to be so easily lifted. She had come, after all, to beseech him.

"Celebrate?" she asked. "Have we got any reason to?"

"We're together," he replied staunchly. "Isn't that enough reason? Come, let's eat."

He poured the wine, and without a toast or any expressed wish, they touched glasses. They ate in silence. Now and then, their eyes met solemnly. The air was heavy with their trouble and with noon heat.

"Take off your jacket," L.B. said after a while.

Her silk blouse clung. She took it off so that the short pearl necklace lay on the flesh between her breasts. Again their eyes met; still without speaking a word, they stood up and went to the couch together.

The sun had moved so far that the room was in shadow, when a rumble of thunder came out of the distance.

"I am thinking of the first time," she said, breaking the dreamlike silence between them. "Do you remember the storm? The thunder was like a roar in the sky, and I was so afraid."

"Of the storm?"

"Of you," she said, "and of myself because I had fallen in love with you."

"Well, you know I had fallen in love with you long before that."

"What are we going to do?" she cried again.

"The first thing we have to do is to be very careful. Norma thinks that you—you are not getting along."

He still cannot say the name "Larry," she thought. That's how deep the pain goes.

"What made her think that?" she asked.

"She dropped in one day and saw you with red eyes."

"Yes, I had been crying."

A sigh so deep that it might have taken all his breath came from L.B.

"Listen," she said, more firmly now. "We'll go away together, anywhere you like. It can be Alaska or down near the Gulf. Anywhere. I can run a dress shop, and you can do something in real estate. We'll manage."

"You make it sound so easy. What about Stevie?"

"He would stay with Larry. I would never take him away, never do that to Larry. And it will be better for Stevie in the long run to be cared for here. Norma will

help. You've seen how she adores him." In a gesture now
become habit, Amanda clasped her hands. "It will be better for me, too, if I leave him now before he gets older
and we have a real relationship. I can part with him now
if I have to," she finished, swallowing a sob.

"What a price to pay," L.B. said, very low. "What a
price."

"Perhaps if we simply tell the truth and take the con-
sequences—"

"Are you asking me or telling me?"

"Both."

"Do you think I could look at Norma and Larry if
they were to know the truth?"

"You wouldn't have to look at them if you went
away," Amanda responded, also very low. And then,
when he did not answer, she cried out again in despair,
"You must see that this has become impossible for me! I
can't live in that house anymore! I have to go back there
in another hour, and I can't bear it. To sleep—in that
room—use your imagination—I can't do it much longer."

L.B. got up and walked as she had done to the window. It is a way of moving free, if only for a moment, of
the place where you are boxed in, she thought. Perhaps
out there in the street, or the forest, wherever you may
be, an answer is written, or so you hope, on the stones or
in the trees. And filled with sorrow because he was suffering, she went over and put both hands on his shoulders.

"To wake up in the morning and find each other
there," she whispered, "for always. Always."

When he turned and put his arms around her, she
thought she saw tears in his eyes. "Give me time to think

of something," he said. "We love each other. We shouldn't, but we do. Give me time to think of something."

"We're having the dickens of a heat wave," her mother said. "It hit a hundred yesterday, and the house is an oven. Are you sure you want to come now?"

What she was really saying, Amanda knew, was, "What brings you here this week, when in all this time you've never made the slightest effort to visit us?"

Somehow Amanda ignored the question by asking another about where she should stay.

"You'll have to stay at the motel on the highway. We're splitting at the seams here. Baby's boyfriend is staying with us until he gets his first month's pay on the new job."

Baby, the youngest of the girls—was she going to be called Baby for the rest of her life?—had been in junior high school just yesterday, or so it seemed to Amanda. And abruptly she felt a warm desire to see them all again. It was probably the first time since, excited and proud, she had left them to go away to the university that she had felt any such longing.

Mostly, she wanted to see her mother. It was not that she expected any specific counsel; L.B. would take care of all that. It was simply that there are times when a woman needs to empty her troubles onto the lap of another woman who will care. And who better than one's mother?

"I'll be taking the usual bus," she said. "I'll wait on the bench at the bus stop till one of you can pick me up."

Larry was upset that he could not go along. "Is your mother seriously sick? What did they tell you?"

"It was a slight attack, my brother said. It might be nothing, and then again it might really be something. But from the way he spoke I had the feeling that I ought to go."

"Of course you should. Listen, there's no excuse for our not going down to visit your folks. We absolutely have to do it in the fall, maybe over Thanksgiving. We'll take Stevie to meet his grandparents and invite everybody to the hotel or motel, whatever it is, for Thanksgiving dinner. Where you going?"

"Upstairs to pack my suitcase. I'll be gone a week, so I'll need things."

"Stay here for a while and watch TV with me. There's a great program coming on in ten minutes."

Lying back in his big chair with his shirt open, he patted his large, pale stomach and belched. Then he laughed.

"Oops, sorry! Too many French fries. I can never stop once I get started. But what the heck, everybody loves a fat man, right? Fat men are good-natured, right? Wouldn't you say I'm good-natured?"

Poor, kind soul, with his innocent grin! It hurt her to look at him as much as it repelled her.

"Yes," she said gently, "yes, you are."

Rip Van Winkle must have felt like this. Nothing had changed. On the bench at the corner of Main and Church, Amanda could see Sue's Beauty Emporium, with bottles of hair goods in the window; next came Ben's Dry

Goods, with shirts, jeans, and overalls in the window. The sidewalks steamed, tar melted where the street had been patched, and everything from the hot, cloudy sky to the unpainted boards was gray.

Right here at this spot she had stood on the day she returned with a diploma in her bag and the very expensive black-and-white carry-on at her feet. Right here she had stood waiting for the bus on her way back north, there perhaps to accept Larry Balsan—if he should ask her to—even though she did not really want to.

Is it good that we cannot see the future, or is it bad?

A horn honked. "Hey, kid, remember me? I'm your brother Hank."

She climbed into the pickup and gave him a kiss. He, too, was the same, with bare, sunburned arms and fair curly hair like hers.

"What brings you here? Troubles?"

The question was startling and might have been taken for sarcasm, but when she looked at him, she saw that it was genuine. Anyway, Hank was not given to sarcasm, nor to irony.

"I only wanted to see you all," she said.

"Well, good. We talk about you a lot, and let me tell you, we're all mighty grateful for the stuff you send. You must have found a gold mine up there."

"No, I make nice money, and I like to share, that's all. Anyway, I really don't send that much."

"Enough to fix up the kitchen. New stove and refrigerator. You keep Lorena's kids in clothes, too. That bum of hers can't even keep them in shoes."

"I'm glad I can help, Hank."

"Want to turn here and take a look at the high school? They haven't had another kid like you since you graduated. Bookworm. Solid A's. People still talk about you."

Solid A's, she thought, but you can still mess up your life.

The road, the trees, and the house, when they reached it, all of these were extending their arms to her. She was being welcomed, not only by the human arms of her blood and kin, but by a sense of safety; the very sameness of it all suggested that nothing ever changed much here, so nothing ever really could go very wrong.

Here it was: the supper table in the kitchen; the menu of okra, ham, and sweet potato pie in her honor; the two yellow hounds waiting for scraps; Lorena's youngest, wearing a wet diaper. With all its defects, from which she had longed to flee, and had fled, it was home. And Mother was the mother who would listen to her and tell her that things really were not all that bad. When mothers kiss, the bruise stops hurting.

Someone said, "You must have brought pictures of the baby."

Of course she had, and so as soon as the kitchen table was cleared, her pictures were spread out on it. Everybody agreed immediately that Stevie was a handsome boy. But why hadn't she brought him along? What about Larry? Why hadn't he come?

"Next time," she promised. "It's quite a job to take a fifteen-month-old baby on a plane, especially a very active one, like Stevie."

"Who's this, the man holding him?"

"Oh, that was on Stevie's birthday."

"But who is he? He looks like a movie star," Baby said.

"He's Larry's father."

"The grandpa!" Baby squealed. "He doesn't look like the grandpas I see around here. This man's gorgeous."

As when a plug is removed and water gushes down the drain, the feeling of ease and safety departed. If at that moment Amanda could have turned and fled, she would have done so. But she spoke brightly with a question about her aunt Eva.

"The last time we spoke, I remember, she had fallen and hurt her knee."

"It was bad there for a while, but she's fine now. And she'd love to see you."

"There are so many people who haven't seen you in years, Amanda," her mother said. "There are Uncle Bob and Aunt May, the Robinson cousins out in Barnville—a whole lot of people, if you're up to it."

"Well, I'll be here for a few days, so if somebody will drive me around, I'll be glad to make visits."

Perhaps what she needed was to think about these other people, the old aunt, the young cousin with the new baby, and the ambitious teenager who reminded her of herself not all that many years ago . . .

On the third day, when she returned from Barnville, her mother was waiting for her on the front porch. They were alone, yet her mother spoke in a low voice, very seriously.

"Why did you tell your husband that I was ill, Amanda?"

"What do you mean?" she asked with a pang of fear in her chest.

"He telephoned while you were gone and asked how I was feeling."

Fool, fool! She had intended to telephone Larry with a report about her mother, and in her addled state had forgotten to do it.

"I needed an excuse to come here. It was silly of me."

"Why an excuse? Are you not on good terms with him, so that you have to lie?"

"No, no. We're fine. But men can be possessive sometimes, can't they? I wanted to come right away, and I knew he wasn't able to leave work. He had been talking about putting it off until Thanksgiving, and I didn't want to wait that long."

A pair of blue eyes behind glasses were examining her. She knew those eyes well; they were not easily fooled.

"There's something you're not saying, Amanda."

"No, really not. Really."

"We all, Lorena and Hank and Doreen—your father, even Baby, all of us—have a feeling that you are in trouble."

The blue eyes were steady in their examination. Above them there was a narrow border of gray hair. It emerged from the scalp beneath a wealth of shining brown hair. Obviously, she was covering up the gray. She was not young anymore. She had never had an easy life and never would have one, whatever future remained. There was poverty. There were Doreen, and Lorena with her troubles, and Baby with another new boyfriend, as yet an unknown quantity. Hank and Bub, for all their decency, were still living at home, getting nowhere. It would be cruel to give her something else to worry over, something that at best she wouldn't be able to help.

"You didn't answer," her mother said. "I'm puzzled why you came home right now. And after so long."

"I guess it was simple homesickness. It's been a long time."

"If you have any big problems, you should tell me, Amanda." As the gentle words were spoken, a gentle smile came into the blue eyes. "Heaven only knows, I've weathered Lorena's problems. And it looks as if they may finally be clearing up. Maybe they are. There's nothing to be ashamed of, Amanda. Nothing dishonorable in having troubles."

Nothing dishonorable. There was no way to tell the story to this mother, or perhaps to anyone, without making it look like a vile and inexcusable affair. This good, righteous mother would never understand. She would struggle, and out of her love, would try to understand, but the wound would be a cruel one, too cruel.

The mission here had been impossible. Amanda got up, kissed her mother, and assured her again: "It was simple homesickness. Believe me. And now that I've seen you all, I guess I'll go back tomorrow."

After the endless, wearying bus trip, there was a long flight delay in Memphis, with nothing to do but buy another magazine or, if hungry, get something to eat. Amanda was sitting in the sandwich shop when Peter Mack came in. They were both surprised, and she was sorry, for her mood was dark while his, she saw immediately, was ebullient.

"Well, of all times and places to meet," he said. "Mind if I join you?"

"Not at all."

"Where've you been?"

"Visiting my family."

"I've been doing the usual. Wonder how late we'll be."

Amanda shrugged. "I've no idea."

"I just phoned Cele to keep in touch with the airport. Have you called Larry? If you need a cell phone, you can borrow mine."

Peter was making conversation, feeling the need to communicate, even about trivia. She wondered what was making him so enthusiastic.

"He's out," she said. "I'll try later."

It was not true. The truth was that Larry had no idea she was coming home today. The plan was to take a taxi from the airport to the place on Lane Avenue, there to telephone to L.B., and then to go home tomorrow.

"It's a good thing we have a day to spare," Peter said. "If this were the third of the month, we'd stand a chance of missing the celebration on the Fourth."

She had completely forgotten the Fourth of July. Indeed, she had been forgetting many things lately: a toothbrush last week, so that Hank had had to get one for her in town; and of all embarrassments, she had not been able to remember the name of Cousin Luke's wife.

Peter ordered a sandwich. When Amanda did not respond to him, he went on.

"Pretty nice of Larry's father to offer his yard for a block party. It was kind of a last-minute thing, Norma said. Only happened the day before yesterday. Those people who usually do it had a sudden illness in the family, and Mr. Balsan very generously offered his place instead."

So I'll have to go to L.B.'s house, she was thinking. Then, catching herself, she explained, "There's a marvelous view from there right down the hill toward the playing field where they set off the fireworks."

"We're still kids, Cele and I. We love it all, 'The Star-Spangled Banner,' the ice-cream cones, and all the sparkle in the sky."

Sparkle in the sky. Larry never used language like that. Now if L.B. were not who he is, she thought, or if I had met a man like this one . . . He might have chosen me instead of Cecile if he had met me at the same time. . . .

"Too bad Larry couldn't go with you," Peter said. "Well, work comes first, doesn't it? It was the same with me. Cele would have come with me, but they're in the middle of a giant fund drive at the hospital. Have you heard there's talk of making her the president of the Guild next time round?" A soft expression passed across his face. "It's a good thing for her, not so much because of the honor, but because the work's important and it fills her days."

So there was still no sign of any baby. She remembered how he had suffered when it was feared that Cele might die. They're probably the best pair of people I've ever known, Amanda thought. He's the kind of man you can talk to. He has the heart and the wisdom to solve things. If I were to ask him, would he have an answer for us?

She had ordered a salad, but having no appetite, had laid down the fork.

"What's the matter, no good?" Peter asked.

"It's too big, and I'm not very hungry."

Had she really, if only for an instant, considered the possibility of consulting Peter? She trembled. Heaven forbid that such mad, reckless words should ever tumble out of her mouth!

Give me time, L.B. said. I'll think of something. And making a mental adjustment, she asked a courteous question.

"I suppose you've been seeing some more of those grand old southern mansions again?"

"Not many this time. Oh, listen. They're calling our plane."

To Amanda's relief, their seats were far apart. Closing her eyes and laying her head back, she let her thoughts stray. On flights from college to home and back, you would often have a talkative pilot who liked to point out places on the earth below them: a lake, a city, and always the Mississippi River. This pilot must be wary of the weather today, she thought, for he had made no reports. But she knew, according to her watch, just about when instead of flying north toward Michigan, they used to head west toward the old campus. And, in the illogical way of straying thoughts, she suddenly had a clear vision of Terry, the high school girl who had walked with her on the nights she left Sundale's. She saw the girl's home again, that simple, tidy home; so peaceful, so secure it had seemed, the very stuff of envy and of dreams! And she wondered what had become of Terry. Perhaps, now and then, Terry wondered about her? Ah, never, never could she imagine what had happened to this old friend!

You are young. You are ignorant, although you do

*not know you are. There are paths and you choose one,
although you do not know where it will take you.*

And, in an instant, came a picture of Stevie with his
smile and a glimpse of tiny teeth. So deep then was her
pain that she started up in her seat; a woman across the
aisle stared in surprise.

She scolded herself: This sort of thing must stop. I
must make myself relax. L.B. will know what to do for
us. Larry must soon get tired of me, anyway. Any other
man, long before this, would have been sick of a woman
who gives him so little. Let him ask me for a divorce.
How can I be the one to do it? How can I crush a man
who is so gentle, so decent, and so good to me? A man
whom I have betrayed as I have? Yes, let him be the one.
It will solve everything—if he asks for it. And then I'll be
free. I'll feel a little less guilty. And it won't matter what
anyone thinks. We will go away. L.B. will know what
to do.

Cecile was waiting at the carousel. Amanda had
hoped to lose Peter in the crowd, grab her bag, and find a
taxi to Lane Avenue. But what a foolish thought, now
that Peter and Cecile knew she was home! Her head was
not even on straight anymore. As might be expected, they
insisted on taking her home, though she wanted to be
alone.

"It's out of your way," she protested, although she
sensed that they were giving her a queer look. "Please let
me get a cab. I don't mind at all."

"Come on," Peter said, leading her by the elbow.
"That's ridiculous. We're driving you home."

In the backseat she sat alone, saying little. When they
had crossed the bridge and rounded the corner at Lane

Avenue, she caught a glimpse of the familiar windows on the second floor. They were dark.

"Isn't there something the matter with her?" asked Cecile when they left Amanda.

"She certainly wasn't herself. At the airport, during the few minutes we were together, she didn't even want me to talk to her."

"Norma swears there's something wrong between Amanda and Larry. She's worried about her brother, of course."

"I hope it's nothing. But that seems to be all you hear these days."

"I know, and I'm just grateful for us. Tell me about your trip. Tell me everything."

When they had finished their dinner, she handed Peter a clipping. "I cut this out of the paper on Saturday. My father said Mr. Roland and the rest all took note of it. Here's a news item, and on this page an editorial."

He read it slowly, nodding from time to time, and read it again before he spoke.

"Casinos. I've heard about that gang in the legislature that's promoting the idea. 'Gang' is right," he said contemptuously. " 'Renaissance,' they call it. 'Kindling a business boom.' Imagine! The wetlands along the river, that whole green little peninsula, turned into a gambling den deluxe. High-rise hotels, entertainment, and shops— all this instead of good housing, green parks, and a bird sanctuary." And Peter flung down the paper.

Cecile soothed him. "The editorial is completely on your side, though. My father is not worried at all. Read the editorial and you'll see."

"I'm not worried. I'm just angry that people can be so destructive. It's the same way I get angry when I see a marvelous old building in the hands of the wreckers."

"Tell me about the marble you went to look at. How was it?"

"Just about perfect. It's coffee with cream, lightly streaked. Very delicate. I was afraid I might have remembered it wrong, but I hadn't. Fortunately, I won't need very much; it's hard to get and it costs a fortune, besides. You know, Cele, it's refreshing to poke around some of these out-of-the-way places. I often think you might call them 'forgotten places.' By accident, for example, I came upon a crumbling balustrade that I'd never seen before. Lucky I had my camera in my pocket. It just struck me as something I might adapt for the semicircular terrace going down to the roadway."

Once, humbly, he had confessed to her his hope that the museum, as part of the project, might find a place someday in the National Register of Historic Places. Indeed, he had even admitted that he thought it had a good chance.

It pleased her to see his face glow like this. He had come so far without anyone's help, as he had always wanted to do. Never mind the "money men" at the banks, who were certainly necessary, but it was Peter who had truly created something grand.

They were on their way upstairs for the night, when the sound of exploding firecrackers tore through the darkness.

"Kids can't wait till the Fourth," Peter said. "I was like that, too."

If we had any, she thought without replying, we'd be taking ours to see the fireworks.

"I suppose Mr. Balsan will be making it a gala event. He likes to do things in style."

The name Balsan made her think again of Amanda, who had been so strange lately. Something was happening to the spirited, winsome girl she had known, and Cecile was sad.

CHAPTER NINETEEN

The sky was still bright when Amanda and Larry left the house. He was slightly annoyed because she had insisted that Stevie was too young to stay up late for the fireworks. She, although gaily dressed in red, white, and blue and prepared to show festive spirits, was actually trembling within. Unless there were to be some way that L.B. could get her aside and talk for a moment, they would have to wait for another long day.

As usual, Larry's annoyance had a short life. "Next year we'll take him with us. And in a few years, though I hate to think of time rushing by so fast, he'll be in high school, going everywhere without us. Hey, did I tell you Norma invited your friend Dolly from the shop? She thinks of everything. Actually, it was Cecile who reminded her to do it, because you've been inviting Dolly to this block party every year, and you must have forgotten before you went away."

Yes, that was like Cele; she thought of everything. Norma did not.

"Why so quiet?" asked Larry.

"I was listening to the music. That's a beautiful song. Turn it louder."

"Oh yeah, a real oldie. 'Some Enchanted Evening.' It goes like this." He began to hum off-key. " '—when you find your true love across a crowded room, then night after night'—something like that. I forget it. It's old as the hills."

Why did he do even the simplest things all wrong? Why, when a person obviously wanted to hear a song, didn't he have enough sense to shut up and let her hear it?

And why is it that somebody else can do the most trivial thing, can make a small, unimportant gesture, and captivate you?

"Time for the news," Larry said. "You want it?"

She sighed. "Yes. Put it on." At least she wouldn't have to talk.

Larry switched off the radio. "Bah! No news. Maybe just as well. No bad news to spoil the holiday. Nice, isn't it, all the flags hanging out? This is really a great neighborhood. Still, if we have another kid or two, Dad's neighborhood, his house, I always tell you, might be better yet."

Suddenly Amanda was interested. "Why? Is he planning to sell?"

"I don't know. Maybe."

Larry cleared his throat. Whenever he did that, for

what reason Heaven only knew, he was about to make an important statement, and she became alert. "Dad and I had a serious talk while you were away. First he asked me an odd question, how you and I get along, whether we do much arguing. I told him no. Oh, we have our little differences, but we're both easygoing, especially you. To come right down to it, you're an easy woman to get along with."

She interrupted. "What made him ask that?"

Larry hesitated. "I think I've made a mistake. I shouldn't have started to tell you. It's something confidential, a surprise. He's going to come out with it himself, tomorrow or the next day, so he asked me to keep it to myself."

How typical of Larry to bungle the story and leave her in suspense! And hiding her frustration, she asked calmly, "What's confidential about a question like that? Go on, tell me the rest."

"Well, all right, but don't dare let this slip. Even Norma doesn't know. So here goes. You won't believe it, but he has turned over the entire business to me, given me all the stock in the company, so now I'm the sole boss. Can you imagine?" Larry cried.

Amanda's heart raced. So they were really going to go away . . . A little smile trembled on her lips.

"I was shocked out of my wits. Yes, I expected that someday when he was old, he'd retire and then I'd step into his shoes. I never expected anything like this. He's a young man, after all. And just like that, Amanda. Just like that," Larry said, snapping his fingers, "you and I are sitting on a pile of money. Hey, are you too shocked to talk?"

His exuberance terrified her. She thought of the second shock that awaited him when he should learn what lay behind L.B.'s grand gesture. And as she imagined his poor face aghast, she felt her racing heart sink in pity.

Since he was naturally expecting some comment, she asked whether this was a sudden decision and what had led to it.

"It seems to be very sudden. You remember my mother's Canadian relatives? Well, one of the cousins, a widower much older than Dad and not well, owns a lot of property, worked hard all his life and wants to take it easy. So he got the idea that maybe my father would like to take it a little easier, too. And he's invited him to be his companion on a trip around the world, then to come back and take over the management of the properties out in British Columbia for him. Well, you could have knocked me over with a feather. And Dad, too. It sounded like a darn good deal, and Dad's accepted."

In front of Amanda's eyes, the road swayed. Something sharp, a bullet or a knife, had pierced her, while something blunt had come down upon her head.

"What did you say?" she whispered. "I didn't hear you. For how long is this to be?"

"Oh, indefinitely. For a few years anyway, as long as this cousin lives. I tell you, I was stunned at first to think Dad would ever leave here, but now that I've been thinking about it these last few days, it seems to be a fantastic idea. Dad's never traveled or done anything but work all his life. So as long as he wants to, why not? We can always visit back and forth."

Amanda, feeling a surge of nausea, remembered to close her eyes against the dizzying glare on the street.

Larry, taking no notice, went on chattering. "Well,

here we are. Look at the picnic spread! You can depend
on getting real food whenever my father's in charge. The
folks on this block won't know what hit them this year.
You can say what you want, but you'll go far to beat this
yard. Why, the trees alone, those blue spruce that my
mother planted! She loved trees. The old house would be
a picture painted white, don't you think so? I know
you've said you'd never want this house, but you might
change your mind—what's the matter?"

"Nothing . . . Something I ate."

Larry took the last parking space at the end of the
street, leaped out of the car, rushed around to the other
side, and opened the door.

"Orange juice and cereal. I don't see how that could
make you—unless the milk was sour?"

She was fighting herself: You can't be sick here; you'll
look like a fool; hold on until tomorrow; he could have
gotten the facts all wrong; tomorrow you'll find out.
Hold on.

People were passing on the sidewalk. She raised her
head in time to hear Dolly's astonished cry. "What's
wrong with Amanda?"

Larry stammered, "I don't know. It just happened. A
sick stomach, she says."

Yes, he could have gotten the facts all wrong.

"It's passing," she said. "Whatever it was, I feel it
passing."

But Larry was too shaken to accept that. "Are you
sure? Came and went just like that? Maybe we should
see a doctor. There are two right on this street: Dr.
Byrnes, and an old retired man, Dr. Slater."

The last thing she needed was a doctor to ask a hundred questions. "It was a momentary thing. A freak thing. I'm sorry," she said firmly now.

"You scared the daylights out of me, honey."

"Oh, this is my friend Joey Bates," Dolly said. "I was so scared I didn't introduce anybody."

Introductions were then made. Amanda looked up into the genial face of Dolly's latest boyfriend, a plumber and volunteer fireman. He looked *nice,* as if he could be trusted. But then, everything was uncertain . . .

"This is Larry's father's house," Dolly explained.

Joey nodded. "Nice place."

"Sure you're feeling all right now?" Larry asked doubtfully.

"Sure."

"Then let's go."

The yard was crowded as people moved up the rise from the front gate toward the rear, where three tables stood trimmed in red, white, and blue crepe paper and loaded with refreshments. Ahead of Dolly and Amanda, Larry was answering Joey's questions about the age of the house and the fence of blue spruce that his mother had planted. Amanda struggled on weak legs.

Suddenly she had an urge to speak. "It wasn't a sick stomach, Dolly. I've had a shock. I can't talk about it now, because probably it will turn out to be nothing. I don't know . . . Do I look all right?"

Surprised, Dolly turned to look. "Why, yes," she said. "Aren't you glad you took the white linen? It looks lovely on you."

"I meant my face. Does it look all right?"

"Of course it does. It's the same as always. What's the trouble, Amanda? Won't you tell me?"

"I can't." Her eyes were searching among the gathering: neighbors, young children, and noisy teenagers, along with sundry familiar employees of Balsan Real Estate. Larry, the friendly mingler, had already been swallowed up among them.

Near the porch stood the Macks and the Coles, along with Alfred Cole. Amanda did not want to waste time talking. There was only one person she needed to see here. Nevertheless, she went over to them.

"Have you looked at the tables?" asked Norma. "Dad ordered sandwiches on baguettes from the French bakery. He's got a bowl of peaches in wine, and a New Orleans ice-cream pie. Leave it to him. This is the fanciest Fourth of July I've ever seen." Exactly as Larry had done, she spoke of their father with pride.

On her hand as she flung it out in a graceful arc, Lester's diamond glittered. It was odd, Amanda thought, that of the three musketeers, the least attractive one owned the best ring. Was it not odd, too, to be having such a strange, irrelevant thought? And most strange of all was that the trees had begun to revolve in the dusk.

She stood still, leaning against the porch railing. The others were talking, their words a meaningless hum in the background, while scattered images, sounds, and sights were racing through her mind: the creak of the swing on this very porch when Larry proposed; white bridal flowers given into her hand at the honeymoon hotel; the thundering storm that first time with L.B.; the room on Lane Avenue.

Take the number 8 bus and get off on the corner near the bridge.

"Is your father here?" she asked Norma.

"Of course he's here. Probably up at the top near the tables."

Abruptly she walked away, too abruptly, no doubt, and they would wonder why. It didn't matter. L.B. was talking to a man tending bar at one of the tables. And still abruptly, she went to him.

"I need to talk to you," she said.

"Not here. Not now," he replied with a slight, worried frown.

"Yes, here and now. Come over near the kitchen door."

When she looked into his face, it seemed to her that she read the answer to the question that she had not yet asked.

"Is it true that you are going away to Canada? Larry just told me."

Now she read his alarm. "I don't know what Larry said," he began, when she interrupted him.

"He said it's supposed to be a surprise, but he wasn't able to hold it in, so don't blame him. Just answer me: Is it true?"

Now she read L.B.'s panic. "I wouldn't call it—I didn't intend a surprise. I wanted to talk to you about it tomorrow and explain, just talk it over between you and me," he said. "But not now. Not here. Please, Amanda."

"Why don't you answer me? It's a quick, simple question. Give me a quick, simple answer."

"God help us both. It's not so simple. Please, Amanda, we're too conspicuous standing here. This isn't the place to talk."

Her legs going weak again, she braced herself against the kitchen door. And once more that terrible feeling of unreality overcame her. Were they really here in L.B.'s yard talking like this, she and he? He, my love, my world?

"I'll meet you tomorrow morning at the place," he murmured. "Let me go now before people notice us."

"All you have to do is say: 'I am going away without you, Amanda. I am telling you good-bye.' Say it. Or say that it's not true."

"Please, Amanda." He was imploring her. "Oh, please. Not now."

"All you have to do is say whether you are leaving me or not." She saw that he was too shaken to speak, but she persisted, letting her voice rise. "Can you tell me it isn't true?"

"I beg you, darling Amanda, let's talk tomorrow."

"Not tomorrow," she said as she walked away. "Not necessary. I have your answer."

A dry sob burned in her chest, the pain of it worse than any pain of childbirth. She wanted to hide someplace where she might cope with herself unseen. A large group of teenagers had congregated in a corner of the yard and were drinking out of paper cups. She walked over to lose herself among them. From where they all stood, she could still see L.B., half a head taller than anyone around him. He was being the gracious host. *Anguish*, she thought: Is that the right word? Surely he must be feeling the same. He must. It had been written in his eyes. How well she knew him! How well. Then why?

Because, came the answer, because in the final analysis he cannot hurt his son. So I must be left to suffer, and he will suffer—perhaps not for too long—in Canada. Anywhere he goes, there will be women who will run to him, women like that girl up near the tables right this minute, who is lifting her pretty face to him. She can't be more than seventeen. . . .

Going back toward the tables, she met Larry looking both irritable and worried.

"I've been looking for you everywhere," he complained. "Are you sure you're feeling all right?"

Feeling all right? I am probably losing my mind, she thought, and replied with a question.

"Who is that girl standing next to your father?"

"I don't know her name. She's summer help, a kid who helps out in the office until September. What's the matter with you? You don't look right."

"Nothing. Nothing. I'm thirsty. I'm going for a drink."

A barman behind two punch bowls explained that one of them was nonalcoholic, and the other was "very alcoholic."

"Red wine, rum, lemon juice—not for kids. Somebody brought it, and Mr. Balsan was pretty upset. That's why I'm supposed to stand here and make sure nobody drinks any who shouldn't."

"Well, I'm overage," Amanda said, helping herself.

"You don't want that size glass, miss," the man said. "Use this one. That's strong stuff. It won't take more than minutes before you'll feel it."

"I want to feel it," she answered as she filled the tall glass. Drink enough, and the anguish may go away. Sit down on that circular bench around that tree, sip slowly, and wait.

But it did not go away. Her whole body from legs to head was burning. Gradually, with purpose and power, a terrible anger over a cruel injustice melded into the anguish. She was sitting in wait for it all to explode when Larry appeared.

"You're behaving so strangely," he cried. "You keep disappearing. We have friends here, and you sit alone with a glass in your hand! What the hell are you drinking, anyway? Your face is on fire. Give me that glass."

"I'm drinking what I want to drink." She got up and went back to the punch bowl. "And if I want to drink more, I'll do that, too."

"Amanda! You never drink. You haven't had even one glass of wine since last Christmas. Give me that."

"Don't you tell me what to do," she said loudly. "Or you either," she added, for L.B. was standing nearby at the other punch bowl.

He stared at her. He had an expression of terror; warning and pleading were in it.

"Don't, Amanda," he said very quietly, so low that he was barely audible. "Don't. It's not for you."

A fresh surge of rage shook her. "And who are you, Mr. Balsan, to tell me what is or isn't for me?" she cried. "Mind your own affairs. I'm nothing to you anymore! Do you hear me?"

Her voice rang so loud that people at the other end of the yard were startled.

In utter astonished disbelief, Larry seized Amanda by the elbow. "You can't talk to my father like that! Have you lost your mind?"

"Your father," she mocked. "You don't know the first thing about your father. Do you know what he's done? No, you don't. But I do. Yes, Mr. Balsan, I do. Oh, you knew, you already knew that last time we met what you were going to do to me. You had it in your mind, but you weren't brave enough to come out and tell me."

Around them, a few dozen people were standing still with curiosity on their faces.

L.B. was keeping control. "Amanda, get hold of yourself. You've had too much to drink, and you're not used to it."

"Yes, I've had too much to drink, but that's not all I've had too much of."

As her voice kept rising, more people became aware that some crisis was in the making. And an instant silence fell as it does when, on the street, a horrible accident has just occurred.

"Yes," said Amanda, "how easy it is to leave the country and forget! Shift the burden, just forget. Forget everything, all the love, the baby I didn't need, yes, yes." In despair and in fury, a stream of words, a torrent of rage, poured out from her mouth, while her hands were clasped together as if in prayer and her body swayed. "Oh yes, a baby. Your baby, L.B., not yours, Larry! Our Stevie—he isn't even yours, Larry! We've been lovers for four years, your father and I." And sobbing, Amanda collapsed onto a bench.

Now, as when inevitable catastrophe approaches, a plane crashing to earth before the onlookers or an avalanche descending upon a helpless village, there came a moment of total paralysis. The stunned onlookers stared at one another as if questioning: Did I really hear what I think I heard?

Then Larry toppled. Friends raced over and led him, tottering, to a tree where he was laid down. Norma was taken to the porch, where Lester, his father, Cecile, and

Peter gave her brandy and did what else they could, which was not very much. L.B., gone ghastly white, was helped into his house by the two doctors. Parents with children old enough to have understood at least some of what they had heard were rushing them away. L.B.'s dogs went frantic in the confusion. Larry, completely crazed, had to be restrained by his friends from rushing into the house to kill his father. Amanda, weeping hysterically, was picked up by Dolly's friend Joey, and taken to Dolly's car.

"Take her home to my house," Dolly ordered, while lamenting, "Oh, my God, my God, I can't believe this," and running to pick up the red shoe that had dropped off Amanda's foot.

Slowly the crowd dispersed, exchanging bewildered comments as they lingered on the sidewalk.

"She must have lost her mind. Or could it possibly be true?"

"I wouldn't have believed it of Balsan. A man like him, in a community like this."

"She was blind drunk. Disgraceful."

"No, tragic. Poor soul."

"But Amanda never drank! I don't understand it."

"They could have had a fight and she just went berserk."

"No. A story like that has got to be true."

"Did you get a good look at Balsan? He was shaking. They were holding him up on the way to the door. I hope he wasn't having a heart attack or a stroke because of this."

"It's a good thing there are doctors here."

In gape-mouthed shock they all drifted out of the

yard. Only the dogs were left to pick up scraps on the grass. The sound of motors starting up and dying away broke the stillness on the street. Those who lived around the neighborhood walked home in the twilight, having lost all interest in watching fireworks. The holiday scene had unraveled.

In a lounge chair on the porch, after a long while, Norma began to revive. Between sobs, sighs, and intervals of silence, she talked.

"You would have to know the mysteries of the universe or the mind of God to understand this. Unless the whole story isn't true! Yes, that's it. For some crazy reason, Amanda made it up."

"No," Cecile said quietly. "I went inside and spoke to Dr. Byrnes. Your father has admitted that it is all true."

Norma covered her face with her hands and whispered, "My father. My father."

No one spoke until she cried out again, "I never told you, Lester, what it really was that I had seen that day. Remember the time in the school theater when I told you I had seen—" She stopped, unable to finish.

Cecile finished for her. "You had seen Amanda and your father on Lane Avenue that day we came back from the airport. Yes, I saw them, too, Norma. I always wondered whether you had, but it was such a strange, unlikely thing that I was sure I couldn't have seen them, that I must have made a mistake. So I never mentioned it."

"Then this is what you meant by people who had betrayed your trust," Lester said, while holding her hand.

"Yes, my father. A good father. A decent, honorable

man. I would tell myself, whenever now and then the memory returned to me, I would think, well, if it was they who were walking there on Lane Avenue, it must have been for some innocent reason, something to do with property. And then I would think it really wasn't them."

The white light from the gibbous moon made everyone look pale green, as if ill. But we really are, all of us are ill tonight, Cecile was thinking. And she thought of her healthy father, who was still in love with her mother after all these years. She looked over at Alfred Cole, whose very presence, although he had scarcely spoken, must be a comfort to his son and his son's suffering wife.

Then she thought with great pain of Amanda and her dear little boy. What could have possessed her? What on earth could have distorted her mind? But then, what about all those clients at social services in the hospital, those who often have such incredible tales to tell? Tales that sounded like nightmares?

"I think I must be in a coma," Norma said. "I've heard that your mind keeps working when you're in a coma. Have we forgotten Larry? Where is he?"

"No, no," Lester soothed. "Some friend took him to his house, to the friend's house."

"But where? Whose?" Norma started up from the chair. "I ought to be with him."

"The friend's name was Willard," Lester said. "I distinctly heard. He was a short fellow with reddish hair."

"That's right. They were in high school together. Jeff Willard. We need to go there right now, Lester."

"No, Norma, you don't need to. You're in no condition to. Stay here and I'll go to Larry. Just give me the address."

"I don't know it," Norma wailed.

Peter stood up. "I'll do it. Stay here," he told Cecile. "You may be needed, too, if anything happens upstairs with Balsan."

After his car had gone out of hearing, the only sound was the cricket chorus. No one spoke; it was as if everything had been said that could be said. In times of dire trouble there is actually very little to say, Cecile thought. We know that, and yet we feel obliged to fill the emptiness with the sound of soothing words. In a way, the cricket chirp says more than any one of us can; it says that life goes on. After the disaster, life continues. Yet it is hardly tactful to say that to anybody who is in the middle of the disaster.

Upstairs there were lights in the big bay window that must belong to Balsan. The doctors were still with him. And curiously, in spite of what he had done, Cecile felt deep pity for him. Do you not feel pity for the man who is under sentence of life imprisonment, no matter what his crime? For surely he will be tortured forever by the thought of what he has done.

Again Norma roused to mourn and rage. "How he loved her! From the first moment he saw her when I brought her here in spring break, he gave her his whole heart. That kind, sweet man, my brother. How could she, I ask you. How could she. I never want to see her again. I swear I never will. She's a slut. Of course it's my father's fault, too, but I blame her more, the more I think of it. It's she who went after him—it has to have been."

No one answered that, either. People take sides, casting blame according to where they stand. Norma, the more she thought about it, would tip the scale, however slightly, in favor of her father. And now Cecile's deep pity went out to Amanda.

A small, chilly breeze arose as the minutes ticked away. From inside the house a clock bonged the hour. An ambulance arrived. Men in white rushed upstairs. Shortly afterward Peter returned with news. Jeff Willard wasn't listed in the telephone book, so Peter had gone to the police station to get the address. At Willard's, he found that Larry had been put to bed. A doctor had come, given him a tranquilizer, and would check on him by telephone in the morning. After that, Peter had gone to Larry's house, paid Elfrieda, who was baby-sitting that night, and asked her please to stay until she heard from somebody tomorrow.

Somebody, Cecile thought. Who, Norma? In her condition? Lester will have his hands full and overflowing. I'll go stay with Stevie tomorrow instead of to the hospital, she decided.

The minutes kept ticking. An unspoken restlessness now began to afflict this group who were waiting for news to emerge from the room above. Nobody wanted to go inside and inquire, yet nobody could think of leaving without having heard something more.

As if emerging out of sleep, Norma spoke again. "A tranquilizer! As well put a Band-Aid on an amputation. It will be a miracle if he ever gets over it."

No one having disagreed with that, Lester changed the subject by addressing Peter. "Working hard this summer? I'm not. We educators don't get rich, but we do have great vacations."

Peter, too, was trying to override the horror with his reply. "I get away on my rescue trips. Old churches, barns, hotels—those are my patients. Right now I'm staying at home working hard, if you can call it work when you love what you're doing."

Two good men, Cecile thought, and was wondering again about the shocking, baffling man upstairs, when Lester spoke.

"There's no use in all of you sitting here. Dad, you have to be in court early, so why don't you leave? And Peter, you've already done so much, running all over town for us. Talk about a friend in need! But go on home now, you and Cecile. It's almost midnight."

So they left the porch and were about to step into their car, when Lester came running with news.

"It's over. He's gone. They were putting him on the stretcher when he had a fatal stroke a couple of minutes ago."

As was only to be expected, the news was in the next day's paper. The terrible event at the Balsan house could never have been omitted, but owing to the fact that the editor in chief was a friend and client of Alfred Cole's, who had pleaded in defense of his daughter-in-law's family, the description of it was decidedly muted. Only the bare facts, which were horrible enough, were given in a short paragraph on a back page.

The obituary was equally brief: Death was the result of a cerebral hemorrhage; the funeral was to be private.

Not reported was the fact that Cecile and Peter had taken Stevie to their house. It was Norma who gave permission, since Larry was in no condition to decide anything. It was difficult enough to prop him up for the funeral.

Norma and he, with Lester and the two doctors who had been present at the end, rode in one car behind the hearse, and stood at the grave as a prayer for love and forgiveness was intoned. Then, accompanied by the doctors, the mourners went to the Coles' house, where Larry was to stay until he should no longer require attention.

Cecile had telephoned Dolly on the morning after the disaster, only to be told that Amanda did not want to see her.

"She's in a very bad way," Dolly said. "Poor thing. I don't recognize our Amanda. When she heard about L.B.'s death, she went to pieces all over again. She surely must have been crazy about that guy. I don't know. I don't think I ever was that nuts about any guy, not that much. They gave me a sleeping pill for her at the drugstore. I would have got the doctor, only they don't come unless you're some big shot, and I can't get her out of the house to his office."

"I wanted to tell her—please tell her that Peter and I are taking care of Stevie. He's at our house with his baby-sitter, and he's quite happy."

"You're a real lady, Cecile. I always said so whenever you came into the shop. No airs about you. Amanda said so, too, only she really doesn't want to see you now. She's so ashamed you'll think she was a no-good bum and a dirty drunk and—"

"I'd never think that she was a dirty anything. It's all

a terribly sad story, and I'm sure none of us will ever really know the whole of it. Please tell her that for me. Shall I just come to your house whether she wants me to or not?"

"I wouldn't do that for a while. She keeps crying that she wants to be let alone. She wants to stay here and hide. I'll keep her as long as she wants me to, until she can at least get on her feet."

"And then what?"

"I don't think she has any idea."

"All right, Dolly. You and I will keep in touch. You have my number? You'll phone me? I'll keep phoning you."

"Yes, yes, I will. Oh, to look at Amanda and hear her, you could cry."

"Isn't it awful?" Mrs. Lyons said when Cecile telephoned the shop. "I came running here this morning the minute I heard. I could hardly believe my ears. A charming, well-educated young woman! And all of her only a surface, with filth underneath. I'm amazed that Dolly took her home. She'd never set foot in my house, I can tell you that."

For a minute or two after the call ended, Mrs. Lyons's indignation was still ringing in the room. So far, the only humane concern for Amanda had been that of Dolly and of Cecile's family.

But as the story spread and grew in the telling, so did compassion spread—along with morbid curiosity. What was going to happen? people asked. Divorce? A custody battle over the child?

"How on earth is that family ever going to find its

way out of this wilderness?" cried Cecile to Peter. "I spoke to Lester. He's not too worried about Norma; he says she's stronger than anybody, herself included, realizes. She's already trying to cope with the Stevie situation. But Larry is a total wreck—understandably—and won't even look at that baby whom he had always adored so much that it was sometimes even a little silly. Won't look at him! 'He isn't mine,' he says."

Peter threw up his hands. "I have no idea. It's a Greek tragedy."

CHAPTER TWENTY

These are the facts," Norma said, "and you have to
face them, Larry. It's been almost a month now. I'm
being frank with you. This bungalow is too small
for Lester and me to share it with you."

She spoke softly, but firmly. It was not because Lester
had ever complained of Larry's presence that she was
making this decision. In fact, it was Lester who kept reminding her that Larry was truly ill. It was simply that,
ill or not, decisions needed to be made and Larry was obviously unable to make them, so she would do it for him.

"Now you have a choice. You can either go back to
your own house, or you can move into—into the other.
You own it now."

"That place? Are you crazy? And see him in every
room every time I open a door? Monster! And up under
those spruce trees where she stood—I hear her voice. It's

shrill, it's awful, and she's standing there with a glass in her hand. No, I'll burn that house down before I'll live in it."

Larry had aged. Perhaps it was true that hair could turn white from shock or fall out, because his hairline had definitely receded. There were lines on his forehead that had not been there before that night. He was a pitiful, shocking sight.

"All right, put it up for sale. Then you'll have to live in your house, you and Stevie. Cele and Peter have kept your baby long enough. They've been marvelous, the best people in the world. But they're not his parents."

Larry was looking past her, past the window and beyond into space. When he spoke, she was barely able to hear him.

"Are you forgetting something? I'm not his father."

"To the world, you are. And to him. Remember that."

"No wonder they—he and she—never fussed over him the way I did. I realize it now."

"To be fair, though it hurts me to say so, she was a good mother in her own way," Lester said.

Larry leaped out of the chair and shouted, " 'In her own way'? Yes, a fine example for a child. Truthful, trustful, moral—let her rot wherever she is. Rot, I said."

No one could say that he was not justified. For a few minutes there was heavy gloom between them until Larry spoke again.

"What is it? Doesn't she want him?"

"Who, Amanda?"

"Yes, yes, who else?"

"We don't know yet," Norma answered. "I've been

told—Cecile heard—that she's in no condition just yet. I don't know. *I* certainly don't want to talk to her."

"Will you take him? Somebody has to, and you love the kid."

Now Lester, intervening, spoke quietly. "There are many things to be considered, Larry. My father says we must remember that Amanda has rights; you have them, too. The first thing, then, in a divorce is the granting of custody."

"A woman like her has no right to have custody!"

"That's for the court to determine."

"I don't want her to have him, you hear me?"

"Why not?" asked Lester.

"Why? Why should a woman like her get her way? It's a matter of principle!"

"But you don't seem to want him," Lester objected, still very quietly.

"I said I want *you* to take him, didn't I?"

The argument circled. Norma and Lester glanced at each other and shook their heads. Poor Larry was not even being rational.

"Maybe you'll be good enough to do something for me," he said abruptly.

"We'll do anything for you, Larry."

"Then get somebody to come to my house and take all her things away. Clothes, books, everything. I don't want to open my eyes in the morning and see anything that is hers."

"I'll do it tomorrow."

"And if it's not too much trouble, Norma, will you buy me a new bed? I'll need to spend only one more night here if you can do that tomorrow, too."

"I'll do that, too. And I'll also bring Stevie home. You can see there's no room here for him and Elfrieda—he needs her because Lester and I are gone all day. Amanda has no place right now, and Cecile still reports that she's in bad condition anyway. Elfrieda is willing to stay at your house, so that's the plan, at least for now." When he did not reply, she reminded him, very gently this time, "He's sixteen months old, Larry, and you're the only daddy he knows."

"I really, really have to talk to Amanda," Cecile said, speaking to Dolly over the telephone. "If she still won't see me, will she talk to me on the phone? Surely she wants news about the baby, doesn't she?"

"I gave her your message that he's at home again with Elfrieda and Larry, and that satisfied her for the time being. Only for the time being."

Cecile was growing impatient—this worry was now in its third week—and she implored, "Tell her I need to talk to her now. Please tell her I'm waiting on the phone for her."

Four or five minutes went by before a weak voice sounded in Cecile's ear. "I know you want to see me, but I just can't face anybody yet. I just can't."

"Even me?"

"Even you. Although I thank you for everything, for taking Stevie to your house . . . tell Peter I thank him so much—I really—" Then the voice broke.

After a minute, Cecile had to resume. "I hate to tell you, but they're getting a lawyer. Alfred Cole's office will handle the divorce. You'll need a lawyer too, Amanda—"

"I know. I need everything, a new job, an apartment

for Stevie and me—I can't think where to turn. I think people are pointing at me. I can't go home and face my family, I can't even tell the truth about the different phone number, even Lorena with her worthless man hasn't done what I've done, I can't stop crying—"

Dolly's voice interrupted. "You see what I mean, Cecile? She can't talk anymore. Hold off. Tell those people to hold off with the lawyer business for a couple of weeks so she can pull herself together. They should have a heart. For God's sake, the poor thing isn't an ax murderer, is she?"

"Your brother has been broken apart," said Alfred Cole to Norma. "He needs help, and badly. He needs to go for some counseling."

"We've worked on that, but he won't do it," Lester said. "He objects to 'washing dirty linen in front of strangers,' he tells us. It sounds absurd to us, but that's the way he sees it."

"Here's a suggestion. Take him away from this environment for a few days. Find an inn with a pool and some hiking trails out in the country. Get him away from the bad memories here. If it lifts his spirits even a trifle, it'll be a good thing."

Norma doubted that Larry would agree. Elfrieda, who quite naturally knew everything about what had happened and who was intelligent enough to report accurately what was happening now, agreed with Norma. Mr. Balsan was living in a fog. He spent most of his time in bed. He refused to answer the telephone; consequently it seldom rang anymore. He ate almost nothing. His clothes were starting to hang loose. And although he was in the same house with Stevie, he rarely noticed the child. In short, he had withdrawn from the world.

So it was with great surprise that Norma received Larry's message. Yes, he would accept their offer; a quiet country inn would be very nice. Lester and Norma would have to do the driving, however, since he did not trust his nerves to do it.

The choice having been left to Larry, they started out on the last week before the Labor Day weekend and headed north toward Canada. Lester and Norma took turns at the wheel, while Larry sat silently in the back-seat, waking only when they stopped at the side of the road to eat the lunch that Norma had packed.

As Elfrieda had reported, he ate almost nothing, but Norma and Lester, merely glancing at each other, made no comment. Sighing, she wondered how long he could go on like this.

The car climbed through foothills into the mountains, leaving full summer behind; the air grew cooler. Spotted here and there among the predominant evergreens were trees whose leaves had already yellowed. Toward evening Larry, rousing from his silence, directed them to turn off into a two-lane, blacktop road leading into what looked like a wilderness.

"Without a map," Lester said cheerfully. "You're quite a navigator."

"I studied the directions in the brochure."

After a few miles of steady climbing, Larry called, "Stop. This is it."

A long log building surrounded by the flowers of late summer lay before them. Behind it were dark blue mountains rising in tiers toward the western sky.

Norma felt instant delight. "Oh, this is beautiful, Larry! However did you find it?"

"Where's the lake?" asked Lester.

"In back of this building. The cabins face the lake. You'll see."

Two small cabins shared a wide veranda. Below them lay the glassy lake, on which no ripples stirred. Above them no leaf stirred in the windless air as Lester and Norma stood entranced.

At the far end of the veranda, Larry appeared at his door. "Like it?" he called.

"Like it?" Lester answered. "Next thing to paradise, that's all. I wish we could eat out here."

"Go on up to dinner. There's supposed to be dancing afterward, if you want it."

"Well, we'll see. But we're hungry. How long will it take you to shower and dress? We're both fast."

"You two go without me. I'm not hungry."

"Now listen to me." Lester strode toward Larry and spoke sternly. "If you want to starve yourself, that's your business, but we came on this trip together, and it's darn rude of you not to keep us company at dinner. That's all."

"I don't mean to be rude, Lester."

"You may not mean it, but the effect is the same. Come on, we'll be ready in twenty minutes. Okay?"

"If you insist, okay."

"I'm amazed that it worked," Norma said.

"Firmness often does work where softness fails. But not always," Lester said ruefully.

Larry entered the dining room dressed neatly for dinner, chose from the menu, and began to eat the food when it came. This was a good beginning. Perhaps,

Norma thought, our little trip really is going to work some wonder, for after the day's long silence, Larry was even making his first attempt at conversation.

"It's a nice place here, I think. Rustic without fake. Look up at the ceiling. The beams are genuine."

"Pine, do you think?" Lester, catching hold of the moment, was pretending an interest he probably did not feel. "They must weigh a ton each."

"Maybe oak," Larry answered. "Pine's too soft."

Lester kept the talk moving. "You might be interested in seeing our library building at Country Day. I'm no architect, of course, but I'm told that it's the nearest thing to an Elizabethan manse that you'll ever see outside of the originals. Let's make a date, and I'll show you. Stop by one day. I know you see enough construction in your business, but this is different."

A thrill of hope went through Norma. Like a normal man, Larry had started to eat and talk. The whole atmosphere in this place was encouraging; bright young couples were noisy, but not too noisy; a lively ten-year-old at the adjoining table was telling about his adventure in a canoe, while Larry was observing a white-haired couple who were being toasted with champagne. He was plainly making an effort to enjoy the evening. He even agreed to come one day with Lester and Alfred for doubles at Amos Newman's house; he had been there, he said, and it really was a beautiful place.

Then all of a sudden he drew something out of his pocket, and handing it across the table, remarked that perhaps they would "like to see this."

To Norma's shock, "this" was a snapshot of Amanda, wearing a long white dress and holding a bouquet, alongside a smiling Larry. In the background were tables with seated strangers, and in the corner a slice of the very fireplace that faced them now.

She could think of nothing to say except, "You chose this place on purpose! Oh, Larry, why?"

"Right in this corner they gave us a wedding cake. Eight years ago this week," he said. "I needed to come back." Then, choking, he stood up, excused himself, and left the table.

"Let him go," Lester ordered as Norma started to follow. "He needs to be alone."

"Maybe so. And yet if I were alone and didn't have you, I wouldn't have been able to live through this horror. Not that I'm doing all that well," she said, feeling the usual sting of tears waiting to be shed.

"But you are doing well," Lester said. "Very well," he repeated, stroking her free hand. "Remember, though, that it is far worse for him than it is for you."

"People say, when a child goes wrong, 'Well, we don't choose our children.' We don't choose our parents either, do we? I'll never, never forgive my father. What he did to Larry was unforgivable. Still, it was she . . . I blame her more . . . I've said this before, and I'll say it again. She lured him."

"Come," said Lester. "Order dessert. Or if you don't want any, let's go to the room."

In effect, he was telling her that enough was enough, and she knew he was right. Her father would have said, "You're beating a dead horse." Such an ugly expression! *Father.* Would she ever want to remember anything about him that wasn't ugly? But she must not afflict Lester with much more of this.

"We'll have dessert," she said. "There's peach pie, your favorite."

At nine o'clock, when they climbed the steps to the veranda, it was already dark in Larry's room. When they switched on the light in their own room, it poured across the veranda, and so revealed Larry standing at the rail looking out.

Lester called sharply to him. "What are you doing there?"

Perhaps the same thought had occurred to him as to Norma, that Larry might be contemplating something terrible. Below the railing lay murderous rocks and the deep lake . . .

"What are you doing there?"

"Nothing. Just thinking." The face that now turned in their direction was gaunt. How old he was! Men of sixty didn't look that old.

"There is nothing worth believing in anymore," Larry said.

"If you would let somebody try to help you," Lester began, "you would find—"

"No, no, you don't understand. There's no help. If a man isn't able to pull himself out of this and save his own self, then he isn't worth saving."

"That's not so," Lester argued. "You need to go back to work, Larry. Work is the ultimate, tried-and-true remedy. I mean that. Find something, some project that's new and difficult. You are the head of a big business—"

"No. It's Lawrence Balsan's business. I want no part of it. I hate his name. From now on, I've told you, I'm Daniel. Remember? Dan. That's my middle name. If anyone calls me Larry, I will not answer. I'm Daniel. You hear me?"

"We hear you, Dan," Lester said.

It was all eerie: the thick darkness, the rustling trees, the lurid, pale stream of light in which the sick man stood. For he was sick, very sick, humiliated in his manhood, cheated and betrayed.

"She never loved me! Norma, Lester, do you know why I wanted to come here? Do you? Because I don't. Maybe I thought I'd find some answer here. She never loved me. Maybe I began to know it eight years ago, right here on the veranda above this lake. Maybe I did, and didn't want to know it. Then again, I'm not sure of that, either. The baby came, and I was so glad—" He began to sob.

"I can't bear this," Norma whispered.

"Go inside," Lester urged. "I'll take care of him."

She was still thinking: What is to be done? I would go to the ends of the earth for him, do anything, say anything, for his sake. He was my mother when our mother died and our father had no time. He was my father when I was mocked in school, kept off the softball team, not invited to a dance . . . He is the soul of kindness and goodness and now he needs me—but what is to be done?

She was racking her brain for some way to distract and mend a broken spirit, when Lester returned.

"Don't unpack anything," he told her. "He wants to go home in the morning. This little trip is not working out. But at least we meant well."

CHAPTER TWENTY-ONE

Dolly's house in Cagney Falls stood in a row of similar small frame houses where, in times gone past, had lived that part of the population that served the great estates. Dolly was sitting on the porch steps, evidently waiting for Cecile.

"She's a little bit nervous about seeing you, Cecile. I've been telling her not to be, but she still is."

"It's been too long. I would have come long ago if she had let me."

"All she does is sit and read or take a walk out toward the country. She won't go near the center of town for fear of meeting somebody who knows her, she's that ashamed. Go on in. She's in the front room. Nobody's home. My mom and Joey and my sister are all out of the house, so you'll have it to yourselves."

You wondered about the differences in people. There was Mrs. Lyons, who had used the word "filth," and then there was Dolly. Mrs. Lyons was the one with sophistication, while Dolly was called the "airhead." Yes, you wondered. And feeling some palpitations, Cecile went inside.

After the first hug and kiss, they sat down and regarded each other almost timidly. Amanda spoke first.

"I didn't think you'd want to touch me. I've set myself apart from decency and decent people."

The statement, so honestly presented, seemed to require an honest reply. For a moment, Cecile considered it before she gave it.

"Yes, you have. But I can despise what you did without despising you. There's a whole other part of you that sees only too clearly, I guess, what you did. So I kissed you, and I still care about you very much."

Amanda bowed her head, spilling the bright, fair hair, which had grown longer, over her sober dark blue shoulders. Her elbows rested on her knees, with her chin held between her hands; in this girlish posture, she had used to sit on the bed while memorizing dates for history finals, so long ago.

"It wasn't just the drink," she said, not looking at Cecile. "I went mad. I went wild. I knew it, but I couldn't stop myself. Now I'll never stop being sorry about the people I hurt. Larry, L.B., everybody." Then after a pause, she asked, "How is Larry now?"

Surely this was a place for truth-telling, so Cecile told it. "Not at all well. Lester and Norma took him away for a few days, thinking it would raise his spirits, but it didn't work. They had to drive him home the next morning."

At this, Amanda raised her head. "But is he able to take proper care of Stevie?"

In this case it would be better to skirt the truth and spare Amanda more pain, thought Cecile.

"Stevie's well cared for," she said.

And that was true; between Norma and the nurse, he was living happily. "Stevie has Elfrieda, he has Norma, and he has Larry, so he's just fine."

"As long as he's with Larry I can be sure he is. I wish I could see Larry and tell him—tell him something, though I don't know how I'd say it." Amanda stopped. "Well, yes. I guess all I could really say is that I'm sorry." She stopped again. "I crushed him. I killed his father, and I haven't left much of a legacy for my child."

No one could refute a single word of all that. Cecile had known that this meeting would be very painful, yet she had not expected to be so moved. And she thought of the day that Stevie had left her house after a mere few weeks' stay. He had been holding the pink stuffed piglet that Peter had bought for him, and he had been laughing about something. He was often full of laughter. There had been such an ache in her heart to see him go! And he wasn't even hers.

"I'd like to talk to Larry about Stevie, but I don't seem to have the courage."

"You shouldn't even try. As soon as the law is involved one is not free to talk about the case; your lawyer does all the talking. Have you got a lawyer yet, Amanda?"

Amanda sighed. "I spoke to a young man who lives across the street here. He's just out of law school this year and he won't charge much. I told him I don't have much money."

An inexperienced young man to argue against Alfred Cole! It was almost cruel. But still, you never know . . .

"I'm all confused, Cecile. I'm not myself. This means that Larry is suing me for divorce, doesn't it? Not the other way around?"

Quite definitely, Amanda was not herself, to ask a question like that.

"Yes, he's suing you. The custody of Stevie will be part of it."

Amanda turned even more pale than she was already. Then she flushed and cried out, "Are they going to take him away from me? Is that what you're telling me?"

"I'm not telling you anything. A judge will decide who is the better parent, where the child will be best off."

There was a long silence. It was as if an enormous heavy hand had clamped down over the room and the two people in it. And then Amanda spoke, so softly that Cecile had to lean toward her to hear.

"I don't suppose anyone could decide in my favor after what's happened."

"I don't know," Cecile replied truthfully. "You're still the mother—"

"He's all I have now," Amanda murmured. "I love him so—I've always loved him but I—somehow I wasn't able to show it as I wanted to." She stood up, walked to the end of the room and back.

"I'll have to fight, Cecile. I don't exactly feel up to it, but I'll do it."

"Of course you will. You're a strong woman."

What else was there to say? I wouldn't give much for her chances, Cecile was thinking as she kissed Amanda and left.

Some weeks later when Cecile opened the front door, the dogs raced to greet her. The two handsome collies had been L.B.'s pride, so Norma had said, but she had no room for them, and Larry would have nothing to do with them. So they had been left in a kennel since that awful night in July.

"In prison," Peter had protested, "through no fault of their own. It's cruel. Let's take them."

A friendly pair, they led her now into his workroom, where they liked to lie under the table next to his feet. It was as if they knew he was their rescuer.

And Peter really was a rescuer, not merely of abandoned animals, either. Through their years together, Cecile had slowly been discovering the depth of his often-concealed kindness. Other people, the man who painted their fence, or a secretary in his office, had often disclosed to her what he had done for their benefit. Hearing her now, he swung around in the swivel chair and immediately, with some concern, asked about Amanda.

"I had planned to visit her again today, but Norma came over instead with news. Her father-in-law's partner has been having talks with Amanda's lawyer. It's pretty clear that Amanda will never get more than visitation rights."

"Did you expect anything more, with her history?" Peter responded.

"Not really. I only hoped—I called the house, planning to talk to Larry today, but as usual he wouldn't come to the phone. Elfrieda said he was still in bed. It was noon, too."

"Complete nervous breakdown, it seems. I wonder what comes next."

"I hate to imagine. He still won't pay any attention to the baby."

"Well, then, he ought to give him up and let Amanda have him, without any more legal fuss or delay. That's my opinion," Peter said stoutly.

"The strange thing is that he won't. He wants to punish her by witholding the child."

"She's the mother! Is there any question that she can't have her child?"

"That will be solved in a long, drawn-out divorce. Oh, lord, why ever did she wreck her life like this?"

Past the window the low sun gilded the grass. Birds, sparrows, jays, and cardinals swarmed around the feeder. "Our backyard is our Garden of Eden," Cecile said suddenly. "Poor Amanda could have had one, too."

"Until she ate the apple, darling."

"Such a bitter apple! Love's not supposed to taste bitter."

Peter smiled. "I know what you're thinking. You're thinking of that poem you always quote: 'How do I love thee? Let me count the ways'—and you're trying to fit it into poor Amanda's story."

"I guess I am," she conceded.

"Well, don't try, darling. You'll never make a perfect fit out of it. You just have to accept that a good person can do something abominable." He sighed. "Let's get down to our own business. Take a look at this." Holding up a long sheet of paper, closely printed, he continued,

"I've been working on it all afternoon. I came home early
from the office, put everything else aside to get this done
right. It's a succinct description of the project, a map in
words. It's a summary for the benefit of bankers who like
to grasp things quickly and get right to the point. Read it
and give me your opinion."

There it was, his beautiful conception, the circle with
the terminal-turned-cultural-center at the hub of the
wheel; the radiating spokes were as clear in her mind as if
they already existed. There were the tree-lined driveways
with bicycle paths and pedestrian paths alongside; the
low-rise inns and comfortable housing behind them ran
to the end, where lay the green open spaces on the edge
of the river.

And there he stood almost glowing, the dear author
of this art. For it was art, and for the second time that
day, though with an entirely different reason, Cecile was
intensely moved.

"It must be a strange feeling when you've worked so
long. I'm thinking of Michelangelo, when he finally com-
pleted the Sistine Chapel."

Peter's laugh exploded. "Wow! Listen to my wife!
Don't ever let anybody hear you say anything that dumb,
will you!"

"The hard work, the dedication are what I meant.
You've put your whole heart into this."

"Well, I can't say I haven't." He looked at the clock.
"I've got to rush back to the office. Some fellow who was
supposed to come tomorrow got the dates mixed. What
about you? Going to the hospital?"

"I'm going to see Amanda, to see how she's coping
with the not-so-good news."

* * *

"I suppose," Amanda said, "that you might call this a just punishment. At least, I know my mother would say so. She was very fond of Larry; she called him a prince. And he really is, he really is a good man—it's a pity . . ."

Cecile was thinking that, if not for Norma's love and care of Stevie, she would be forced to reveal the truth about Larry's condition. And yet, perhaps not, for her parents had told her that Alfred Cole was certain of the outcome, regardless of Larry's condition—short of outright insanity. *Amanda will never get custody, not in this city's courts,* he had declared. And Alfred Cole knew what he was talking about.

Amanda had steadied herself. At the clinic, Cecile had often witnessed, and marveled at, the way some people can lift themselves out of the pit and show great bravery in the face of bad news.

"Yes," Amanda repeated, "just punishment."

"Your lawyer agrees about the outcome, then?"

"Yes. He's very bright, and he's gotten other opinions, besides. My morals, you see."

"There was nothing wrong with your morals until—"

Amanda raised her hand. "Enough, Cecile. Thank you for all the good things you've done, but don't make me cry again. I have to start life over, and do better."

Now it was Cecile who needed to cry. For goodness knows what reason, she seemed to see Amanda sitting there in Dolly's chair, wearing the Sundale uniform she had worn long ages ago.

"If L.B. were here, Cecile, he would hope I would let Larry keep the baby—and I understand. To lose a wife, a father, and then a child—a child he so adored—it's too much. And Larry is vulnerable, anyway. Did you know that about him?"

"No. I thought quite the opposite."

To lose a baby you have held in your arms, Cecile thought, must be—must be the worst, worse than my twins. And she could not help but ask again whether there truly was no use in fighting the case.

"Not at the cost to everybody's health, and money. And what good would it do for me to have visitation rights when Larry hates me so? Of course he must, and Stevie would feel it. No, a clean break is best for him."

Amanda got up and opened the window, where a large brown moth was desperately fluttering.

"It was trapped," she said, "and I had to free it. It was trapped, like me that day I sat on the bench across from the post office after the doctor had told me I was pregnant. Does it sound too stupid for me to say that I can relate to a moth? I need to go far away. Far. Then perhaps I'll forget." A sad smile touched her mouth and receded. "You don't really believe that I'll forget."

No, Cecile did not believe it. There were some things that would never leave you; she herself had ceased to lament her unborn twins, but would she ever forget them? She looked about at the dim, mole-colored room and out toward the sleepy street. "Yes, if you need to leave here, go. Go to work, Amanda. Fill your mind."

"I have a job offer, and I'm accepting it. Dolly talked to one of our customers about me, and she knows somebody in California who'll take me into her dress shop." Again Amanda showed that wan, small smile. "I'm said to have a flair for clothes, but the funny thing is that I'm not a clotheshorse anymore and haven't been for a long time. All that changed when I—when I was with him."

"You can say the name," Cecile said gently. "You mean Mr. Balsan."

"With L.B. We read together and we talked about the music we'd hear and the places we'd see if—if things were different. I have never met a man like him, except maybe your husband." And clasping her hands in the gesture that Cecile remembered so well, Amanda cried out, "I know, oh, God, how I know that what we did was a moral horror! If I—if we had known what hurt would come of it, we would have stopped. But I want you to think of one thing if you ever do think of me: We loved each other. We had no right to, but we did. And for us two it was a beautiful love. We loved each other until the very last day." For a moment Amanda's voice broke. "I understand now why he had to leave me. It was because, in the end, he could not hurt his son. He was a good man, L.B. was, and always had been. I can't believe he's dead. I think of him every day, and I will always think of him."

Was it not astonishing that there could be any beauty or truth in an affair as sordid as this?

"And what about you, Cecile?" Amanda asked.

It was almost time to end the sorrowful meeting. What was done could not be undone. And so, after answering a few innocuous questions, Cecile did bring it to an end.

"Let me know where you'll be," she said as she embraced Amanda. "I'll be here for you if ever you need me."

At the bottom step she looked back to where Amanda stood in the doorway. She was the brightest object on the little street, as she always had been everywhere.

Suddenly Cecile was tired. This morning she had faced Amanda's grief, while now in the afternoon she was facing Norma's anger. Sometimes, no matter what the subject with which she tried to divert Norma, it always returned to this fundamental anger. Even the dogs had led her back to it.

"I used to be fond of them, but I can't stand the sight of them now. In my—" Obviously unable to say the word *father*, she stopped and resumed, "—in the house they always lay under a table or under the piano. I see they still do."

Cecile looked over to where the two dogs were dozing. Even those innocents were too much for Norma in her bitter rage.

"I can't understand how you could bring yourself to visit Amanda. If I didn't know you so well, I'd say it was a bit—well, disloyal of you."

It was the second time Norma had said it, and Cecile gave the same answer. "Not at all. I couldn't simply let her disappear, could I? Think about it."

"I'm thinking about it and I could, gladly, with great pleasure. She's nothing but a slut."

"As I sat there today, Norma, I suddenly saw her walking in at our door, the country girl come to the university with her old, banged-up suitcase and her head of curls."

"I don't want to think about that, Cecile. I'm not like you."

"Well, she hasn't hurt me the way she's hurt you."

"No, you'd be different even then. Peter would, too. You're well matched, the two of you. Sometimes I think you're the best people I've ever known. And sometimes you're so good that you wouldn't even avenge an injury, which is stupid."

"Don't make saints out of us," Cecile said firmly, "because we're not. I'm only saying that Amanda is something more than a tramp without a conscience. She's a complicated human being, as we all are."

"And I say again that this kindness of yours can go too far. I don't give a damn. If it wasn't against the law, I'd shoot her, and I don't mind saying so. What she's done to my brother! I'm going to fight for him and Stevie and care for them as long as I live. I'd do anything for either one of them."

Norma was a fighter. Strange, Cecile thought, that I never realized how small she is, there in the low chair with those poor legs stretched out. Why, she's been defending those legs all her life! She's accustomed to fighting.

"Have another cup of tea. It'll soothe you," Cecile said.

So they sat for a while and talked, keeping to neutral subjects such as Norma's Latin textbook for beginners. Soon it would be time for Norma to leave, and five o'clock could not come soon enough for Cecile.

Sometimes, she thought as she closed the front door, it is easier to work with troubled strangers at the hospital than to be involved with one's oldest friends.

"What kind of a day did you have?" Peter always asked when he came home.

"A complicated one. I came away with such an ache, after seeing Amanda! You would have, too. It wasn't just a fling, Peter, although most people would think so and I had thought so, too. They really loved each other. They really did. And yet it was so utterly wrong. And then in the afternoon Norma came by."

"What, again?"

"It seems to help her to vent her worries. She wasn't too pleasant, I can tell you that. Of course, she's absolutely frantic about Larry. He's become a total recluse. She thinks he's ashamed to go back to the old office, but he has no other place to go to, and he needs to get out of the house. He needs to be revived. To be inspired."

"Poor guy." Peter frowned and shook his head. "Let me think. I might have an idea or two. You know what? The man I'm seeing this afternoon is having me restore a wonderful little 1910 theater out in Watersburg. He also owns a row of decrepit stores out there that he wants to gentrify because the whole area is changing. That might be a good thing for Larry. It's right in his line. You can tell Norma about it. I've got another thing in mind, too. Tell Norma I'm serious. I'll find something. Poor guy," he repeated.

CHAPTER TWENTY-TWO

"Y ou cannot believe," said Norma to anyone who asked, "what has been happening to Larry. After the summer's disaster, we thought he was losing his mind. And he was. We were witnessing a complete breakdown. And then, after going through hell, we got the idea—actually, it came from a psychologist, a friend of Lester's—of presenting him with a definite plan for work, something spelled out that would equal or surpass anything his father had ever done. And you know, I think that's what has finally appealed to him, the thought that he could surpass his hated father. So, having grown up with real estate and construction, I got together three or four possibilities for him to mull over, condominium developments, a mall—big possibilities. Larry always knew how to put through a deal, how to pull a syndicate

together and get the financing; in fact, a lot of the Balsan
work these last few years was not L.B.'s, but his.

"He's actually made an office out of the den. The
computer was already there, but now he's added a telephone extension and a fax. Obviously he's working hard
on something, but he doesn't tell me what it is, and I
don't ask. It's enough to see a small smile on his face
again. We had given up hope, I tell you. I'll never forget
the day—it's only a couple of weeks ago—when for the
first time he picked up Stevie and hugged him the way he
used to do. Stevie had come downstairs from his nap and
run to me. So I looked at Larry and I said straight out,
'You're all he has. I've told you that. Do you realize it?'
And Larry looked back at me, and he burst out crying,
and picked up Stevie and kissed him.

"I'd been going over there every day, you know, to
check on Stevie, but there's no need for that anymore. I
only go now and then, the way normal relatives do. Now
that Larry is beginning to rally—imagine, he was carving
a Halloween pumpkin for Stevie yesterday—I can lead
my own life again.

"By the way, when you see him, be sure to call him
'Dan.' He's very insistent about that. A new life needs a
new name, I guess. It's really a miracle."

CHAPTER TWENTY-THREE

O n a quiet autumn evening with winter about to descend, Peter and Cecile, walking homeward hand in hand and holding flashlights, saw a car in their driveway.

"Why, it's your father's car!" Peter exclaimed. "Did you expect him?"

"Not at all. I wonder—"

"Of course! Roland and Baker are in New York this week, tying the final knot with the big lenders at Bishop National. And your father's so excited that he can't wait till tomorrow to tell us about it."

"So this is it? The knot tied?"

"Yes. They're the major players in the whole deal. That's where the big mortgage comes from."

"It seems to me this has all taken forever."

"Just about four years. That's not long when you

consider the enormous size of the project, the dickering with all the owners, some guy who holds out for his crazy price because he knows you need six feet of his property, the court cases, environmental commissions, the local politicians, the zoning people—four years is par for the course. As for me, I'm only the architect. All I had to do was sit down alone and think." He squeezed her hand. "I'm terribly excited, Cele. You'll probably have to tie me down when I see them turning the first shovelful of earth."

Harriet was standing on the walk when they reached the car. All out of breath, she rushed her words. "Amos is already sitting on the doorstep, he's so impatient. He's so upset! I had to take the wheel away from him. I couldn't even allow him to drive."

"Why, what is it?" cried Cecile.

"Let's go in. No, nobody's died. He'll tell you. I didn't want him to come here. Tomorrow would have done just as well."

"Stop it, Harriet!" Amos, red of face, was almost incoherent. "Open the door, hurry up, and let's sit down."

Once in the living room, he himself stood, and almost choking on his words, delivered his message.

"You won't believe it. You won't want to, but it's authentic. Listen to this: At a quarter past seven, Roland called from New York. They've dropped us. Bishop National has dropped us. Good-bye. Finished. Out."

"I don't understand," Peter said.

"Out!" Amos roared. "What don't you understand? Don't you know what 'out' means? No loan. No mortgage. The deal's over."

Never had Cecile seen her father so distraught. His face

was now an alarming purple, and his Adam's apple, always prominent, was threatening to burst out of his neck.

Peter was sitting stiffly, as if he were numbed, while Cecile and Harriet looked to him to deny the shock that Amos had given.

Frowning as people do when confronting a puzzle, he said quietly, "But we had an agreement, written and signed."

"No, no, no, it's not that simple!" Amos waved his arms, sweeping all argument away. "We had dozens of agreements, didn't we? Dozens of smaller packages, but the major loan, the guarantee that covers everything else—oh, listen! We're not lawyers here, and it's too complex and I'm exhausted. Listen, it's this way. Let me make it short. Perhaps Bishop National was the roof of the house with everybody else inside. What good is a house without a roof?"

"You're saying then that it's all over?" asked Peter, still quietly. "All these years, all this work, thrown away just like that?"

"From our point of view, yes, but not from theirs. They're going ahead with the terminal and the acreage. Oh, they're going ahead all right! Except not with us."

"Then with whom?"

"We don't know. Roland swore he wouldn't leave New York until he found out. But what's the difference who it is?"

Cecile was having a claustrophobic moment. You've traveled a long, long road, she thought. You're sure of your direction, you're riding cheerfully on your way, and then suddenly there's a high wall with no exit.

On the pretext of letting the dogs out for the night, she got up and went outside. Peter's voice was sounding in her head. Was he saying this right now in the room she had just left, or was she remembering some past, intimate confession?

This is the most thrilling work I have ever done. It has filled my mind and my days.

I must not cry, she thought, steeling herself before going back inside. Amos and Harriet were already leaving, Harriet saying again that they should not have come.

"We disturbed your sleep for nothing. What can you do about it tonight? But Amos insisted."

"All right, I'm sorry," he said. "But if I should hear anything later tonight, do you want me to phone you?"

"Please do," said Peter.

They went upstairs. Cecile hardly knew what to say, and apparently he did not know, either. Because it was too early to go to bed, they settled into their easy chairs, each with a book. After a long while, after she became aware that he, like herself, had not turned a page for many minutes, she spoke.

"Darling, it could be a great mistake, a misunderstanding. It could be something temporary that will be settled tomorrow. Those things happen. Something tells me that's all it is."

"There's no point guessing," Peter said. "Let's try to sleep."

He had hardly finished the sentence, when the telephone rang. When he answered it, she watched his face for a clue. It stiffened and froze. When, after little more than a minute, he put the receiver back, he was stunned.

"There's no mistake, Cele. It's gone. Gone to the Balsan Real Estate Company. Larry Balsan. Can you believe it?"

The next day's newspaper had a full spread of news and editorial comment about the enormous project on the railroad property. In the dark early morning, after a night without any sleep, Peter and Cecile laid the paper on the kitchen table between them and read, as one might read about the death of someone dear whom one had seen just yesterday, a description of Peter's plan.

"It is a highly original scheme. In place of the usual urban grid, the pattern is circular, with the terminal as the center. From there the streets radiate as far west as the river, and north toward the bridge, which provides a link with a revived Lane Avenue."

In total dismay, in total shock, they raised their eyes to each other. Then, without speaking, they returned to the printed page.

"Alfred Cole, attorney and yesterday's spokesman for the Balsan firm, characterizes the proposal as 'one of the most important projects ever undertaken in this city, perhaps even in the state. It will revive commerce, create employment, and bring new prosperity to a benighted area.' Mr. Cole also provided what he termed a 'very rough diagram,' showing the wheel-like appearance of the plan, the spokes to be lined with condominiums, shops, and high-rise international hotels as far as the spot where the circumference reaches the river. There it is expected that a spectacular casino will be erected."

Not all the editorials and comments agreed with that

estimate. Some of them even decried the commercialization of what could instead be turned into a pleasant neighborhood, with the wetlands left intact and green. But even these agreed that the idea of the circle was a "stroke of genius, a masterpiece," or it was "dazzling," or it had "a Parisian grace."

Peter's lips were trembling. In alarm, Cecile reached over and grasped his hand. Then, with a surge of grief, she laid her head on his shoulder and wept.

For a long time they sat together. At last she got up, wiped her eyes, and brought a pitcher of water to the table. Each of them poured a glassful, drank, and stared out of the window.

"Who could have known?" she asked. "It has to be a crazy coincidence."

His reply was so rough that it startled her. "Can't you read? It's theft, pure and simple. Even the language is mine: *rotunda, axis, rotation,* my descriptions of the museum in the terminal, and all my final summary. Coincidence!" Staring fully at Cecile, he demanded, "Who was here? Who's been in this house?"

"I don't understand what you mean."

"I mean that someone was in my workroom. Which Balsan was it? Or which friend of theirs? Who gave it to them?"

"Peter, I cannot imagine. You know that the door locks automatically when anyone leaves that room. It's the same kind of door that they have in hotels. So who could get in without a key?"

"Now let's get this straight. Think like a detective. Who in that Balsan family ever comes to this house?

Norma and Lester haven't been here or anywhere together since they've had Larry on their hands. And Larry—Dan—hasn't been here since last summer. That leaves Norma, having lunch with you. You probably left the door open, propped open with the vacuum cleaner or something, and she snooped."

"I don't use a vacuum cleaner when I'm having a guest, Peter. So that's no solution."

"Then the only other one is that you talked. Not on purpose, for Heaven's sake, but just carelessly, the way people do."

"You should be ashamed of yourself," she said, "first, to think that I would be so stupid or careless. And second, to subject Norma to suspicion is horrible."

"Well, if you don't want me to suspect her, that leaves you. You dropped some hint to somebody—oh, innocently, of course. I didn't say on purpose, for God's sake, but you did it. You had to. How else did it get to Balsan?"

Cecile was furious. "Easy to blame your wife, isn't it? You wouldn't dare blame Mr. Baker or Mr. Roland."

"I would dare blame anybody, Cecile, and you know damn well I would. But as it happens, neither Baker nor Roland ever saw my summary. Even your father never actually laid eyes on that last draft. I'm going to call him right now. I need to go over and talk to him. We have to talk."

When Peter came back from the telephone, he reported that Amos was already on his way here. "You'd better get dressed," he said curtly, and left her. A few seconds later she heard the vicious slam of the workroom door.

* * *

Amos's emotions were exhausted. Wearily, he listened to Peter's accusation and Cecile's defense, and wearily he chided them both.

"What's the sense in this talk? I hate to admit that the signs all point to you, Cecile. There is no other way this stuff could have leaked out! You talk too much. Women always talk too much. Your mother does. I love her dearly, but she's a woman, and so are you."

Cecile, too, was exhausted. There was no use trying to refute such an outrageous, silly statement out of a time long past. *Women talk too much!* Well, let these two men talk! She would close her eyes and settle back to listen.

"With hindsight," Amos said, "we can see that we shouldn't have dallied so long with Bishop National. But for safety's sake, to avoid exactly what has happened— and there's the irony—we wanted their signature to the effect that they would go through with the deal if our design should meet with their approval. Lord knows there wasn't any risk in that. And we would have their guarantee on the money. Who can be a more respectable outfit than Bishop National?"

Peter's voice was hollow. "A couple of days' delay. What's that poem? 'For want of a nail, the battle was lost'?"

Amos sighed. "Baker's made a lot of inquiries around town. He must have been on the phone all night. It seems that Balsan's been going after our local lenders for over a month. He's agreed to take a little less in the way of loans and to pay a little more interest. I have a hunch, and Baker agrees with me, that a lot of these people who've been doing business with Balsan for thirty years felt sorry for Larry and were happy to help him get on his feet, after all the scandal and tragedy. All the more so because it wasn't going to cost them anything. In fact, it was going to cost them a good deal less, as I just told you."

"Besides," Peter added, "he also brought them that 'highly original' design."

"Yes, and having Alfred Cole's contacts didn't hurt, either," Amos said bitterly.

Cecile roused herself to return Peter's insult. "You mean that there isn't any fight left in either of you? Why don't you sue?"

At that Peter jumped in his seat. "Very, very smart, Cecile. On what grounds shall we sue, when it's obvious that you gave the whole thing away to your dear, trusted friend? Your little musketeer?"

Cecile shouted at him. "I am so hurt, so angry at you that I can't even look at you. Accusing me—"

"I'm not 'accusing' you of anything. You're not the criminal here. You're only a woman who talks too much. You didn't *mean* to ruin all my work, you only—"

Here Amos interrupted. "This is a waste of energy, and you're giving me a worse headache than I already had before I got here. Listen to me. Alfred Cole is a friend of mine, and he comes to my house for tennis most Saturday afternoons. He's due today. I want to have a friendly talk with him, probe a bit, and get the lie of the land before we make any decisions."

"Be careful," Peter warned. "He's a lawyer. With all respect to you, you're not used to verbal combat."

"Well, you're not, either. But you stand at the heart of the problem, and you should be there, anyway. And you should be there too, Cecile."

"I had every intention of being there, even if I wasn't wanted," she retorted.

Alfred Cole, dressed for tennis with his racket on his knees, took a long, thoughtful look over the spreading lawns and the remnants of summer roses, still dotted here and there in Amos Newman's garden. When he spoke again, his tone of puzzlement bore a trace of temper, or so it seemed to Cecile.

"I thought I came for tennis," he said, "but here we sit, just talking and getting nowhere."

"It's not 'just' talking," Amos corrected him. "It's highly important to us"—this with a nod toward Peter—"as I'm sure you must understand. It's of the essence, as you lawyers say."

"I could understand if I knew anything about it. As I've tried to explain, I'm only the lawyer for Dan Balsan. I haven't the slightest knowledge of where this design originated, other than in Dan's head."

"Did you know nothing," asked Peter, "about the diagram that was in the newspaper?"

"Nothing."

"I'm telling you that it is my diagram, Mr. Cole."

"If that is the case, then somebody must have given it to him to copy. Or else, it is sheer coincidence."

Now Amos intervened. "Alfred, how many years have we known each other? Don't we go back as far as June six, 1944? Let us be frank with each other now. This is no coincidence, and we both know it."

"We're talking in a circle, Amos. Let's go back to the beginning." And turning toward Peter, Alfred said quietly, "The only other person who was familiar with your work was your wife. She had total access to it, she and nobody else. This you admit. Therefore it follows that she talked about it—to whom we can only guess. She alone knows the answer."

All eyes were on Cecile. They pressed, they peered, they bored into her, and they were suddenly so intolerable that she stood up and walked away.

The steps from the terrace led down to the "long walk" that she had trod as a bride. At the far end, where the improvised altar had been, there was now a little gazebo in which on a summer afternoon one might sit in the shade with a book. Here in the quiet, with the yellow leaves drifting and the sweet recollection of the past, here all was peace.

But there was such a roaring in her head! It was hopeless; every one of them, from Alfred Cole who was the enemy, to the others who were not, had arrived at the conclusion: Cecile was the cause.

Even her mother had asked gently, "Are you sure that you never let anything slip? I know how you two trusted each other."

Yes, Mother, we did. Once there were three of us, remember? And we all trusted each other. Of course, we were very young . . .

When the throb and roar subsided, she got up and walked back to the terrace. Voices had risen during her brief absence, and the atmosphere was hot.

"Do you realize what's been done here?" The deep bass belonged to Amos. "A good man has been given a blow enough to topple him. Pour paint on an artist's masterpiece! Plagiarize an author's book! Seize a scientist's latest experiment and claim it as your own! It happens all the time."

"My wife trusts," Peter said. "If she did reveal what should not have been revealed, an honorable woman would not have taken advantage of her trust. I have the impression that Norma is very clever. She could have wangled it out of Cecile. She is the only one of the Balsans who has had any contact with Cecile."

Cole rose from his chair and shouted. "If you're going to persist with your absurd accusation, if you're going to sue, at least have the decency—since you talk about decency—to sue Dan Balsan. Leave my son's wife alone. You have no right to accuse her. It's a crime."

"Don't shout at us," cried Amos. "You're in my home. Have some respect."

"You brought me here under false pretenses. I came to play tennis." Alfred, crying back, flourished his racket. "So go ahead. Bring suit. You stand as much chance of winning as a snowball in hell. Go ahead. Go to court. Make fools of yourselves. Make a fool of this young woman, Cecile. You admit she's the only person who has access to your papers. If there is any guilty one, she's it. Guilty of having a loose tongue. She could have prattled to a dozen women, for all you know."

Amos's cheeks were burning. "Leave my premises. Leave," he ordered.

"I've left," Alfred snarled from partway down the walk. "And if you ever come within a thousand miles of me you'll be too near."

Transfixed, they stood and listened until the last sounds of Alfred's engine had died away.

* * *

When you are in a car and so distraught that you are not capable of speech, the best means of avoidance is to play some music, Cecile thought, and that was exactly what Peter was doing. She understood better than anyone could that he was feeling a loss akin to a death. She understood too, after they arrived home, why he walked straight to his workroom and shut the door.

Yet she tried to make contact. "You haven't eaten all day. You'll have a headache."

"And you think that putting food in my stomach will cure this headache?" he answered.

At least he had not finished the sentence as he might have: *this headache that you caused.* But she had not caused it! Of that she was as certain as if her life depended on it. She had her own share of weaknesses and faults; forgetfulness and carelessness were not among them. It was a terrible thing to be falsely accused and have no way, no way at all, of proving that the accusation was false. Yes, of course he would ultimately forgive her, but how could he forget? Always this knowledge would lie between them, a chronic ache in each of their hearts.

Hours later, Peter had not yet come out of that room. Cecile had not been able to read, to do a household chore, or to lie down. The sun was low in the sky and very golden when she had the idea that a long walk might help her. Yet the aftermaths of that day, the ugly scene with Alfred Cole and the feel of Peter's anger, were too heavy; her legs felt too weary for any country walk. Yet she could not sit still, either.

"Walking the floor," it was called whenever the nerves

would not let the body rest. Back and forth through the rooms, down the hall and out onto the porch she went. Passing the window of Peter's office, the one that gave onto the porch, she peered in to see what he was doing and saw him at the long table that served as drawing board and desk. His arms were folded on the table and his head rested on his arms. An open newspaper lay beside him. Very likely he had been trying to read and had given up the attempt. Pity ran like a soundless sob in her chest.

Suddenly, where the pity lay, where the ache lay behind her eyes, something struck her, and she stood transfixed. The light, the golden light of late afternoon, was beaming low under the roof of the porch and through the window where the newspaper lay. She had only to bend a few inches to read: East Side Hockey Team Chooses Captain. Tax Bill Fought in Committee. Then a whole column, the full length of the page, about a burglary. She could read it clearly.

In a frenzy, she ran inside and pounded on the office door.

"What on earth?" Peter said as he opened it.

"Give me your summary. Your design. Quick."

"What's the matter with you? Can't you at least let me have an hour's rest in peace?"

She ignored his words. Seizing the precious summary from the chair on which, in his despair, he had apparently cast it aside, she placed it precisely on top of the newspaper.

"Now come outside to the porch. Please. I'm serious, Peter."

Reluctantly, he went, looked where she told him to look, and turned away.

"So? What about it?" he demanded.

"Don't you see? This is how Norma saw it."

"Ridiculous. To begin with, she was never alone in this house. At least, that's what you claim."

"I never said she was never left by herself for a couple of minutes. I went to the door when the mailman came, I went to the bathroom, didn't I? Norma was always agitated. She often walked up and down, and one day—"

"And one day she got the idea—"

"Will you let me finish, Peter? Look how the sun comes through that slit between the louvers. It aims like an arrow at your window. Of course, you have to catch it at just the right time. The right time of day and of year. In another season or another hour there's too much shade here, and it's too dark to read. But right now, look." Her thoughts and her tongue were racing. "Here's yesterday's paper with the quotes. She's changed some words so that they won't be exactly like yours. They sound like her: *circumnavigate,* where you had *go around.* That's the way she talks. Look back at the rest of it, Peter. There's your diagram. It isn't exactly the same, but ninety percent of it is."

Peter scoffed. "She took a chance too, didn't she, standing here all that time with a pencil and paper while you were getting the mail in at the front door? This sheet of mine measures fourteen inches in length, with narrow margins. That's a lot of print to copy. And I doubt that she came fortified with the right kind of camera, or any camera. No, think up a better one, Cele."

"Peter! Listen to me! She didn't copy. She memorized. Norma has a photographic memory."

"Don't tell me she can memorize all this."

"She can. She can remember a whole page of history, dates and all, in two minutes. We used to marvel at her when we roomed together. If Amanda were here, she would tell you."

Rarely now did she speak that name. It had a sad, far-away sound, like a chime that lingers in the air.

"Cele, search your memory. Can you swear that you never accidentally—"

Again it was too much, and she began to cry.

"For God's sake, don't cry! I can't stand it. Don't cry. I won't ask you again. It's settled, it happened, you made a terrible mistake, and we can't do anything about it. Just stop crying."

A slender pencil of sunlight was moving around the corner, leaving the desk and Peter's summary illegible in shadow. Looking into his face, she saw that he was in furious distress, and at the same time, he wanted to control his anger because he loved her. She knew, too, that she was asking him to accept something that was very hard to believe. A photographic memory, though not impossible, was too rare, and rarer still in a case like this one, with all the details of the complicated diagram. And so she could easily envision those future moments in which silently, against his will, these terrible doubts would arise in his mind again and assail him. He would be careful not to reveal them, in order to keep the peace of the house, but they would be there all the same. If only there was somebody who could confirm what she had just told him about Norma!

For a few moments, she stood quite still. Then, suddenly, a new thought came flashing. "I want you to listen to Amanda."

"Listen to Amanda? What is this? What are you talking about? Why the devil should I talk to her? Anyway, you said she's gone to California."

"She might not have left yet. I want you to get onto the extension, Peter, and listen. Go into the hall. I'm asking you this very, very earnestly. Please. Oh please, just do it for me."

As she called Dolly's number, she was aware of Peter's agitated breathing on the other phone; she could see the black disapproval on his face as clearly as if he were still standing next to her.

"She's upstairs packing her things," Dolly said. "You've just caught her. She's taking a night flight to California. I'll get her."

"You called to say good-bye again?" asked Amanda.

"Well, yes, but—well, no, not exactly. I called you to ask you for a favor. You'll think it's crazy. But it isn't crazy. It's very important. I know you're in a hurry, so I won't take time to explain. Peter's on the other phone, and I want him to hear you answer something about Norma."

"I don't want to do this," Peter said.

"Please, Peter. Please. It's very simple, Amanda. Just tell him—us—what you know about Norma. Is there anything unusual about her?"

"My goodness, that's a strange question. Unusual? You mean her legs?"

"No, no. Think hard."

"That she was uncomfortable around men?"

"Something else."

There was a pause. "Well, she had a good sense of humor, I remember."

"True. Anything more?"

"I'm trying to think. Oh, she's very smart."

"True."

"An exceptional student."

"In what way? Can you describe?"

"Well, for one thing, she had a photographic memory. She could look at a page for a couple of minutes, recite what she'd read, turn to the next page, and do it all over again. She could really have gone on a game show or something."

"Thank you, Amanda. That's exactly what I wanted to know. Exactly. Now I won't keep you. Have a safe trip. And send me your address in California. I'll keep writing to you about Stevie. Good luck."

The phones clicked off, first Peter's, and then Cecile's. When he came back into the room, she saw by his lowered glance that he was embarrassed.

"Extraordinary," he murmured as if to himself.

This was hardly the time and surely not a subject for any feelings of triumph or for any words like "I told you so." In troubled silence, then, she waited for him to speak.

"I—everyone, but mostly I—need to apologize for—for doubting you. For me not to believe you—it was an attack on you. I attacked your intelligence when I let myself think you could have given my work away even by accident. You, of all people! I'm ashamed, and I'm sorry, Cele. I'm sorry more than I can ever say."

A small, wan smile crept over her lips as she answered him. "Think nothing of it. My parents attacked me, too." The little smile receded. "But none of that matters much now, does it? The terrible question is: What are we going to do?"

"File a suit, I should say. Get a lawyer. Get one of the best in the city."

"If this were any other case, we'd no doubt go to Alfred Cole. Can you believe it?"

In deep disbelief, they were immobilized, standing in the center of the room just looking at each other, when the telephone rang.

It was Norma's voice that came over the wire in voluble lament. "I just heard what happened at the Newmans' house. Those terrible accusations, when it's all sheer coincidence! You know it is, Peter. Oh, hasn't my poor brother been through enough without being assaulted like this?"

"Nobody's assaulting your poor brother, Norma. And I really don't want to discuss it with you, anyway," he said.

"We can make an appointment."

"No, really, Norma. I'm sorry, I don't want to talk to you at all, and I'm going to hang up right now."

Cecile made a sudden resolve. "I'm going to talk to her. I'm going to call and ask her to meet me someplace, neither here nor at her house, but on neutral ground, like the library or the park."

"It will be nasty, and nothing will come of it. You won't get anywhere with her. You'll only upset yourself. Anyone who's gone this far isn't going to give up what she's stolen, no matter how you appeal or reason. Don't do it."

"Just the same, I'm going to try."

Norma was nervous, a nervous enemy. On the hard bench, she kept shifting from one haunch to the other. Plainly, she would have liked to get up and run away from the eyes that Cecile was deliberately fixing upon her. One could almost, in an ironic way, feel sorry for her and her predicament.

"You know you're lying, Norma. And you know that I know exactly what happened: You were pacing back and forth as usual, and you saw what I admit should have been better hidden—oh, what's the use? Why don't you simply admit it? We don't have to take legal action. We're decent people, and we can find a decent way to settle this."

Even as she spoke, she was aware that all this repetitious talk was futile, as Peter had predicted. There was no "decent way to settle" that would not involve Balsan's complete withdrawal, and that was not about to happen, not with Norma in charge. Nervous or not, she was immovable. If Amanda were here in person, *she* could testify to Norma's ability. But that was absurd. Poor Amanda, to stand up in court in this city as a reliable witness?

Yet Amanda would never have done what Norma had done. Amanda had heart. She could easily have taken the baby away from Larry and left him, yet she had not done it to him.

Norma, she wanted to say, *remember the three musketeers? Why are you doing this to my dear Peter and to me? He has always been so kind to you. Only a few months ago, he—*

But she had already said enough. They both had, and it was time to end the talk, time to leave. So, without any mention of seeing each other again and without even a handshake, they parted.

Often in the days and nights that followed, through a jumble of meetings, consultations with lawyers, and the incessant ringing of the telephone, Cecile had bitter thoughts. How stupid life could be, how frustrating, haphazard, and unjust! Was it not incredible that a friend as dear and *sisterly* as Norma could have done what she did? And was it not senseless that Amanda's love affair could have reached into Peter's life and turned it around?

The air was heavy with unanswered questions. Their brittle speech and their silences were tense. And one day, driven by worry and impatience, Cecile burst forth.

"What's the problem? Why the delay? It seems so simple. What are we waiting for? We've already wasted two weeks."

"It's not that simple," Peter answered grimly.

"Why isn't it? I don't understand. It's a theft. What's complicated about that?"

"Because, as we've been told, they will claim that you talked freely about the idea. You thought it was interesting that Larry had had a similar idea, which Norma had discussed with you. It was all a very friendly interchange of ideas. And anyway, his plan is not exactly like mine—"

"No, of course it isn't. She was clever enough to change it just a little bit, wasn't she?"

Peter sighed. In all their years together, she had never heard him sigh as often as he had been doing during these past weeks.

"Well, our lawyers are evolving a strategy, and it doesn't go so fast. That's all I can say at this point," he told her. "And you should know that although the lawyers are fairly certain that we would win in the end, it's you who would be deeply involved, as you can see from what I've just been telling you."

"Well, and if I were, I wouldn't mind."

"You don't know what it's like to be examined and cross-examined in a courtroom. The opposite side would try to make you look like a fool. Do you really want that?"

He was thinking of her! He whose achievement had been smashed as a city is plundered, was thinking of her! And filled with a tremendous surge of protective love, she cried out. "I don't care, I told you! I want revenge. We'll go to court and we'll fight. I'll fight. Go back and tell them all. Tell the lawyers, Roland, my father, everybody."

Intensely moved, he put his arms around her and did not answer.

More days went by. They were well into the third week of their troubles, and because he was involved in them every day, inevitably without having reached any conclusions, she ceased to question him. He came home at all hours; their late supper was eaten in front of the television, which was something they had rarely done before. Understanding that he had as yet nothing to tell her, she kept a worried silence, only turning upon him now and then her worried glance.

More days passed. And one evening, when Peter

opened the front door, she saw in his face that he at last had something definite to say.

"Sit down," he said. "We've reached a decision. We're dropping the case. We're not going to sue."

"What? What are you saying?"

"You heard. The lawyers, your father, Roland, and all the rest of them have agreed. It's over."

His tone was grim, and she was appalled. "Why? Because of me? Because I would be dragged into it?" Yes, that must be the reason. Her husband and her father were shielding her. . . . "What do you think I am? A coward, a delicate lady who has to be protected? You ought to be—"

"No. Your father might have had such thoughts, but he's of a different generation. I would have let you struggle through it because I know you and how courageous you are. We stand together, you and I. No, the reason is something else, and nothing to do with you. The partners simply do not want to be involved in years of litigation. We would probably win. Yes, almost undoubtedly we would. But it would cost a fortune. And it would waste time that the other investors feel they can spend more prudently on another venture. It won't be as grand as this one, but it will be a lot more profitable than tying themselves up in the courts with this. That would leave me to go it alone, and obviously I can't afford to do that. So that's it, Cele. It's settled. From their point of view it certainly makes sense. And when you think about it, it makes sense from ours, too. It's simply not worth the wear and tear on the spirit."

She burst into tears. "Your work, your vision—it was your brainchild!"

"Children die," he said.

There came a long moment during which they looked into each other's eyes. And suddenly there passed across his grave, still face that old, brave smile, the kind he had shown to her when they lost the twins.

"There's still a beautiful world out there in spite of all," he said. "We've lived and loved before there was this project, and we'll do it again." He held out his arms. "Cele, darling, come to me."

More than once, as the years went by, Norma became aware that Lester sometimes looked sharply in her direction, whenever the "coincidence" happened to be mentioned. They would probably have had a few rough times if the subject had been pursued, but neither of them wanted any rough times. Nor did Alfred Cole, so noted for his keenness as a litigator. It was a subject best not talked about.

It was, however, not always possible to keep it from intruding into one's thoughts. Unfortunately, well-meaning people—or are they merely intrusive gossips?—love to come running with information that they are sure will be interesting to you.

And so in the course of time Norma learned that Amanda had done very well in California.

"I remember," someone said at a dinner party, "she could make you feel that the world was a happy place. There was so much life in her. And she was brave. She went out there, swallowed her medicine, and started all over again. Made a place for herself in the community—good work at the hospital—that sort of thing."

"She owns her own dress shop in Sacramento," another reported, "and I heard she's going to open a branch in the suburbs. Her house is absolutely charming, somebody told me. She entertains beautifully, and naturally with all her sparkle she's in no want of men."

At that point, apparently to their embarrassment, the speakers recalled that Norma was at the table, so the subject of Amanda was immediately dropped.

With looks like those, that body, that head of curls, Norma thought, almost anything is forgiven, isn't it? Once, speaking of Amanda, Cecile had said that Peter had called her "a magnet." And even Lester, my own husband, she thought, had tactlessly reported to her when somebody had told him how Amanda took care of her parents and was known for her charities in California.

Why didn't people remember instead that she had killed my father and almost killed my brother? No, they prefer to talk about her sweetness, smiles and her blond hair!

Fortunately, though, California was a long distance from Michigan, so Norma was highly unlikely to glimpse Amanda while crossing a street. This, however, was not the case where Cecile was concerned.

At a restaurant in the city one evening, who should stop at Norma's table but Mrs. Lyons, chatty as ever.

"I saw your friends Cecile and Peter Mack the other day. Aren't they the most wonderful couple? And those beautiful children! Isn't it strange how, right after people adopt, they have their own? The nice thing for the Macks is that their adopted boy actually looks a bit like their own two girls. Such a lovely family! Do you see much of them?"

"We don't see them at all," Norma said, sounding stiff and not caring that she did.

Mrs. Lyons's eyebrows went up a fraction of an inch. "Oh! I thought you were such good friends."

"We were."

"Oh, really? I didn't—" And then her companion, possibly seeing Norma's reaction, drew her away.

Yes, I suppose it's too bad about Peter, thought Norma. To be in sight of the prize, for surely he had been on the way to national acclaim, must be terribly painful. But he is doing well enough with his restorations, they have their family, and that's more than many people have.

A good fairy must have blessed Cecile at birth. She had a father who deserved respect, a lasting, passionate love from Peter, and with it all, a fair degree of beauty. That should be enough. It's far more than I ever had.

Why should I worry about Peter and Cecile? She wasn't even a loyal friend to me and my brother. Shedding tears over Amanda!

No, I did what I did for Dan. I gave him a miracle cure that saved his sanity. His buildings stand high in a dozen cities. They don't have any particular artistic merit, but they've made him prominent enough to become a household name. It's wonderful to see him traveling around with Stevie. He's so proud of the handsome boy!

People say that Stevie is the image of his grandfather—but it is better not to think about that, too.

Think instead about the fortune that has allowed Dan to become a philanthropist, especially in the cause of children from broken homes. This fortune, so he told me once, amounts to two billion dollars. Well, he was always good to me, and I have been good to him.

There are days, though, when memory hurts me, as it can when certain music dies away. And then, from the top shelf of the closet I take a small framed photograph, and stare again at three young women standing together in cap and gown on a sunny lawn.

EPILOGUE

"Two billion dollars," said the narrator. "That ends the story."

The afternoon had faded. The sun was a ruby line on the horizon, and the Atlantic was still battering the rocks below as the two old men, who had met so accidentally after such a long, long time, sat looking at each other.

"So, Amos, what do you think now about Balzac's 'crime'? Was this a real crime? She didn't, after all, exactly—"

"No, not 'exactly.' "

"Can't it be seen simply as a pitiable struggle for survival?"

A wry expression crossed Amos's face and faded into a small, ironic smile. Perhaps time as it often does, and memories as they often do, were softening life's sharp, mean edges. Human nature! It hadn't changed since the days of ancient Rome, and long before then, too.

"I suppose," he said, "like most things in this world, Alfred, it depends on the point of view. So I guess I will answer 'both.' It was both."

ABOUT THE AUTHOR

Belva Plain lives in northern New Jersey. She is the author of the bestselling novels *Evergreen, Random Winds, Eden Burning, Crescent City, The Golden Cup, Tapestry, Blessings, Harvest, Treasures, Whispers, Daybreak, The Carousel, Promises, Secrecy, Homecoming, Legacy of Silence, Fortune's Hand,* and *After the Fire.*

Be sure to look for . . .

HER FATHER'S HOUSE

The unforgettable new novel from the
New York Times bestselling BELVA PLAIN

*When a terrible lie has been told out of love,
can it be forgiven?*

Some choices are destined to shape the course of
our lives forever and for Donald Wolfe, this is
one such choice. Donald's daughter is the light
of his life, so when his flawed marriage begins to
fail, he has to decide—shall he consider a step
that would force him into flight and a life of
hiding—for his daughter's sake?